Welcome to Newton, a perfect town…
Where the kids get perfect grades… And everyone
seems perfectly happy – all the time…

Except newcomer Henry Ward isn't buying it. With
a pair of misfit friends, he's determined to expose the
dark secrets lurking behind Newton's bright façade.

But asking questions about Newton and
the corporation that owns it can be dangerous.
The doctors in the sinister medical centre on the hill
have a procedure called "adjustment" for kids
who don't fit in…

And Henry and his friends have just gone to the
top of the waiting list.

ALSO BY ANDREW TAYLOR
(WRITING AS A. G. TAYLOR)

METEORITE STRIKE
ALIEN STORM
ENEMY INVASION

THE ADJUSTERS

ANDREW TAYLOR

USBORNE

For Henry

First published in the UK in 2012 by Usborne Publishing Ltd.,
Usborne House, 83-85 Saffron Hill, London EC1N 8RT, England.
www.usborne.com

Text copyright © Andrew Taylor, 2012

The right of Andrew Taylor to be identified as the author of this
work has been asserted by him in accordance with the
Copyright, Designs and Patents Act, 1988.

Cover artwork by Elisabetta Barbazza and Eamon O'Donoghue.
Skull image © Don Farrall / Getty Images

The name Usborne and the devices ♈ ⊕ are Trade Marks of
Usborne Publishing Ltd.

A CIP catalogue record for this book is available from the British Library.

ISBN 9781409540533 JFM MJJASOND/12 00845/1

Printed in Reading, Berkshire, UK.

It's no fun being dead.

The cold steel of the mortuary table against your naked skin...
A black, plastic sheet draped over your body from head to foot...
Your arms and legs immovable as iron girders...

Is this it? Is this all there is?

But then the sound of people moving around the table...
Metal objects clattering around in a tray... Trolley wheels on a
tiled floor... Someone vigorously washing his hands... Muffled
voices...

You take a breath. A terrible mistake has been made.

You're not dead.

You're alive!

You try to call out, but your lips won't form the words. Your
tongue feels thick and useless, like a piece of raw meat in your
mouth. You desperately try to raise your hand, but your limbs
just aren't answering your brain's command.

Without warning the sheet is whipped to one side, leaving
you exposed on the table. A brilliant light is shining in your
face but you can't turn away. Can't even blink. Your eyes swim
with tears, slowly becoming accustomed to the glare. In your
peripheral vision you see sterile, white walls and a lamp angled

down, a scene reminiscent of every medical drama you've ever seen on TV. On a metal trolley to your left, instruments are laid out in a neat row: scalpels, clamps, curved suture needles, a drill...

You try to scream, but can't.

"So, how are you liking it here so far?" a man's voice says as two figures approach the table. They are both dressed in surgical scrubs. The taller of the two wears a green cap from which grey hairs protrude. The other man is completely bald. Their lower faces are obscured by masks.

"Very stimulating," the bald-headed one replies. "Different to Hope General, that's for sure."

(You want to cry out: Help! Help me! I'm alive!)

The grey-haired surgeon chuckles. "In a good way, I hope."

(Please! Help me!)

"Of course!" bald-head replies hurriedly. "This is the cutting edge. It's everything I've ever dreamed of." He turns his attention to the instrument trolley. "Are you going to use the laser scalpel?"

(Listen to me! Can't you see my eyes are open?)

"No," grey-hair replies. "Call me old-fashioned, but give me the electric saw any day."

You direct all your willpower towards making your lips form a word. And your body finally begins to obey...

"Puh..."

The effort required to form a single syllable is superhuman, but you can't give up. You mustn't give up.

"Puh... Puh-leeez..."

"Hey," says the bald-headed doctor, looking round in surprise.

"This kid's awake! Should I give him more sedative?"

"No need," grey-hair replies. He picks up something that looks like a power tool from the trolley: a handheld instrument with a circular cutting blade on the top. He presses a button on the side and the serrated edge begins to spin at high speed.

You want to leap from the table and run screaming for help... This can't be happening...

But there's no escape...

"Puh-leeeez... I'll be g-g-g..."

Grey-hair leans in, blocking out the light of the theatre lamp. The buzzing motor of the electric saw fills your ears.

The surgeon smiles down at you. "Yes. Yes, you will."

The blade of the power tool approaches. There is a squeal as it makes contact.

And then incredible pain...

And then darkness.

1

The gas station had a sad look to it: rusting pumps, a faded sign and peeling paint around the shopfront. At the grimy shop window, a white-haired attendant with a beard that touched his shirt front peered out, as a Toyota Land Cruiser piled high with packing boxes pulled up by the diesel pump.

"Would you look at those prices," said Jennifer Ward, a dark-haired woman in her mid-forties who was sitting at the wheel of the car, checking out the cost per litre chalked up on a board by the door. "Welcome to the country, kiddo."

Kiddo. In the passenger seat, Henry Ward sighed. "Mom, I'm fourteen."

Jennifer looked at her son and gave him an expression of mock hurt. *"Well, excuse me!"*

Despite himself, Henry laughed. That had been dad's line whenever he said something out of turn.

"Do me a favour and fill her up, huh?" Jennifer gave him a fifty from her pocket. "And get me a Diet Coke?"

"Yes, Your Majesty."

Henry opened the passenger door into the searing

September afternoon, a late summer heatwave. The air con in the rented Toyota had made him forget it was thirty-five degrees outside. He looked back at his mom through the window and pulled an agonized face. She waved at him to get on with it. Henry moved to the back of the car, flipped open the gas cap and then grabbed the diesel nozzle from its cradle. The thick plastic handle was almost too hot to hold, even though it had been in the shade. As Henry slotted it into the gas tank, the bell of the shop door jangled.

"What do you think you're doing?" the attendant snapped, hobbling across the forecourt as fast as his legs would carry him.

Henry froze. There was anger in the old man's voice. *What?* he thought, looking down at the pump in his hand. He had it inserted properly. When he pressed the trigger he could feel the gas beginning to flow. Perhaps the old geezer just didn't like how he looked. For his age, Henry was tall and over the last year had broadened out as a result of being on the swim team at school. Recently he'd noticed people beginning to look at him differently, especially old people when he was out and about – like they were sizing him up as some kind of a threat. Was that it?

"You see a *self-service* sign anywhere?" said the old man, peevishly snatching the pump from his hand.

"Oh, I'm sorry," said Henry and took a couple of steps back.

"Well?"

"Uh…well, what?"

"How much do you want?"

"Oh, right. Fill her up." Henry held out the fifty.

"Pay at the counter."

Henry looked back towards the shop window and the empty seat by the till. The old man stared into space as he began to fill the tank. The numbers on the pump ticked up agonizingly slowly. Henry shuffled in the heat as a second vehicle, a sandy-coloured police cruiser, drove onto the forecourt. It pulled up by the shop and a trooper who seemed as tall and wide as a door emerged from the front. He wore a light-brown uniform and a wide-brimmed hat that gave him something of the look of a cowboy, albeit one without a horse. The biggest handgun Henry had ever seen rested in a holster on his hip.

"Be with you in just a minute, Dan," the old man said in an altogether more pleasant fashion than when he'd spoken to Henry.

"Take your time, Clyde," Trooper Dan drawled. "Ain't no hurry."

Henry became aware of the cop casting his professional gaze over the Toyota and bringing it to rest on him. The trooper stared right at him, like he could read thoughts. Henry looked back at the expressionless mouth and mirrored shades. The cop kept staring at him.

The moment stretched on...

I haven't done anything wrong here, Henry thought indignantly, but found himself looking away all the same. The trooper made a little noise, something like a snigger. From the corner of his eye, Henry saw him lean against the hood of his cruiser and pop a stick of gum in his mouth. *Jesus,* Henry thought. *Could that guy be any more of a cliché?* The trooper started staring at him again.

"Do you have a bathroom?" Henry asked the old man for an excuse to get away from the cop's X-ray gaze.

"Yep."

It became clear the old man wasn't going to say anything else.

"Can I use it?"

"Yep. Round the back."

"It's not locked?"

The old man looked at him as if he was crazy. "Now why would I want to lock the toilet? You think there's somethin' in there worth stealin'?"

Henry shrugged. "I guess not."

"You guessed right."

The old man turned his attention back to the pump. Henry walked round the side of the shop, ignoring the cop's eyes following him all the way. Out back, a small building made of corrugated iron stood on the far side of a dirt yard. Someone had written RESTROOM on the side in big white letters.

Nice, Henry thought as he walked across the yard, scuffing up little clouds of dust as he went. *This dump has got real character.*

Six months before, when his mom had lost her job, she'd warned him that they might have to move from the city in order for her to find work. It was the recession – apparently people had to relocate. At the time Henry had imagined another city, or at least a large town. She was the manager of an IVF lab, helping couples who couldn't have kids get pregnant. Then the job with Malcorp came up – a job that involved moving to live at its facility in the isolated north of the state. The nearest big town was thirty kilometres away from the place they'd be living for the next year at least...

Newton County. Aka Hicksville.

Henry had spent the weeks since his mom got the job praying that something else would come up. He didn't mind moving, even though it would mean starting all over again at a new school...new friends...new teachers... No, there was actually something exciting about that. He could keep in touch with his old friends online and visit from time to time. But the thought of being an hour's drive from a sports stadium or a games store was pretty hard to bear. And although Mom wasn't letting on, Henry knew she was thinking the same thing (no doubt wondering when she'd ever get another of those skinny lattes that she'd once bought every morning from the coffee shop directly under their city apartment).

But a different job hadn't come up. So here they were, driving through the sweltering heat to one of the most deserted parts of the state... Getting eyeballed by bored local cops and about to sample the delights of rural plumbing...

Henry pushed open the toilet door with some effort. The hinges had come loose, making the bottom scrape on the floor. Inside it was dark and hot. Flies buzzed and there was an acrid smell of urine in the air. Wrinkling his nose, Henry reached out and flipped the light switch on the wall. A fluorescent tube in the ceiling flickered into life, revealing a single cubicle and a disgusting-looking urinal against the wall.

"Man, this is nasty," said Henry as he pushed the door shut behind him. But the decision of whether to use the urinal or risk the stall was cut short as something moved in the corner. Henry spun round, expecting to face anything from a trapped bird to a rat…

It was a girl. About his age.

She had long, blonde hair that looked as if it hadn't been brushed in a week. Her face was smeared with dirt, as were her clothes – a plain white smock and a pair of boots that were two sizes too big for her. She stood, pressed into the corner by the sink, unmoving and wide-eyed. Henry's gaze flicked to a plastic bracelet on her left wrist, the type they give you in hospital.

"Oh," he said a little stupidly as he backed towards the door. "I'm sorry…"

The girl's mouth fell open. "No!" she cried, rushing towards him. Before he could grab the handle, she placed herself against the door so he couldn't exit. "Don't leave me."

"Okay," Henry said, holding up his hands. This girl was strung out. "Are you alright?"

Her eyes filled with tears.

"It's okay," he said. She was clearly in some kind of trouble. A runaway, maybe? She certainly didn't look as if she belonged at the gas station. Beyond the mess of hair and the dirt on her face, Henry could see she was pretty. Beautiful, even.

"Really?" she said with an edge of pure desperation to her voice. *"Can I trust you?"*

He nodded. "What's your name?"

The girl looked at him blankly, as if confused by the question. He read the tag on her wrist.

"Gabrielle Henson," he read. "That's you, huh?"

"Yeah," she replied, holding his gaze intently.

"My name's Henry Ward…"

"Do you have a car?"

"Uh… Yeah."

"I need to get out of here."

"You're hitch-hiking?"

The girl rubbed her temple violently with the heel of her palm, revealing a series of needle marks along her inner arm. "I just need to get away. Will you help me? Take me with you?"

"Sure," Henry said, wondering at the same time what his mom was going to say when he turned up with a strange girl out of the blue. But of course she would see that the girl needed help and would know what to do. He wondered how long she had been hiding in the heat and stench of the gas station toilet. There were scratch marks on her exposed knees and lower legs, as if she'd been running through brambles.

"Thank you," said the girl. She placed a slender hand on his shoulder and leaned against him as if exhausted. "I don't know what I would have done if you hadn't shown up."

"We're going to Newton," Henry said, "perhaps you can get a lift with us and then—"

"No!" she said, pushing away from him so forcefully he almost fell back. "Not Newton!"

"It's okay…"

She shook her head emphatically, backing into the darkened corner once more. "*Not Newton…*"

Henry was about to argue that if she wanted a lift, that was where they were headed, when a fist banged twice on the other side of the door.

"What's going on in there?" It was Trooper Dan's deep voice.

The girl stifled a gasp. She shook her head violently at Henry and held her hands together, as if praying for him to stay quiet. Suddenly everything began to make sense to him: *the hospital gown, the bracelet, the track marks on her wrist…* He'd known students like her at his last school. Usually rich kids in trouble with drugs who got shipped off to secluded and very expensive rehab clinics for months at a time. Was she an escapee from some private hospital hidden away in the woods? And if so, shouldn't he tell the cop so she could be taken back?

Please, the girl mouthed and there was something so desperate about her that he couldn't betray her trust. He'd get the trooper away from the toilet, and then talk to his mom about it… She'd know what to do…

Okay, Henry mouthed back at her and a pathetic look of relief passed over the girl's face.

The trooper banged on the door again. "Open up right now!"

"Alright!" Henry called through. "Just washing my hands!"

He gave the girl a final look. The sheer terror in her eyes was something he wouldn't forget for a long time. What was she afraid of? The cop? Getting dragged back to rehab? From what he'd heard, those places were glorified holiday parks – everyone sitting around the pool drinking juice. Henry pulled the door open, flicking off the light to hide her from view as he did so. The trooper towered in the opening, hands on his gun belt.

"Is there something wrong, officer?"

The trooper looked him up and down like he was a bug. "What's going on in there?"

Henry raised an eyebrow and said, "It's a toilet?" He'd been questioned by cops before – city cops, not some hick deputy either – and he wasn't about to fold like a little kid. Obviously this guy had come looking for him, hoping to find him up to no good in the outhouse. Well, he'd be out of luck there.

"Don't be smart, son."

"Sorry, sir," Henry replied, bringing it down a little. *Have to play him just right.* He moved forward, pulling the door shut behind him.

"Been smoking in there?"

"No, sir."

"Takin' drugs?"

"*No!*"

"Someone else in there?"

"Uh, no."

"You don't want to lie to me." Henry could almost feel the cop's eyes boring into his skull from behind those mirror shades.

"No one," Henry said and immediately regretted it...

The corners of the cop's mouth twitched and he moved forward swiftly, kicking the door open with his boot. Before Henry could protest, the trooper grabbed a little torch from his belt and started shining it around the darkened toilet.

"Well now, what's this?" the trooper said as the beam fell on the girl cowering in the corner. There was a grim satisfaction in his tone now he'd proved he'd been lied to.

"Hey, she's sick," protested Henry, stepping forward.

The cop pointed a finger in his face without even looking round. "Two paces back *right now* or I will put you *on your ass*."

There was something so hard in the trooper's voice that Henry found himself stepping back immediately. The man might be a small-town cop, but Henry didn't doubt he could knock him down with a flick of his little finger.

"Get yourself out here," the trooper commanded, aiming the torch beam right in the girl's face. When she didn't move, he added, "Don't make me come for you."

Ever so slowly, the girl walked towards the door, her head bowed. When she got within a metre, the trooper reached out and grabbed her arm, as if worried she'd try to bolt past him. Without another word, he began marching his prisoner across the yard towards the gas station.

"Where are you taking her?" Henry demanded, following after them. "What's she done wrong?"

"Stay out of this," the trooper snarled without looking back. "Or I'll have to take you in too."

They rounded the side of the building and the cop headed straight for his cruiser, pulling open the rear door with his free hand. By this time, Jennifer Ward was out of the Toyota and walking towards them. Henry ran over to her.

"She's in trouble," he said, indicating the girl as she meekly got into the back of the patrol car. Since the cop had banged on the toilet door, all the fight seemed to have drained from her. "We have to help!"

Henry's mother gave him a hand motion that said *cool down*, before turning her attention to the trooper. "Excuse me, officer. Is there a problem here?"

Trooper Dan slammed the back door of the cruiser shut and replied, "No problem, ma'am. Nothing for you to concern yourself over."

"That girl asked for our help," Henry persisted. "She's scared."

"Please," Jennifer Ward said to the cop, "what's going on here?"

"She's a runaway," said Trooper Dan, the bored tone in his voice making it clear he didn't have to tell them anything at all. "Danger to herself and others. I've been chasing her all over these woods for the last two days. Now I can take her back to her family. *No thanks to some people…*" He directed his gaze towards Henry.

Henry glanced at the girl in the back, wishing that she would try to get out of the cruiser or something, but she merely stared at her lap. He turned towards his mother. "She was hiding out back." Then added in a whisper, "*She's terrified of this guy.*"

Unexpectedly, the trooper reached up and whipped off his sunglasses, revealing a pair of piercing, blue eyes. He was an incredibly handsome man, like some kind of model or old-time film star, but Henry thought he'd seemed more human before he removed the shades. His blue eyes were now locked on Jennifer Ward. They had all the warmth of an iceberg.

"I asked your son a question pertaining to this troubled young lady," he said, "and he lied to me. That's a no-no in my book. Interferin' in a police investigation, we call it." He said the word *police* with heavy emphasis on the first syllable: *poh-leece.*

Henry began to protest, but Jennifer Ward placed her hand on his shoulder. "Henry, it's okay. She's going back to her family."

"Mom…"

"*Henry.*" Her tone left Henry in no doubt that the discussion was at an end.

"Are we finished here?" asked the trooper.

Jennifer Ward looked at him, annoyance flashing in her eyes for the first time. "I'm sorry, officer. Is answering a few questions too much trouble for you?"

Trooper Dan's blank expression didn't waver. "You've got a full load there, ma'am," he said, staring at the boxes piled in the back of the Toyota. "Are you moving to Newton County?"

"Yes," Jennifer said, obviously a little taken aback by his change of tack.

"Well, you'll find that around here, people follow the rules. And they teach their kids respect for authority." *Oh-thor-rit-taay.*

"Now, what is that supposed to mean…?"

But Trooper Dan was already climbing into the front of the cruiser. The door slammed and the engine roared into life. The cruiser peeled away, sending up a cloud of dust from the forecourt floor. The last thing Henry saw of the girl was her face looking at him through the back window of the car. She mouthed something, but he couldn't make out what it was.

Barely controlling her rage, Jennifer Ward said, "Well I never! That was one rude son of a—"

The shop bell rang as the white-haired attendant stuck his head out. "That'll be forty-seven dollars."

Jennifer took a deep, calming breath. "Pay him and let's get out of here, Henry."

As she returned to the car, Henry passed the fifty to the attendant, telling him to keep the change. It was only then he realized what the girl had mouthed to him as the cruiser sped away.

A single word.

Run.

2

"**W**hat were you thinking, lying to a cop?" Jennifer was saying five minutes later as the Toyota sped north once more. "I mean, haven't we discussed this enough?"

Henry sighed and leaned back against the headrest. Since leaving the gas station he'd been getting the third degree, most of it centred on the fact he'd tried to conceal the presence of the girl from Trooper Dan. "Yes, Mom. We have been through this enough."

"You're very lucky not to be in the back of that patrol car as well," Jennifer continued as the Toyota negotiated another tight turn through the forest. The road had become narrower since they'd left the gas station.

"She needed help!"

"And that is what that cop was giving her."

Henry gave her an incredulous look. "Did he look helpful?"

Jennifer sighed, but didn't argue. "There *was* something weird about that guy."

"Ah-ha! I knew you felt it too!"

"But that's just county policing… They're obviously a little bit…rough and ready."

"A little bit?"

"Okay, a lot," Jennifer admitted. "All the more reason not to rile him up. I thought that getting out of the city would put an end to all this. I can't be worrying about you getting into trouble with the police all the time…"

Henry groaned. *Not this again.* "Mom! I got picked up once."

"And you got a reputation…"

"Oh, please…"

"A name for yourself at your school! Everyone knew!"

Henry shook his head and looked out of the window at the trees passing by. Six months before he'd been caught spray-painting a fence down by the railway and his mom just wouldn't let it drop…

He'd always been artistic and it had actually been Mom who had encouraged him to join the arts club at school. But that's where he'd met Skiv and Nas, two kids from his year whose idea of art wasn't exactly watercolours on canvas. Henry was soon accompanying them on their nocturnal trips to the deserted building sites and train yards of their neighbourhood, where they released their artistic impulses with spray cans and markers on any available piece of wall.

The funny thing was, Henry found that he was a natural – much better with a can than his friends, who could only manage the most basic designs. Their work was little more than tagging, crude symbols depicting their names – something that held no interest for Henry. He was too busy bringing to life characters from his imagination – monsters, robots, dragons, ninjas. In his spare time he was reading about the graffiti art scene and how some artists used stencils and had their work exhibited in galleries...

Then the red and blue lights of a cop car had come out of nowhere one night. Skiv and Nas melted into the darkness, leaving Henry to take the blame. When they sat him down in the interrogation room he'd naïvely tried to explain that what he was doing was art... That he only inked on bare walls no one was looking at anyway... But the cops didn't share his viewpoint. The others had been tagging all over the area, including bus stops, shopfronts and doorways, and the officer who interviewed him seemed convinced that Henry was the culprit. When he protested that he wasn't a tagger, the cop in charge had leaned into his face and demanded names. Who had been scrawling their symbols all over his beat?

Henry took the blame.

It was his first offence, so he was let off with a warning: if he was caught inking again, however, or even in possession of spray cans, it would mean prosecution. That wasn't the worst thing, however. The worst thing was the hurt in his mom's eyes as she collected him from the station. And then the ongoing lack of trust. He wasn't allowed out in the evenings after that. If he was going anywhere she'd double-check on him. Of course, if Henry had wanted to carry on his nocturnal activities, there was nothing she could have done to stop him – he was almost fifteen, not a kid any more, after all. But Henry wasn't like that. He didn't want to hurt or embarrass her, although he wished she could understand that. She seemed to regard what had happened as some kind of massive failing on her part...

"I hoped that coming out here would get us away from trouble, I really did," Jennifer continued as the Toyota took another turn way too fast. Whenever she drove angry she was heavy on the gas. "But trouble seems to follow us around."

Henry sighed. Sometimes she could be hyper melodramatic. "Do you remember when you asked me to tell you if you were being a crazy ubermom? Well, this is one of those times."

Jennifer Ward looked as if she was going to carry on arguing, but then without warning let out one of her short, barking laughs and the tension broke.

"Okay, okay," she said grudgingly. "I guess we've got better things to think about today."

Henry looked at her and smiled with more than a little relief. "Who do you think she was?" he asked after a moment. "The girl, I mean."

Jennifer shrugged. "Maybe an escapee from a lunatic asylum. A psychotic ex-cheerleader looking for young men to ensnare..."

Henry groaned.

"You were lucky that trooper came along when he did, kiddo. I might never have seen you again. She was pretty good-looking, huh?"

"Mom!"

"I'm just saying that a nice-looking young man like

you should have a girlfriend. Perhaps in Newton…"

Henry pretended to bang his head against the dash. "Can we go back to giving me a hard time about the cop, please?"

They reached the outskirts of Newton less than ten minutes later. The tall fir trees thinned out and they crossed a bridge over a fast-flowing river, before coming to a pristine sign that read *Newton – where it's nice to be nice!*

"Well, this is it," Jennifer said as they passed.

"Yeah," Henry said unenthusiastically.

His mother reached across and put a hand on his shoulder. "Chin up, Henry. It's going to be okay. Wait till you see where we'll be living. You're going to go crazy."

"Uh-huh." She'd been telling him that for the last few weeks, but he was yet to be convinced. He'd seen the Malcorp induction brochure for new employees and the pictures of the *worker's complex*. It looked like toy town.

Newton itself was small – with a population of only a couple of thousand people. Practically every Malcorp employee lived within the facility, while the residents of the town worked mainly in the service industries, the shops and restaurants that catered to their needs.

"Would you look at this place?" Jennifer said as the Toyota pulled along a main street lined with tiny shops that had names like *Olde Curiosity Shoppe*, *Full of Beans* and *Newton Style*. Everything looked newly painted, like it had been created just yesterday, although the style was that of small-town America from fifty years ago. A Disneyland version of real life.

"Quaint," Henry said. He didn't mean it as a compliment. People walked along the row of shopfronts, taking their time browsing in the sun.

"This place is so clean!" Jennifer exclaimed. "Not a bit of graf— I mean, I literally have not seen a speck of litter since we drove in here."

"That's amazing, Mom."

"Oh, stop being such a grouch. Look, there's a cinema!"

They passed a single screen theatre. The letters above the door read *BACK BY POPULAR DEMAND:* HIGH SCHOOL MUSICAL 3.

"It just gets better and better," Henry said.

They reached the end of the high street and, after passing a few more houses with immaculately kept front gardens, took a new road leading out of town. After about a kilometre they came to a high brick wall that stretched into the woods in either direction. Double iron gates next to a sign that read *Malcorp Research and Development Complex* blocked the way ahead. As they pulled up, a uniformed guard appeared from a hut by the gates.

"Let's hope this guy is as friendly as everyone else we've met so far," Henry muttered.

"Shut up," Jennifer hissed as she lowered her window.

"Good afternoon," the guard said, leaning in. He was a chubby guy, spilling out of his uniform. A name badge on his chest read *Hank*.

"Hi," Jennifer said. "Oh, I've got a letter… They told me

I'd need it to get past the gates..." She reached across and started rummaging in the glove compartment.

"It's okay, Mrs. Ward," Hank said pleasantly. "We're expecting you. Just drive on through and park in the visitors' area. Mr. Mallory will be right along to give you the tour."

"Great... Hold on. The owner of the company is going to meet us?"

Hank grinned. "Mr. Mallory likes to welcome all new employees in person." With that, he stepped back and touched a remote on his belt. The iron gates swung inwards and Jennifer drove through.

"Mr. Mallory, jeez!" she said, checking out her hair in the mirror as she swung the Toyota into one of the parking bays marked *VISITOR*. "If I'd known the big boss was going to meet us..."

"Calm down, Mom," Henry said. "You'll be fine."

They emerged from the car into the sunlight. The temperature had dropped, perhaps because the facility was located on one of the highest points in the area. Now the afternoon was pleasant, a different world from the intense heat and dust of the gas station. They were standing in a small parking area located on the edge of the Malcorp grounds. Manicured lawns and lines of trees stretched away to the north, while a high wall behind them appeared to encircle the whole compound. Single storey buildings stood here and there among the trees, linked by little roads and pathways.

"Hmmm," Jennifer said appreciatively. "Good to be out of that car."

"Look," Henry said as a vehicle approached along the nearest road. It was a four-seater electric car just a little bigger than a golf buggy, with large, spherical wheels. A grey-haired man with a neatly trimmed moustache sat in the driver's seat.

"Hello there!" he called as he pulled the buggy up beside them.

He leaped out with the energy of a much younger man, revealing himself to be tall and broad shouldered beneath his tailored suit. There was something boyish in his manner. Henry imagined that he'd look right at home in a scoutmaster's uniform.

"Nice to see you again, Jennifer," he said, extending a hand for her to shake. "And you must be Henry. My name's John Mallory and I've heard a lot about you."

"Great," Henry said uncertainly as he shook Mallory's hand. For a brief second the fingers closed around his in a vice-like grip. *The old guy must work out*, he thought.

"Well, let me give you the five-dollar tour," Mallory said, indicating the buggy. "Just leave the keys in your car. I'll have someone drive it round to your unit." Jennifer looked unsure about this and Mallory laughed. "Don't worry, nothing will go missing. This isn't the city. Is that all your stuff?"

"The rest is being shipped in the week."

"Of course." Mallory turned his attention to Henry. "Well you look almost old enough to drive. Would you mind?"

"Sure."

Henry climbed behind the wheel while his mom and

Mallory got in the back. The buggy was a simple automatic with stop and go levers on the side of the wheel.

"U-turn, driver," Mallory said, leaning back and smiling at Jennifer. "Don't spare the horses. We'll take a look at where you'll be living first."

Henry sent the buggy in a wide turn and Mallory directed him back up the road towards the nearest set of buildings. Despite himself, he was pleased that Mallory had asked him to drive the vehicle. Perhaps the tour wouldn't be so bad after all.

"This facility was built less than a decade ago, as I'm sure you know," Mallory said. They passed a similar buggy going in the other direction. Two guys in pristine lab coats waved and smiled. "In those days Newton was a town of less than five hundred residents, and slowly dying like so many small towns this far north. Over the years the jobs moved abroad and the people moved to the cities. Since we came the population has increased fourfold, new businesses have opened and we've invested over a million dollars in building works." He rattled this off like it was a speech that he'd given many times before. "We like to give back to the local community."

"This is a rather remote place to locate the headquarters of your business, Mr. Mallory," Jennifer said. "Do you mind if I ask why you chose Newton?"

"Precisely because it *is* remote," he replied. "We could have set up in one of the big cities, or even a medium-sized town, but that was never the idea. Quality of life is what we offer our employees."

"That's very noble."

"Not noble," Mallory said, "*sensible.* It's good business to have happy employees. Happy families. Successful kids." He leaned forward to speak to Henry. "Someone told me you were quite the star in the pool at your last school."

Henry shrugged. "I was in the swim team. I don't know about *star…*"

"Oh, don't be so modest! We've got an Olympic-sized pool that you're going to love. I'll arrange an introduction with Coach Tyler." Mallory pointed to a large building in the distance. "That's the education complex. Kindergarten right through to high school. Three hundred students, small classes. Everyone gets their own laptop – staff and students."

"Laptop!" Jennifer said in the back. "Sounds cool, huh, Henry?"

"Yeah," Henry replied uncertainly. In his experience, *school laptop* meant a machine the weight of a sink loaded with software from the turn of the century…though something told him it might be a different story here.

"Lecture hall, computer suites, orchestra room," Mallory continued, like he was checking items off a list. "*Art studio.*"

Henry looked round and saw Mallory's eyes glinting with a kind of mischief.

"Do you like *art*, Henry?"

"Yeah," he replied cautiously. Something told him that Mallory knew everything about his previous run-in with the cops. "When I get the chance."

"Well, you'll find plenty of chances here. *Within the studio.*"

Jennifer hurriedly changed the subject. "When does school start again, Mr. Mallory?"

"On Monday," he said, all the intensity gone from his voice as he sat back. "That gives Henry a couple of days to get settled in. Make new friends. And, please, call me John."

She gave an uncharacteristic giggle. "Okay…John."

Henry looked round at her and the wheels of the buggy scraped a low wall bordering the roadway.

"Woah, eyes on the road, chief!" Mallory said with a laugh as Henry turned his attention back to the steering wheel.

"Sorry."

"And here we are," Mallory said, indicating a group of a dozen two-storey houses built on a slight incline. They were made of blue-painted wood and glass and their roofs sloped all the way down to the ground on either side. They looked as if they'd been plucked straight from the side of some Swedish lake. "We call these the blue lodges, for obvious reasons. You're number six." He pulled a key card from his pocket and passed it to Henry. "I'll let you explore by yourself, while I show your mom where she'll be working. How does that sound?"

Henry looked round at Jennifer, who nodded to him. A dark-haired kid dressed in black jeans and a band T-shirt emerged from behind one of the lodges. He started walking across the grass, squinting at the sun as if it hurt his eyes.

Mallory stood up in the back and waved him over.

"Christian!"

The kid's dark expression immediately brightened and he ran over to the buggy.

"Henry, this is Christian," Mallory said by way of introduction. "His family arrived here just a couple of months ago, so he's a newcomer too. Isn't that right?"

"That's right, sir," Christian replied.

"Perhaps you'd like to show Henry around. Take him to the *cool places* to hang out in the complex. How does that sound to you?"

Christian's perky expression didn't waver. "Swell!"

Mallory smiled approvingly. "Off you go then."

Henry climbed out of the buggy. Mallory took over the driver's seat and Jennifer joined him in the front.

"You boys behave yourselves now," Mallory said, sending the buggy speeding off across the grass away from the residential area. "Don't do anything us olds wouldn't do!"

"Sure thing, Mr. Mallory!" Christian called after him. The buggy disappeared over an incline and the boy looked at Henry for the first time. The fixed grin on his face had melted away. "Got any smokes?"

"Uh, no."

Christian shrugged and reached into his pocket to produce a crumpled pack of cigarettes. "Let's go to your place. My dad's on to me."

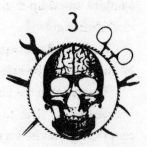

3

"The first thing you've got to learn about Malcorp," Christian said, "is that it's easier to go with the flow than against it." He was sitting on the marble kitchen counter in Henry's new home. Periodically he would take a drag on the cigarette and then blow the smoke at the extractor fan in the ceiling, which he'd turned on full. "Know what I mean?"

"I guess so," Henry said. "Do you want to smoke that outside?" He knew that if his mom came back and smelled smoke in the kitchen he'd be explaining himself all evening.

Christian shook his head. "Security cameras catch you every time. Whole place is full of them. Sure you don't want one?"

"No. Those things'll kill you."

Christian blew more smoke at the fan and began a coughing fit. "You're probably right," he said with effort. "But I find it's important to hang on to some vices."

He jumped off the counter and tossed the cigarette butt into the drain before hitting a button on the wall. A garbage crusher whirred furiously for a few seconds. Christian slapped his hands together and grinned at Henry. "And the evidence is gone."

"Right," Henry said looking around the kitchen. Every appliance, every surface appeared brand new, never used.

"You're from the city?" Christian asked.

"Yeah."

"Well, you can forget that life. You have to make your own entertainment here."

"What about Newton?" Henry asked.

Christian pulled a strangulated face. "You've seen Newton, right? Oh, it's a party town, as long as your idea of a party is shopping for socks followed by a trip to the garden centre."

Henry laughed and walked through to the lounge. It was about as big as their entire apartment had been back in the city and was decked out with a huge TV, Blu-ray surround sound and even a games machine. Large windows set high in the wall caught the afternoon sunlight, bathing the room in a golden glow that matched the wooden walls and warm colours of the furniture. It looked like something from a *better homes* feature in a magazine.

"Yeah, there are some perks," Christian admitted, coming to his side. "But believe me, after a couple of weeks here, you'll be going crazy."

"Yeah? My mom has been saying I'd go crazy when I saw this place," Henry said with a smile.

Christian flopped into an armchair. "You know what my dad's been saying to me?" He put on a gruff, enraged voice. *"Show some appreciation for what you've been given, you little punk. Have a little respect for your elders."*

Henry raised an eyebrow at him. "You obviously get on well."

"Oh, yeah. He's one of those *follow the rules, respect for authority* guys. We've got a lot in common."

Henry frowned. "That's the second time today I've heard that."

"What?"

"Follow the rules, respect for authority."

"From who? Mr. Big-shot Mallory?"

"No. Some small-town cop who gave me a hard time on the way here."

"He wouldn't happen to be about three metres tall and have aviator shades for eyes, would he?"

"That sounds like him."

"Trooper Dan."

"You've run into him?"

"Not up close, thank god," Christian replied. "He swaggers around Newton, *enforcin' the laaaw.*" He said these last words in an exaggerated drawl that was a pretty good impersonation of the cop's accent. "Got something going on with Mallory."

"What's Mallory got to do with the cops?"

Christian looked at him as if he was being dense. "Malcorp *owns* Newton. So what Mr. Mallory says goes and Trooper Dan makes sure that it happens. Drop a piece of litter on the high street and old Dan will make you pick it up with your butt cheeks, boy."

Henry laughed. "So that's what all the *yes, Mr. Mallory…*

no, Mr. Mallory was about out there, huh? You worried Trooper Dan is going to make you pick up one of your cigarette butts while it's still alight?"

"Being a teen rebel comes with certain risks," Christian replied, spreading his hands. "Just don't underestimate Trooper Dan. From time to time reporters show up in Newton uninvited. You know, trying to get the inside scoop on what goes on in Malcorp's toy town? I've heard they tend to wake up the next day on the county line with seven bells of crap beaten out of them."

"Right."

Christian shrugged. "Don't believe me if you don't want to, just don't say I didn't warn you." He pushed himself out of the chair with a grunt of effort. "Come on, I said I'd introduce you to the robots…I mean, the locals."

Henry checked his cell phone as they walked across the grass towards the leisure centre. He'd had no reception since about half an hour before they'd got to Newton.

"Forget it," Christian said. "You can barely get a bar, even in town."

Henry held up the cell and waved it around. "Is there a law against cell towers round here?"

"Funny, huh? This place has every modern convenience except phone reception. They say it's the trees, but I think they don't want us communicating with the outside world."

Henry gave him a look as he pocketed the phone. "That sounds kinda paranoid."

Christian shrugged. "And we haven't even started talking about how they read your emails."

"Right," Henry said with a laugh. Then he noticed that the other kid wasn't smiling. "Wait a minute. You're not kidding?"

"About the emails? No. And that's not to mention the censorship of certain websites from the facility internet connection. If Malcorp doesn't like a site, you don't get access."

"I don't believe it."

"Don't take my word for it. Ask Mallory or one of his suits. They'll give you ten good reasons why the web should be censored. Number one is how it's *for the safety of our children*, as I remember."

"What is this, North Korea?"

Christian snorted. "Yeah. With jocks." He indicated a tall, blond kid approaching from the leisure centre.

"Hey there," the newcomer said pleasantly. "You must be Henry Ward. Coach Tyler told me to head over and show you the pool."

"That's where we were headed, Blake," Christian said with a real edge to his voice.

The big kid looked at him without any sign of malice. "It's just you were late, so…"

"Late?" Christian snapped. "This isn't a town meeting. We're not on a schedule."

"It's okay," Henry said, trying to work out what the problem was. Perhaps Christian didn't like jocks – and Blake was just about the most stereotypical jock he'd ever seen. "We were going there right now."

Christian shrugged. "Well, Winklevoss is here, so I'll skip the rest of the tour. I've got better things to do." With that, he stuffed his bony hands in his pockets and trudged away in the other direction.

"Hey, come on, dude!" Blake called after him. "Don't be like that!"

Christian flipped a finger in their direction without looking round.

Blake shook his head. "Sheesh, that kid's got a real attitude problem. Anyone would think he's got something against us sporty guys."

Blake spoke with such innocence that Henry wondered for a moment if the boy was joking, but his face was deadpan. Despite Blake's size, there was a childish quality to his manner.

"Well, his loss if he doesn't want to join the swim team," Blake said as they carried on towards the leisure centre. "Or any team for that matter. Goodness knows, me and the other fellas have tried hard enough to make him feel welcome, but I guess there's just no helping some people."

"I guess not," said Henry, trying to decide what he found stranger, Christian's affected rebel act or Blake's way of talking like a kid from a 1950s sitcom.

Blake led Henry through into the sports centre, pointing out the track and field areas, the football and baseball pitches, and finally the gym and pool. Mallory hadn't been lying – the pool was Olympic-sized, housed in a spectacular glass building. Most of the twelve lanes were occupied with swimmers powering through the water. Over to one side was a dive pool. As Henry and Blake walked towards the middle of the room, a teenage boy leaped from the high board, executed a perfect triple and hit the water like an arrow.

"Woah!" Blake said, pumping his fist in the air as the kid broke the surface. "Way to go, Steve! Nice dive!"

The kid in the water grinned and waved.

"We've got a pretty solid programme," Blake said to Henry as they walked on. "I'm not on the swim team myself – I'm all about football – but I've heard Coach Tyler is the best."

Henry nodded. The facilities were impressive. "So what competitions has the team entered?"

"Well, we have a sports day at the end of every school year. And the coach is always throwing races into the mix—"

"No," Henry interrupted. "I mean, what trophies has the team won?"

Blake looked at him blankly.

"You compete against other schools, right?"

"Why would we want to go to other schools to swim? We have the best facilities in the state right here!"

"You mean you don't take part in any competitions outside Newton?"

"There's more to being part of a team than just winning trophies, Henry," Blake said.

The patronizing tone in the other kid's voice annoyed Henry suddenly. "I know that, *Blake*. But healthy competition increases motivation."

"Well, I think you'll find we have all the motivation we need right here at Malcorp."

Henry frowned. He'd never heard of a school team that didn't get involved in local competitions. "What about the football team then? Who do they play?"

Blake laughed as if the answer was obvious. "Simple. We have two teams and they play one another every Friday night. I tell you, there's been some pretty exciting games this year…"

"You must be Ward! I can spot a swimmer's physique a mile off."

Henry turned to see a stocky, middle-aged guy walking towards them. He wore a faded pair of track pants and a T-shirt that read *Malcorp Swim*.

"This is Coach Tyler," Blake introduced them.

The coach reached out and gave Henry a predictably bone-crushing handshake. "I'm looking forward to getting you in the pool. How about a trial sometime this week?"

"Sounds good," Henry said, and the coach gave him a wide grin, revealing a row of crooked teeth. It seemed to Henry that this man was the most normal person he'd met all day. He liked him immediately.

"Friday afternoon then," the coach confirmed. Blake grinned at him too.

At least the locals are friendly, Henry thought, but then he remembered the girl from the gas station. What had she said?

No, not Newton.

"Hey, do you know a girl called Gabrielle Henson?" Henry asked impulsively.

The coach shook his head. "Don't know the name. She a friend of yours?"

"Not really," Henry said, suddenly feeling a bit stupid for asking. *What was she to him?* "Just someone I met. She gave me the impression she might be from Newton."

"Well, she isn't a swimmer. Might be in one of the compulsory classes, but I mostly only remember the kids with an interest." He looked over at Blake. "Is there a girl called Gabrielle Henson at the high school?"

Blake turned and Henry saw that the blood had drained from his face.

"Yoo-hoo, Blake!" the coach said, waving his hand at him. "Anybody home?"

"Huh?"

The kid called Steve had been listening to their conversation from the side of the pool. Now he pulled himself out, dripping water. "No, coach," he said, wiping his eyes as he stood. "There's no girl with that name here." Something in the kid's tone made Henry certain that he was lying.

Blake looked at Steve and then said unconvincingly, "That's right, coach. Never heard of her."

The coach shrugged at Henry. "Well, there you go. Perhaps she *was* talking about one of the other towns around here."

"Perhaps, but—"

He was interrupted as a kid across the dive pool shouted

to the coach that he had a telephone call. The man excused himself, reminding Henry to be at the pool on Friday afternoon after school. As he hurried away, Henry turned back to Blake, who was suddenly unable to meet his eyes.

"Tell me about Gabrielle Henson," he said.

Blake kept looking at his feet, so it was Steve who answered. "Didn't we make it clear? She doesn't go to school here." His manner was sharp and unfriendly.

"That's funny," Henry said, not backing down, "because I met her this afternoon in a gas station toilet. She was on the run and looked like she'd been living rough for about a week."

"And you think she's from Malcorp?" Steve said, as if the very idea was distasteful. "A girl who hangs around gas station toilets?"

"She seemed familiar with Newton," Henry replied.

Steve sniggered loudly. "You're new, so I'll make this nice and simple for you. The hick kids from Newton get scholarships to the school here in the facility, but mostly they just sit at the back of class and look stupid. It makes everyone feel better, I guess. Maybe she was one of those. I wouldn't remember."

"Take it easy, Steve," Blake said meekly.

"I'll take it easy when I feel like it," he snapped, before turning his attention back to Henry. "Any other stray skanks you ran into that you'd like to ask about?"

Henry gave him a smile and took a step forward, noting with satisfaction that Steve tensed. Despite all his nastiness, he was nervous. *But why?*

"Word of advice," Steve continued, pulling himself up a little taller. "If you want to fit in around here, don't go asking questions that you know are going to make people uncomfortable."

Henry frowned at him. "What are you talking about?"

"I think you know."

"I don't have a clue but perhaps you'd like to explain…?"

Henry stopped dead as something caught his attention in the dive pool behind them. A younger kid had just gone off the board, but there was something all wrong. Something in the way he was falling – tumbling rather than diving. A cry split the air as the kid spun gracelessly and smashed into the water…

Everyone around the pool watched in shock as the kid sank into the water, arms and legs outstretched. Unmoving. The kid touched the bottom of the dive pool.

"Where's the lifeguard?" Henry said, looking around wildly and not seeing one. Beside him Steve and Blake were watching the kid in the pool with dumbfounded expressions. All around, other kids had stopped to look but no one was doing anything.

"Someone's got to help him!" Henry said to Blake, who looked at him with a confused expression, as if at a loss what to do. Steve was staring at the water with eyes wide, his earlier aggression gone.

Shaking his head, Henry looked round at the other end of the pool and yelled, "Coach!" Then, kicking off his shoes, he took a breath and dived into the pool.

He entered the water perfectly and kicked away powerfully with his legs, angling down towards the bottom of the pool where the kid was resting. It took just a few seconds to reach the boy, who was several years younger and slightly built, which would make getting him to the surface easier. However, Henry knew from a life-saving class he'd taken the year before that the actual act of getting a person in trouble out of the water could be extremely dangerous for the rescuer. In a panic a flailing limb might knock you unconscious, or they might struggle and drag you down too.

Henry swam round so he was behind the kid and placed his hands under his shoulders. His lungs were starting to burn and this only got worse as he began to pull the stunned kid up from the bottom of the pool.

Come on! Henry thought, gritting his teeth and looking up. The dive pool was necessarily deep and the surface looked a million miles away.

They rose, metre by metre. The kid was like a lead weight trying to drag him back down again, but Henry wouldn't give up. Using all his strength, he kicked his legs even harder…

And with a gasp of relief, broke the surface. For a moment he merely floated there, getting much needed oxygen into his lungs. Then, checking the kid's head was above water, he began to swim on his back towards the edge of the pool.

"What happened?" Coach Tyler said, reaching down to pull the kid from Henry's arms as he made the side.

"Bad dive," Henry said breathlessly. A sudden wave of exhaustion swept over him. The coach quickly grabbed his arm to stop him going under the water.

"That's it," the coach said as Henry pulled himself out of the pool with his help. The other kid was lying on the floor, breathing but barely conscious. "Call the school nurse!" the coach yelled at a stunned-looking girl. She went running to the office and the man turned his attention back to the half-drowned boy. "It's a good job you were here, Henry. I sure as hell didn't see any of these other champs jumping in to help."

"Maybe you should do some life-saving lessons," Henry said, looking around and noticing that Blake and Steve were no longer by the side of the pool. In fact, it seemed they were no longer in the building. While he'd been saving the kid's life, they'd just walked away.

"What's the matter?" the coach asked from the kid's side. "You okay?"

"Yeah, I'm okay," said Henry, shaking his head in disgust at the other two boys. "I'm just fine."

4

"**Y**ou're a hero," Jennifer Ward said as she scooped another spoonful of pasta into his bowl at dinner that evening. As usual when something happened to her son, her answer was to start piling food onto his plate. "I don't know what that coach was thinking. Where was the supervision?"

"It wasn't his fault," Henry said. "He was called away. Accidents can happen in a few seconds, Mom."

"All the more reason to keep your eye on the ball. And what about those other boys not even jumping in to help?"

Henry took a mouthful of pasta and nodded. "Yeah, it was weird. Like they didn't know what to do or..." He struggled to find the words. "It was like they weren't even bothered."

At the other end of the kitchen table, Jennifer shook her head. The boxes from the car stood unopened all around. After what had happened at the pool, they'd decided to leave the unpacking for tomorrow. It had been a long day.

"Well, that coach had better give you a place on the team, that's all I can say," she added. "Or I'll be having words with him."

"*Mom.*"

"Okay, okay. I'll stay out of it!"

Henry thought for a moment before saying, "The strange thing was I started asking them about Gabrielle—"

"Who?" Jennifer interrupted.

"The girl from the gas station. Blake and Steve acted like they didn't know her. But I know they were lying."

His mother looked across the table at him with concern, before managing a smile. "What makes you think that?"

Henry shrugged. "I could just tell. That's all."

"You *are* going to try to fit in here, aren't you, Henry?"

He frowned. "What's that supposed to mean?"

"Just that it's important to make friends in a new place… A new school…"

"You don't believe me," he said.

"I—"

"You think it's in my head."

Jennifer looked down, choosing her words carefully. "No. But we've both had a long day. And then there was the incident at the pool…"

"They were lying to me *before* that. Something was wrong, I know it."

Jennifer smiled at him suddenly. "Just like your dad. Always a million questions—" She was interrupted by a loud knock on the front door. She rose from her seat, looking positively relieved at the distraction. "Now who could that be?"

As she went through to the lounge, Henry pushed his

plate away. *Of course, if something was wrong here, it had to be in his head.* He felt angry at her for never believing him. He wasn't a kid any more. And he wasn't in the habit of making up stories.

"Henry, you've got a visitor."

He turned to see Mr. Mallory standing beside his mother in the kitchen doorway. The man strode towards the table and stretched out his arm like a javelin.

"Put it there, son."

Feeling just a little stupid, Henry rose from his chair and placed his hand in Mallory's.

"I hate to think what would have happened at the pool without your quick wits," Mallory said, looking into Henry's eyes with great intensity and pumping his hand up and down. "The coach told me all about it. In fact, the coach and I had a very frank discussion about safety at the pool."

Henry coughed uncomfortably and pulled his hand free. "It wasn't the coach's fault. And someone else would have jumped in if I hadn't been there…"

Mallory waved his hand through the air as if dismissing that argument. "From what I heard, everyone else stood around like a bunch of starched shirts while you took charge."

Behind Mallory, Henry caught sight of his mom beaming and giving him the thumbs up.

"In fact," Mallory went on, "there's someone here who'd like to say a few words to you." He turned his head towards the lounge. "Blake! Get yourself in here!"

Blake ran into the room, coming to a halt a few steps behind Mallory.

"Well? Get on with it!" Henry was surprised by the way Mallory's tone changed completely when he spoke to Blake. It was like he was talking to a naughty five-year-old. Blake practically cowered as he stepped forward.

"I'm sorry for not helping you rescue Danny from the pool," he said, looking down at his shoes. "It all happened so fast. I was…uh…"

"Say it," Mallory ordered, his voice low.

"I was a coward."

Henry looked over at his mother, who seemed equally taken aback. He'd never heard anyone refer to himself as a *coward* before. It was clearly something Mallory had put into the kid's mouth.

"Do you forgive me?" Blake asked.

"Forget it," Henry said, trying to make light of it. "There's nothing to forgive."

Mallory reached over and placed a large hand on the back of Blake's neck. "Well, that's all settled then. I know you and my grandson are going to be the best of friends, Henry. And you'll be a good influence on him too."

Henry looked at Blake, who had raised his head for the first time since setting foot in the kitchen. *Grandson.* That figured.

"Run along and get your homework done," Mallory ordered and Blake trotted towards the door.

"See you in class on Monday, Henry!" Blake said as he passed Henry's mom, who watched him go like he was from a different planet. Henry had to smile at that.

"Now, first thing tomorrow," Mallory said, laying his hands lightly on Henry's shoulders, "I want you to get along to the medical centre to be checked out by my head physician."

Henry shook his head. "Really, I'm fine…"

Mallory's hands suddenly became very heavy on his shoulders. "But I insist. You put yourself through a traumatic experience. Just a standard medical to make sure everything's okay." Mallory glanced round at Jennifer. "And it's company policy following an incident."

"He'll be there," Jennifer said pointedly.

"Excellent," Mallory exclaimed, moving towards the kitchen door. "Dr. Chancellor will expect you at 9 a.m. Now I'll leave you both to your unpacking."

Henry could have left it there, but found himself calling out across the room, "Mr. Mallory!"

The big man stopped in his tracks and looked round. A slow smile spread across his face. "You're going to ask me about Gabrielle Henson."

Henry nodded. His mother looked daggers at him.

"You're a very astute young man," Mallory said with a chuckle. "I can see there'll be no keeping things from you."

"Everyone said they hadn't heard of her."

Mallory sighed and reached into his pocket. He produced a fat cigar, placed it in his mouth and began to chew on it without lighting up.

"Gabrielle and her family are from Newton," he said. "And Gabrielle, as you might have gathered, is a rather disturbed young lady. Her mental problems are exacerbated by her addiction to several illegal drugs. Very difficult for her family, who are old-fashioned types, to say the least. When we came here, Malcorp tried to help her fit in to our school system – without much success, I might add. I even had our psychiatrists offer counselling, but the girl wouldn't take it." Mallory removed the cigar from his mouth and looked thoughtfully at the chewed end. "Then the bad behaviour around town began. Theft. Vandalism. Accusations."

"Accusations?" Jennifer asked.

"Against some of the boys living here in the facility," he said. "I'm sure I don't have to paint you a picture. There was nothing to it, of course. Gabrielle was just looking for a bit of attention, I guess. And for a while she got it. Not an easy time for the boys."

"Probably not an easy time for her, either," Henry said, trying to reconcile Mallory's version of events with the terrified girl he'd met just that afternoon.

"So you understand why Steve and Blake were a little thrown by your question," Mallory continued, as if he hadn't heard the last comment. "We all thought we'd heard the last of her. A couple of weeks ago, she took an overdose and got herself hospitalized. Then she promptly ran out of the facility. Stole a car from town, but didn't get very far – we found it crashed in a ditch a few kilometres down the main road. After that I guess she just ran into the woods and lived rough until Trooper Dan picked her up this afternoon."

"Where is she now?" Jennifer asked.

"Being cared for by our doctors tonight," Mallory replied. "I paid her a visit just before I came here. She says she wants to make a fresh start. That she's going to accept some counselling support this time. We live in hope." He held up the cigar and laughed unexpectedly. "I used to smoke five of these a day, but I gave up before they killed me. Still like to keep one in my pocket, though." He put it back in his mouth and clamped his jaw down on the end.

Jennifer looked at Henry and smiled. "Mystery solved?"

He shrugged.

"Goodnight," Mallory said. "And thank you again, Henry. Malcorp owes you a huge favour."

He turned and left through the lounge. Jennifer walked over and put her arms around Henry. "My hero son."

An hour later, having helped his mom unpack their bedding and just a few other essentials, an exhausted Henry walked up the stairs to his new room. He'd left Jennifer sitting on the couch watching the late news, but he knew she'd be asleep within ten minutes herself.

His bedroom was as lavishly equipped as the rest of the lodge, with a large bed, a brand-new PC workstation and mini home-theatre system. There was even an electric guitar and amp in one corner. Henry didn't play, but on picking up the sleek, red and white Stratocaster, had decided that if he did nothing else while at Malcorp, he was going to learn.

It was only as he undressed and reached for the light that he noticed the envelope – it was stuck to the outside of the bedroom window with a piece of tape. Frowning, Henry opened the window and looked out. Someone had climbed the sloped roof of the lodge – a lot of effort to place an envelope on his window. He reached round and pulled it off the glass, opening it as he returned to his bed.

Inside the envelope was a handwritten note:

Heard about what you did at the pool. Sorry for being weird before – didn't know if you were one of us or not. Meet at "Full of Beans" in Newton, 7 p.m. tomorrow – Christian.

We need to talk about Gabrielle Henson.

Henry sat back in bed and was about to crumple the note, when he noticed something else scrawled on the other side, as if an afterthought.

PS – If you go to the medical centre, don't let them scan your brain.

He shook his head and thought about tossing the note in the bin. Christian was crazy, even by the standards of everyone else he'd met that day. But right now he was one of the few people Henry knew in Newton, and that had to count for something. He folded the note and laid it on his bedside table.

5

"**Y**ou should see the equipment they have in that lab. Absolutely cutting-edge stuff, not like the last place I worked. They must have spent millions…"

Henry was barely listening to his mom's words as she drove them to the medical centre in the buggy they'd been assigned the following morning. Despite his exhaustion, he hadn't slept well last night. His head had been spinning with thoughts of Gabrielle, the story that Mallory had told him and Christian's strange note.

"Hello!" Jennifer said, leaning into his ear. "Is anybody in there?"

Henry gave her an embarrassed smile. "Sorry. I'm still half asleep."

"Don't tell me you're worried about the medical exam?"

"No!" Henry paused. "They're not going to need a blood sample, are they?"

Jennifer laughed. "Just like your father. Scared of a little needle…" Her voice trailed away, as it often did when she started thinking about her husband. Henry reached over and touched her arm.

"It's okay, Mom."

"Yeah," she said, brightening. "And I can't see why they'd need blood. You're clearly as fit as a fiddle."

"I don't see why they need to do this test at all. Can't I just—"

"No," Jennifer said firmly. When he gave a groan of frustration, she added, "Come on, kiddo. Do it for your old lady, huh? Mallory insists and I need to keep on his good side."

"Okay, okay."

"Who knows, you might get a pretty young nurse."

Henry shot her a look. His mother smiled back at him innocently.

"And afterwards, you can walk back to the lodge and unpack the rest of those boxes."

"You're not hanging around?"

"Have to head over to the lab. Start getting things organized."

Henry nodded, the beginnings of a plan starting to form in his mind. Once he was dropped off at the medical centre, he'd walk into reception, wait around until his mom drove off and then slip out. It wasn't that he minded going to the doctor, it just seemed so unnecessary – especially on his last free day before starting at a new school.

The buggy rounded another set of anonymous glass and metal buildings and the medical centre appeared before them. It was located on the highest point within the Malcorp complex, on a hill covered around the base with thick trees. Beyond the trees it was possible to see a high fence encircling a windowless, concrete building – a stark contrast to all the others in the complex. A gravel driveway ascended through the trees to an open gate in the wall.

"That's different," Henry said as the buggy ascended the driveway. "You're going to work in that place, Mom?"

"No!" Jennifer replied, sounding relieved at the fact. The featureless façade of the medical centre was decidedly uninviting – like a vault or mausoleum of some kind. "The IVF lab is on the other side of the complex. And it has windows."

They reached the end of the driveway and pulled up in front of the main entrance: a set of wooden double doors over three metres high. Closed-circuit TV cameras on either side of these doors scanned the buggy as they stopped. One of the doors opened a crack and a tall, thin man with slicked-back hair and a spotless white coat emerged from the building.

"Henry Ward?" he asked, approaching the buggy. In one hand he cradled a device that looked like an iPad, only smaller and thinner. "I'm Nurse Levin. I'm here to take you directly to your medical exam."

The look of disappointment must have been evident on Henry's face, because his mom slapped him on the shoulder. "No getting out of it, kiddo."

Henry climbed out of the buggy and she turned it round fast, kicking up gravel on the driveway. "Don't forget the unpacking!" she yelled over her shoulder as she sped away.

"Great," Henry said. So much for his last day of freedom before Malcorp High…

"Let's get inside," Nurse Levin said, leading the way back to the door. "Dr. Chancellor doesn't like to be kept waiting."

Passing through the giant entrance doors, Henry found himself in a high-ceilinged reception area where every surface appeared to be made of marble. As Levin briskly led the way to a door on the other side of the area, Henry realized that the place was missing something that had been present in every other doctor's surgery he'd been to. A reception desk. Clearly visits to the medical centre were by appointment only. It also felt distinctly chilly inside the building after the heat of the morning. Maybe it was all the marble. The interior was bright, despite the lack of windows. Henry looked up at the ceiling and made out large globe lights throwing out the ridiculous amount of illumination necessary in a building with no natural sunlight.

Levin reached a glass door and swiped a key card through a reader, ushering Henry through as it slid open. They walked into a corridor lined with steel doors marked only with numbers. He turned right, into another corridor. And then another. Levin didn't drop his pace for a second and offered no conversation as they made their way through the building. Soon Henry was completely disoriented and couldn't have found his way back to reception if he'd wanted to. The doors and corridors looked identical to him and he was beginning to wonder how Levin found his way around, when the nurse stopped in front of a door marked 603.

"Here we are," Levin said, throwing the door open.

Henry walked through into a small examination room. Like everywhere else in the building it was windowless, lit by a globe in the ceiling.

"Why don't you strip down to your underwear and I'll go through the preliminaries," the nurse said, tapping the tablet screen with his finger.

Feeling more than a little self-conscious, Henry took off his T-shirt, folded it and laid it across the back of a chair in the corner.

"Just a few background questions," Levin said, an apologetic tone in his voice, as Henry sat in another chair and began to remove his sneakers. "Any previous injuries or medical conditions?"

Henry pulled off his socks and placed them in his shoes. "No."

"Not taking prescription drugs at the moment?"

"No."

"Non-prescription drugs?"

"Uh…no."

"Smoke?"

"No."

They went through a list of about twenty other questions, at the end of which Henry was sitting in his boxer shorts, arms folded across his chest, shivering from the chill in the room.

"Last question," Levin said. "Have you ever been in trouble with the law?"

Henry frowned. "What has that got to do with the medical exam?"

"It's just a standard question," Levin said with a smile. "If you don't want to answer…"

"No," Henry said before he even knew he was going to lie. "I've never been in trouble with the police."

"Great," Levin said, tucking the tablet under his arm. To Henry's surprise, the nurse stepped forward and slapped him on the upper arm. "You're going to do fine. Dr. Chancellor will be along in a moment."

With that, he exited the room.

Alone, Henry rubbed his arm where Levin had slapped him – for a slightly-built guy, he had some strength behind him. He looked round forlornly at his pile of clothes on the other chair. The room seemed to be getting cooler by the minute. Everything about the inside of the medical centre was cold and hard and sterile. Even the floor felt uncomfortably cold against the bare soles of his feet.

Time passed…

Henry wrapped his arms around himself and considered putting his T-shirt back on. But the doctor could arrive at any minute, so he sat as he was. Goosebumps formed on the exposed skin of his arms and legs.

He began to wonder how long he'd been sitting there. Ten minutes? Twenty? It occurred to him that they hadn't passed a single other person on their way through the medical centre. Was it possible he'd been forgotten?

He decided to see if anyone was around outside. Rising from the chair, Henry moved towards the door, feeling surprisingly stiff.

He didn't make it.

Halfway to the door his head spun and his knees buckled. It felt for all the world as if he'd just finished a two-kilometre swim. Henry threw his hands out to break his fall as the floor came rushing up to meet him…

"He's coming round."

Henry recognized the voice as belonging to Nurse Levin. He opened his eyes and squinted against a bright light that shone in his face.

"Where am I?" he asked, licking his dry lips. He was lying down on some kind of padded surface. He tried to sit up and a woman's hand touched his chest, holding him down gently but firmly.

"Do not try to sit up," the woman said. Her voice had a strong Eastern European accent and the commanding tone of a doctor. Henry opened his eyes a little more against the light and saw Dr. Chancellor (identified by a badge on the lapel of her white coat) for the first time. Although he was lying down, Henry sensed that she was tall. She was also blonde and strikingly beautiful, although her face had a cool, calculating look to it that made him feel a little uncomfortable. Not least because he was lying practically naked on a table in front of her.

"Your heartbeat is elevated," Chancellor said, running a soft hand over his chest. "Are you still feeling light-headed?"

"Uh, a little," Henry said, looking round at Levin, who was standing on the other side of the table. "What happened?"

"You passed out in the examination room," Levin said. "We found you lying on the floor."

"Has this happened before?" Chancellor asked, removing a pencil light from her pocket and shining it in his eyes.

"No," Henry replied.

Unexpectedly, the doctor ran a hand through Henry's hair, caressing the curve of his skull. Henry realized that he must have looked more than a little shocked, because in his peripheral vision he saw Nurse Levin suppressing a smile.

"You have a beautiful cranial structure," Dr. Chancellor said, feeling under the back of his head and then removing her hand. "Highly developed."

"Thank you," Henry said uncertainly.

Dr. Chancellor turned to Levin and said, "Put him in the scanner."

As she strode through to an adjoining room that could be seen through a glass window, Levin wheeled the table upon which Henry was lying towards a large, cylindrical machine in the corner.

"What's going on?" Henry demanded.

"Relax," Levin said. "You had a dizzy spell and it's probably nothing, but better safe than sorry."

Henry twisted his head back so he could get a better look at the machine. It was the size of a car and made of smooth, white plastic. There was a circular opening at the front. Levin wheeled the table towards it.

"Hold on a minute," Henry protested as the table made contact with the machine and locked in place. Then Levin pushed something and the surface on which Henry was lying slid forwards so only his head entered the opening of the machine. Blue lights set into the circular headspace began to glow all around. "What's going on?"

Levin patted him on the shoulder reassuringly. "We're just going to take a couple of brain scans. Lie still and it will all be over in a moment."

Henry's blood ran cold as he remembered the words of Christian's note: *Don't let them scan your brain.*

"This isn't necessary," Henry said, trying to sit up. He found this was not possible as his head was in the machine and Levin had taken hold of his ankles so he couldn't wriggle out. "Could someone call my mom?"

"Just lie very still."

The blue lights suddenly glowed brilliant white and Henry involuntarily closed his eyes. Even with them closed he could sense the glaring light, which seemed to be boring into his skull. He opened his mouth to cry out...

And suddenly the table was being pulled away from the brain scanner. Levin grabbed his arm and pulled him into a sitting position.

"All done!" the nurse said, looking round at the control room. Through the glass, Dr. Chancellor gave an *okay* sign and then disappeared through another door.

"Uh, is that it?" Henry asked, blinking as his eyes readjusted.

"That's it," Levin said. "Looks like you have a minor ear infection, which caused the dizziness. Probably the result of jumping in the pool yesterday."

Henry looked round at the scanner. "You diagnosed an

ear infection with that? Did you even look at the results?"

Levin didn't answer. He dumped Henry's clothes on the table beside him. "Get dressed and let's get you home."

"But what about the examination?"

Levin looked at him as if he was being slow. "You just had it."

Less than ten minutes later, Levin dropped Henry off at his lodge in one of the medical centre buggies. As Henry climbed out of the passenger seat, the nurse snapped his fingers.

"I almost forgot," he said. "You mentioned something about wanting us to contact your mother…"

"Yeah," Henry said, remembering with some embarrassment the way he'd panicked during the scan.

"I guess she should know about the ear infection. Normally we'd recommend bed rest for a couple of days. Maybe a high-fibre diet with prunes…"

"Don't worry," Henry blurted out. "I'll tell her myself."

"You're sure?"

"Really sure."

Levin put the buggy in gear and gave him a little salute. "Be seeing you."

As the buggy zipped away, Henry turned back to the lodge and a day's worth of unpacking, having already decided not to tell his mom anything about passing out in the centre. She didn't need the worry. And he didn't need the prunes.

6

The Full of Beans coffee shop in Newton looked as if it could have been a popular place to hang out once upon a time. The walls were painted in warm reds and browns and every piece of available hanging space was filled with arty black and white photographs. The tables and chairs were made of funky-looking 60s-style plastic, while more comfortable sofas lined the edge of the cafe. A column in the middle of the room was plastered with posters for local bands, theatre productions and classified ads. However, all of them were faded and peeling; the newest were for bands that had played the town over three years before. As Henry entered through the main door and looked around the empty tables and chairs, he decided that whatever life had once been at Full of Beans, it had gone somewhere else a long time ago.

Following his strange experience at the medical centre, Henry had spent the day unpacking. By the time his mom had arrived home from the lab, most of the work was done. As his mom had prepared dinner, she'd started questioning him about the medical exam. He'd told her that it was fairly standard stuff: sight and hearing tests, look right and cough, the usual. His mom had accepted this and after they ate had agreed to let him meet up with Christian without the slightest objection. He'd been a little surprised by this after the months of being grounded in the city, but she obviously assumed nothing could happen to him in sleepy old Newton.

The town was a twenty-minute walk from the gate of the Malcorp complex, where he'd signed out with Hank the security guard. If he'd wanted, he could have borrowed a buggy from the gatehouse and driven it along a special track that ran parallel with the main road, but Henry preferred to walk. He'd been cooped up in the house all day and felt like he needed the fresh air. After the incident at the medical centre he hadn't felt dizzy again – hopefully a sign that the ear infection wasn't serious. He didn't want anything to delay his return to the pool, or spoil his chances when he tried out for Coach Tyler at the end of the week.

He needn't have worried. The early evening walk to Newton had left him feeling great – no dizziness at all. The air was fresh and clear, the temperature just right and there wasn't a car in sight. As he listened to the breeze blowing through the firs and the sound of cicadas buzzing, Henry had admitted to himself that Newton County had some things going for it. Things that the city couldn't offer.

What it didn't have was nightlife – that much became clear as he reached the edge of town. At 7 p.m. the streets were deserted. Every shop along the high street was shut – with the exception of Full of Beans. And that was completely empty. It was beginning to look like his mom's instincts were correct: he couldn't get into trouble here even if he wanted to.

As he stood inside the doorway of the deserted cafe, he looked around for Christian. It wasn't hard to see that he wasn't there. At the counter, a fourteen-year-old girl with short-cropped black hair was reading a paperback book beside a large, chrome coffee machine with an Italian name emblazoned on the front. The girl didn't look up as he entered, as if she was used to people walking through the door, taking one look at the empty place and then walking right back out again. Feeling uncomfortable, Henry moved across the room to the counter.

"Hi," he said, looking down at the girl as she turned a page. He noticed that her hands were flecked with many different colours of paint and her fingernails were bitten short.

"Hi," she said, looking up at him without much interest. "What can I get you?"

Henry eyed the industrial-sized coffee machine and wondered when it had last been used. "Just a Diet Coke, thanks."

The girl pushed herself off the counter with an audible sigh, opened a bar fridge and removed a glass bottle. She unscrewed the top and placed it on the counter in front of Henry. "Three bucks."

Henry passed the money across to her.

"Want a glass?"

"No thanks."

"Anything to eat?" The girl waved a hand over glass

containers filled with cookies behind the counter.

"No." For all he knew the cookies were as old as the band posters on the column.

"Take a seat then," the girl said, waving him away dismissively. She already had her head stuck in the book again.

No wonder this place is so popular, Henry thought as he turned away from the counter. *It must be the friendly service.*

To his surprise, Christian was now seated at a table in the corner of the cafe away from the window.

"I didn't hear you come in," Henry said as he joined him at the table.

Christian spread his hands. "I'm like a ninja."

"You hang out here much?" Henry asked, looking around the deserted interior.

"I like to be sociable," Christian replied, leaning forward as if he wanted to speak confidentially and was afraid of someone overhearing. "How was your medical exam?"

"How did you know about that?"

Christian tapped the side of his angular nose. "Sources. Did you meet Dr. Chancellor?"

"Yeah."

"I'd like her to examine *me* sometime," Christian said with a grin that quickly faded away. "But actually I wouldn't. Because she's a psycho Nazi doctor."

Henry frowned at him. "What is that supposed to—"

"Did they give you a brain scan?"

"Yes, I—"

Christian banged his fist on the table with enough force to make Henry jump in surprise. The noise echoed around the empty cafe.

"What the hell did you let them do that for?" Christian demanded, leaning even closer. "Wasn't my note clear?"

Henry leaned in as well. "I had a dizzy spell. I passed out. What was I supposed to do?"

"You *passed out*?"

"I picked up an ear infection when I jumped in the pool yesterday. It affects balance."

Christian shook his head as if he didn't believe a word of it. "You were drugged. Did they give you pills to take?"

"No."

"Something to drink?"

"No!"

Christian reached over and started examining Henry's left arm.

"What are you doing?"

"Looking for injection marks," Christian replied.

"They did not give me an injection," Henry said, pulling his arm back. Christian was acting even stranger now than he had the day before, when he'd walked away from Henry and Blake.

"Then what's that?"

Henry looked at a red mark Christian was pointing to on his upper arm, just under the sleeve of his T-shirt. He pulled up his shirt and looked at the mark more closely. The skin looked inflamed and there was a red point in the centre.

"It's just a mosquito bite," he said. "Must have got it as I walked here tonight."

"That's an injection mark."

"It is not…" Henry stopped dead as he remembered the way Nurse Levin had slapped him on the upper arm before leaving him in the examination room. He was pretty sure the slap had been on the exact same spot where the so-called injection mark was now coming up. Could Levin have had some kind of syringe concealed in his palm? Had they drugged him? Henry shook his head and laughed to himself. He was getting caught up in Christian's paranoid fantasies – it was pretty easy to do. "Why would they want to drug me?"

"To get you inside the scanner," Christian replied. "Not much reason to conduct a brain scan as part of a normal medical exam, right? But for someone who has passed out in their waiting room…"

Henry played along for the moment. "And what is the purpose of the brain scan?"

Christian grinned enigmatically at him. "Well, that's the million-dollar question, isn't it?" He pulled a folded piece of paper from his pocket and passed it across the table. "Take a look at this."

Henry unfolded the paper. It was a printout of a news story from the internet entitled *Polish Doc Struck Off for Gene Crimes*. Scanning the article, he made out that it was about a Dr. Chenowski of Krakow University who had been accused of violating international law in the attempted cloning of human babies. Chenowski had fled the country and was wanted by Interpol for multiple breaches of the international agreement on genetic engineering. At the top of the paper, someone had scrawled in black pen: *Think this is our woman – Fox*.

"So?" Henry said, passing the paper back to Christian.

"Dr. Chenowski now works for Malcorp," Christian said. "Except she changed her name to Chancellor."

"Oh come on! Chenowski's a wanted criminal!"

"She's got a new identity."

"And what makes you so sure it's her?"

Christian produced another printout, this time a grainy black and white image of a dark-haired woman surrounded by police officers. The caption underneath read: *Chenowski arrested outside Krakow clinic*. Again the paper was marked with the name *Fox*. Henry strained to make out the face of the woman, trying to match it with what he'd seen of Dr. Chancellor.

"It's her, right?" Christian insisted.

"Chancellor has blonde hair."

"She dyed it!"

"I can't tell from this picture. It's way too blurry."

"How about this?"

Christian passed him another web news story, auto-translated from the Polish and dated from the early-nineties, the headline: *Beauty Contest Crowns Local Girl*. The story was about eighteen-year-old Magda Chenowski, a medical student who had won a beauty pageant in the city of Lodz. The picture showed a stunning, tall girl wearing a ribbon and clutching a bouquet of flowers.

"Right?"

"She's twenty years younger!"

"It's her!"

Henry tapped the same handwritten note on the top of the story. "Who's this Fox?"

"My contact."

"Your contact?"

"Fox feeds me information."

"It sounds like Fox is feeding you bull. Who is he?"

Christian shook his head. "I can't tell you. Not until I know you better."

That line again. It was the final straw for Henry, who decided he'd wasted enough of his evening on Christian's fantasies. For all he knew, the kid *was* Fox and had pulled the stories off the net himself. He was clearly in need of a friend and perhaps thought that inventing a story about psycho doctors in Malcorp was the way to get one. But he was sorely mistaken.

"Where are you going?" Christian asked, his face falling as Henry rose from his chair.

"I think I've heard enough."

"But I have more evidence!" He grabbed Henry's arm in desperation. "You have to listen! There aren't many of us left!"

"What are you talking about?" Henry demanded, pulling free.

"There aren't many...*normal ones* left."

Henry couldn't suppress a laugh. "Okay, Christian. Perhaps I'll see you at school tomorrow, huh? Don't drink too much coffee. You don't need it."

With that, he turned and strode to the door, determined to get home as quickly as possible and get an hour in on his PS3 before he had to hit the sack. But something caught his eye as he put his hand on the door…and it stopped him in his tracks.

Hanging by the door was a framed photograph, one among about a hundred in the cafe. But this one wasn't of a band or a film star or a cafe scene from the 1930s. And it stood out because it was colour, not black and white. It showed two teenage girls, smiling and laughing at the camera and dressed up as if they were preparing to go out for a party. Henry recognized them both.

One was Gabrielle Henson, the terrified girl he'd met at the gas station.

The other was the girl who'd served him a Diet Coke just ten minutes before.

Reaching out, he plucked the photo off the wall and slowly turned back into the cafe. The girl behind the counter had closed her book and was looking directly at him, one eyebrow raised.

"I'm Fox," she said. "And we need to talk."

7

Five minutes later, Henry and Christian were sitting on a worn-out couch in the tiny apartment above the coffee shop. The girl calling herself Fox had closed up the cafe (Henry guessed that she wasn't expecting any other customers that evening anyway) and led them up a narrow staircase behind the counter into the cluttered lounge. Every surface was piled with books, ornaments or stacks of paper, as if the contents of an apartment three times larger had been squeezed inside. Having ordered them to sit down and be quiet just as brusquely as she served coffee, the girl had promptly disappeared into a back room and had not re-emerged.

"What's going on, Christian?" Henry asked finally. The other kid had been unusually silent since they'd ascended the stairs.

"Fox has the answers," he said, almost in a whisper. "Patience."

"*Fox*," Henry repeated. "What kind of name is that anyway?"

Christian shrugged. "Just an internet handle she uses, I guess. Her real name's Michelle or something."

"Uh-huh," Henry replied, looking around the apartment. The kitchen was separated from the living area by a narrow counter; dirty dishes were piled in the sink. As in the cafe downstairs, the walls were covered with framed pictures – although these were a mixture of watercolours and oils, not photographs. One of them, a painting of a forest – black trees stark against a burning sky – caught his eye. He stood up to look at it. It was really good. And it was signed *Fox* in the bottom right-hand corner. He remembered the paint stains he'd noticed on her hands earlier and looked around at the other pictures. At least half of them appeared to be by her.

One of the bedroom doors opened and the girl slipped through quickly, as if she didn't want them seeing what was on the other side.

"Did you paint this?" Henry asked, pointing to the picture of the forest.

"So?" the girl said defensively, like she was expecting him to make fun of her over it.

"I like it."

"Know a lot about art, do you?" Without waiting for a response, she walked through to the kitchen and started running water into the sink.

Henry looked at Christian in exasperation. "Maybe I should get going."

"Just hold on," Christian said. "You want to find out about Gabrielle, don't you?" He looked round at Fox, who had her back to them and was placing dishes in the sink. "Henry had a medical exam this morning."

Fox stopped what she was doing and looked round with new interest. Picking up a towel from the counter, she dried her hands and moved towards them.

"What happened?" she asked.

Christian nodded encouragingly and Henry related the tale of his trip to the medical centre, even though he was impatient to know more about Gabrielle.

"He was drugged," Christian added after Henry explained how he'd passed out on the floor of the examination room.

"*I had an inner ear infection*," Henry argued. "It can cause dizziness."

Fox, who had listened intently up to that point, said, "So you let them scan you?"

"I didn't *let them* scan me," Henry shot back. "I passed out. They were worried about me."

"You seem fine now," the girl added.

"Well, yes…"

"And you've never passed out before?"

"I've never had an inner ear infection before."

"So *they* say."

Christian nodded as if Fox's arguments were making perfect sense. Henry thought back to the examination and how it seemed they hadn't even examined the scan before making a diagnosis. He asked cautiously, "So, what *was* going on then?"

Fox paused a moment before answering. "We think that's how they change you. The doctors at Malcorp, I mean."

75

Henry looked at them in confusion. "Change? Change who?"

Christian waved a hand at the front windows of the apartment. "All the kids in Newton. And all the kids at the Malcorp complex."

Fox nodded. "We think the doctors at Malcorp medical centre are altering them somehow."

Henry laughed out loud at the absurdity of the idea. "What do you mean, changing them? How exactly?"

"Turning them into good little boys and girls," Christian replied. "Drones who do everything they're told all the time. You've met Blake and the others, haven't you?"

"Yeah, but…" Henry thought back to the kids at the pool. Their weirdly detached manner. The way Mallory had treated Blake like a five year old and he'd just taken it. Henry shook his head. "Okay, they're a little…odd. But what you're saying sounds crazy. Anyway, I came here to find out about Gabrielle Henson – not them."

"Why are you so concerned about her?" Fox snapped, studying him with her intelligent eyes.

Henry shrugged. *Why am I so concerned about her?* he thought. It was a fair question. "I don't know. I met her and she seemed to be in trouble…"

"And you just can't resist a damsel in distress, right?" Fox said sarcastically.

"What can I say? I'm a hero like that." He paused. "Honestly, she asked for my help and I felt that I could have done more. That's all."

Fox's expression softened. "Did she seem okay? I mean, did she know who she was?"

Henry could tell from her voice that Fox was honestly concerned about her friend. "She was in a bad way," he said carefully. "Looked like she'd been living rough, but apart from that... She was talking to me until..."

"Trooper Dan grabbed her," Christian finished.

"But Mallory told you she's back and everything's okay, didn't he?" Fox pressed. "So why are you still asking questions about her?"

"I..."

"Or didn't you believe him?"

Henry opened his mouth to protest, but then stopped. He realized that she was right. Deep down, he just didn't believe Mallory's story. There was something about it that just didn't fit with the terrified girl he'd met at the back of the gas station the day before.

"Mallory said she was disturbed," Henry explained. "She was into drugs."

Fox laughed harshly. "Drugs! And where do you think she got them from out here?"

"She made accusations against boys from the complex."

"She was dating a guy," Fox said. "He changed overnight. Didn't want to see her any more."

"That happens."

"No, he *literally* changed overnight – said he had to devote time to his studies. Wouldn't even talk to her. Gabrielle began asking questions around the complex and that's when she started getting scared…"

"And then she disappeared," Christian finished for her.

"We used to meet up after school," Fox continued. "One day about a month ago, she just didn't turn up. So I called her mom and she told me that Gabrielle was sick and had been admitted to hospital in the complex. When I asked if I could visit her, she told me that I was a bad influence and to stay away from her daughter. She told me that Gabrielle was sick in the head and the Malcorp doctors were going to make her all better." Fox's face twisted with anger at the memory. "*She's* the one who's sick…a mother talking about her own daughter like that. And do you know what the scariest thing was? I could tell she actually believed the crap she was saying."

Christian nodded. "Malcorp putting words into her mouth. We think that's how Mallory works it. Picks parents with some hard-line ideas about raising their kids in the first place and exploits them."

"*Exploits them?*" Henry said.

"You know," Christian continued, "plays on all their natural fears that the big bad world is going to turn them into drug addicts or criminals the moment they're out of their sight. Mallory tells these parents he can make their kids perfect, upstanding citizens or something. Everyone's happy."

"Look," Henry said, "I know you want to believe that there's some conspiracy going on here, but the truth of the matter is that Gabrielle Henson is a kid who got her heart broke and went off the rails…"

Fox snatched up the photograph of her and Gabrielle and thrust it into Henry's hands.

"We've been friends since kindergarten," she said, her face flushed with passion. "Since long before this town had even heard of Malcorp. And I'm telling you that Gabrielle Henson does not have mental problems. And she is not into drugs." Her voice choked and she fought to keep talking. "She's my friend."

Henry looked down at the photograph in his hand. The two girls certainly looked normal enough. *Happy.* They were several years younger in the picture and he noticed for the first time that it had been taken in the cafe downstairs. In the background the tables were filled with customers. Henry looked up at Fox. She was glaring, as if daring him to argue with her. It was hard to reconcile this spiky character with the younger girl in the photo.

"I'm sorry your friend has problems, whatever they are," he said gently, handing the picture back. "But I'm sure you'll see she's okay now she's back with her family…"

Fox frowned at him. "Gabrielle isn't back with her family. I went round her place earlier today and she isn't there."

"Well, maybe they're keeping her at the medical centre for observation…"

Christian removed an item from his pocket and held it up. "What do you say we find out about that? Tonight."

Henry saw he was holding a Malcorp key card.

"This will get us into the Malcorp medical centre," Christian explained. "Swiped it from my dad a few weeks ago. He thought he'd lost it. It's time someone found out what's really going on in there."

Henry held up his hands. Suddenly everything was moving too fast. "Now hold on…"

Fox moved closer to him. "Gabrielle's somewhere in that centre. If we could just talk to her for a while, we could find out why she ran away. I need to know why she didn't come to me when she escaped the first time."

Henry held her gaze. "I've been to the medical centre and it's just a clinic. There's nothing going on. And if the students at Malcorp are a little strange… Well, it's just because they're the kids of pushy parents. You know, high achiever types."

"You don't believe that," Christian said. "I heard about the pool. Blake and his friends just walked away when that kid was drowning, right?"

Henry glanced at him. "They just didn't have life-saving training, that's all."

"They didn't have the programming! They're…" He struggled to find the words. "Replacements! Robots! They don't do anything they're not ordered to do!"

Henry sighed and walked to the door. He'd heard enough. He couldn't believe they'd almost got him believing their insane ideas.

"I'm going home," he said.

"But we've got more to show you!" Christian said.

He made to follow Henry, but Fox threw out a hand. "Let him go. He'll be one of them as well in a week or so. For all we know, he already is."

For some reason, these last words cut Henry and he paused as he opened the door. Then, with a shake of his head, he flew out and down the stairs, away from the pair of weirdos as fast as his legs would carry him.

8

Henry's first day at Malcorp High began at 8.30 a.m. on Monday. As he walked across the manicured grass in the direction of the school buildings, along with scores of other kids, the events of the evening before seemed increasingly like a strange dream. He hadn't told his mom about Fox and Christian's plan to break into the medical centre, of course, or any of their strange ideas for that matter. He didn't want her worrying about the delusional locals he'd somehow befriended just a day after arriving at the complex. Although she was trying hard not to show it, he could tell she was stressed about the new job. The last thing he wanted was her thinking that he'd fallen in with a *bad crowd* again. And he certainly didn't need the hassle of her lecturing him about it either.

The walk to school took less than ten minutes. The other students were dressed in green and gold school uniforms and ambled along like any other kids Henry had seen – not like robots at all. Henry had yet to receive his uniform, so he was dressed in the smartest pair of trousers he had and a plain white shirt.

"Hey there, newbie!" Blake ran over and fell into step

beside him. "Pumped about your first day?"

Henry gave him an exaggerated look of excitement. "Yeah! I can't wait!"

"I can tell you're joking," Blake replied with a laugh. "But seriously, the school is pretty neat. Have you checked out your timetable yet?"

Henry shook his head. "I guess I'll get that when I arrive."

Blake pulled a small tablet PC, bearing the Malcorp logo, from his blazer and tapped the screen, navigating to a student list and Henry's name. He got the timetable up on screen and handed it across to Henry.

"You'll get an eDiary," Blake explained. "All the students have them."

"Cool," Henry said, examining the machine. "What games does it have on it?"

Blake gave a snorting laugh and punched him on the arm. "Kidder! But seriously, we'd better get you to the uniform shop before we go to class."

"That's okay. I'll pick it up at recess."

Blake looked at him as if he was being crazy. "No way! We need to get you in the school colours! You don't want to stand out, do you?"

With that, he snatched the electronic diary from Henry's hand and jogged on ahead.

"No, I guess not," Henry said and ran after him. Blake might be just about the straightest kid on the face of the planet, but at least he wasn't crazy-delusional like the other acquaintances he'd made.

And at the moment, that counted for a lot.

* * *

The school was divided into three areas: one for nursery and infant kids, another for juniors and finally the high school. The uniform shop was located at the back of the high school area, which gave Henry the chance to check out the building as Blake led the way. Like everywhere else in the Malcorp complex, the place was spotlessly clean and looked newly built. Clearly things were replaced the moment they began to wear, right down to the light switches and door handles.

An ear-splitting siren sounded and kids started scurrying for class, although Henry was surprised by the lack of noise within the building. The corridors of his last school had been deafening in the moments before class began, as students yelled, argued and shouted last minute messages to one another. Seconds after the siren stopped in Malcorp High, complete silence had fallen over the corridors.

At the uniform shop, Henry was issued with a pair of black trousers, a grey shirt and a green and gold blazer and tie. The woman behind the counter told him that a spare set would be sent to his lodge and his mom would be billed. Henry took his new clothes and put them on in a tiny changing room, checking the tie in a mirror on the wall. His last school hadn't had a uniform, so the blazer and tie felt weird. Henry stared at his reflection and sighed.

"You look *soooo* cool."

He swiped the curtain of the changing room and jumped to find Blake standing right there, waiting eagerly.

"Man, you look great!" Blake exclaimed and pumped his fist in the air. "One of us! One of us!"

"Right," Henry said, putting his old clothes into his bag and slinging it over his shoulder. "We should get going. Don't like being late on my first day."

"That's the spirit," Blake said as they walked alongside one another down the corridor. He consulted his diary. "Hey, we've got class together! French." His face fell. "Man, what a way to start the day!"

Henry looked at him and smiled. "Have we found something you don't like about school?"

"It's just…I've been studying that darn language for six whole months and I don't seem to be making any progress."

"Well, six months isn't long," Henry replied. French was actually one of his favourite subjects. He'd had it at his last school since he was twelve, clearly a lot earlier than they started here. He'd found, to his surprise, that he had a real facility for language and had been top of his class in both French and Spanish for most of the last two years. To let Blake know he was no slouch when it came to languages, he added, "*La pratique rend parfait.*"

Blake looked at him and roared with laughter. "Nice accent, Jean-Claude! Where did you learn that, a *Pink Panther* movie? Jeez, you're a kidder!"

Henry was still puzzling over what that was supposed to mean as they reached the classroom door and Blake pulled it open. The entire class was silent, heads down over thick textbooks while a prim-looking woman stood at the front, casting her eyes over them. She turned her gaze on Blake and Henry as they entered.

"*Pardon, Mademoiselle Chabrol,*" Blake replied in perfectly accented French. "*J'ai dû prendre Henry pour aller chercer son uniforme.*"

The teacher gave Henry an unimpressed look. "*Et ce nouveau spécimen ne parle pas pour lui-même?*" Doesn't he speak for himself?

There was a smattering of laughter around the room, which was silenced by a stern look from Mademoiselle Chabrol. Henry had worked out, despite the speed at which the teacher had rattled off her question, that it was his turn to speak.

"*Je m'appelle Henry Ward,*" he said, trying to sound as fluent as possible. "Uh…*je suis un student nouveau dans votre classe…*"

"*Oui, oui,*" the woman said with a dismissive wave of her hand. "*Asseyez-vous et ouvrez le livre à la page cinquante-six. Nous lisons* À la Recherche du Temps Perdu." As she turned away, she muttered, "*Mon dieu, il y a du travail à faire avec celui-ci.*"

Blake nodded to two spare desks at the back and they sat down. Henry picked up the book in front of him, which was almost a thousand pages long, and flicked through. It was written in incredibly complex French – far more advanced than anything he'd ever been asked to read before in class. He looked at Blake who, like the other twenty students, had become engrossed in the French text. He turned towards the front and saw that the teacher was regarding him with a look of barely disguised contempt.

"*Avez-vous un problème, Monsieur Ward?*" she called across to him. "*Préféreriez-vous quelque chose de plus simple à lire?*" *Would you prefer something easier to read?* She held up the French equivalent of a *Janet and John* book, causing more giggles around the room.

"*Non, mademoiselle,*" Henry replied firmly. He looked down at his book and pretended to read.

"How long did you say you've been studying French?" Henry asked Blake at the end of the period, as they walked to the next class, which was maths.

"Six months," Blake replied. "You were struggling, I could tell. But don't worry, you'll soon get up to speed. Mademoiselle Chabrol is the best."

"Yeah. She seemed like a…really nice lady."

"How's your maths?"

"Not bad," Henry said with a lot less certainty than he might have done an hour earlier. "Do you know what we're studying this term?"

Blake held open the door for him to enter the maths class. "Nothing too difficult: quadratic equations with integer coefficients."

Heart sinking, Henry took a seat as the teacher at the front began to chalk up equations on the board that looked as if they belonged to the space programme. He was left behind from the beginning, while the rest of the class had no problem answering the most complex questions. In fact, they seemed to have the answers even before the teacher asked them, hands shooting into the air, desperate to provide the solution. Henry surreptitiously looked around for anyone else who was struggling, but saw no one. Every student was switched on, alert and fully engaged. In a normal class there was certain to be a couple of kids sleeping through things at the back, but this class was nothing like normal. Christian was nowhere to be seen, leading Henry to wonder if he'd been put in the wrong stream – was this some kind of genius-level group he'd been placed in by mistake? And if so, where were all the normal kids?

The remaining classes of the day were exactly the same.

In History the teacher presented a text written in Old English that Henry might have had a chance of following if the class hadn't whizzed through it as if it was an easy reader. Science was an analysis of Einstein's $e=mc^2$ that left Henry behind after about two minutes. It was a relief when the final class of the day came around: Phys Ed. *Finally, something I can do,* Henry thought with relief as he got into his kit in the changing rooms.

"Tough day, Ward?" a familiar voice asked from a couple of lockers down. He looked round to see Steve, the kid he'd met at the pool. "I saw you in French class. What was it you said? *Uh…je…suis…un…student…*"

Several of the other boys in the changing room laughed.

"Leave him alone, Steve," Blake said, appearing at Henry's side. Steve waved his arm as if it wasn't worth it and started talking to his mates in low tones. They cracked up at something he said. *Great*, Henry thought, *even the jocks around here are smarter than me.*

"Ignore him," Blake said.

"What is with this place anyway?" Henry asked quietly, unable to keep the frustration from his voice. Academically, he'd never been one of the high achievers, but he was comfortably above average. Top of the class in a couple of subjects, like French... Or at least, he had been. He'd always felt sorry for those kids who seemed to struggle with every new thing that came along, but during the course of the day, he'd gained a fresh sympathy. He'd *become* one of them. "Were those classes supposed to be for geniuses or something? Because I am no genius."

"Geniuses?" Blake asked, genuine confusion in his tone. "Oh, you mean the gifted and talented kids? No, they have different classes by themselves. Y'know, more difficult stuff."

"Right," Henry said, slamming his locker shut. He was beginning to suspect that behind Blake's apparently guileless exterior, there was something altogether smarter going on. He could sure as hell speak good French, for one. And hold his own in a conversation about Einstein's theory of relativity. But so could most of the other kids at Malcorp High, it seemed. And if these were the average kids, what were the gifted and talented like?

They ran out of the changing rooms onto the sports field to meet the gym instructor, a middle-aged guy with greying hair who looked fitter than most of the kids in the class.

89

He sent them on a warm-up jog around the field and then called them back in with a blast from his whistle. Henry pushed his way to the front of the group. This was one lesson where he knew he could make a good impression, and he intended to do so.

"Sports day coming up in less than a month," the instructor said, his accent clipped and British. "So, we're practising middle distance events, starting with the three thousand metres."

There were a few theatrical groans around the group, which the instructor acknowledged with a grin.

"Yes, I know this is your favourite, so let's put on a good show." He pointed at Henry. "New kid, try to keep up. But don't push it, okay?"

"I'm fine, sir," Henry said. He'd run cross-country at his last school for a while. He could manage three kilometres.

The instructor slapped his hands together. "Okay. Everyone line up. And remember, it isn't a race!"

The class ran over to the track and as he joined them, Henry noticed a lone figure sitting atop the bleachers. Christian. Typically, his uniform looked as if it had been dragged through a hedge and he was missing his tie. He raised his hand and offered a little salute as he saw Henry looking.

"Good luck," Blake said, nudging his arm.

Henry looked round at him. "What did he mean? *It isn't a race.*"

Blake gave him one of his innocent looks. "Well, it isn't. Sports are non-competitive at Malcorp High." He bent slightly, preparing for the start along with the rest of the class. "Don't worry, you'll get used to it."

"Non-competitive," Henry repeated as he prepared for the start as well. Then something occurred to him. "What about the football teams? How do they do non-competitive?"

"Easy. They just take turns winning."

Before Henry could respond, the instructor raised his starting pistol and fired. The class started off and Henry sprinted in line with them. Competitive or not, he intended to do well.

Putting his head down, he caught up with Blake and passed him with ease. To his surprise he also passed Steve, who was at the head of the group, a second later. Then, without having to push himself too much, he found himself steaming ahead of the rest of the class. Looking over his shoulder, he saw the twenty or so other boys running together in a huddle as he moved steadily away from them.

"Ward!" the instructor yelled across the track, as he came to the bend. "Slow down, dammit!"

Almost tripping over his feet in confusion, Henry slowed his pace until the others caught up with him. Steve shot him a murderous look as they passed.

"Get with the programme!" he hissed.

Henry fell back until he was jogging alongside Blake, who looked at him and said, "We run as a unit. I should have explained."

As they completed their first lap of the track, the instructor fired his gun into the air again. On this signal every boy in the group doubled his running pace. Surprised by this sudden change, Henry found himself struggling to keep up. By the time he'd caught up with Blake, the instructor had fired his gun once again.

The group doubled its pace once more. Getting wise to what was going on, Henry was ready to increase his work rate this time and had no trouble keeping up. Blake nodded his head and said, "Now you're getting the idea."

Henry almost laughed with relief. Finally, a class where he wasn't a million light years behind everyone else…

The starting gun fired again.

The group broke into a full-on sprint. Henry kept with them as they tore around the track. After a revolution at this sprint pace his heart was racing and he was gasping for breath, but the group showed no sign of slowing. Casting a look at Blake he was surprised to see him at full sprint and not in the least fatigued. In fact, he hardly appeared to be out of breath. None of the class did.

The starting pistol fired again, barely audible to Henry above the blood thundering around his temples. The group actually increased its pace once more. They completed another circuit of the track. By this time, Henry's head felt as if it was going to explode with the blood pulsing around it from the effort of the prolonged sprint.

The gun fired again. The runners' speed increased…

Henry gasped and tried desperately to keep up with them. He managed another two hundred metres before his legs simply gave way. He collapsed on the grass beside the track, barely able to get breath into his lungs. For a moment he lay on his back, before a wave of nausea overcame him and he rolled over and vomited.

"Difficulty keeping up, newbie?" the instructor said, appearing at his side. He showed little concern at Henry's condition.

Henry wiped his mouth and looked round as the class flew by on another lap of the track. After almost two thousand metres they were still running like they were in a hundred-metre sprint. "I'm fine," he said.

The instructor gave a snorting laugh and walked away. Face burning as much from humiliation as from the blood pumping like crazy around his body, Henry turned towards the bleachers.

The spot where Christian had been sitting was empty.

9

"**T**hey really need to get a grip on their sterilization procedures. I mean, no wonder they're having contamination issues when there aren't even no-touch soap dispensers in the lab." Jennifer Ward paused briefly to spoon cornflakes into her mouth before she carried on talking at a mile a minute. "I really think I'm going to be able to raise their fertilization rate by four to five per cent without having to break a sweat…"

"That's great, Mom," Henry said, pushing his cereal around in his bowl distractedly.

The last two days at Malcorp High had followed the same pattern as his first. In every class he felt lost with the sheer complexity of what was being studied and the speed with which the other students moved through the material. Even the jocks, like Blake and Steve, left him for dust. Just as he thought he was getting a handle on a subject, they'd move onto something else that he'd never even looked at in his last school. From what he could gather, they were studying college-level material in all subjects.

Jennifer stopped talking and looked at her son with concern. "Listen to me, rattling on. How's things, kiddo?"

Henry gave her a smile. "Great. Just great."

"You are a terrible actor," she said. "What's up?"

Henry shrugged. "You know. School stuff. I'll get a grip on it…" He didn't want to admit that he was struggling in class – in *all* classes. He'd never had problems in school before. A couple of subjects, maybe. But not *everything*.

"If you want me to talk to your teachers…"

"Mom!"

"Okay! Okay!"

She reached round and grabbed a note from the fridge.

"I forgot to say. Your friend Christian dropped this round while you were in the shower. I asked him to come in, but he said he didn't want to wait."

Henry reluctantly took the note from her hand and unfolded it. It said: *How's class? Coming round to our way of thinking yet?*

"That kid is not my friend," Henry said, scrunching the note in his fist and throwing it at the trash.

"Over here, Henry!" Blake yelled across the lunch hall.

Carrying his tray of food, Henry approached the long table near the windows looking out across the sports field. It was the nicest spot in the room and, he'd quickly learned, the exclusive domain of the in-crowd at Malcorp High. Steve and most of the football team sat along one side, with a collection of cheerleaders who looked like they'd stepped off the front cover of a magazine.

As he approached the empty place next to Blake, the

six-foot quarterback on the other side placed his foot on the seat.

"Henry's okay," Blake said, giving him a look. The quarterback reluctantly removed his foot.

Henry sighed and looked at Blake. "If this is a problem…"

"Hey, you're one of us!" Blake said, waving him into the chair. "Or at least, you're going to be. Right?"

"I guess," Henry replied as he sat down. This really wasn't his scene. Looking along the table, he met the eyes of everyone else in the group. Steve and several of the others were staring at him with barely hidden hostility.

"My grandad said we should help you fit in," Blake said, loud enough for the entire table to hear.

It was like a switch had been thrown. Frowns turned to smiles the length of the table. Hands were raised in greeting.

Henry raised a hand back. "Uh, nice to meet you all."

Only Steve was still staring at him frostily.

"Y'know, you've been seen with that kid Christian again," Blake said. "You don't want to get associated with that freak."

Henry felt the need to defend the other kid. "Christian's not a freak. Just a little…unusual."

Blake laughed. "That's my definition of a freak." His attention wandered across to the far side of the hall and his expression turned to a frown. Henry followed Blake's gaze to a table where a group of pretty normal-looking kids were sitting.

"When's the last time that kid got a haircut, d'you

think?" Blake asked, referring to a boy whose hair was only slightly shaggy.

"We should remind Principle Carpenter about the school regulations on hair length," the cheerleader to his left said.

Blake nodded. "Why don't you do that, Stacy? And mention uniform standards at the same time. Half of the student body look like hobos, walking around with their shirts hanging out."

This caused laughter around the table. Henry found himself surreptitiously reaching to tuck his own shirt in.

"We could start a poster campaign!" Stacy exclaimed.

"I'll get the football team to do uniform checks in the halls," the quarterback added, cracking his knuckles.

Henry looked at Blake, who grinned and took a bite of pizza. "It's all about standards, Henry. Our crowd has to set the tone."

"Our crowd, right," he replied, glancing down the table at Steve, who was whispering with one of his friends. "He doesn't like me much."

"Don't mind, Steve," Blake said. "It's just the way he's put together. Suspicious of outsiders, but once he gets to know you—" He stopped at the sound of a crash from the other side of the hall.

Henry looked round with the others. Near the food line a tall, skinny kid had dropped the contents of his tray on the floor. As they watched, the kid started walking in a circle around the pizza and fries on the floor, rubbing the side of his head vigorously with the palm of his hand, like there was something inside he wanted to get out. Silence fell over the hall as the kid stopped circling, reached down and grabbed a handful of fries from the floor and stuffed them into his mouth.

"Jesus," Henry said.

Blake nodded to the other end of the table. Steve and two of the larger boys from the group rose and started across the hall to the kid, who was now on his hands and knees scooping up food from the floor and eating it.

"What's wrong with him?" Henry asked as they watched Steve and the others grab the kid. The boy gave no resistance, going limp like a rag doll as they pulled him towards the exit.

"Tommy?" Blake said as the others turned back to their lunches as if nothing had happened. "He had an accident a few weeks ago."

"Accident?"

Blake tapped the side of his head. "Got hit during football practice. Knocked something loose. Know what I mean? Steve will make sure he gets taken care of."

Henry raised an eyebrow at that, but said nothing, wondering what getting *taken care of* by Steve would entail. Unsettled, he finished his lunch quickly, made an excuse about having a book to pick up from the library and left the hall.

It was chance that Henry's first lesson after lunch took him right past the school medical room, but what happened next wasn't. With the image of Tommy from the lunch hall still in his head, Henry found himself stopping in the corridor outside, when he should have been carrying on to class. *What had happened to that kid?* On impulse, Henry walked through the open door rather than carrying on by.

Like everything else at Malcorp High, the medical facilities went way beyond the norm. "Can I help you?" a woman's voice asked as he looked around. His attention fell on the door marked *Recovery Room*.

Henry turned to see a pinch-faced woman in a nurse's uniform staring at him from a reception desk.

"I'm…I'm a friend of Tommy's."

The nurse looked at him suspiciously. "He's not here."

Thinking on his feet, Henry grabbed a textbook from his bag. "I've got his French homework from Mademoiselle Chabrol. I could just take it in…"

"He's been taken for observation. And who are you…?"

"Thanks," Henry said, ducking out the door.

Aware of the nurse's footsteps following him, he fast-walked down the corridor and turned the corner. Through the windows looking out over the front of the school, he saw a pair of white-uniformed orderlies loading a trolley onto the back of one of the medical centre buggies. Tommy was strapped onto the trolley, his skull wrapped in a bandage. He seemed to be conscious because his eyes were open, although they were blank, staring up at the sky as he was put in the buggy.

Henry shook his head, even more unsettled. As he struggled to rationalize his thoughts, the feeling of being watched crept over him. He turned away from the window just in time to see someone disappear swiftly down to the other end of the corridor and round the corner.

A hand fell on his shoulder and he started.

"Woah!" Christian said, holding up his hands. "Jumpy!"

Henry took a breath. "Don't sneak up on me like that."

"Can't help it. Told you, I'm like a ninja." He nodded through the window to where the buggy was pulling away. "Quite a scene in the lunch hall. Another member of the student body with a screw loose."

"He had a football injury," Henry countered, desperately wanting to believe the story he'd been spun. "Probably concussion."

"*Football injury?*" Christian said incredulously. "Did he look like much of a footballer to you?"

Henry thought back to the tall, lanky kid. Christian had a good point. And Henry couldn't deny the bad feeling that was growing inside him. Taken by itself, the Tommy incident was just a little strange…but it wasn't just that, was it? Bit by bit, this place was really starting to get to him: the odd behaviour of the kids in general, the fact most pupils seemed to be geniuses, and the way that Blake and his friends were at pains to make him think that everything was *just swell* at Malcorp. *Just how weird does it have to get here before you start believing Christian might be right?* he wondered.

But letting himself believe in crazy conspiracy theories could surely only lead to a world of trouble – which was something he *really* didn't need right now.

He swallowed down his doubts and said, "Look, perhaps Tommy just—"

But before he could finish, Christian turned and started walking away up the corridor. Henry frowned.

"Hey!"

Christian didn't look back, disappearing around the corridor. *Is everyone crazy around here?* Shaking his head, Henry turned in the other direction…

And that's when he saw Steve, staring at him through the doors at the far end of the corridor. He held Henry in his glaring gaze for a couple of seconds, before turning away.

10

Friday afternoon couldn't come round fast enough for Henry. It brought the promise of the swim trial with Coach Tyler, the only teacher at Malcorp High who didn't look at him like he was some kind of bug crawling around their classroom. When the last period finally ended, Henry was the first out the door and running across the school grounds to make his meeting with the coach.

Upon arriving at the pool, he found the last class finishing up and getting changed. Henry got into his swim gear, taking a locker at the far end of the changing room as far away from everyone else as possible. He'd talked enough with Blake and his crowd that week – all he wanted to do now was get in the water and swim until his arms and legs ached.

The changing room began to empty out fast and by the time Henry pushed his uniform into the locker, the place was silent. As he slammed the locker shut, however, a cry of pain split the air. Henry looked towards the showers – that was where the noise had come from. There was another cry and the sound of laughter. Grabbing his towel, Henry walked towards the noise.

As he rounded the side of the shower, he saw Christian sitting under one of the taps. He was fully dressed, but his clothes were soaked. Someone had turned the showers on him and blood was pouring from his nose – he was trying to catch it in his hands. He looked completely defenceless. And right in front of him was Steve, standing with clenched fists and five of his followers at his back. As Henry watched, Steve raised a fist to hit Christian again…

"Hey!" Henry yelled. "Why don't you pick on someone who actually wants to fight you?"

Steve's hand stopped in mid-air. He looked round. "Are you still here? Haven't they flunked you out yet?"

"They're letting me stay on until I kick your ass. They're going to give me special credit."

Steve laughed and shook his head. "Your comebacks are lamer than your grade average. I'm gonna give you one chance. *Walk away*."

Henry looked down at Christian, who was wiping his bloodied nose, and then back to Steve. "I don't think so."

On the floor, Christian looked up and shook his head slightly, as if to say that Henry shouldn't even think about fighting Steve. Henry ignored him. He'd never been one to start a fight, but he wasn't about to walk away from one either.

Steve bent down, grabbed Christian by the back of his shirt and practically threw him across the shower towards Henry. As Christian landed heavily against the tiles, Henry wondered just how strong the other kid was. Could it be that he was jacked up on steroids? Did that explain the aggression? He'd seen it before – jocks getting into drugs to enhance their bodies and their performance, and becoming completely strung out in the process.

Steve started forward and his gang came with him. Two of them disappeared towards the back of the shower and Henry had no doubt that they were moving round the changing room to cut off his retreat. *Well, you're into it now,* he thought.

Taking the initiative, Henry stepped forward and swung at Steve's chin, hoping to end it with one blow. With lightning speed, his opponent caught his fist and squeezed. Henry gasped in pain as the bones in his hand were crushed. In desperation, he flailed his left fist at Steve, causing the bully to release him – but only for a second. In a blur of motion, he grabbed Henry's throat in his vice-like grip and slammed him against the tiles, knocking the air from his lungs even as his fingers tightened on his windpipe. Within seconds Henry found himself gasping for breath, fight draining from his arms and legs.

"If I killed you," said Steve, his voice unnaturally calm, as if the act of violence had no effect on him, "do you know who would care?"

Henry struggled to get free, but the fingers around his neck tightened inexorably. There was no escape. Stars began to explode behind his eyes. Christian pushed himself off the floor and flew at Steve, but two of the others held him back.

"No one," Steve went on. "Absolutely no one at all."

On the verge of passing out, Henry realized he had no

chance of tearing free of Steve's grasp. Instead, with the last of his strength, he reached up and gripped the shower head on the wall above him. Using it for leverage, he raised his legs and kicked Steve in the gut. With a look of surprise, the boy flew back against the far wall, hitting the tiles hard. For a second he stared at Henry, clearly shocked that he'd been thrown off. Then he tensed to fly at him again...

"What the hell is going on here?"

Everyone stopped at the sound of Coach Tyler's voice. He stood at the far end of the showers, his expression a mixture of shock and anger.

Steve gazed back without expression. All aggression had drained from him in an instant. "Nothing, coach," he said. "Just about to get out of here for the day."

As if on a silent command, both he and his gang walked from the shower as one. Coach Tyler made to follow them, exasperation written all over his face.

"It didn't look like nothing! If I find out you've been fighting in here, I'll ban you all from the pool for a month!"

There was no response, merely the slamming of the changing room door as they left. The coach took a deep breath, clearly fighting to control his anger. He turned to Henry, who was standing against the wall, rubbing his throat.

"Are you okay?"

Henry nodded. He wasn't about to show he'd taken a beating.

"What about you?" the coach asked Christian.

"Nosebleed," the kid replied. "Happens all the time."

"Right," Coach Tyler said, before turning his attention to Henry. "We'd better do the trial another day. Next week perhaps."

"No, coach!" Henry protested. "Please. I'm okay."

Tyler regarded Henry carefully and slowly nodded his head. "Fine. But if you're not in the pool in two minutes, you can forget about the trial."

With that, he turned and left. Henry looked at Christian, who was standing by the wall. "Are you okay?" he asked. "What was that about?"

"I'm just fine," Christian replied, starting towards the door. "Steve and his friends don't like kids who don't fit in. Not that you care."

Henry felt a surge of anger. "Hey, I just saved your ass!"

Christian stopped on the edge of the changing room. "Big deal – Steve and his goons will be around on Monday to beat the crap out of me all over again. But you're not worried about that, are you?"

"*Christian…*" But he was already out of the door.

Henry went to the nearest sink and splashed water on his face in an effort to clear his head. He rubbed his neck. He'd seen fights before and heard all sorts of exaggerated threats thrown around, but there was something truly weird about the calmness with which Steve had attacked him.

And when Steve said he was going to kill him…Henry had absolutely believed it.

* * *

After the long school day and the incident in the changing rooms, the water of the pool was wonderfully cool and refreshing. The place was empty apart from a few kids taking turns on the high board over at the dive pool. The surface of the lap pool was perfectly still as Henry dived into the deep end and started on a few easy-going laps to warm up. On his fourth turn, he upped the pace, working his arms and legs harder, powering to the other side where Coach Tyler had appeared with a stopwatch in his hand.

"Not bad," the coach said. "Good arms, but your breathing needs work."

Henry nodded. Although it had only been a couple of weeks since his last swim, he felt out of practice.

"Why don't you show me what you can really do?" the coach asked. "What's your best stroke?"

"Breast," Henry said, pulling himself out of the water and moving into the starting position by the edge, so the coach could see how he entered the water.

"Okay then," the coach said, resetting the stopwatch. "Get ready."

Henry stretched and then bent into starting position...

Bare feet slapped across the tiles, approaching the lap pool. Henry looked round as Steve took position at the head of one of the other lanes.

"This pool's closed for a try-out," the coach told him coldly. "Go to the dive pool if you want a swim."

Steve gave no indication he'd heard, merely pulling a pair of goggles down over his eyes.

"Fine," the coach muttered, before leaning down so he could whisper in Henry's ear. "*Show that son of a bitch what you can do.*" With that, he stepped back and raised his hand. "Four laps on my mark…ready…set…go!"

Henry sprang from his starting position and entered the pool perfectly, arms forward, cutting the water like an arrow. For a few seconds he powered along underwater, before breaking the surface to take a breath. Looking left, he saw the shape of Steve a couple of lanes down, neck and neck.

Focus, Henry told himself, concentrating on the co-ordinated power in his arms and legs… *Breathe… Stroke… Breathe…*

Suddenly the other end of the pool, a hundred metres from their starting point, loomed up. Henry dived… turned…kicked away from the wall…

And then he was on his way back down the pool. *Time to pull away,* he thought, aware of Steve executing the turn at the same time as him. He started working his legs harder, keeping the rhythm of his arms steady… He sensed he was pulling away, but Steve was on his right now and he couldn't see for sure.

Nobody's faster than me in the pool, Henry told himself. *Nobody.*

The next turn came up. Once again he executed it perfectly, seeing that Steve was going into the turn a good two seconds behind him. *Time to consolidate…* He kept up the pace all the way through the third lap, even though the muscles in his legs were starting to burn. He knew he should hold something back for a final push, but he wanted to beat Steve on the third lap…and wanted the other kid to see he was beaten…

He hardly paid attention to his opponent as he streamed down the lane, so intent was he on getting every iota of speed from his limbs. So it was only as he approached the third and final turn that he saw it…

The shape of the other boy racing ahead in the parallel lane… Somehow making it to the turn before him… Suddenly no longer seconds behind, but seconds ahead…

No way! Henry thought as he made the turn. Unable to resist, he looked up, seeing that Steve was now almost halfway down the lane on his way to the finish. *Got to catch up.* In the following seconds he pushed himself harder than ever before …

And it still wasn't enough.

By the time he slapped his hand against the far end of the pool, Steve had pulled himself up out of the water and was waiting for him with his arms folded. He wasn't even breathing heavily, despite the incredible exertion of the last few minutes. Gasping, Henry leaned against the edge and tried to get some much needed air into his lungs.

"Great time," the coach said, kneeling down beside him and examining his stopwatch. Then he stole a glance at Steve, who turned and walked away, his face an emotionless mask.

"Not great enough," Henry said, splashing water on his face.

"You look exhausted," the coach said. "Get dressed and meet me in my office."

"But the rest of the trial!" he protested.

"Kid, you're done in," the coach said with a sigh. "Too bad. I really wanted to see you beat that guy."

He turned and walked away. Henry balled his hand into a fist and pounded it against the water.

It seemed Malcorp High wouldn't even allow him to be good at the one thing he was best at.

Five minutes later, Henry found the coach sitting in the small office that looked over the pool. The room was crowded with papers, sports magazines and all manner of other junk. As he walked in, the coach pointed to a chair in the corner. Henry removed a stack of old newspapers from the seat and sat down.

"Sorry, coach," he said quietly. "Guess I didn't make the grade, huh?"

"I made you a coffee," the man said, passing over a mug to Henry. "Thought you could use one."

"Thanks," Henry said.

The man reached into his desk, removing a bottle of whiskey. He poured a measure into his own coffee mug. "You didn't see that," he said as he replaced the bottle.

"Uh, no, coach."

The coach considered him for a moment, and then forced a smile. "Congratulations. You just made the swim team."

Henry frowned. "But I got beaten…"

"In any other school I've taught in, that time you did would have put you at the top of the team."

"Steve's better."

"Yeah," the coach admitted. "I'd never seen anything like it until I came to Malcorp High."

"He'll win you gold medals," Henry said. "Perhaps you should be spending your time on him."

The coach smiled. "But that would mean spending time *with* him."

Henry burst out laughing.

"I probably shouldn't say that about a kid on the swim team," the coach added.

Henry shrugged. "Well, I might be fast, but I'll bet I'm the slowest swimmer in this school. I just don't know what's going on."

"Neither do I," the coach replied. "I took this job six months ago, thinking it would be a nice, quiet gig up to my retirement. The level of sporting and academic achievement at this school surpasses any place I've ever worked. And I've worked at some good schools. But everyone seems to regard it as normal. They don't even want to compete in the local leagues. What the hell is with that?"

"I don't know, coach."

"Not the slightest interest. From the students or the faculty. News kids that do show some competitive edge lose it after a few weeks. Like this place sucks it out of them." The coach leaned forward and pointed a finger at Henry. "If you swim for me, we're sending you to a county trial. And *you're* gonna win me some medals. Think you can handle that?"

Henry nodded. "Sure thing, coach."

Coach Tyler nodded approvingly and sat back in his chair. "I know one thing: these kids might be good, but there's no joy in what they do. Know what I mean?"

"Yeah," Henry said. The man had a point. Most of the students he'd met…they were brilliant at everything, but it never seemed a big deal. Just cold, clinical perfection. Blake was the only one who had shown any normal enthusiasm, but thinking back, Henry thought there was something fake about that too. Almost like he'd been going through an act for Henry's benefit.

"You'll do just fine, Henry," the coach said, finishing his drink and pouring another. "And if you don't, that'll be just fine as well." He took a sip from his mug and pulled a face. "You know what? I've got ten kids on the team who come here after school every single day. Never miss. They swim laps so long and so fast they should be on the bottom of the pool with exhaustion. Then they get out of the water, say, *Thank you, coach*, and go home. You understand what I'm saying?"

"I'm not sure, coach…"

"At my last school, I think half my time was spent coaching kids in the water. You know what the other half was spent doing? Chewing them out over being late. Giving them pep talks when they wanted to quit. Listening to them blub because some boy or girl broke their heart." He looked out over the dive pool, where a few kids were still swimming. "But this lot… They never have any problems. No doubts. No distractions. It ought to be a dream job."

"But it isn't?"

"Half the time I think I needn't be here at all."

Henry considered this. "The other teachers around here don't seem to mind."

The coach shook his head. "Well, I wouldn't exactly call those people teachers, Henry. Most of them have never set foot inside a classroom outside Malcorp High. They're *facilitators*, or at least that's what they call themselves. I'd hate to see how they fared in my old school back in the Bronx." He thought it over for a moment, remembering some other time, then looked at Henry. "So I want you to do something for me. Show up late for practice once in a while. Forget your kit. Slack off during training so I can ball you out. Can you do that for me?"

He laughed. "Sure thing, coach."

The man smiled at him, then said, "Go on, get outta here. Training is Monday, 5 p.m. sharp. And if I ever catch you fighting in my changing rooms again, I'll put your ass in a sling."

As Henry opened the door, the sound of music began to echo across the pool from speakers set high into the ceiling. Henry listened and heard it playing dully outside as well, as if it was being broadcast across the entire complex. The sound was distorted, but there was something familiar about it. It took him a second or two to realize that the tune was "The Star-Spangled Banner".

"Here we go," the coach said, reaching into his desk for a top-up from his whiskey bottle. "Every Monday morning, every Friday afternoon. Without fail."

Around the dive pool, kids had emerged from the water and took position by the side. They stood absolutely still, staring into space as the music played, almost as if they were in a trance. Henry found himself wincing as the music played. There was something discordant about it that he just couldn't put his finger on. The effect was grating, but the kids around the pool didn't seem to sense it. If anything, their expressions were serene.

"Jesus," the coach said, taking a swig from his mug, "that has got to be the worst version of our national anthem ever."

Henry nodded and walked towards the changing rooms, past the kids standing like statues around the edge. He looked at the face of one of the girls as he crossed in front of her. Her eyes were half-closed, but beneath the lids he could see her pupils flickering from left to right.

Like the eyes of a dreamer in REM sleep...

11

Henry had spent a whole week at Malcorp High now and, as much as he'd tried to ignore it, his anxiety had grown from one day to the next. He just couldn't get the events at the pool out of his head, and it seemed Coach Tyler was no wiser than he was. So if Henry wanted answers, there was only one place to go.

He hammered on the door of the coffee shop, which was showing the *closed* sign, even though it was midday on a Saturday. Through the window he'd seen someone moving around in the darkened lower area and he was sure it was Fox.

He banged his fist on the door again.

After a moment the girl approached and studied him through the glass.

"What do you want?" she shouted, an accusatory tone to her voice.

"You said you had evidence about what's going on at Malcorp," Henry replied. "Show it to me."

"What brought about this change of heart? Things not going so well at school? You thought we were delusional, remember?"

Henry looked round. The shopping street was quiet enough, considering it was a Saturday afternoon, but he still didn't want to have this discussion out in the open. "Can I *please* come in?"

Reluctantly, Fox opened the door and allowed him into the cafe. Inside, it was pleasantly cool after the heat of the day and the walk he'd taken from the complex. The smell of yesterday's coffee lingered in the air.

"You're not opening for lunch?" he asked, looking around the interior. The chairs were still on the tables.

"Business is slow," Fox said with a shrug as she locked the door. "But if I'd known you were coming, I'd have baked a cake." She walked through to the other side of the counter. "Come on up, I guess."

He followed her up the narrow staircase to the apartment above the cafe. In the light of day it looked just as cluttered as the last time he'd been there, but there was something warm and lived-in about the place. It made Henry think of his old apartment in the city. It had been way too small for him and his mom, but he'd begun to miss the old place since he'd been at Malcorp.

"Take a seat," Fox said as she moved through to the kitchen. "Something to drink?"

"Just some water," Henry said, sitting down on one of the sofas. "I didn't see you in school this week."

The girl poured a glass from the tap and brought it over. "That's not surprising. I wasn't there."

"You were sick?"

"I don't go to school."

Henry frowned. "What do you mean? You've dropped out?"

"Malcorp High didn't agree with me," she replied. "And since the Newton school closed down, it's the only option. Anyway, I've got the cafe to look after."

Henry sipped his drink. "I can see you're real busy with that."

Fox said sharply, "If you just came to be sarcastic—"

"Okay, sorry. Why didn't the school agree with you?"

Fox grinned wryly at him. "Well, I'm sure you can guess yourself. Finding the curriculum a little challenging?"

Henry put the glass of water down amidst the clutter on the table and sighed. "I'm not stupid… But I just can't seem to keep up…"

"Don't beat yourself up about it," Fox said. "We've all been there."

"So what *is* going on?" Henry asked.

Fox raised an eyebrow. "You're sure you want to hear this?"

"Try me."

She walked to a bookshelf and pulled out what looked like a thick, leather-bound photo album. Opening it up, she took a seat beside Henry and passed it across to him. He looked over the page she'd opened, which was covered with newspaper clippings and stories printed from the web.

"What is this?" he asked.

"Research," she replied. "On Malcorp. Just read it."

* * *

For the best part of an hour, Henry worked his way through the scrapbook.

There was background information about Malcorp... How John Mallory founded it in the late seventies as a software company. How it had developed an operating system that almost became the industry standard for home and business computers, before Microsoft bought them out for millions in the mid-80s. With the proceeds of that sale, Mallory had diversified his company into the area of bioscience, getting involved in the cutting-edge field of genetically modified foods. One story covered Malcorp's seed engineering sector, and how it held patents on ninety per cent of the grains used in the United States – this one company could hold the agriculture industry to ransom. If the farmers didn't buy their GM seeds from Malcorp, they were pretty soon driven out of business.

Then there were the reports of Malcorp's other scientific interests, including low-cost IVF (Henry guessed that's where his mom came in), stem-cell research and the development of next generation prosthetic limbs for troops injured in Afghanistan. Some articles were critical of the company, focusing on several scandals in their biotech labs, where scientists had been accused of breaching safety guidelines in the use of stem cell and cloning technology. Others were gushingly positive. There were plenty of people around who believed that, with its use of science to improve farming and medicine, Malcorp was going to save the world from poverty and hunger. Fox had certainly been thorough in her research and Henry wondered how long it had taken her to collate all of the information.

One story in particular caught his eye. It was a recent interview with John Mallory that had been grabbed from the *Financial Times* website. In it he spoke about an education revolution he believed was going to occur during the 21st century. The reference was brief but something about Mallory's fervent tone stuck in Henry's mind.

He looked at Fox. "So Mallory's interested in education?"

"*Very* interested," Fox replied. "I started at Malcorp High when I was twelve, back when it was just a normal school. Then something began happening. Kids from Newton were offered a part in an accelerated learning course that promised to turn them into geniuses over a few weeks or something. They signed up and were taken out for special classes. And guess what?"

"It worked?"

"Only too well," Fox said bitterly. "Pretty soon everyone was signing up. Getting taken out. And when they came back they were all little Einsteins. After that the classes changed too. If you hadn't been in the programme, you couldn't keep up. No way."

"So more kids signed up?"

"Or were signed up by their parents," Fox added. "I mean, who wouldn't want a genius for a son or daughter?" She paused, remembering. "But when they came back they weren't just smart... They were different. I've seen kids who'd been friends since kindergarten hardly speak to one another any more. It wasn't that they'd fallen out – had an argument or something. They'd just gone cold. Like they didn't have any connection any more, nothing to say. There was something missing."

Henry thought back to some of the strange behaviour he'd seen over the past week and understood what she meant. He remembered how the coach had described the students at Malcorp high. That same word. *Cold*.

"When new kids come to town they're given a week or so to realize they're not going to fit in," Fox continued, "then they're handed the sign-up sheet for the *special programme*. A few, like Christian, hold out, even though their parents soon start begging them to sign. Others try to run away. They're never seen again…or they come back *changed*. Gabrielle and me and some others formed a group against the special programme. One by one, we'd watched our friends change since Malcorp arrived. They were still there in the same classes as us, but they may as well have been different people. That wasn't going to happen to us. We weren't going to lose each other…or ourselves. So we signed a pact that we wouldn't sign up, no matter how bad things got at school or how much pressure we were put under." She sighed. "I'm the only one left."

She reached over and produced a photograph from the back of the book. It showed Fox and Gabrielle on the very sofa they were sitting on now. There were two other kids he didn't recognize, but another he did. It was Blake…and he had his arm around Gabrielle's shoulder.

"Blake was Gabrielle's boyfriend?" Henry asked incredulously. "The one who broke her heart?"

"You know him?"

"Mallory's grandson? Yeah, I've met him. I bet the head of Malcorp just loved his grandson hanging out with your little anti-capitalist brigade."

"We're not anti-capitalists," Fox said, shaking her head. "Blake was a cool guy... Before."

"Cool guy." Henry thought of the kid's submissive behaviour around his grandfather and his complete loyalty to Malcorp. Now he had heard everything.

Henry closed the book on his lap and tried to process it all. A few days before, he could have dismissed everything that Fox had told him as crazy. But not after what he'd seen around Malcorp High that week. And if kids like Blake were anything to go by, there was certainly something weird going on. He didn't know if they were giving them drugs or hypnosis sessions, but Malcorp was doing something to the kids at the high school.

And Henry was becoming certain of one thing: if he just sat back and did nothing, he'd be next in line for the *special education programme*. And then what would happen? Would he become excellent at everything he did? Would he be able to swim as fast as Steve...but be cold and detached and lacking in joy?

"So, what do we do?" he asked.

"We need to get the story out there," Fox said. "I've made contact with a reporter from the city. A guy called Richardson. He's coming here to meet with me on Monday morning. I'm going to tell him everything."

Henry wondered how that conversation would go – telling a seasoned journalist about a supposed Malcorp plot with nothing more than a scrapbook and a few old photos. "We have no real evidence they're doing anything strange to these kids…"

"That's why we need to get to Gabrielle," Fox said. Her eyes sparkled with animation and Henry could see the passionate determination behind her cool exterior. "They're still holding her in that medical centre, I'm sure of it. She'd never sign up for the programme of her own free will. It must have been her parents forcing her into it. If you and Christian can just get in to see her… Get her to talk about what's been going on—"

"Wait a minute," Henry interrupted. "What do you mean *me and Christian*? You're not coming with us?"

Fox gave an embarrassed look. "I'm…uh…kind of banned from setting foot inside the Malcorp complex." When Henry looked at her questioningly, she continued, "I staged a little protest outside the main gates a few months ago."

"About the medical centre?"

She shook her head. "Malcorp has been buying up businesses all over Newton for years. Every shop on the high street is owned by them. We're just about the only independent left and every month they send their suits along, trying to pressure us into selling." She coughed. "And I might have thrown a balloon filled with red paint at Mallory's Rolls-Royce."

Henry couldn't stop himself from laughing, imagining the look on Mallory's face as the paint bomb hit his expensive car.

"So I'm not exactly welcome in Malcorp any more," Fox went on. "In fact, I think that fat security guard on the gate has orders to shoot me on sight."

"Well, I wouldn't worry too much about him," Henry said. "Hank looks like he spends more time in the doughnut shop than he does at the range."

Fox laughed at this and said, "You're okay, Ward. I formally forgive you for acting like an ass before."

"Oh, thanks."

"Don't mention it. So, you'll do it? Christian's got the key card, but he can't go by himself."

"Why not?"

Fox shrugged. "He's scared. Wouldn't you be?"

Before Henry could answer, the door to the bedroom opened noisily and a middle-aged woman in a wheelchair appeared in the doorway. She was wearing a dressing gown that had seen better days and her greying hair was pulled back in a loose ponytail. She looked at Henry and smiled.

"I thought I heard company."

"Mom!" Fox said, rising from the sofa and going to her. "I thought I told you to call if you needed anything."

"I wanted to see the guest!" the woman said, pushing the wheels of her chair so she scooted quickly across the lounge, almost colliding with Henry. "I'm Mary Layton," she said, extending a hand.

As Henry took her hand in his, he noticed that her skin was incredibly white and there seemed to be no weight to her. "Nice to meet you, Mrs. Layton."

"And it's nice to see Fox making some friends. She never has anyone round any more…"

"Thank you!" Fox muttered under her breath. Henry wondered if her mother always called her by her nickname.

"I know it doesn't look like it, but this used to be the most popular place in town," Mary Layton said, a melancholy tone to her voice. "The cafe used to be full every evening. That was before Malcorp started buying everywhere up – people don't seem to go out so much these days." She looked down at her legs. "And before I had my…problems." She reached out and touched her daughter's arm. "Now Fox has to keep things going until I'm better."

Fox smiled and touched her mother's hand. "It's okay, Mom." She looked round at Henry. "We're going to sort everything out. Right?"

He nodded, surprised to find that he really believed it when he said, "Yes, we are."

Five minutes later, Fox led Henry down the stairs again and through the cafe to the door. Mrs. Layton had just finished quizzing him about his mom, where he'd lived before and how he'd met her daughter. She seemed like a nice lady, but Fox had clearly been eager to get him out of there. As she was about to open the door she gave a sharp intake of breath and stepped back into the relative darkness of the shop. She grabbed Henry's arm and pulled him back too.

"What is it?" he asked.

"Trooper Dan," she replied. A second later the police cruiser passed by on the street outside, crawling along the high street. Behind the wheel, Henry made out the cop's head turning left and right as he passed, scanning the sleepy town for any sign of trouble.

"Malcorp's eyes and ears in Newton," Fox said quietly. "It's best he doesn't see us together."

Henry nodded and looked round at her. She was still holding onto his arm and they were pressed close together in the shadow cast by the window frame. Although the cruiser had passed, neither of them moved.

"What's wrong with your mom?" Henry asked.

"Multiple sclerosis," Fox replied. "It's a brain disease that attacks the nervous system. Mom was diagnosed six years ago. It comes and goes…"

"Your dad—"

"Left us just after she was diagnosed. Can you believe that? He's got a new family now. But he does send a card at Christmas."

"I'm sorry," Henry said again, not knowing how else to respond.

"Yeah, so am I," she said, her voice becoming hard and businesslike again. "Just get to Gabrielle and get us something we can use to shut down whatever Malcorp is up to."

"Okay."

"Tell Christian *Project Alcatraz* is a go."

With that, she pulled open the door and pushed him out onto the street. As it slammed behind him, Henry started back down main street, blinking in the afternoon light.

12

"I'm here to see Christian."

The man who had answered the door was wearing a grey suit that looked crumpled from a day's work, even though it was Saturday. The tie around his neck was loosened and the top button of his shirt was undone. In one hand he held a glass of Scotch loaded with ice.

"Well, there's a first time for everything, I guess," said the man, who Henry assumed to be Christian's dad. He stepped back and Henry entered the lodge, which was identical in construction to his own, except it was located on the other side of the complex.

"Christian!" the man hollered after taking a sip of his drink. "You have uh…a…friend to see you." He looked round at Henry. "You *are* a friend, right?"

Henry nodded. There was no response from within the lodge and the man shouted again. This brought the sound of a door slamming and movement from one of the bedrooms.

Feeling more than a little uncomfortable, Henry cast his gaze over the lounge and was surprised to see that one wall was devoted to a display of sporting trophies. Running, football, swimming awards, they were all there – along with photographs of a confident-looking kid posing with various teammates and coaches, or caught in action on the sports field. For a moment he thought it was Christian, but on closer inspection he saw that it was a different kid, although they looked remarkably similar.

"My eldest, Simon," Christian's dad said upon seeing Henry look over the trophy collection. "He's at Yale on a rowing scholarship. Quite the sportsman. That's him with his football team a few years back." He looked at the picture wistfully. "A real all-rounder. Do you play... uh...?"

"Henry. I swim."

"Outstanding!" the man said with a little too much excitement. "Outstanding! Maybe you could get Christian involved. It would be nice to see him do something other than lounge around on the couch for once."

There was an embarrassed cough from the kitchen doorway and Henry looked round to see Christian's mother standing there. Her hair was tied back in a neat bun and she was wearing an apron smeared with flour. She looked like something out of a black and white sitcom.

"Christian just hasn't found his sport yet," she said softly.

His dad snorted and took a hefty swig of Scotch. "Well, it's about time he did. Too bad he doesn't have more of his brother's gumption..."

"Don't embarrass Christian in front of his friend, dear!" she said, looking daggers at her husband.

He chose to ignore this and turned to Henry. "You're a sportsman, Henry. You know what I'm talking about. A young man needs an outlet for his energies! Christian's problem is…"

He stopped in mid-sentence, realizing that his son had appeared in the doorway leading through to the bedrooms.

"Don't let me stop you, Dad," he said. "Why don't you tell him all about what a disappointment I am compared to Simon the super-athlete? Henry may as well know. Everyone else does."

Christian's dad looked as if he was about to snap back in response, but then he merely shrugged and walked to a bar in the corner to fix himself another drink. Christian turned his angry gaze on Henry.

"What do you want?"

Christian flopped onto a beanbag in front of a TV in his bedroom that was playing a PS3 game. Henry hung back at the doorway and looked over the room. Compared to Christian's scruffy, goth image, it was surprisingly neat and ordered. Books lined the walls and a study desk in the corner was piled with school textbooks. He turned his attention to Christian, noticing that the evidence of his altercation with Steve's gang from the day before was coming out as a nasty bruise under his left eye.

"Well?" Christian demanded, pressing the PS3 controller to resume his racing game. "This had better be good."

"I went to see Fox. She showed me the stuff you've collected about Malcorp."

"And?" Christian didn't remove his eyes from the screen as he took a corner at high speed.

"I believe you."

Christian paused the game again and looked round at Henry.

"I'm *starting* to believe you. Something weird is going on here."

"Really?" Christian asked. "You didn't seem too enthusiastic to get involved before."

Henry stepped into the room and closed the door. Feeling more than a little stupid, he said, "Fox says *Project Alcatraz* is a go."

For the first time that Henry could recall, a grin broke Christian's face. "I knew you'd come round!"

Clapping his hands together, he moved to the door and shot the bolt. Then he went to his desk and pulled out a roll of documents that was taped to the underside. Henry joined him at the desk as Christian spread out what looked like a map.

"This is a plan of the Malcorp complex," Christian explained, waving a hand over the sheet. "It shows the location of all the external security cameras. We can use it to get to the medical centre without being picked up by the bad guys."

"Where'd you get this?" Henry asked, before answering his own question. "Let me guess. Stolen from your dad."

"From his briefcase, actually."

"What is he, head of security or something?"

Christian shook his head. "He's in non-human resource management. Whatever that is."

Henry studied the map. It showed every building in the complex, along with the location of the cameras. There were other underground buildings marked as *security substations*. "What are those?" he asked.

"Underground security bunkers. Emergency communication stations in case something happens at the complex. But let's just worry about the medical centre for now."

"What about once we're inside?" Henry asked. "We won't be able to avoid the cameras then."

"Don't panic," Christian said. "My dad is always bitching about security around the complex – how just about anyone can walk in most places if they've got a pass. The lobby's unmanned at night and half the guards are like that guy Hank on the front gate. They fall asleep at their posts, so they're not even watching the cameras most of the time."

"Let's hope they're sleeping tonight," Henry said. "Or *Project Alcatraz* is gonna be over real fast."

"I know I haven't been giving you much time, kiddo," Jennifer said as she placed a dish on the draining board. "But now things are getting settled at the lab, I promise I'll be around more."

"I'm fine, Mom," Henry said. He picked up one of the plates and wiped it with a towel.

"I know it can be difficult settling into a new place... A new school..."

"Mom, I'm fine." The last thing Henry wanted was to worry her about what was going on. He still half thought Fox and Christian's idea was crazy. What would his mom say if she knew he was thinking of breaking into the medical centre that evening? Although it wasn't really *breaking in* when they had Christian's dad's key card, was it...?

"Because you know if you were having any kind of problems, you could talk to me about them."

Henry looked round at his mother. She gave him an embarrassed smile.

"The principal gave me a call about your progress."

Henry felt his face redden. "What did he say? That I'm some kind of special needs case?"

"No, Henry. Just that you had some catching up to do."

"Mom, there's something not right at Malcorp High."

She raised an eyebrow. "Come on, kiddo. Just because they have higher academic standards than that rundown place you used to go to in the city."

"I liked that school."

Jennifer Ward dried her hands on the towel and placed them on her son's shoulders. "It's nothing to be ashamed of. Nobody's saying you're stupid—"

"Oh, thanks!"

"Principal Carpenter even said you might qualify for a special programme they run to help new kids get up to scratch."

Henry took a step away from his mother. "Special programme?"

"Yeah," she continued. "Extra classes and the like. He wants to talk to us next week about getting you signed up."

"Signed up."

"It's no reflection on you, Henry, really. The principal says that most new kids sign up for the programme within a couple of weeks."

Henry backed towards the door to the lounge. "I'm going out this evening. Is that okay?"

Jennifer Ward's face fell. "Sure, but—"

Henry turned and left, not wanting to hear any more. Malcorp was already trying to sell his mom on the *special education programme*. And that meant only one thing.

Time was running out.

13

Henry and Christian moved silently between the trees lining the lower levels of the hill where the medical centre was located. At 9 p.m. the sun had gone down and the road leading up to the centre was deserted.

"The only camera we have to worry about is the one on the gate," Christian said as they stopped near the wall. "It's monitored by the central security room. The cameras around the building aren't watched at night. Security's slack."

Henry nodded, eyeing the two-and-a-half-metre-high wall. "Okay, we'll go over the wall." He began to move...

"Hey!" Christian hissed.

Henry looked round.

"You might be able to jump that wall, but I'll need some help!"

"Come on," Henry said, running to the edge and cupping his hands to give the other kid a boost. Christian clumsily put his foot on Henry's hands and tried to reach the top of the wall.

"It's higher than it looks!" he whispered as he struggled to pull himself up.

"Just climb!" Henry hissed, giving him a push. Christian made the top, albeit with a lot of fuss…and promptly fell over the other side with a small cry of shock. Then there was silence.

"Christian!" Henry called, as loud as he dared. "Are you okay?"

"I think I landed on my phone."

Henry shook his head and took a few paces back from the wall. He ran, caught the top with both hands and pulled himself over in a single motion. He landed on the other side beside Christian, who was rubbing his back with a pained look on his face.

Henry looked towards the main entrance of the building. Like Christian had suggested, there was no sign of any guards on patrol.

"Are you sure that's going to work?" Henry asked as Christian removed his dad's key card.

"We'll soon find out." He took out another item – a small digital recorder – and checked it over.

"Where'd you get that from?"

"Fox. She used to be involved in the school paper back when there *was* a school paper. Fancied herself as a proper journalist or something." Looking satisfied the machine would work, Christian slipped it back in his pocket. "She thought we could use it to tape what Gabrielle has to say."

"Well, let's just concentrate on finding her first," Henry said, suddenly wishing Fox was there with them. There was something calm and collected about her manner that would have steadied his nerves. He couldn't escape the feeling that they were about to get into serious trouble – who knew how Mallory would react if he caught the sons of two of his employees breaking into one of his buildings? And what would it mean for his mom's new job? But then he remembered everything that had happened since he'd started at Malcorp High...all the weirdness and frustration...and he knew he had to get to the bottom of whatever was going on.

"Let's go," Henry said and they moved towards the main entrance. There were no cars or buggies parked out front. Henry eyed the closed-circuit TV camera as he silently pushed through the heavy front door into the reception area. He hoped Christian was right about no one watching the security feed. Like his last visit to the centre, the interior of the marble-lined reception felt several degrees cooler than outside. The globe lights in the ceiling had been dimmed slightly, probably because the centre was closed for the day. Nothing moved.

"Over there," Henry said, nodding towards the door that led into the main part of the building. They ran across to it and Christian held the key card above the reader.

"Fingers crossed," he said and swiped the card.

A green light flashed on the side of the reader. Henry grabbed the door handle and pushed. It opened and they stepped through into the anonymous corridor beyond.

"We made it!" Christian hissed excitedly in his ear.

"We still have to find Gabrielle," Henry replied, looking at the corridor stretching into the distance. "If she's here, that is."

"She's here."

Henry led the way down the corridor, past the unmarked doors on either side to a set of double doors at the end. They pushed through into another corridor with turnings to left and right. Henry tried to remember the way he'd been taken on his previous visit to the centre and came up blank.

"Look!" Christian said, indicating a sign on the wall opposite. It was a basic map of the medical centre marked *Staff Evacuation Plan*. It showed their location in relation to the three wings of the building: *patient care...operating theatres...research labs*. "I guess we head for patient care."

Henry nodded and studied the map. The quickest route to the patient care area was to go straight ahead, through the operating theatres. It would take them right to the other side of the building, but he suddenly felt very out of place in his jeans and T-shirt. They hadn't run into anyone yet, but there had to be someone around in the building. If there were patients, then there would be nurses or doctors in the centre round the clock. They needed to find some way to blend in a little better.

A solution presented itself as they reached the end of the corridor. A sign before another set of double doors read *Masks and gowns must be worn before entering theatres*. On the other side of the door a line of green surgical gowns and masks hung on a rack.

"Perfect," Henry said, grabbing one of the gowns and tossing it to Christian. The gowns covered their bodies from shoulders to ankles, hiding their clothes. Henry slipped a mask over his nose and mouth and looked round at Christian, who had done the same.

"You look stupid," Henry said.

"Look who's talking."

"If we bump into anyone, just keep your head down," Henry ordered. "Hopefully they'll just think we belong here."

Christian nodded and they started forward again. The corridor had widened out here, and there were signs pointing to various operating theatres on the walls. They went through another set of double doors and found themselves passing a long observation window that looked into a darkened operating theatre. Henry peered through the glass, making out the shapes of machinery and racks of surgical tools in the dimness.

A door flew open and the lights in the theatre flicked on without warning.

Just in time, Henry grabbed Christian's shoulder and pulled him to the floor so they couldn't be seen through the window. On the other side of the glass it was possible to hear muffled voices and the sound of a trolley being wheeled into the theatre. Christian pulled Henry's arm and nodded his head towards the other end of the corridor, but Henry gave him a hand signal to stay put. He wanted to see what was happening on the other side of the glass.

Ever so carefully, he raised his head so he was peeking through the window. Inside the operating theatre two doctors in surgical scrubs were moving around a table. On the table a white sheet covered the unmistakable shape of a person. There was some kind of frame at the top of the table, designed to keep the sheet off the patient's head, but the angle Henry was looking from made it impossible to see anything else.

One of the doctors, a grey-haired man whose face was obscured by a mask, leaned over the end of the table with a scalpel in his hand. His partner, a bald-headed doctor, said something that was inaudible through the glass. The grey-haired doctor poked at something under the sheet with the scalpel and the body on the table twitched violently. The other doctor moved round, lifted the sheet and checked the patient's hand, which was secured to the table at the wrist by a Velcro bond. Then he checked the patient's ankles, which were similarly bound.

Henry frowned as he watched the doctors step away from the table. *What were they doing? And why was the patient strapped down?*

The grey-haired doc looked at his watch, said something, and the two men moved towards the doors. As they exited, grey-hair tossed the scalpel into a nearby sink.

"That was too close!" Christian said. "Let's get out of here before they come back."

"Wait," Henry said. "I want to get in there and take a look."

Christian pulled down his face mask and stared at him as if he was crazy. "You what?"

"There's something wrong. They've got that patient strapped to the table."

"We're not here for this…"

"We're here to find out what's going on, right?"

"I guess."

"Come on then. I think we can get into the theatre through those doors up ahead."

Henry rose, but Christian stayed where he was, looking sheepish.

"What's the matter?" Henry demanded.

"I...uh...don't like the sight of blood. And operating theatres kind of freak me out... I get sick just watching *House*..."

"Okay, okay," said Henry, aware that time was ticking away and the surgeons might return at any minute. "Just wait here. I won't be long."

Leaving Christian, he moved swiftly to the end of the window and took a door into another corridor that curved round the side of the theatre to the entrance. Pausing to listen for the sound of the doctors coming back, he opened the door and slipped inside.

The operating theatre was silent and Henry was aware of his footsteps as he approached the table the patient was lying on. There was movement at the window and Henry looked round to see Christian stick his head up and give him a *make it fast* signal with his hand. Henry nodded and walked slowly towards the table.

As he passed the patient's feet he said softly, "Hello? Are you awake?"

There was no response. Where the doctor had checked the patient's wrist restraint the cover was raised, exposing an arm. There was a pattern of injection marks above the patient's wrist and Henry was reminded of Gabrielle when he'd met her at the gas station. He'd taken the needle marks on her arm as evidence of drug abuse – but had she merely been a patient at the medical centre? And what had she been injected with?

Henry moved round the table so he could get a look at the patient's face under the raised cover. What he saw made him freeze with shock… He blinked twice, trying to process the image… It was like something from a horror movie…

The patient was a little older than him. The kid's eyes were closed and his face looked peaceful enough, which was surprising as the top of his skull was missing. The top of his head had been cut away just above the eyebrows, exposing the delicate grey matter of his brain resting in the skull cavity. A metal frame was locked around his neck and jaw, holding his skull off the table.

A wave of nausea rose in Henry as he looked over the glistening surface of the kid's brain, but he just couldn't look away. Flecks of blood and white bone matter stood out on the ridged, grey surface…

Henry took a step back, colliding with a metal rack of surgical instruments. The rack went flying and collided with the wall. Scalpels and clamps clattered noisily against the tiled floor.

As if disturbed by the noise, the eyes of the kid on the table flicked open – wide and staring and full of horror…

The kid's mouth opened and he moaned two desperate words…

"Help…me…"

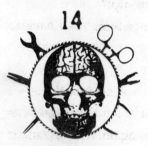

14

Henry stood staring as the horrific figure of the kid on the table continued to plead with him for help. The kid thrashed against the bonds holding his wrists and ankles in place.

"Help…me!"

Moving forward, Henry took hold of the Velcro restraint around the kid's exposed wrist and tore it open. The kid immediately grabbed Henry's arm, nails digging into his flesh.

"It's okay," Henry said, moving round to the head of the table. "You're going to be okay." The kid's exposed brain had been hard enough to look at before, but now his eyes were open and he was conscious, there was something obscene about it.

"What…what have they done…to me?" The kid rolled his eyes, as if trying to see the top of his head.

Henry shook his head, not knowing what to say.

"I want…to get up…"

"That's not such a good idea," Henry said, looking at the frame holding the kid's head in place.

The kid waved his free arm around frantically and

started screaming. "Let me up! Let me up!"

"No!" Henry said, trying to silence him. "You have to be quiet!"

THUD.

Henry spun as something slammed against the glass observation window. On the other side, Christian was raising his fist to bang the glass again. He mouthed something.

They're coming!

At that moment, the door at the end of the corridor flew open and a security guard burst through. Christian barely had time to back away before the guard was on top of him. Henry was powerless to do anything as his friend was rammed against the window. Christian's nose smacked it hard and he slid down, leaving a smear of blood on the pane.

"Christian!" Henry yelled.

The door to the operating theatre clattered open and the bald-headed surgeon appeared, framed in the opening. He looked at Henry with wide eyes. "Who the hell are you? What are you doing here?"

Henry backed away, looking around for some means of escape. He noticed a door on the other side of the theatre. By now, the surgeon had snatched up a syringe gun and was lunging at him. Henry grabbed a table and heaved it towards his attacker. The surgeon went flying amidst surgical instruments, letting out a cry of pain as his hand came down on a scalpel on the floor.

Not wasting another second, Henry threw himself at the

door to the rear of the theatre, hoping it didn't just lead to a cupboard. To his relief he found himself in another corridor and he ran without thinking.

A door crashed open further down the corridor and a man's voice shouted at him to stop. Henry pushed through a set of double doors to get away. Christian was caught – the best thing he could do now was get out of the building and tell everyone what he'd seen in the operating theatre. He didn't know what the hell the doctors thought they were doing, but he knew it wasn't right.

And it had to be stopped.

Henry started trying doors along the corridor. The first two were locked, but the third led into a darkened room. He locked the door behind him and looked around. He was inside some kind of lab full of long workbenches and large, glass-fronted machines. Many of the machines were covered in dust sheets and there were toolboxes lying around, as if the place was being upgraded. Despite this, it reminded Henry of the time he'd visited his mother's workplace. A horrible thought occurred to him: could *she* be involved in all this? Did *she* know what was going on in the medical centre? He immediately dismissed the thought. One of his mom's favourite words was "ethics". She was always going on about the *ethics* of this or the *ethics* of that. No way would she want to be involved in anything that was happening at the medical centre...

He moved to the back of the lab and found another side door. He tried the handle... Locked. The main lab door rattled as one of the guards tried to open it. There was mumbled discussion on the other side – clearly the guards didn't have a key. *Good*, thought Henry, *that buys me some time.* He needed some kind of tool to force the side door open...

The lab door shook on its hinges as something heavy smacked the other side. The guards were throwing themselves against it.

Henry reached for a toolbox lying on top of a large, cloth-covered object on the nearest workbench...

The lab door juddered as the guards hit it a second time. One of the hinges came loose from the wall with a grinding sound.

As he picked up the toolbox, the cloth slipped down to reveal a tank that was filled with a dark, yellowy liquid. In the half-light, Henry made out several objects suspended in the murk and peered in to make out what they were... They seemed strangely familiar...

Human brains?

Four of them hanging in suspension. Henry gasped.

The guards hit the door again, but somehow the last hinge held. One of the men on the other side let out a yell of frustration.

Henry grabbed a hammer from the toolbox, went to the side door and slammed it down on the handle twice with all his might. The lock smashed on the second blow.

There was a crash from the other side of the room and the main door flew off its hinges. Two security guards staggered into the room, carried by their own momentum, and collided with a workbench. Behind them, the grey-haired doctor waited in the doorway.

"He's there!" the doctor yelled. "At the back of the lab!"

In a desperate effort to buy himself time, Henry grabbed the edge of the tank and heaved it over. There was a mighty crash as the glass shattered, spilling its contents across the floor of the lab. Then Henry threw his shoulder at the door. It swung open and he tore out into the night. A second later he was running across the gravel.

From behind him, he heard the voice of the doctor cry out: "The specimens! Forget him! Pick them up! Get them off the floor!"

Henry put his head down, realizing that he had come out on the other side of the medical centre. A door clattered open somewhere to his right and footsteps crunched on gravel. A torch beam flicked through the darkness at the back of the centre. He moved low and fast to his left, following the building round towards the front once more. There was no other way out of the complex. The surrounding wall was too high to climb on all other sides.

Making the front without being spotted, Henry paused at the corner of the building and scanned the way ahead. The courtyard in front of the centre was deserted and the gates were still open. Was it some kind of a trap? Surely they had to be expecting him to come this way.

Another torch beam flickered behind him and he broke from cover, heart thundering in his chest…

He sprinted for the gate and flew past, along the driveway and into the cover of the trees, pulling off the surgical gown and mask as he ran. Henry didn't look back, although he could hardly believe he'd made it out. Then cold realization struck him – he'd left Christian behind, not just with the guards, but with those doctors. Did they have Christian strapped to a table already? Were they cutting his skull open even now, ready to remove his brain?

He had to rescue his friend. And he was going to need help…

15

"**M**om!" Henry yelled, bursting through the front door of their lodge. He was breathless from running and covered with sweat. If the guards hadn't identified him by sight, then they would have probably got it out of Christian by now – one way or another. He shuddered, thinking of the methods those doctors might use to extract information. It was only a matter of time before they showed up at the house.

"Mom, Christian's in trouble!" he yelled again, moving through the lounge, which was in darkness. Something didn't add up. Henry checked his watch and saw that it was only 10 p.m. Mom never went to bed so early… And she would have certainly waited up until he got back…

A light was on in the kitchen and he moved towards it, pushing through the swing door. And froze in shock at what he saw…

His mom was sitting at the table, a glass of wine in one hand, laughing as if someone had just told a joke. Her other hand was on the table, almost touching that of a man seated beside her.

John Mallory.

"Henry!" Jennifer Ward said in surprise, pulling her hand back from the table as if she'd been caught doing something wrong. "I didn't expect you back so soon!"

Henry advanced into the room. "What's going on here?" he asked, aware that the question was pretty stupid. It was clear enough what was going on. His mom and the head of Malcorp were having some kind of wine-drinking, hand-holding date in the kitchen while they thought he was safely out of the way for a few hours.

"You're covered in sweat!" Jennifer said, rising from her seat and moving over to touch his forehead. "Are you sick?"

Henry turned from her to Mallory, who sipped his wine and gave him a concerned look.

"Are you okay, son?" Mallory asked.

Henry looked back at his mother. "What's he doing here?"

Jennifer gave her son an exasperated look. "John…Mr. Mallory popped over to see how we were settling in…"

"What, does he want to be your boyfriend or something?" Henry asked, aware of the nastiness in his voice. "He's like sixty years old!"

"Henry!" Jennifer snapped, anger in her voice.

Mallory pushed his chair out and half rose. "Perhaps I should be going…"

"Stay right there!" Jennifer said, before turning back to her son. "How dare you speak like that to a guest in our house…"

She stopped at a heavy banging on the front door. Henry

looked round and his mom must have recognized his anxiety at once. She placed a hand on his arm. "What is it? What's going on?"

The banging came a second time. Mallory rose swiftly from his seat. "I'll get that," he said, sounding relieved for the chance to get out of the kitchen. He moved through to the lounge before anyone could argue.

As he left, Henry turned back at his mom. "I have to tell you something," he said urgently.

"And I have to tell you you're bang out of line!" she hissed back. "How dare you act like a spoilt ten year old and embarrass me? And so what if I want to have a glass of wine with my boss?"

"Mom, I'm sorry…"

"And he is *not* sixty, goddammit! Do you know how difficult it is to meet decent—"

"Mom! I'm sorry!" Henry said this with enough emphasis to make her stop. "I have to tell you something. *Please*."

Jennifer took a deep breath. "Okay."

"Christian and I broke into the medical centre this evening—"

"You did WHAT?"

"Those are Malcorp security guards at the door. They're chasing me because we got inside and saw some things we shouldn't. They got Christian, but I managed to run away…"

Jennifer put her hand against her temple and looked at Henry with wide eyes. "This is not happening. Tell me this is a joke, Henry."

"It's no joke, Mom," Henry said, feeling suddenly ashamed that he'd kept everything from her. He looked through the gap in the kitchen door and saw Mallory talking to one of the security guards. At any moment they'd be marching in to take him away. "Listen, Mom, you have to believe me. This is going to sound crazy, but—"

"You mean more crazy than my son breaking and entering my boss's property?"

"Yeah. Malcorp is doing something to the kids around here. That special education programme the principal told you about is just a cover for some kind of experiment they're running…"

"Henry…"

"Just listen to me! I saw a kid inside the centre. He was strapped down to a table and they'd cut the top of his head off! They were gonna do something to his brain!"

Jennifer opened her mouth to say something, but stopped as the kitchen door swung open again. Henry backed away, expecting to see a guard there – but there was only John Mallory. He looked at them with a neutral expression.

"John, I'm so sorry," Jennifer said. "Henry started telling me some crazy story…"

Mallory held up a hand. "It's okay. Really. I sent the guards away. I thought it better that we clear up this misunderstanding ourselves." He turned his attention to Henry. "What do you say?"

"You're not going to get away with this," Henry replied. "I've seen what goes on inside your hospital."

Mallory actually smiled at him. "And what *is* going on exactly? What am I getting away with?"

Henry was momentarily at a loss for words. The head of the conspiracy that he and Fox and Christian had uncovered was standing in his kitchen, asking him to explain what he thought was going on.

And he found he didn't have the answer.

"Maybe we should take a look at the medical centre," Mallory said, glancing at Jennifer. "And I think there's someone your son should meet."

With that, he held open the kitchen door and waved his hand through. "Come on then."

Henry was about to protest, but his mom shot him a look that made it clear he was treading on very, very thin ice. Without a word, she walked past Mallory. Powerless to do anything else, Henry followed her through the lounge and out to a waiting buggy. As the head of Malcorp emerged from the lodge and climbed behind the driver's seat, Henry could have sworn he saw a glint of pure satisfaction in the man's eyes.

16

"I am so sorry, Mr. Mallory," said the red-faced head of security as the Malcorp boss strode into the medical centre reception, closely followed by Henry and his mom. "I don't know how this could have happened."

"Well it did happen," Mallory said brusquely. "I'll be conducting a full review of security here at the centre. Then I'll decide whether or not you get to keep your job. Now get out of my sight."

The security head looked so downtrodden as he disappeared across the other side of reception, Henry actually found himself feeling sorry for the man. He'd clearly caused him some big trouble...maybe even cost him his job. But Henry reminded himself what was going on in the medical centre. All in all, not a bad job to lose.

Mallory led the way to the door into the main part of the centre and swiped his key card. They passed through into the now-familiar corridors beyond.

"Tell me this was all that Christian kid's idea," Jennifer said, leaning in so she could whisper to her son. "Tell me you were easily led in this."

"Mom," Henry said, shaking his head. "It was my

idea as much as his."

"How did you get in then?"

"Christian's dad's key card…"

"Well then, it sounds like he had more of a hand in things than you did."

"It was both of us, Mom," Henry said firmly. Mallory looked over his shoulder and actually smiled at him.

"Sticking up for your friend," Mallory said. "I like that."

Henry gritted his teeth. Clearly Mallory wanted to keep on his mom's good side – not wanting to jeopardize future date nights, no doubt. *Yuk.* Well, they'd see what she thought of him when the truth came out about what was going on in the centre. The only thing Henry couldn't work out was why Mallory was so eager to take them right to the scene of the crime…

They passed through one set of double doors after another until they reached the corridor with the observation window. The operating theatre was fully illuminated, with the table in the centre. The sheet still covered the patient on the table.

"That's him!" Henry said to his mother, trying to keep his voice calm. "That's the kid with his skull cut open!"

Jennifer looked at Mallory with an apologetic expression. "I can't believe they poked around in here." She turned back to Henry. "Do you have any idea how much damage you could have caused walking around in an operating room? The infection risk you posed?"

Henry opened his mouth to argue, but Mallory started

down the corridor again. "I think the easiest way to get to the bottom of things would be to take a look at this patient, don't you?" he called over his shoulder.

Jennifer gave Henry a murderous look as they followed him through the door at the end and into the operating theatre.

They stopped in the doorway and the bald surgeon who had cornered Henry in the theatre approached. Henry noticed that he had a bandage on his left hand from where he'd fallen on the scalpel.

"How's the patient?" Mallory asked.

"Doing just fine," the surgeon said. "Considering the circumstances."

"Can we take a quick look?"

The surgeon walked to the table and wheeled it round so they could see the patient beneath the sheet-covered frame. Henry's eyes widened as he saw that the kid's head was now resting on a pillow, not clamped in a frame. There were thick white bandages covering his skull.

"His head was cut open – I could see his brain," Henry protested, turning to his mother.

"This young man was in a motorcycle crash earlier this afternoon," the surgeon said, directing his words to Jennifer. "Wasn't wearing a helmet, so we had to practically reconstruct his entire skull. I'm afraid your son walked in halfway through the procedure. It must have been a bit of an eye-opener…"

"No," Henry protested. "That's not right!"

Jennifer placed a hand on his shoulder. "Henry…"

He pulled free, looking round at Mallory and the surgeon. "They're lying! That's not what I saw!"

"Henry, I have had enough…"

He looked round at the glass where Christian's head had bounced off – they'd cleaned away the blood smear. Then he thought of the lab he'd fled into… The vat of brains that had shattered…

"We have to look in the lab!" he said, jogging across the theatre to the door on the other side. Behind him his mom and Mallory protested, but he ignored them. There was no way they could have cleared that mess up so quickly….

He pushed through the door and ran down the corridors, closely followed by the others. When he came to the lab door, which was still off its hinges, he ran through.

Inside, the grey-haired surgeon was fussing over a tank of water as security guards mopped up the floor. Henry advanced further into the lab, pointing at the tank.

"Look!" he said to his mom, pointing to the tank. "They're growing…brains!"

Jennifer and Mallory joined Henry as the grey-haired surgeon looked round in surprise. Mallory let out a low, guffawing laugh.

"Dr. Chricton," he called across the lab, "would you be so good as to show us what you've got in that tank?"

The surgeon grumbled something before reaching into the tank and removing a dripping object that looked like a large, grey sponge. "My sea-cucumber experiment was almost ruined, Mr. Mallory! I suggest you improve your security arrangements!"

"You can be sure of it, Dr. Chricton!" Mallory gently took both Henry and Jennifer's arms and led them back to the doorway.

Feeling stupid as hell, Henry said, "I know what I saw..."

His mother gave him a withering look, but Mallory merely placed his hands on Henry's shoulders and looked into his face. "Are you sure? I mean, are you *really* sure? Couldn't it have been that you saw that poor kid lying on that table with his brain hanging out and got a little spooked?"

Henry looked down at his feet.

"You got chased by the guards," Mallory continued. "Things were moving fast and you made a mistake. Is that at least a possibility?"

Henry took a deep breath. "Yeah."

Mallory patted his shoulder and looked at his mom with a wink. "Everyone's allowed to get a little screwy from time to time."

"What's going to happen next?" she asked, voice full of concern.

"Well," Mallory said, "the breach of security was a serious issue, but more for my men than for Henry or Christian. And no real harm was done, I guess. Although I would suggest that a world-class grounding is in order..."

"Oh, you can bet on that," Henry's mom said emphatically.

"Then I guess we can call this matter closed," Mallory said, turning his attention to Henry. "I'd just like to know one thing. We caught your accomplice in this little scheme and he's back with his parents right now. Was Christian the only other person in on this?"

Henry looked into the man's penetrating eyes. "Yeah. Just him and me."

"That's the truth?"

"*Yes.*"

Mallory slapped him on the shoulder. "Then I guess you'd better see what you came looking for."

He started down the corridor again, leaving a confused Henry to follow behind. They passed down a few more corridors into an area signposted *Patient Care*. Here the corridors were less anonymous than before, with numbers on the doors and even plants in pots arranged here and there. A female nurse passed them and smiled warmly.

"Is she awake?" Mallory asked.

"Yes," the nurse replied, "but it's getting late."

"We won't be long."

Mallory knocked twice on a door to his right. A female voice called through for him to enter. Mallory opened the door, but rather than entering himself, waved Henry through. The room contained only a hospital bed and a couple of chairs. In the bed, a girl was sitting propped upright on pillows, watching a sitcom on the TV with a smile on her face.

Gabrielle Henson.

She turned towards Henry and her face lit up in recognition. She grabbed the TV remote and muted the sound.

"I know you," Gabrielle said. "We've met before."

For a moment, Henry didn't know what to say. It was unmistakably the girl that he'd met just a week earlier, but she was a million miles away from the terrified figure he'd encountered in the gas station toilet. Her hair was neatly combed and washed now, blonde locks cascading around her shoulders. Her expression was relaxed, happy even, and she regarded Henry with a calm openness that he found surprising. As she continued to stare at him he found his face reddening a little.

"Is your name Henry?" she asked.

He nodded. "We met…uh…in a toilet."

Gabrielle gave a little laugh and put her hands to her mouth. "Oh my goodness! What must you think of me!" She looked down at the bed sheets in embarrassment. "I was going through a bit of a bad spell…" Henry guessed she was referring to the "drug problem" Mallory had told him about.

"Now, now, my dear," Mallory said, entering the room to stand beside Henry. "You have nothing to feel bad about. We're allowed to get…"

"…a little screwy sometimes?" she finished for him, as if it was a line she'd heard before.

Mallory laughed and waggled a finger at her. "You are too smart by half." He turned to Henry. "Why don't you two get reacquainted? I want to have a quick word with your mom."

Mallory walked out, closing the door behind him. Henry felt suddenly foolish standing in the room of the girl he'd broken into the medical centre to find. He realized that he really didn't know her at all. And she looked like she needed anything but rescuing.

Gabrielle patted the mattress beside her. "Come and sit down."

Henry walked over and perched on the side of the bed uncomfortably as the girl studied him again.

"Is it true what they're saying?" she asked.

"What?"

"That you and another kid broke into the centre to... *rescue me*?" She said the last two words as if they were ridiculous.

Henry felt himself blushing again. "I guess. The last time we met, you seemed so afraid."

Gabrielle shook her head, remembering. "Phew! Was I strung out that afternoon! I'd been living rough for the best part of a week. I don't know what would have happened if you and Trooper Dan hadn't come across me."

Henry frowned. From the way she told it, it was like the cop had saved her.

"You seemed pretty afraid of that cop at the time," he ventured.

Gabrielle rolled her eyes. "Afraid? Why would I be afraid of Trooper Dan?"

"So what happened after he took you away?"

She frowned at him. "When?"

"He put you in his cruiser and as you were driving away you told me to run..."

"I was pretty strung out, wasn't I...?"

"But what happened next? Did he bring you back here?"

Gabrielle's serene features crumpled into a frown. "Back here? I..." She fell silent as she tried to remember. "Something..." Her voice broke.

"What is it?" Henry pressed, leaning closer. "What's wrong?"

Gabrielle looked at him and smiled. "I'm sorry for being so silly. I guess I'm just so happy to be back here with my family. They come to visit me every day, you know. And I'm going to be able to go back home next week if I keep up this good progress!"

Henry sat back.

"What's wrong?" she asked. "You look so disappointed."

He shrugged. "I guess...you're not like I remember from that afternoon."

Gabrielle smiled at him uncertainly. "You'd prefer me to be a drugged up runaway with cuts all over her legs?"

"No! It's just...can I ask you a favour?"

"Shoot."

Hesitating only a second, Henry reached out slowly and brushed Gabrielle's hair away from her forehead to expose the skin underneath. It was unmarked – no trace of scarring. If she'd been operated upon during the last week, the evidence would have been there to see. But there was nothing.

"What did you expect?" Gabrielle asked as he lowered his hand.

Henry shook his head. "I don't know. I was just being stupid." Suddenly everything he'd done that evening seemed pretty stupid.

The girl leaned over unexpectedly and placed a kiss on his cheek. "That's for coming to rescue me," she said as she pulled away. "Even if I didn't need rescuing. Now, can I ask you something?"

"Anything," Henry said. Suddenly it felt a lot hotter in the room.

"Come see me after school tomorrow? I get lonely in here."

"Okay."

Gabrielle smiled and sat back on the pillows with a yawn. "I'd better get some shut-eye. All this lying around makes me sleepy."

Henry rose from the bed and walked to the door, knowing that even though things seemed square with Mallory and he had managed to see Gabrielle Henson after all, the night was far from over.

He still had plenty of explaining to do to his mom. And if he knew her at all, she was gearing up to give him the lecture of a lifetime.

In a room located deep within the medical centre, John Mallory stood before a bank of security monitors and watched as Jennifer and Henry Ward exited the front of the building and were escorted down the drive by one of the guards. Although there was no sound on the video feed, he could clearly see that Mrs. Ward was giving her son one hell of a talking to.

"Was he telling the truth?" Dr. Chancellor asked, appearing at Mallory's side.

"About what?" her employer asked without taking his eyes from the screens.

"About him and the other boy being the only ones who knew about this."

Mallory considered for a moment. "No. The Christian boy is an idiot, and Ward hasn't been here long enough to plan something like this. Someone's been feeding him information."

"Who then?"

"Well that's the question, isn't it?" Mallory looked at his head doctor, pulling a chewed cigar from his pocket and clamping it between his teeth. "But I'm betting if we give Ward enough rope, he'll lead us right back to that girl who repainted my Rolls. Put Trooper Dan on it."

A look of concern darkened Chancellor's perfect features. "Is that wise, if outsiders are involved? They could have spoken to anyone! And Trooper Dan is impossible to control...unpredictable. This girl, Gabrielle, is showing signs of rejection as well. I need more time to adjust the implants. They are not stable."

Mallory frowned at her. "Why, Magda, you sound as if you're having doubts about our project." He reached out and stroked his hand down her face. "So beautiful. I really don't think you'd get on so well in a Polish jail, do you?" He moved his hand round so that he was gripping the back of her neck. "Perhaps you need to be reminded who got you your nice new identity and who allows you to conduct all your experiments in a...non-judgemental environment." Chancellor struggled against Mallory's grasp, but he held firm, pushing his face in hers. "Nothing happens in this town without me knowing about it. They have no evidence. They haven't told anyone squat. And Trooper Dan will do as he's told, just as long as you keep feeding him his medicine. The adjustment process works. A few subjects need a little more...tinkering...that's all."

The doctor pulled free from Mallory, eyes blazing with anger. She made an effort to control herself and said, "What do you want me to do?"

"Proceed as planned with the boy in custody," Mallory said. His voice was hard and commanding now. "His parents have already signed the release forms. And put Trooper Dan on Ward's ass."

Chancellor looked him deep in the eyes. "And the girl in Newton?"

Mallory removed the cigar from his mouth and studied it thoughtfully. "If she's involved...tell Dan to have a little talk with her."

17

Early Monday morning, Henry knocked on the door of Christian's lodge. He'd spent the last thirty-six hours locked down in his room. His mom had made it clear the only reason he'd be leaving their new house for the foreseeable future would be for school. She'd convinced herself that the whole thing with the medical centre was her son's way of trying to sabotage their move from the city. And after meeting Gabrielle Henson, Henry was beginning to wonder if she had a point.

Everything that had happened since he'd arrived in Newton had been ultra-strange, but hadn't part of him been secretly pleased about that? He'd never wanted to leave the city and finding problems with their new home was something that, subconsciously, he'd been almost happy about. Gabrielle. The school. Mallory's conspiracy to turn the local kids into...something. All good reasons for them to pack their bags and head back out of Newton County as fast as possible. Following the events of the weekend, he'd resolved to stop believing in crazy stories and try to fit in.

He hoped Christian was feeling the same way.

The door was answered by Christian's dad, who was still in his dressing gown and unshaven, like he had no intention of going to work that day.

"Is Christian there?" Henry asked. "I wondered if he wanted to walk to school."

"*You*," the man said, looking at Henry with barely contained anger. "Don't you think you've caused enough trouble?"

Henry took a step back as Christian's dad advanced on him through the doorway. The man's hands were bunched into fists.

"Stay away from my son. And stay the hell away from my family…"

Christian's mom appeared and placed a restraining hand on her husband's arm. "Come back inside, George."

To Henry's relief, the man nodded and allowed her to usher him into the house.

"I just want to know if Christian's okay," Henry said as she began to push the door shut.

"Christian is going to be just fine," she said firmly. "He just doesn't need bad influences like you hanging around. He's going to be a good boy from now on. Goodbye."

The door slammed shut.

For a moment Henry just stood there trying to process everything. He hadn't expected to be the most popular person with Christian's folks, but clearly they had the impression that the break-in at the medical centre had been his idea. *Great*, he thought as he turned and started walking in the direction of the school. *Thanks for sticking up for me, Christian.*

Things didn't get any better when he got to school. As he walked through the gates and approached the main building he had a feeling that something was wrong. Looking round the yard, he realized what it was…

Every kid was staring at him.

Shaking his head, Henry shouldered his school bag and doubled his pace. News travelled fast around Malcorp. But as he passed the car park, he was pleased to see someone he could rely on to be friendly – he hoped. The coach was climbing out of an ancient Chevy that looked as if it hadn't been cleaned since the last century.

"Coach!" he called, running over as the man started in the direction of the pool.

"Henry," the coach said, just glancing in his direction. "When I told you to act like a normal kid, I didn't mean making an enemy of the head of Malcorp."

Henry started. "How—"

"Internal memo to all teaching staff emailed through yesterday morning," the man said quietly, as if worried someone was listening in. "It appears you're a bad influence and to be watched for *disruptive tendencies*. I don't know what you did…and I don't want to either…but you've just become public enemy number one in the eyes of Malcorp High."

"Great," Henry muttered. So much for John Mallory's promise to call the matter closed.

"It gets better. You're banned from all extra-curricular activities and clubs for the foreseeable future."

"So that means—"

"No swim team, kid," the coach said with a sigh. "More than my job's worth to be seen breaking an edict from John Mallory himself."

Henry tried to hide the disappointment in his voice. "That's okay, coach. I understand."

The man stopped walking and gave him a questioning look. "You must've done something pretty extreme to get Mallory worked up like this, I'm guessing. Tell me you had a good reason."

"I thought I did at the time."

"But now you're not so sure?"

Henry shrugged. "The evidence suggests otherwise."

The coach gave a guffawing laugh. "The evidence? What about your gut, kid? What's that telling you?"

Henry frowned. "I don't know."

"Well, perhaps you should start listening to it more. When I'm not sure about something, I always listen to my gut. It's never been wrong. Apart from one time when it was just indigestion."

Henry laughed despite himself. The coach nodded and carried on towards the pool.

"You'd better get to class," he called over his shoulder. "You're in enough trouble already. I'll see you at swim practice tomorrow afternoon."

It took a moment for Henry to process that. "But I thought…"

"It's more than my job's worth to let you on the team? Maybe I just don't like my job enough."

Henry watched the coach walk on for a moment before turning back to the school. At least someone was on his side. As he approached the building he ran through everything in his mind. John Mallory had lied about calling an end to the matter – he'd informed his teachers…*so what else had he lied about?*

Suddenly, Henry's gut was beginning to turn over, and rather than feeling annoyed with Christian, he started feeling worried.

First class of the day was English, which was just about the only lesson he could keep up with. The week before they'd started *Hamlet*, which Henry was actually enjoying, much to his surprise – even if they'd been expected to read the entire play for homework that weekend. His grounding and loss of PS3 privileges had left him with plenty of time for that.

"So what is the message of *Hamlet*?" the balding English teacher said, casting a piercing gaze over the class. "What is Shakespeare trying to tell us?"

A girl in front who Henry recognized as one of Blake's crowd raised her hand. "Be grateful for what you've got?"

The teacher nodded. "Very good, Stacy. Anyone else?"

"Try to fit in?" someone else suggested. "I mean, if Hamlet hadn't gone round causing problems for his uncle, he wouldn't have gotten in trouble."

Henry burst out laughing. The teacher's head swivelled to look at him.

"Something funny, Mr. Ward?"

"Well, Hamlet's uncle was a murderer," Henry said, aware of heads turning in his direction. "He killed his father. Right?"

"There was no evidence of that," Stacy snapped at him.

"The ghost told him," Henry said.

"Don't you think that sounds a bit delusional?" she countered, turning back to the teacher. "Hamlet needed to accept the authority figures in his life. Then there might have been a happy ending."

Heads nodded all round. On the other side of the class, Steve said, "It's like kids who run around breaking into places they shouldn't."

There were sniggers around the room. Henry reddened. *Had everyone in the school received Mallory's memo?*

The teacher smiled at Stacy and Steve. "Well done, both of you. You've clearly understood the morals of the play very well. It has a clear message that we're happier when we accept the given rules of the place where we live." He was looking directly at Henry as he said this. "Some people try their best not to fit in – like Hamlet. If only he'd worked with his uncle rather than against him."

"He shouldn't have gone poking around in business that didn't concern him," Stacy added.

"That's right," the teacher agreed. "Because what happens at the end of the play?"

"Everyone dies," Steve said, and looked round at Henry with a grin.

The teacher turned to face him also. "Henry Ward. Do you agree?"

"Uh," said Henry, well aware that every single student in the class was looking at him now. Their faces were expressionless, but their eyes were all the same: judgemental, almost predatory, waiting for him to say the wrong thing. The room felt suddenly suffocating. He had to get out. Henry reached down and grabbed his bag from under his seat. "I have to go…to the toilet…"

The teacher began to protest, but Henry was already through the door and running along the deserted corridor towards the nearest exit. And he almost made it…

"Henry!" a familiar voice called out as he reached the door. He looked round to see Blake approaching down the corridor with the quarterback and several others from his crowd.

"Hey," Henry said, trying to sound casual. There was a hardness to Blake's features that he hadn't seen before. "What is this? Uniform patrol?"

"I heard about your break-in at my grandfather's medical centre Saturday night," he said. "I guess you think you're pretty smart, huh?"

Henry shook his head. "No, it's—"

Without warning, Blake struck out with his fist, catching Henry across the jaw. There was enough force behind the blow to send him staggering back against the door. He hit the frame and lost his footing, landing clumsily on his backside. Behind Blake, the members of the football team laughed and high-fived one another.

"That's for the kid whose operation you interrupted," Blake spat, fists still clenched. "Johnny's a friend of ours!"

Henry struggled to his feet. "Blake, I—"

Blake shook his head in disgust and held open the door. "You haven't got many friends left around here, Ward. Maybe you ought to think about cleaning up your act."

Henry wiped a hand across his mouth. His fingers came away bloody. Shouldering his bag, he started towards the exit.

"There's nowhere to run," Blake called after him. "Your friend's been fixed and you will be too!"

Henry stopped and turned round slowly. "What was that?"

Some of the confidence drained from Blake's face, as if he knew that he'd spoken out of turn. "Just get out of my school until you've sorted out your...attitude." He started backing away. The other boys did the same.

"What's happened to Christian?" Henry demanded. "Where is he?"

Rather than respond, Blake merely turned and walked off around the corner, closely followed by his gang.

"Answer me!" Henry demanded, his voice echoing through the deserted halls of the school. There was no response. Henry kicked the wall in frustration. "Crazy sons of bitches!" he cried aloud, before taking a breath and composing himself. Getting mad wasn't going to solve anything.

Mallory was a liar after all. And Christian was being held…somewhere.

He ran to the main door and pushed through into the daylight outside, headed for Newton.

Like the coach had said, it was time to start listening to his gut.

The house stood alone at the end of a track that was easy to miss from the main road. Few of the residents of Newton, even those who had lived there since long before the arrival of Malcorp, knew of the place. And newcomers to the town were sure to miss the track, which meant that Trooper Dan's residence was practically hidden from the world… silent…forgotten…

And that was exactly how he liked it.

Except on that morning, the giant cop wasn't enjoying the peace and seclusion so much. He was suffering one of the splitting headaches that plagued him from time to time and with increasing frequency. The bottle of pills prescribed to control the brain aches was empty, as he'd found out when he shuffled to the bathroom following yet another sleepless night.

He'd managed to get into his uniform in a haze, and then staggered downstairs to the kitchen to start preparing his usual breakfast of bacon, sausage and three eggs. He didn't get any further than the kitchen table, where he slumped with his head in his hands for what seemed like a very long time.

The headache was so bad, in fact, that he didn't even hear the car pull up out front until its door slammed as someone emerged. Rising from the seat at the table, Trooper Dan removed his Magnum from the holster on his belt and moved to the hall, taking aim at the door as it opened...

Dr. Chancellor stepped through. Being confronted by a man aiming a gun directly at them would startle most people, but the doctor barely reacted. She gave Trooper Dan one of her stern looks.

"What do you think you're doing?"

He lowered the weapon and stumbled back through to the kitchen as she followed him down the hall. "I have a headache," he said as he retook his seat.

Chancellor placed an old-fashioned leather doctor's bag on the table in front of him and removed a pencil light from her pocket. "Is that a reason to shoot anyone who walks through the front door?"

"You didn't knock."

Dr. Chancellor shone the light in his eyes – first the left, then the right. "Have you been feeling dizzy again?"

"Yes."

"You've been the taking pills?"

He slammed his fist on the table so suddenly that the doctor actually jumped this time. "Yes, I've been taking them, dammit! And I ran out two days ago. If you'd brought my prescription on time I wouldn't have this headache..."

"Shhh," Chancellor stroked a hand through his hair. "So much going on in Dan's poor little skull."

He looked away from her. "You didn't answer my calls."

"I was very busy at the clinic. You forgive me?"

"Do you have my pills?"

Chancellor smiled and reached into her bag. "Yes. And something else. A special treat because you've been such a good boy."

Trooper Dan looked round at her. "What is it?"

Chancellor removed a syringe and a glass bottle filled with a clear liquid. "Something to make you feel big and strong again. And very little pain. The effects should last for a few days. Roll up your sleeve."

He did as he was told as she poked the needle through the top of the bottle and filled the syringe. The doctor wiped his arm with an antiseptic swab and positioned the needle over the vein. "There's something we need you to do for us."

"What?" the trooper asked, eyes locked on the syringe.

"A kid has been causing trouble around the complex. We think he is linked to the girl from the coffee shop. You know who I am talking about?"

"Yes, yes, I know."

"We need you to keep an eye on them. Find out what they are up to. You understand?"

Trooper Dan clenched and unclenched his fist. "Yes, goddammit. Don't talk to me like I'm an idiot."

"And if the girl is poking her nose into Malcorp business…"

Dr. Chancellor slid the needle into his arm and depressed

the plunger. Trooper Dan's eyes seemed to go completely black and his fist slowly unclenched.

"...Mr. Mallory wants you to talk with her."

"Talk with her," the cop repeated, his voice distant as a numbing sensation overtook the pain coursing through his skull. For the first time in hours he felt relief. Then he felt a sudden surge of energy – his old power returning. He grinned.

Chancellor removed the syringe, wiped the broken skin clean with the swab and stroked his skull once more. "That's a good boy. Do as you are told and I will bring all the medication you could ever need."

"I could ever need," Trooper Dan repeated.

Chancellor took a bottle of pills from the bag and placed them on the edge of the table. From beneath the floor there came a thudding sound.

"What is that?" the doctor asked as she picked up her bag.

"Huh?" Trooper Dan asked distractedly as the sound came again. Then his eyes snapped back into their usual focus as the drug kicked in, sharpening his senses. "Oh, just some reporter I caught snooping around. He actually stopped on the road to ask me for directions to Newton. That was a real bad decision on his part, don't you think?"

"What are you going to do to him?"

Trooper Dan's face became deathly serious. "Take a wild guess."

"Mr. Mallory wants a report on the girl before you take action," Chancellor said. "Is that clear?"

"Crystal."

"Good. See you soon, Dan. If the headaches get worse, give me a call."

Dr. Chancellor walked from the kitchen. Trooper Dan sat motionless, listening to the slam of the front door, then to the sound of her car as she drove away. Then the thudding from the basement distracted him again.

"Okay, okay," he said, rising from his chair. "I'm coming."

He walked across the kitchen and opened a door. Stone steps led down into the basement, which was in darkness until he flicked the light switch on the wall.

The reporter was where Trooper Dan had left him at the bottom of the stairs – tied to a chair with a piece of tape over his mouth. He was a middle-aged guy who was just fat enough to be called overweight. His cheap grey suit was covered with dust and flecked with blood here and there. He'd managed to topple the chair to one side and was now lying on the floor, squirming around in an effort to get free.

"What are you doin' on the floor?" Trooper Dan asked. "Didn't I tell you to sit still?"

The reporter made muffled sounds as the cop walked into the centre of the basement, grabbed the back of the chair and hauled it upright with one hand. The reporter looked at him with wide, desperate eyes. Trooper Dan leaned forward.

"I'm gonna ask you some questions, mister," he said in an altogether different tone from the one he'd used with

Dr. Chancellor. His accent was thick once more – the epitome of a small-town sheriff. "And you're gonna give me the answers or we're gonna have a fallin' out. You hear me?"

The reporter nodded his head frantically.

"Now the first word I want to hear out of your smart city mouth when I take off this tape is the name of your contact in Newton. Understand?"

Another nod. Trooper Dan reached to tear the tape off, but stopped as something buzzed in the inside pocket of the man's jacket. The cop reached inside and removed a cell phone. He flipped the front and a text message opened up.

Where r u? Waiting at coffee shop – Fox

"Hmmm," Trooper Dan said and snapped the phone shut. He smiled broadly at the reporter. "Well, looks like I don't need you after all." He reached behind his back and removed a hunting knife from a sheath concealed on his belt.

The reporter's eyes widened even further as he saw the blade. From beneath the tape he gave a muffled scream.

18

"**O**uch," Henry said as Fox dabbed his split lip with a wad of cotton wool soaked in antiseptic. She looked at him like he was being a baby and continued to clean the cut.

"You have a real way with people, Ward," she said. "Is there anyone at Malcorp who doesn't want to punch you out?"

Henry clenched his jaw and said nothing. He might have reminded the girl that it was because of her and Christian that everyone wanted to punch him out in the first place. He was sitting in the room above the cafe, having run all the way from Malcorp High. To his surprise, Hank the guard hadn't given him any trouble when he had passed through the main gate in the middle of a Monday morning, but that didn't mean his movements wouldn't be reported back.

As Fox continued to clean the cut, his gaze fell upon an easel in the corner. An oil painting was in progress – it was of Newton's main street. Shoppers with thin, distorted bodies were walking along it. The odd thing was they all seemed to be peering directly out of the picture. Somehow, it reminded Henry of the way all the kids had stared at him in the playground.

"I just started it the other day," Fox said. For once there was a note of shyness in her voice. "I probably won't finish it…"

"You should," Henry said as she closed the lid on her first-aid box and returned it to the kitchen. "I like it."

"What happened on Saturday night, Ward?" she asked. "I was worried about you… Both of you. Christian was supposed to give me a call after the operation but I didn't hear anything. I've been trying to text that reporter, but he's not answering either."

Henry took a deep breath and walked over to the front window. The street outside was as quiet as ever.

He said, "We got inside, but the guards caught up with us."

"What did you find in the centre?" Fox asked, unable to keep the excitement from her voice.

He related the story of how he'd been chased from the centre and then taken back by Mallory and his mom. He told her about the kid who'd apparently been in a motorcycle crash. How despite his promise to keep things quiet, Mallory had turned the high school against him. He even told her about the "sea cucumbers".

"Sea cucumber research!" Fox said. "How dumb do they think we are?"

Henry shook his head. "Mallory had me convinced I was imagining things. I guess I wanted to believe him – to believe that everything is okay. Now I don't really know what to believe…"

"What about Gab—"

Henry held up a hand to stop her. "Mallory took me to see her."

Fox's mouth fell open. "You saw Gabrielle?"

"She's in the medical centre, apparently recovering from her latest 'drug binge'."

"Gabrielle does not take drugs!" Fox said, anger rising in her voice.

Henry sighed. "*I* believe you, but *she* doesn't. If you ask her, she'll tell you all about how Trooper Dan and everyone at Malcorp stopped her from running off the rails."

"Then they've done something to her..."

"She seemed completely happy – in fact she asked me to come visit her again this afternoon. No evidence of scars on her head, nothing. I just don't get it."

Fox stood up and began to pace, agitated. "They're controlling her somehow. They've got her locked up in there and she's afraid. I knew I shouldn't have trusted you and Christian to get the job done."

"Hey, Christian got smacked in the face pretty bad," Henry protested, remembering the blood on the operating theatre window. "For all I know he was seriously hurt. Back at the school Blake let something slip... I think they're holding him somewhere – maybe in the medical centre. He said they'd *fixed* him and I was next."

Fox shook her head. "I should have gone myself."

"Well, you seemed pretty happy for us to walk into danger while you stood around painting pictures..."

"Watch it!" Fox interrupted. "Or you're gonna get hit

in the mouth for the second time in one day!"

Henry threw up his hands. "I don't need this," he said. "Christian's in trouble and I'm going to find out where he is. If you're just going to give me a hard time, I'll go by myself." He walked out of the door and down the stairs.

A second later, Fox ran after him. "Ward, wait!"

He stopped at the bottom of the stairs and looked round. Fox almost tripped into him.

"I'm sorry," she said. "That was out of line."

"Yeah, it was."

"So what are you going to do?" she asked. "Run over to the medical centre and demand to see Christian? Is that the plan?"

Henry shrugged. He didn't know what his plan was, but he felt responsible for his friend. While he'd spent the last two days feeling sorry for himself, god knows what they'd been doing to Christian. *Fixing him.*

"Well, what do you suggest?" he asked finally.

Before Fox could respond, a hammering on the front door of the cafe made them both look round. Henry looked past the door at the bottom of the stairs, half expecting to see his mom standing outside, demanding to know why he wasn't in class.

But it wasn't his mom.

It was Trooper Dan.

19

"I'm afraid we're closed, officer," Fox said as she opened the coffee shop door a crack.

Trooper Dan pushed his way through and stepped into the cafe, looking around the darkened interior without bothering to remove his shades. "I'm not here to drink coffee."

"Okay," Fox replied, closing the door after him. She cast a glance towards the counter and the half-open door to the stairs, where Henry was standing out of sight, peering through the gap between the door and frame.

"Something wrong?"

She looked round at the cop, who was studying her closely. "Why would there be something wrong?"

"You seem kinda tense," he said, hooking his thumbs into his belt. "There was an incident at the Malcorp complex Saturday night. You wouldn't know anything about that, would you?"

Fox gave him a hard look. "Why would I?"

The cop opted not to answer that question, walking across the cafe as if he owned the place. Henry moved a little further into the shadows behind the door, convinced for a second that the man was staring right at him. But then Trooper Dan's gaze moved on as he stopped at the counter. He dragged a gloved finger along the top of the coffee machine, picking up dust that he wiped away with disgust. "Business a bit slow, huh?"

"Is this some kind of inspection?" Fox asked coldly. "Because I think you're outside your jurisdiction."

The cop looked round at her and his lips curled into a mocking smile. "*Jurisdiction?* My, what a big word for a little girl." He moved along the counter, past a tray of stacked coffee cups, and stared at one of the photographs. "Shouldn't you be in school today?"

"I dropped out."

"Well, that figures. Must be difficult managing this place. What with your momma being a cripple and all."

Through the gap in the door frame, Henry saw Fox's rage. *Just keep it together,* he prayed. He could see the cop was trying to wind her up. Get a reaction.

"My mother is *not* a cripple," Fox said, her voice low and controlled.

The trooper gave a snorting laugh. He leaned back against the counter and nudged the edge of the tray that rested on the top, sending the pile of stacked cups crashing to the floor on the other side.

"Hey!" Fox exclaimed, moving towards the counter. As she passed, Trooper Dan caught her arm and pulled her back. Fox gave a cry of surprise and tried to struggle free, but the cop held her firm.

"I know you were involved with the break-in Saturday night."

"Prove it!"

"I don't have to. The whole town knows you're a troublemaker. It's about time you and your white-trash mother accepted Mr. Mallory's offer and sold up."

Fox stuck her chin out at him defiantly. "Or what? You'll come and break some plates as well?"

Trooper Dan grinned at her. "Oh, I'll do more than break plates."

She let out a cry of pain as he tightened his grip on her arm.

"What's going on?" Henry said, pushing open the door and stepping out behind the counter.

The cop released Fox's arm and she ran round the counter beside him. Henry stepped forward so he was between her and the cop.

"Well, I might've known you wouldn't be far away," Trooper Dan said.

Trying to disguise the fact his heart was beating as fast as a racing car, Henry said, "You were harassing her. I saw it."

"Then perhaps she'd like to file a complaint," the cop answered, his voice deadpan. He looked at Fox. "Do you want to make a complaint, miss?"

Henry looked at Fox, who shook her head imperceptibly. "No. I don't want to make a complaint."

Trooper Dan gave Henry an arctic smile and walked back across the cafe. "I'll be keeping an eye on you both, you can be sure of it."

With that he turned and walked out of the door, slamming it so hard it seemed the glass in the window would shatter.

Alone in the cafe, Henry and Fox breathed sighs of relief.

"You shouldn't have come out like that," Fox said. "Now he knows we're together in all this."

Henry gave her an exasperated look. "He was twisting your arm half off!"

"I'm used to Mallory's men coming round and breaking the crockery every month. It's their way of letting us know we're not welcome in Newton."

"If you made a complaint..."

"Complain to who? Mallory? The town councillors? They're all in Malcorp's pocket." She paused, biting her lip. "It is interesting though."

"What is?"

"Well, if there's nothing funny going on at the medical centre," she said, "why do you suppose Trooper Dan showed up here to hassle me about the break-in?"

Henry leaned back against the door frame, rubbed his forehead with his hand and groaned.

"What's the matter?" Fox asked with concern.

"*You're* the matter," he said and then waved his hand around the shop. "This whole place...Newton and Malcorp is the matter... I really wanted to believe that nothing was going on here. So my mom could have a good job and be happy here. I wanted to believe that Gabrielle Henson was fine and that Trooper Dan was just a normal small-town cop. And that the kids in my school were just…really, really clever… And that Mallory wasn't…" His voice trailed away.

"Say it," Fox pressed.

"Experimenting on the brains of local kids," he said. Out loud it sounded insane. But despite his efforts over the weekend to believe otherwise, everything he'd seen – the kid with his head cut open, the weird behaviour, the lies, the threats – pointed to one conclusion. He'd read a Sherlock Holmes book once where the detective had said that when you eliminate all the rational explanations, whatever's left is the truth, no matter how crazy it sounds. Which was just a fancy way of expressing what Coach Tyler had been saying about listening to his gut.

"So," Fox said, all businesslike, "the break-in didn't help us. Christian has disappeared and they've still got Gabrielle. We need a new plan. More evidence."

Henry nodded. "My mom's going to be watching me like a hawk and so is everyone else in the Malcorp complex. Sneaking around isn't going to be easy."

Fox thought for a moment before saying, "You keep your meeting with Gabrielle. See if you can find out where they're holding Christian while you're in the medical centre. And maybe you can get Gabrielle to tell you what happened to her."

"I already tried – she doesn't remember."

Fox reached into her pocket and withdrew the photograph of Gabrielle and Blake she'd shown him the other day. She handed it to him.

"Give her that. Perhaps it will jog her memory."

"What about you?"

Before Fox could answer, her cell phone vibrated and she pulled it from her pocket. She looked at Henry and grinned as she read a text message.

"It's my missing reporter. He wants to meet me outside town."

Henry frowned. "Why?"

"Sounds like he had a run-in with Trooper Dan. Says he wants to meet this afternoon. Somewhere discreet."

"I should come with you."

Fox shook her head. "No. Go and talk to Gabrielle. Find out where Christian is. I'll deal with the reporter – see if I can get him to hang around long enough for us to get some real evidence."

Parked in the shadows of an alleyway across the street, Trooper Dan watched as Henry Ward emerged from the coffee shop, took a look around to make sure he wasn't being followed and headed off up the street. He fought the urge to follow the kid. He would be dealt with later. His orders were for the girl.

Through the glass-fronted door he saw her shoot the bolts, as if she believed that a few locks would stop him if he really wanted to get in. Then she disappeared inside, no doubt to get ready for her meeting with the reporter. He smiled to himself and sat back to wait.

Soon his prey would come to him.

20

"So, you're playing hooky?" Gabrielle said.

Henry smiled at her turn of phrase, which seemed strangely old-fashioned. It reminded him of the way Blake spoke. He laid a card down on the sheet and took another from the deck, slotting it into his hand. They were sitting on the bed in Gabrielle's hospital room, playing a game called rummy that she'd been trying to teach him for the best part of thirty minutes. His trip back to the medical centre had been uneventful – barely a nod from Hank on the main gate. Upon entering the centre, snooping around the corridors for any evidence of Christian's presence was curtailed by a nurse who insisted on escorting him to Gabrielle's room. And she was now waiting outside to make sure he didn't take any unscheduled trips around the facility on his way out. So much for that plan.

"What makes you think I'm playing hooky?" Henry asked as she examined her hand and exchanged two cards of her own.

"Well, you're here at 2 p.m. on a school day."

"You got me."

"You're right I got you," she said, laying her hand down. Four aces and three kings.

"I'm no good at card games," Henry said, scratching his head. She'd beaten him four times in a row.

"Neither am I normally!" Gabrielle exclaimed, scooping up the cards and shuffling them. "I mean, I used to get beaten every time before…" Her voice trailed away and she was silent for a moment. Her hands stopped shuffling the cards.

"Before what?" Henry asked.

Gabrielle looked at him in confusion.

"You said you used to get beaten all the time before something," Henry pressed. "Can you tell me what you meant?"

Gabrielle gave a little giggle. "I don't know what I'm talking about." She looked down at the cards in her hands and started shuffling furiously.

"What do you remember before you came here?" Henry asked. "To the medical centre, I mean."

She shrugged and started dealing the cards. "I was pretty crazy, I guess. I ran away. Took drugs. Shall we play?"

Henry picked up his cards and examined his hand. "What kind of drugs?"

"Huh?"

"What kind of drugs were you taking? Where did you get them from?"

Gabrielle's face darkened. "Why do you want to go asking me nasty questions like that? I thought you came here to make me feel better…"

"Did you ever meet my friend Christian?" Henry asked quickly, changing the subject as the door opened a crack and the nurse peered in, checking on them.

"Christian?" Gabrielle said, brightening again as she organized her cards. "I think I met him once or twice. Kind of an outsider, don't you think?"

The door creaked closed. Henry smiled and exchanged a couple of cards. "You could say that. He disappeared."

"Disappeared?" Gabrielle laid down a six and picked up another card.

"After Saturday night when we broke in. He hit his head on some glass and I haven't seen him since."

Gabrielle watched him as he laid down another card. "Perhaps they brought him here."

Henry looked at her sharply. "What makes you say that?"

"Well, he was injured, wasn't he?"

"You've seen him here?"

"No, I haven't seen him," Gabrielle said, a note of annoyance rising in her voice. "My, you ask some persistent questions! I thought you were coming here to make me feel better, but all these questions are just making me feel upset."

Henry reached out and touched her hand. "I do want to make you feel better. But I just want to know what happened to my friend. And to you. You seemed so terrified the first time we met…"

"When I was on drugs."

"What drugs?"

She sighed in annoyance. "Well, if you must know..." She laid her cards face down on the bed. "You know something? I really don't remember."

"And I bet you don't remember where you got them from, right?" Henry said, sensing he was onto something. "Or what you did when you took them?"

Gabrielle shook her head slowly, eyes fixed on him. "Can we talk about something else? *Please?*"

"Okay," Henry said. "Tell me about Fox."

Gabrielle brightened. "Oh, we've been friends since kindergarten. She's great. Do you know her?"

Henry nodded.

"How is she? How's her mom?"

"She's good," Henry said. "Her mom is still sick."

"It seems so long since I saw them. Not since..."

"Not since you ran away," Henry finished for her. "Do you remember why you ran away?"

"No, I..."

Henry took the photo Fox had given him from his pocket and laid it between them, where the cards had been.

"Oh," Gabrielle said, her voice small as she reached down and picked up the photo of her and Blake and the others. "That really seems a long time ago."

"You were all friends."

"Yes, we were."

"But something changed," he pressed. "Blake didn't want to talk to you any more. So you started asking questions around Malcorp."

Gabrielle shook her head. "I don't remember..."

"And that's when you started to get scared. Fox told me you were scared."

"That was just the drugs making me crazy. I started believing some strange things."

Henry said carefully, "Gabrielle, I think you've been told that you had problems you didn't really have. I think you found out some things about Malcorp that made you frightened and that's why you ran away."

"But everyone says…"

"They're lying to you."

"My mom and dad?" she said incredulously. "The doctors? Mr. Mallory? You know, for someone I only just met, you claim to know an awful lot about me and my family."

"Think about it! Do you remember anything about what happened while you were on the run? Do you remember—"

"No," Gabrielle said, cutting him dead. She collected up the cards and laid them on the bedside table. "I don't want to talk about these things."

"Why not?"

"Because they make me feel bad, Henry! Confused! And I don't want to be confused any more. I just want to be normal – like everyone else. My mom says I'm going to get good grades now and be able to go to college, just like she always wanted me to… I think you'd better just leave."

Henry didn't move. "I need to know, Gabrielle. I've been here just over a week and this place is starting to drive me crazy. Almost to the point I don't know what to believe.

But I know one thing."

Gabrielle met his eyes. "What?"

"We're all in danger," he said seriously. "Mallory and all the rest of them are lying to us about something. Christian has disappeared and I have to find him. You got close to the truth – perhaps closer than anyone. That's why they had to catch you and bring you back here."

Gabrielle shook her head. "Trooper Dan rescued me. Drove me back here. Mr. Mallory was waiting to see me with that doctor…"

"Chancellor."

"They took me downstairs…"

"Downstairs in this building?"

"Yes, I think so. Down in some kind of an elevator. A big elevator…"

"Go on," Henry encouraged. If there were floors under the medical centre, then that was probably where Malcorp undertook its real business. And it was there that its biggest secrets lay.

"I can't," Gabrielle said, rubbing her forehead. "It's too hard and it hurts."

"Open your eyes!" Henry said. "They've done something to you! They've done something to all the kids in this place!" He tapped the picture of Blake. "They changed your boyfriend and you ran away before they could change you too. Now they've got Christian and I'm next on the list."

Gabrielle reached round the side of the bed and pressed the call button for the nurse three times in quick succession.

"What are you doing?" Henry asked.

"I want you to leave, right now," she said, picking up the photo and thrusting it at him.

"Gabrielle…"

"Now! Before I have you thrown out!"

Henry left the photo on the bed and got up to leave. As he walked to the door, he paused and looked back. Gabrielle was staring at the wall to avoid eye contact with him.

"You said you wanted to be normal," he said. "Well, I think it's normal to be afraid and to make mistakes and to not be the best at everything."

Gabrielle didn't look at him. The door opened and a nurse appeared.

"It's alright," Henry said, brushing past her. "I'm leaving."

Trooper Dan had parked his cruiser at Romero's Point, a scenic lookout to the south of town that gave a fantastic view of Newton, as well as the sprawling Malcorp complex that grew like a circuit board out of the unspoilt woodland. He kneeled by the danger sign attached to the safety railing. It had been put in a few years before after a couple of drunken kids had almost fallen into the valley one evening. In his arms he held a scoped rifle that he used during duck-hunting season.

Although today he wasn't hunting ducks.

Leaning forward so that the railing supported the barrel of the rifle, he looked through the telescopic lens at the picnic site two hundred metres below. There were two tables with benches and an ancient gas barbecue that looked as if it hadn't been used in years. A trash can by the car park spilled over with rubbish; it hadn't been emptied in months.

A movement caught Trooper Dan's attention and he angled the rifle round, picking up Fox as she cycled across the car park, right on time for her meeting. He kept the scope crosshairs on her as she leaned the bike against one of the tables and looked around, like she was expecting the reporter to emerge from the trees. After about a minute, she took a seat on a bench and removed a cell phone from her pocket, checking for a message from the reporter. The cop knew she'd be out of luck there.

Feeling his trigger arm getting a little stiff, Trooper Dan shifted his grip on the rifle and then re-aimed at the girl's skull. From this distance she wouldn't even hear the gunshot when he pulled the trigger. To anyone standing nearby it would seem like her head had just decided to explode for no apparent reason. The girl stood up and began to pace around impatiently, looking left and right, no doubt suspicious that the picnic spot was a lonely, deserted place to meet. Trooper Dan smiled as he tracked her, keeping the crosshairs in position, enjoying the feeling of having complete power over her life and death...

Except... *What was it Dr. Chancellor had said?*

Keeping one eye on the girl, Trooper Dan removed his cell from his pocket and called Mallory's private line. The elevated position on the hill was one of the few places in the area where uninterrupted coverage was guaranteed.

"Mallory," the man answered on the second ring.

"I have the girl in my sights," said Trooper Dan, wondering if Mallory realized how literally he was speaking. "She contacted a reporter and is waiting to meet him. Should I take her out now?"

There was silence on the other end of the line.

"Mr. Mallory?"

"Not yet. I want to see what she and Henry Ward do next. If she was stupid enough to contact a reporter, I want to find out who else they've told."

Trooper Dan gritted his teeth, looking down the scope at the girl once more. All he had to do was pull the trigger and...

"Are you listening to me?" Mallory demanded. "Take no action against the girl at present. She and Ward are going to learn how to behave themselves."

"And if they won't?" Trooper Dan asked. He watched as Fox picked up her bike and started back across the car park. She had evidently got sick of waiting. He kept his sights on her as she cycled back towards the road. Any second now she would be out of view... Out of his control...

"Then you can do what you like with them," Mallory continued. "But not until then."

The girl disappeared into the distance. Trooper Dan relaxed and lowered the weapon.

"What about the reporter?"

"The usual. Cut him loose."

The line clicked dead and Trooper Dan placed the cell back in his pocket. Standing up, he walked back to the cruiser and laid the rifle across the hood. Then he walked round the vehicle and opened the back door.

"Get out," he said.

The reporter, who was lying on the back seat with his hands tied, struggled from the car. He flinched away as Trooper Dan removed the knife from behind his back once more. The cop grabbed the reporter roughly, turned him around and cut through the rope that bound his wrists.

For a moment the reporter stood dumbly, not even bothering to remove the tape from his mouth. Trooper Dan replaced the knife in its sheath and looked at him without expression. He stepped forward and flung out his hands...

"Boo!"

The reporter turned and ran, following the railing towards a narrow pathway that led down the hillside. As he ran, he ripped the tape away and began yelling at the top of his lungs, a sound that was halfway between a sob and a scream.

Trooper Dan walked slowly back towards the front of the cruiser. The headache from that morning had begun to come back, throbbing faintly at his temples, so he removed the bottle of pills from his pocket and popped two in his mouth. He was only supposed to take one at a time, but that just didn't seem to work any more.

He closed his eyes and stood there for a while, enjoying the feel of the cool breeze against his skin. Up this high there was always a chill in the air, no matter how hot it got down in the valley...

Trooper Dan opened his eyes slowly, remembering that he had to do something. Something had to be wrapped up...

Picking up the rifle from the hood he walked back to the railing and looked over. The reporter had made it almost halfway down the hillside, still screaming, not that there was anyone to hear him. Shaking his head at the sight of a grown man crying like a little boy, Trooper Dan took aim, lining up the crosshairs with his head, and pulled the trigger smoothly...

The reporter's head burst like a water balloon and his body fell off the path into the surrounding bushes. For a moment it was possible to see his corpse falling through the undergrowth, but then there was nothing. It probably wouldn't be found until the following spring, when the walkers came back to the area.

Trooper Dan walked back to his car.

A few seconds later, the cruiser roared away from the lookout at high speed.

Fox pedalled hard back towards town, keeping her eyes on the treacherous turns in the road in case any speeding idiots came round a blind corner too fast. Drivers never seemed to look out for cyclists...

But more than that, she still felt spooked from the picnic site.

The fact that Richardson, the reporter, hadn't turned up was one thing. She kept on telling herself that he was just delayed, or that he'd simply decided he couldn't be bothered to turn up. Some other story had come up. However, it didn't feel right. And when she'd been sitting on the bench at the picnic site, she hadn't been able to shake the feeling that someone had been watching her.

She was so preoccupied with these thoughts that she didn't hear the police cruiser until it was almost on top of her…

Cycling to the side at the last moment, she looked left in time to see the sandy-coloured vehicle steam past at full speed, just centimetres away. It didn't slow for a second, taking the corner up ahead with such pace that the wheels on one side seemed to lift. Then it was gone.

As it had passed she'd caught sight of Trooper Dan staring right at her through the window…

Fox stopped on the side of the road, taking several deep breaths to compose herself. One thing was certain in her mind: whatever had happened to the reporter, he wouldn't ever show up. Trooper Dan had got to him first. The realization chilled her to the bone.

She'd brought someone into the events in Newton and he'd suffered because of it. Maybe died even. She thought of Henry and Christian and the very real danger they'd put themselves in. Perhaps the sensible thing was to turn away… Pretend nothing was going on…

Fox shook her head. She wasn't going to let them frighten her off. Because that's what men like Mallory and Trooper Dan relied on: others being too scared to fight back.

Someone had to take a stand. And who else was there? The thought of what lay ahead terrified her, but somehow it made her start pedalling towards Newton at double the speed.

21

Henry arrived back at the lodge an hour before school normally finished, fully expecting to find his mother waiting for him there. The nurse from the medical centre would have told Mallory that he'd visited Gabrielle when he should have been in school. And Mallory, in turn, would have told his mom. As he opened the front door, he braced himself for another lecture…

But the house was silent. The kind of silence that belongs to an empty place.

"Mom?" Henry called as he walked through to the kitchen, though he'd sensed already that she wasn't there. He was off the hook for a while, he guessed, but it was only delaying the inevitable.

Then he saw the note on the kitchen counter, written in his mother's recognizable, blocky handwriting.

Business trip came up – will be away for a couple of nights. Don't think this lets you off the hook – Mr. Mallory will be keeping an eye on you. Don't give him a hard time. Will call later. Love, Mom.

Henry's relief that his absence from school would probably go unnoticed was quickly replaced with concern for his mother. A business trip? Why now? And where had she gone?

He picked up the phone by the fridge and dialled her cell. It rang five times and then went to the messaging service. Henry frowned. Her cell phone was always by her side and if she saw it was him ringing, she always picked up.

"Hi, Mom," he said after the beep. "Is everything okay? Give me a call back."

He hung up and was about to walk away when the phone started ringing. He snatched it up. "Mom?"

"It's John Mallory," the voice on the other end answered.

"Oh."

"Did you get your mother's note? She's gone to Chicago for a couple of nights. They're having a few issues at our lab there that I think she can help with. She felt real bad that she didn't see you before she left."

"Right," Henry said, still finding it hard to believe that she'd gone without speaking to him.

"She tried to find you in class," Mallory said. "But you weren't there."

Henry closed his eyes. Of course he wasn't.

"I was feeling sick, so I left early."

"Sure you did," Mallory said and Henry felt he could detect just the slightest hint of amusement in the man's tone, as if the whole thing were a massive joke. *Or some kind of game. A game where Mallory was in complete control.* "I'd like you to come to dinner with me this evening. I'll send a car to pick you up at seven."

"I can get my own dinner, thanks."

"I'm sure you can. But I'd like to get to know you a little better and I promised your mom. What do you say?"

Henry was silent for a moment. He looked around the empty house, wondering what would happen if he walked out right at that moment...went to Newton and stayed with Fox. Would the guards on the gate try to stop him from leaving? He couldn't escape the feeling that this was his one and only opportunity to get out. But Mallory had the answers to what was going on at Malcorp... And this was perhaps the best chance he'd ever have to get them.

"Fine," Henry said. "That would be good. I'll look forward to it."

He sensed that Mallory was smiling on the other end of the phone as he said, "Not half as much as I will."

Mallory's residence was on the northern edge of the Malcorp complex, a single-storey building made of glass and concrete in a harsh, modernist style. As the man had promised, a buggy had arrived at Henry's lodge at 7 p.m. sharp. It was driven by a guy in a black suit who introduced himself as Wilson, Mallory's butler. Henry took a seat in the back of the buggy and sat in silence as Wilson drove them across the complex. The butler wasn't a chatty type, but Henry guessed he wasn't supposed to be.

They arrived at Mallory's house less than five minutes later, driving into an underground garage that appeared to be at least as large as the building above. As Wilson steered the buggy down the entry ramp, lights came on automatically, revealing rows of vintage sports cars – convertibles with gleaming, pristine paint jobs. On the other side of the garage was a line of brand-new vehicles, Lamborghinis, Porsches, the biggest Hummer he'd ever seen and several motorbikes that looked as if they belonged on a racetrack. Every vehicle was spotlessly clean, like they'd been taken out of the showroom and never used.

"Wow," Henry said as he climbed out of the buggy.

"You like cars, son?"

It wasn't Wilson who had spoken, but Mallory himself. Henry turned to see the man descending a flight of stairs on the far side of the garage. He was dressed as casual as he got – in a pair of jeans and a sports jacket.

"I guess," Henry said.

Mallory grinned and stuck one of his unlighted cigars in his mouth. "Well, maybe I'll let you take one of these for a spin when you're a little older. Come on up!"

Henry followed his host up the stairs into a brightly lit room that appeared to run the entire length of the building. Along one wall, floor-to-ceiling glass windows looked out across a terraced garden and an infinity pool. From the elevated position of the residence, it would be possible to stand in the pool and look out across most of the Malcorp complex. Henry wondered if that was what Mallory did when he was alone in the house – gaze over his empire like a king.

"Dinner is ready when you are, Mr. Mallory," Wilson announced, appearing at another doorway.

"What do you say, Henry? You hungry?"

"Yeah," he answered, trying to sound casual. Actually he was starving, having missed his lunch.

"Over here," Mallory said, giving Wilson a nod as he led Henry towards the other end of the room.

The interior of the main living space was subtly divided into different zones, Henry noted, as they approached a dining table set for a meal. Just beyond was a group of leather sofas, arranged around a giant television that appeared simply to be hanging in the air. Beyond that there were bookshelves filled with leather-bound books that seemed slightly out of place against the hard lines of the rest of the interior. It was cool and beautiful, but there was something unforgiving about the place.

Mallory ushered him into a seat at the table, which Henry noticed was laid for three.

"Blake will be joining us in a minute," Mallory said as he took a seat to Henry's left. "You don't mind?"

"Why would I?" Henry replied, remembering his last meeting with Blake. If the kid tried anything again, he'd be ready for him this time. He looked down at the expensive silverware and then at Mallory, who was studying him with an interested expression. Henry hated to admit it, but the man reminded him of his mother in that respect – they were both scientists and from time to time both had the habit of looking at you like you were a participant in some kind of live experiment.

"I've got to apologize for taking your mom from you, Henry," Mallory said as Wilson appeared and filled their glasses with water from a jug. "We had a little emergency at the Chicago lab. Contamination incident. I needed someone to deal with the problem fast. It took a lot of persuading to get her to fly out without speaking to you."

"That's okay."

"If you'd been contactable, I would have suggested you went along with her. We had my private helicopter pick her up from right outside your lodge."

Henry nodded, coming to a realization: for some reason Mallory was trying to impress him. The house, the garage downstairs, stories about helicopter trips to the city. It was like he was trying to sell him on something. But what? That Malcorp was a great place to be? That he should be his new dad?

"Oh, well, next time maybe," Mallory went on, unfolding his napkin and laying it across his knees. "And don't worry about playing hooky from school. It can be our little secret. We'll just tell your mom you were taken sick and sent to the medical room, alright?"

Henry nodded as Mallory gave him a conspiratorial wink. *Still trying to get me on side,* he thought. *Make me an accomplice in a lie. Have to play along…see if he'll let something slip about Christian…*

Blake appeared and stood beside the table as if waiting for some order. He didn't look at Henry or Mallory, keeping his eyes fixed ahead as Wilson set out their entrées on the table.

"Looks great, Wilson," Mallory said, looking down at his plate as if he hadn't even noticed Blake's presence. "What the hell is it?"

"*Escargot de Bourgogne*," the butler answered.

Mallory raised his eyebrows at Henry. "How's your French, kid? Wilson would rather cut out his tongue than read a menu in plain English."

"Burgundy snails," Henry said, thinking of his difficulties in French class at Malcorp High. Was this Mallory's reason for picking the starter? Or was he just reading too much into everything?

Mallory turned his attention to Blake. "Sit yourself down. You're late."

"Sorry, sir," Blake said as he took a seat opposite Henry. Wilson melted into the background and they began to eat. Henry had never had snails before and, although the idea of eating something that you might find crawling across a rock in your backyard repulsed him a little, they actually tasted great. Kind of like earthy prawns. As he ate, he caught Mallory casting glances at him and once again felt he was being tested. On the other side of the table, Blake cleared his plate in a mechanical fashion, chewing each mouthful without expression. When they had finished eating, Wilson reappeared and cleared their plates.

In the break between courses Mallory made small talk about swimming and asked Henry about his last school. Blake sat in silence, neither sullen nor uninterested in the conversation. He was merely blank, as if someone had put him on mute. Mallory was pleasant and seemed genuinely interested in his responses, but Henry couldn't help feeling the entire thing was leading up to something. That the whole meal…the polite talk…was just a prelude to the real purpose of the evening.

"We'll have dessert later," Mallory informed Wilson as he cleared the main course plates. He patted his stomach. "Give this one some time to settle."

"Very good, sir," the butler said, backing away with the plates.

Outside, the sun had practically set, casting red light across the floor that softened the straight edges of the room. In the stillness of the evening, Henry thought the place actually seemed inviting – but perhaps that was just the effect of the food. At Mallory's suggestion, they moved to a set of leather sofas angled to look out over the pool, which was perfectly still and catching the glow of the dying sun. Wilson reappeared and lit candles on a low table in front of them.

"Very romantic," Mallory said wryly as the butler disappeared once more. "So, what do you think of my home, Henry?"

For a moment, Henry wondered if he was asking him about the building or the complex or the whole area, even Newton. Mallory owned everything, after all. "It's amazing," he said, looking around the interior.

There must have been something in his tone that suggested uncertainty, because Mallory added, "But?"

Henry looked at him and shrugged. "I guess I'm just used to living in the city. Things are a bit less…ordered there."

Mallory snorted. "You can say that again. Kids going off the rails on drugs. The effects of vandalism on every street corner. Virtual no-go areas for law-abiding citizens."

This was said with such vehemence that Henry didn't know how to respond. Mallory put a forced smile on his face, but it did nothing to soften the moment.

"I guess it's natural," he went on. "People are weak. They'd rather feed on one another than strike out and make a decent living for themselves. So they turn to crime."

Henry frowned. "I'm not sure it's *weakness*…"

"Then what is it?" Mallory snapped back.

"People have lost their jobs. They're living in poverty…"

Mallory waved his cigar-hand at Henry dismissively. "Excuses! My father died when I was six years old, leaving my mom to bring up four kids by herself. Do you think she started thieving? Used her bad luck as an excuse to start taking crack?"

"No, but—"

"When I was thirteen years old I dropped out of school and got a job so we wouldn't be thrown out on the street," Mallory said. "By the time I was twenty I had a degree in chemical engineering. If I can do it, anyone can."

"Not everyone is as strong-willed as you, Mr. Mallory."

The man smiled at him and nodded his head, accepting the point. "And that's the problem, isn't it?" He turned to Blake, who sat a little straighter in his seat, as if coming to attention. "Roll up your sleeve, Blake. Let's give Henry a little demonstration of the real power of will."

Blake did as he was told without a word. Mallory nodded to one of the candles on the table before them.

"Hold your arm over it."

Henry watched, wide-eyed, as Blake leaned forward, clenched his fist and held his forearm directly over the flame. A smell of singeing filled the air as the hairs on his arm burned away. Blake looked straight ahead throughout, expressionless, eyes unwavering.

"Make him stop," Henry said after almost twenty seconds. A horrible smell of burning skin had begun to spread through the room.

"Why?" Mallory said. "He doesn't seem to be in any discomfort."

"It's burning him!"

Mallory looked at his grandson. "Do you feel the need to stop, Blake?"

"No, sir," the kid replied, his voice even.

Henry looked in disbelief as the skin of Blake's arm began to blister and blacken. Any normal person would be screaming with pain by this point. Blake's arm trembled and, for the first time, Henry saw his eyelids flicker.

"Stay strong!" Mallory snapped.

"Yes, sir!" There was stress in Blake's voice now. Almost a full minute had passed...

Unable to take it any longer, Henry jumped from his seat and pushed Blake's arm away from the candle. As he did so, his own skin came in contact with the flame and pain shot up his arm. He snatched his hand away. Blake rose from his seat, facing Henry down, fist clenched.

"Enough!" Mallory ordered, and immediately Blake's expression softened once more. "Go and find Wilson. Get him to attend to that burn."

"Thank you, sir," Blake said, nodding to his grandfather. "Goodnight, Henry."

With that, he simply walked away. Henry shook his head and turned to Mallory. "I'm going home now. I've seen enough."

"Sit down." Mallory leaned forward and lit his cigar from the same candle that Blake had used to scorch himself. A smell like burning tyres wafted across the table.

"I want to leave right now…"

"Sit your ass down!" There was no nicety to Mallory's voice this time, just a hard command.

Henry looked at him, but then did as he was told, seeing little other choice. He was in the man's home and didn't even know the way out. Mallory had him where he wanted him. He began to seriously regret not fleeing when he'd had the chance.

Mallory puffed on his cigar and grinned at him, as if reading his thoughts.

"Too late to run, kid," he said. "Now let's talk turkey."

22

"I thought you gave up smoking," Henry said. His heart was racing, pumping fear-fuelled adrenaline around his body, but he was determined not to let Mallory see he was scared. Suddenly he felt like he was trapped in the very centre of a great web – with the spider sitting right opposite him. All he could do was keep Mallory talking and look for a way out.

"That's just what I tell my doctor," Mallory replied. He rose from the sofa, moving to the window where it was now dark outside. "Tell me, Henry, what do you understand by the phrase *technological singularity*?"

Henry shrugged, remembering an article he'd read in *Wired*. "It refers to a time in the future when supercomputers will start changing technology so fast, we won't be able to keep up with things. We'll all end up living for ever in the brain of some machine, right?"

Mallory sucked on his cigar and blew smoke at the glass. "Something like that. Typical nerd-head thinking: that we're all gonna merge with our laptops." He turned back to Henry. "But they are right about being able to live for ever. Just not through building better machines."

Henry could tell the man wanted him to ask the question. "How then?"

Mallory tapped the side of his head. "By building better brains. *Better bodies.* Neuroscience is the future, kid. I realized that twenty years ago when I began Malcorp. Re-engineer the human brain, put it in an enhanced body, and you've got something that will always be superior to a computer."

"That's what all this is about, isn't it?" Henry said. "The kids at Malcorp High. You've...been changing them."

"We call it *adjustment*," Mallory said. "And the change is only for the better, let me assure you."

"You're making them like Blake? Robots that will put their arm in a fire for you at your command?"

"Sure, they'll do that," Mallory answered. "But they can also run a mile at the speed of an Olympic sprinter, without getting out of breath. They can learn a new language overnight with a neural download. They'll never voluntarily choose to do things that are harmful for them, like take drugs or smash their cars off the side of the road."

"Sounds like they don't have a lot of choice in the matter."

Mallory sighed and came back to the sofa, sitting opposite Henry. "My own son died of an overdose at the age of twenty-five. Did you know that?"

Henry shook his head.

"He left behind a two-year-old kid and a wife, who was heading the same direction as him – to a life wasted by addiction." Mallory shook his head slightly, remembering.

"My son was the product of a privileged lifestyle. I tried to give him everything I never had: private education, opportunities to travel, the best toys money could buy. It was…a mistake. Do you know what it taught him to be? Dependent. An addictive personality always looking for the next fix – whether it was drugs, or booze, or the next car he could crash. When I took Blake from my no-good daughter-in-law, I vowed that no grandson of mine was going to grow up to be a weak-assed…"

Mallory's voice trailed away, lost in the memory. Henry studied him, not knowing how to respond to this revelation. He found himself wondering what happened to Mallory's *no-good daughter-in-law*.

Mallory smiled at Henry. "I should have dealt with you the moment you started poking around my medical centre, son. Do you know why we're having this conversation right now?"

"No," Henry said.

"Because I see a lot of me in you. You've had a tough ride, not like most of the kids around here. And you lost your father, just like I did. Your mom told me all about how—"

"Don't talk about him," Henry said, anger rising.

Mallory held up his hands. "It's okay. I know he was stabbed trying to stop a woman being attacked on the subway. He was a hero. Someone who wasn't afraid to step in when he saw something was wrong."

"I don't need you to tell me that," Henry said coldly. It had been two years since the cops had come to their apartment with news of his father's death, but sometimes it felt like just yesterday. An open wound that would never heal. It was one thing to listen to Mallory's insane ramblings about technological singularity and changing brains and his messed-up family, but it was something completely different to hear him talking about Henry's own father. It felt obscene. "He did what anyone else would have done. He tried to help someone in trouble."

"Trust me, there aren't many people like that any more." Mallory leaned towards him, becoming even more intense. "Don't you see, Henry? You're like him and that's why I need you."

Henry frowned. "What do you need me for?"

"You saw it yourself," Mallory continued, "the day you rescued that kid from the pool. Practically every adjusted kid at Malcorp High can outrun, outswim and out-think you, without breaking a sweat. Their enhanced brains allow them to run their bodies at one hundred per cent efficiency. Give them an order and they'll follow it to the letter. But put them in an unusual situation…and they shut down. We've improved just about every facet of their beings, but there's one thing we haven't been able to isolate: *initiative*. And you've got that in spades, Henry. So has your little friend at the coffee shop in Newton…"

Mallory grinned as Henry started.

"Yes, we know all about her," Mallory went on. "And we know all about her plan to bring in some half-assed *investigative journalist*." He said this as if they were dirty words. "He isn't coming, by the way." Mallory paused to register the effect of his last statement, while Henry struggled to prevent his feelings from showing on his face. "I think it's time you faced facts, Henry. This thing is too big to fight. The land for fifty kilometres in every direction is owned by Malcorp. There's nowhere to run. Nowhere to go. The best choice you can make right now is to join us."

Henry looked at him in disbelief. "You want me to sign up to be...*adjusted*?"

Mallory sat back. "That's right."

Henry's mind went into overdrive. *Mallory didn't want to kill him. He wanted to adjust him!* And to Henry, that sounded like a fate *worse* than death. Somehow he had to get out of the building, out of the complex and to Fox. If Mallory knew what she'd been up to, it was only a matter of time before he went after her too. His best option was to stall Mallory for as long as possible...keep him talking... maybe get down in that underground garage somehow, grab a bike...

"I'm waiting for your answer, Henry," Mallory said. "I'm not going to wait all night."

A thought occurred to Henry. "Why?"

"Why what?"

"Why are you asking me? You scanned my brain during my first visit to the medical centre, right? Why not just..."

"Take what we want by force?" Mallory sighed. "We could do that. Believe me, *we have done that*. For the good of the subject and with full parental consent, you understand."

"They sign up to have their kids altered?" Henry asked sceptically. "Just like that?"

"Oh, you'd be surprised how many parents share our views. And I hand-pick workers for the Malcorp complex based on their family history. You know, problem kids… broken homes… Like you and your mom."

Henry bristled at this but didn't react.

"These are people who are only too willing to accept a solution to their family problems, whatever the cost," Mallory continued. "They've suffered for too long under the burden of badly behaved and low-achieving children. We offer a way out and they're only too glad to take it."

"Right," Henry said, casting a glance back in the direction of the stairs to the garage.

"And once the parents are on board, it's easy enough to persuade the kids to sign up as well. I mean, what choice do they have, short of running away like your friend Gabrielle? Of course, it's useful if they fully accept that adjustment is for their own good. Parental pressure and advice from our counsellors usually works in the end. We've found that a willing subject…one who consents to the adjustment process of their own volition…has a far higher acceptance rate for the hardware upgrades and greater operational efficiency overall. Naturally, those who won't consent are still put through the process, with reduced operational parameters unfortunately. It's still a big improvement on how they were before, even if they have the occasional glitch."

The occasional glitch. Henry guessed that explained the kid who had flipped out in the lunch room at school. One of Mallory's less willing subjects, no doubt.

"Of course, it's a complicated process and different subjects have different reactions. Not all of them follow the predicted programme at first, but we're ironing out the problems."

"You're talking about people like they're machines," Henry said and found himself thinking of Christian. Had Mallory's doctors got inside his head already? Had it been done with his father's consent? Christian's father had seemed so disappointed with him... Was he just another parent who was deluded enough to think that letting Mallory mess around with his kid's brain would give him the son he always wanted?

"But we *are* machines, Henry," Mallory said. "We just haven't been perfected yet. I want you to consent to adjustment, son. I've got great plans for you. You've got so much more potential than the average kid that comes here. I'm talking about our next-generation implants – the highest level skill sets implanted to complement your unique talents. You'd be a god among men. Hell, one day we might even be calling you...Mr. President. Just think how proud your mom would be!"

Henry looked at Mallory, trying to process everything he was saying. "You seriously think I'm going to agree to that?"

"It's the only way it's going to work, Henry. We ain't putting our new hardware in the head of someone who's going to fight it." He gave an annoyed sigh. "Hell, Blake and Steve would tear my arm off for this opportunity. Now Blake's a good soldier, but he doesn't have the spark to run our newest upgrades to the full. And Steve, well his reaction's been a little...shall we say...erratic from the start, but then he was one of the first to be adjusted. We've made a few improvements since then." Mallory seemed to drift off for a moment, but then snapped back to attention and pointed a finger at Henry. "I'm offering this to you. Because you've got something I want...*unlimited potential*."

Henry tried to hide his disbelief. Mallory was clearly mad enough to think he would go for his proposal. He decided to change the subject, still playing for time. "Where's my mother? What have you done with her?"

"Calm down. She's having a lovely time in a five-star hotel in Chicago. When she returns in a couple of days, she's going to find a son she'll never have to worry about letting out of her sight ever again. Who'll never get in trouble with the law for vandalizing public property in some pathetic show of teenage rebellion..."

Henry looked away in disgust, but deep down he was relieved. His mom knew nothing about this. "She'd hate what you're doing. She'll be able to tell something's wrong..."

Mallory laughed harshly. "Really? Or do you think she'll just be so happy that you're starting to fit in, get top grades and make friends that she won't notice anything at all? You're a disappointment to her, Henry. Given more time, I'd have persuaded her to sign you up just like all the others – most of them don't ask too many questions about what we really do. Just as long as it works. But you've forced my hand with all your running around and plotting."

Henry held his gaze. *"Don't ask many questions?"* You don't know my mom very well, do you?"

Mallory snorted. "Face it, Henry! She's sick of you! You're just like the rest of your generation. All we hear about is how bored you all are with your easy lives and violent games and lectures about the environment we messed up. How we all ought to shape up and understand you better." Mallory sat forward and pointed an accusing finger at Henry. "Well I've got news for you, son. We're the ones who are sick of *you*. And *you're* the ones who are going to shape up."

"I'm guessing you weren't a hippy when you were young," Henry said.

"Hippies!" Mallory exclaimed. "God, I hated the hippies! Then the punks…metal-heads…goths…new romantics… nerds…emos… They make me want to goddamn puke!"

"You're a psychopath."

Mallory looked at him sadly. "Can't you see I'm trying to do what's best for everyone? I'm trying to give hope to desperate parents. All I'm asking you to do is give adjustment a try. What's your answer, son?"

"Go shove it." Henry grabbed the edge of the coffee table and lifted it, throwing the entire thing towards Mallory. The glass top shattered and he had to shield his eyes against the flying glass shards.

"Stop!" Mallory yelled, but Henry was already up and running for the stairs leading down to the basement…

"Blake!"

Mallory's grandson stepped from the shadows, too fast

221

for Henry to avoid – he'd obviously been waiting there all along. A fist like an iron girder slammed into his gut and Henry doubled over, gasping for breath. Blake grabbed him round the neck with one hand and pinned his arms behind his back with the other. Henry struggled, but the other kid was superhuman, restraining him effortlessly. Wilson the butler appeared with a syringe in his gloved hand…

"Let me go!" Henry said, fighting for breath as Blake's hand tightened around his neck.

"It's too bad you didn't buy into the programme, Henry," Mallory said as he approached from the sofa. "You could have been a pioneer, our shining star. But we can always use one more soldier – and one less troublemaker."

Wilson jabbed the syringe into Henry's arm and depressed the plunger. Henry felt the liquid enter his bloodstream and a second later his vision began to swim. Blake released his grip and Henry staggered forward, his legs no longer able to support him. Now he was on his hands and knees at Mallory's feet, struggling to stay conscious.

"Please…" was all he could manage to say.

"Don't fight it," Mallory said. "When you wake up you're going to love Malcorp and all this will seem like a bad dream. We're going to fix you."

"No…"

The floor rushed up and slammed Henry in the face.

23

In the beginning, there was pain... And then there was light... And then the feeling of being strapped to a table...

Henry sensed someone moving around him so he kept his eyes closed, even though he'd been slowly coming round for a few minutes. He flexed his wrists carefully; they were bound tightly to the table. The air around him was cold. There was only one place he could be – the medical centre.

"I know you're awake," a vaguely familiar voice said. "You can open your eyes."

Henry did just that and tried to look round, but his head was held in place by some kind of strap. From the tiled walls and equipment in his peripheral vision he could tell he was in one of the operating theatres. Adrenaline began surging through him and he strained against the bonds that held his arms and legs. No use.

"Easy," the man said, stepping towards the table so Henry could see him. "Remember me?"

Henry stopped struggling and focused on a bald-headed man, who was dressed in surgeon's scrubs. He held up his left hand, which was heavily bandaged, and wiggled his fingers in a kind of wave. Henry remembered him now: the doctor who had confronted him in that very theatre just a few days before. He'd slipped on a scalpel and cut his hand.

"That's right," the bald doctor said, seeing the recognition in Henry's eyes. "Looks like I might have a little nerve damage from the cut. Not good news for a surgeon, is it? I mean, we kinda need our hands to be in full working order."

Henry licked his lips, which were incredibly dry. He wondered how long he'd been out. "I'm sorry," he began. "I didn't mean to…"

"Oh, you'll be sorry alright," the doctor said, leaning close so his round, doughy face filled Henry's vision. "Why do you think you're awake right now? Huh? I brought you out of sedation so you can be fully conscious for your operation."

"Operation?" Henry tensed the muscles in his right arm… If he could just pull free somehow…

"We're going to cut open your skull," the doctor leered down at him. "And you're going to be fully aware, right up to the moment we start cutting into your brain. Your own front-row seat. How does that sound to you?"

Henry twisted his head back as far as it would go and yelled, "Help! Somebody help me!"

The doctor smiled and patted Henry on the shoulder. "Don't waste your breath, kid. There's no one round here who gives a damn." He grabbed a trolley loaded with surgical equipment and wheeled it closer to the table so Henry could see: drills, scalpels, and weird-shaped extraction tongs.

"Please don't do this," Henry said, aware of the pleading, desperate tone in his voice. "I'll be good from now on."

The doctor chuckled. "That's what they all say. Right up to the moment we open up their craniums. I'm going to go prep your brain implant, Henry, which should give you some time to think about the horrible fate that awaits you when I come back. You might want to spend the time rehearsing some new ways to beg me not to do it."

Henry's face twisted in rage. "Screw you."

The doctor waggled a finger on his injured hand at him. "Potty mouth. We'll have to change that, won't we?"

With that, he walked from the theatre. Henry lay still for a moment, stunned by the unforgiving silence that had returned to the room. They were really going to do it. When the theatre door opened again, the surgeons would come in and cut him open...

Henry thrashed madly against his bonds and screamed for help again and again. In the back of his mind he knew it was no use...that he was just playing the sadistic doctor's game by showing how desperate, how terrified he was...

After a minute or so he stopped struggling, though he was still breathing heavily and covered with sweat. *Come on, think!* he told himself. *There has to be a way out.*

He looked at the trolley to the left of the table, trying to view the surgical equipment with fresh eyes. Rather than instruments of torture, maybe they could help him to get the hell off the table. The scalpels…cut through the bonds…

With all his strength, Henry arched his body up and slammed it to the side. The table moved a couple of centimetres towards the trolley. He did it again. The table moved a little more.

"Come on!" Henry hissed through gritted teeth. He rocked the table a third time. It moved far enough to hit the edge of the instrument trolley…sending it rolling half a metre away. Henry slumped. "No…"

The double doors to the theatre opened and someone approached the table. Henry clenched his fists and fought against the restraints once more, even though he knew all hope was lost…

But suddenly there was a blonde-haired girl beside him, in ordinary jeans and a T-shirt.

"Henry!"

Gabrielle leaned over him and reached round the side of his head to release the strap holding it in place.

"Are you okay?"

He almost cried with relief. "Jesus, I thought you were one of them coming back… Untie my arms!"

Gabrielle reached over and undid the straps around his head and wrists. With his upper body free, Henry sat up as she freed his ankles.

"How did you find me?" he asked.

Gabrielle looked at him. "I did as you said. *I opened my eyes.* And I stole a key card from a nurse."

Henry frowned, trying to make sense of what she was

telling him. "But how did you know I was down here?"

"There was a big commotion about an hour ago, so I snuck out of my room. I saw them wheeling you in here on a stretcher. You were all trussed up, so I guessed you weren't coming of your own free will."

"You got that right," Henry said. "But the last time we spoke, you didn't believe anything was wrong."

She blushed a little. "I know. But then I got to looking at that photo you left, the one of me and Blake, and I started remembering. They've done something to me…and I want to know what it is."

"Let's get out of here before that doctor gets back," Henry said, swinging his legs off the table. He tried to stand up and his knees buckled. It felt as if he'd been in bed for a week. "I can barely walk," he said, wondering just how long he'd been out. "What time is it?"

"It's about nine," Gabrielle replied.

"Nine?" Henry repeated in confusion. *Had he really only been here an hour?* "What day?"

"Tuesday evening," she said.

Henry shook his head. He'd been sedated for almost twenty-four hours – no doubt while the doctors made the final preparations for the adjustment process. He took a breath and flexed his legs, feeling the strength coming back to them. "He could be back at any moment."

"Yeah," Gabrielle said. "But we should find you some clothes first."

Henry looked at what he was wearing – a green hospital smock. "Good point," he said.

Voices sounded in the corridor outside. The surgeons were coming back.

"What do we do?" Gabrielle whispered.

Henry looked at the instrument trolley. Scalpels… saws…an injection gun… He snatched up this last item and a vial of clear liquid that was lying next to it. Fumbling a little, he slotted the vial into the gun. It hissed as the seal broke. A tiny needle appeared near the muzzle.

"What's in that?" Gabrielle asked.

Henry looked at her. "I guess we'll find out, won't we? Hide over there. We mustn't let them raise the alarm."

Gabrielle ran across the theatre and ducked down behind a metal workbench near some lockers. Henry jumped back on the table and lay down with the injection gun in his right hand, concealed at his side.

As the theatre doors opened once more, he heard a murmuring of voices and footsteps approaching. There were at least two people entering the room. Wheels screeched on the tiles, as if they were pushing a heavy piece of equipment along. Henry lay very still on the table, hoping they wouldn't notice the loosened bonds before they got close enough for him to jab them with the gun. He needn't have worried. The surgeons, bald and grey-haired, were more interested in the machine they'd brought into the room. It looked like a large water tank on wheels. As the grey-haired surgeon continued to fuss over the tank, bald-head walked back towards the table… *No doubt planning to give me another friendly talk,* Henry thought, flexing his grip on the handle of the gun…

The bald surgeon leaned over Henry once again. "Well, how are we feeling about...?"

His voice trailed away as his eyes registered the loosened wrist restraints. Henry moved lightning-fast, twisting round and pressing the muzzle of the gun into the man's throat. He pulled the trigger and with a barely audible hiss a dose of the liquid was delivered.

"Help..." bald-head managed to whisper, before his face went slack, his eyes closed and he crashed to the floor, unconscious.

Henry looked round at the other surgeon, who had turned from the tank and was staring in shock at his fallen colleague. Then he noticed that Henry was rising from the table, ready for a fight.

With a little cry, the surgeon turned and ran.

He almost made it to the door, before Gabrielle threw herself from her hiding place at his legs. The surgeon went down with a cry, hitting the floor with his face. He tried to get up, but Henry leaped from the table and jumped on his back.

"No, please, don't," grey-hair pleaded as Henry jabbed the syringe gun into his side and pressed the trigger twice. The surgeon yelped in pain, struggled a little, and then lay still. Not wasting a moment, Henry grabbed his ankles and dragged him over to the other doctor. Second by second he felt the strength returning to his arms and legs.

"Is he dead?" Gabrielle asked.

"Just stunned," Henry said, tossing the gun back on the trolley. "Nice tackle. You play football?"

"I have older brothers," she replied and produced a pile of clothes from a locker, which she held out to him. "I think I found your stuff."

"Thanks," Henry said. Gabrielle turned her back while he got out of his hospital smock and dressed quickly. Then they turned their attention to the unconscious doctors.

"How long will they be out?" Gabrielle asked.

"I don't know." Henry had been wondering the same thing. "We need to tie them up."

Gabrielle started looking around the room. "How about this?" she said, going to another locker containing shelves of surgical gear. She grabbed rolls of rubber tubing and held them up for Henry to see. "I think they use these for making tourniquets. They're really strong."

"Great!" Henry said, taking one roll from her and using it to bind grey-hair's wrists behind his back. Gabrielle was right – the tubing was like a giant, unbreakable rubber band. He tied the man's ankles too, before securing the other doctor. Gabrielle handed him a thick roll of surgical tape to cover the men's mouths. If they did come round any time soon, they wouldn't be calling for help.

"Let's get out of here," Gabrielle said.

Henry made to follow her, but then the glass tank the doctors had wheeled into the theatre caught his eye. The liquid inside was a yellowy colour, but there was something floating inside the murk. At first he thought it was a squid, but then he saw that it was more spider-like, with a round, flat centrepiece from which eight thread-like legs extended.

"What is it?" Gabrielle asked.

"I don't know," Henry said. He stepped forward and pressed his face to the glass. On closer inspection he saw the thing floating inside wasn't an insect, but some kind of machine. The "body" was no bigger than a dime, while the "legs" were each as long as his little finger. Was this an implant of some kind? The thing that allowed Mallory to control all the kids in Newton? And were they going to put it inside *his* brain? He reached out and tapped the glass. The thing twitched...its legs moving... A wave of nausea rose in him...

"Are you okay, Henry?" Gabrielle asked, placing a hand on his shoulder. "Henry?"

Gabrielle's voice brought him back to the moment. He reached up and, flipping a latch, opened the lid on the top of the tank. A thick, musty smell assaulted his nose.

"What are you doing?" Gabrielle asked anxiously. "Don't touch it."

Henry looked at her and then back at the spider-like thing floating in the tank. He knew one thing. "It has to be destroyed," he told her. But how?

The answer was sitting on the instrument trolley: a handheld electric saw. Henry snatched it up and pressed the button on the side. The circular blade began to whir as he hurried back to the tank. He tossed it, still whirring, into the liquid. There was a crackle and a flash as the drill sent a burst of electricity through the tank. The legs of the spider-like implant jerked and then went still. It floated to the bottom of the tank and lay there, followed moments later by the saw.

"That should do it," he said quietly.

Gabrielle's hand slipped into his as one of the doctors moaned in his sleep. "Can we go now, Henry? *Please?*"

"Yeah. Let's get the hell out of here." He grabbed her hand and they ran from the theatre along corridors, Gabrielle leading the way.

"There's an elevator up ahead," she said. "We're two floors down."

Gabrielle used her stolen key card to get them inside the elevator, pressing the button for the ground level. The car rose swiftly and the doors opened a second later onto another unfamiliar corridor. She led Henry to the left, where a set of double doors blocked the way. Henry tried the doors, but they wouldn't open. Instead of a card reader, there was a fingerprint scanner on the wall.

Gabrielle pushed the doors uselessly. "These were open before!" she cried.

The sound of heavy footsteps along the corridor made Henry wheel round. Someone was coming. They were trapped!

24

"**G**uards!" Gabrielle said, panic in her voice. Henry looked round for a way out, or at least something to fight with. His gaze fell upon a ventilation grille set into the wall at floor level. It was big enough for them to fit through.

"Quickly!" Henry said, pulling the grille away from the wall with some effort. "In here!"

Gabrielle slid into the ventilation shaft and Henry followed, pulling the grille back into place behind them. The footsteps of two security guards approached the locked doors. In the shaft, they held their breath as one of them touched a finger to the scanner and they passed on through.

"We can go through these vents to avoid the door," Henry said, looking at the shaft stretching ahead. It was wide enough for them to wriggle through on their stomachs. The going wouldn't be easy – but at least they wouldn't run into more guards. He looked round at Gabrielle, who was lying behind him. "We can make it."

She smiled at him bravely. Henry started crawling along the shaft, looking for a way out. Through the next vent he heard the sound of two male voices.

Henry pressed his face to the vent and peered into a room filled with equipment that looked like it belonged in a recording studio. Two technicians were seated at a deck filled with control dials and sliders. Monitors in front of them showed audio data arranged in blocks of sound.

"What is it?" Gabrielle whispered.

"Some kind of recording facility," Henry whispered back.

One of the technicians placed a pair of headphones on his head and nodded to the other. "Let's get the Friday broadcast finished," he said. "Mallory wants the theta wave pattern increased."

"That could be dangerous," the other technician said. "We're already seeing signs of psychosis in the older kids."

The first technician shrugged. "He's the boss. And he said he wanted more obedience."

"Okay then," the other replied, pressing a button. A track began to play softly in the background. Henry recognized it immediately – the strange version of "The Star-Spangled Banner" Malcorp High broadcast at the beginning and end of every week. The technician adjusted something and the sound became even more distorted.

"Bringing in Mallory's message," the other tech said, clicking a mouse to add another audio file under the main track. Henry strained to make out Mallory's voice speaking on the track...

"...*you love Malcorp...love and respect your parents...your teachers...the employees of Malcorp...you will not question* anything we do…you will obey without question…you love Malcorp…you will obey without question…"

"Taking it down to sub-audio level," the first tech said and Mallory's voice faded out. "Increasing the theta wave frequency by fifteen per cent."

"Okay," replied the second tech. "Now shut it down before it gives me a nosebleed."

"Yeah." The first tech nodded, rising from his seat as he cut the audio. "I need a coffee."

In the ventilation shaft, Henry looked back at Gabrielle. "That music. They're using it to control the kids in the complex. There's a subliminal message running through it."

A sudden scratching sound came from further down the shaft. Gabrielle started. "Do you think there are rats in here?" she said. "I want to get out."

Henry nodded and led the way further along the shaft, looking for another vent that they could climb through. Turning a corner, he came to a grille that looked into a darkened room. With just a little pressure, he managed to pop it out and slide it to one side. The room was silent as he slipped out of the shaft and turned to help Gabrielle. They stood up behind a low counter and looked around – the room was a lab of some kind. The main lights were off, but illuminated dials and read-outs glowed from equipment laid out on workbenches. Looking around, Henry could see it was some kind of production facility – complete with glass vats full of the spider-like implants hanging in suspension.

Got to record the evidence, Henry thought. He remembered

his smartphone, which was still in the pocket of his jeans. Useless for making a call within the complex, of course, but perfect for collecting evidence.

Gabrielle tugged on his shirt. "I don't like this," she hissed. "We need to go."

Henry looked back at her. "We will. Let me just get a couple of shots." He held the phone up to the vats and snapped off some photos of the floating implants. He had to smile. Fox was going to go crazy over this.

"Someone's coming!" cried Gabrielle, grabbing his arm and pulling him back. They ran behind the counter and ducked down just as the lights in the laboratory flicked on blindingly full. Gabrielle squeezed herself back into the vent and beckoned for Henry to follow, but the sound of a familiar voice from the doorway made him pause. Moving to the end of the counter, he peered round the side and saw Mallory enter, along with a group of men and women in suits. He was addressing them as if they were on some kind of tour. Several of the guests were decked out in full military uniforms, as if they were high-ranking commanders of foreign armies.

"Henry!" Gabrielle whispered. He looked round and held up his hand. He needed to see what was going on. From the vent opening, Gabrielle gave him a desperate look, but she stayed where she was. Waving at her to stay calm, he turned his attention back to the room...

Mallory strode into the middle of the area and gestured for his guests to assemble in a semicircle along one wall. He waved a hand at the equipment and the giant vats.

"This is the main operations area," Mallory said proudly. "Two years ago we began experimenting on rats, developing a neural modification system that allowed us total control over their central nervous systems. Motor functions. Behaviour. Learned skills. We achieved complete control. Stage two was work on primates, followed by stage three: human subjects. As I'm sure you can appreciate, there's a massive leap between controlling a rat brain and that of a child."

The group erupted into conversation. Mallory allowed the chatter to go on for a moment, then silenced them by raising his hand.

"I know you have a thousand questions," he said, "which is why my staff will be on hand for the rest of your stay to take you through the process – including my head physician, Dr. Chancellor." He indicated the doctor, who had appeared in the doorway of the lab. "She'll be able to explain the technicalities of the adjustment process from a medical-scientific perspective – within reason. We're not going to give away all of our secrets, of course. You can also get a look at some walking-talking test subjects at our high school. Our staff don't just work here, they've been among the first to sign their kids up for neural adjustment." He laughed and pulled a cigar from his pocket. "We're not in the business of making new people. We're in the business of making *better* people. Does anyone have any questions?"

One of the men, a short guy with a hard face and small, round glasses walked from the group towards the implant vat. He tapped the glass, making the spider-machines wriggle, and looked round at Mallory. "I want a better look at one."

Mallory nodded at Chancellor, who crossed to the tank and removed the lid. With a pincer tool, she carefully reached inside to retrieve one of the implants.

"We call it the SPIDIR," Mallory said, as the doctor removed the dripping implant from the tank.

"SPIDIR?" asked a man in a green general's uniform, complete with a chest full of medals.

"Stands for Skills/Personality/Intellect Direct Instruction Receptor," Chancellor said, holding out the machine for the man to see. As he reached to take it from her, she held it back. "Please. It is very delicate."

The short man looked at Mallory, who sighed.

"Why don't you tell our guests how it works?" Mallory said to the doctor.

"The SPIDIR is embedded into the brain matter of the subject," Chancellor said, holding up the implant for everyone to see. "The central receiver" – she pointed to the round "body" section – "is linked in to the central cortex. The receiver picks up instructions and information from us sent via theta wave technology. The information is transported from the central receiver to the ganglions…" She indicated the eight dangling "legs", which were wriggling madly in the air. "These ganglions link into each of the major sections of the brain."

Beside the counter, Henry angled the phone so the camera was focused on the action and pressed *record*. The video of Mallory should get someone in the FBI or the CIA or at least the police interested. What they were saying was incredible. This SPIDIR device had clearly been implanted in the brains of every adjusted kid in Newton – controlling their actions at the whim of Mallory and his doctors... adjusting their personalities and moods...

"Our scientists have already cloned a brain from stem cells," said another member of the audience, a guy in a suit who had the same military bearing as the others nonetheless. "How is this different?"

"Your scientists might be able to clone a brain," Dr. Chancellor said, moving towards the group. "But to what end? I am sure you are aware, a cloned brain is merely an empty vessel. Devoid of knowledge, memories, skills. Even if you implant it in a donor body, you create nothing more than a zombie – a creature without thoughts."

"Why go to the trouble of cloning a brain when you can improve what's there already?" Mallory said, waving his cigar at the vat. "A scan is taken of a subject's brain, pre-operation. This is to ensure the subject is viable and to gauge the best implantation points for the..." He struggled for the word.

"Ganglions," Chancellor said.

"Ganglions," Mallory repeated. "This allows for maximum control and responsiveness from each subject. As I'm sure you can appreciate, every brain is different."

"But what is the purpose of all this messing around in brains?" an Italian-sounding woman asked.

Mallory shrugged. "Imagine being able to copy the

knowledge and skills of your best scientists. Your most gifted soldiers. And then implant that knowledge into the bodies of... How shall I put it? *Less productive* members of your societies. The neural patterns of a gifted and loyal warrior can be copied simply by scanning the subject's brain, loaded into the SPIDIR...and then implanted into the brain of a test subject. Creating an equally gifted soldier."

This caused a stir among the audience. Henry remembered the scan they'd given him and he felt a chill – had his knowledge, his memories been mapped onto one of these SPIDIRs? Mallory had told him he wanted his initiative. Could that aspect of his personality already have been tapped and put into someone else's brain? And would that brain think like him? The thought made his flesh crawl.

"But that's only the beginning," Mallory continued, seeing he really had the attention of his audience now. "Once implanted with a SPIDIR, the subject gains two massive advantages: increased intellectual capacity and the potential for us to implant a wide variety of information. Give me a day, and I can create a subject who is fluent in twenty languages...able to solve the most complex mathematical problems... Or with our military programmes, a soldier willing to push his body to breaking point at your command." Mallory nodded at them. "That's right. *Your command*. Every Malcorp SPIDIR comes with certain fail-safes built in – most importantly complete, unquestioning loyalty to the controller."

"You're talking about brainwashing," a British-accented man said. "It doesn't work. Our scientists have been trying to develop it since the 1950s."

Mallory looked at him. "So has the CIA – and you're quite right, brainwashing in the traditional sense doesn't work. But it does with our SPIDIR implants." He nodded to Dr. Chancellor. "Let's give them a demonstration."

The doctor walked to the door and opened it. Henry stifled a gasp as Christian appeared. So they had experimented on him... A wave of remorse and guilt washed over Henry. How could he have left his friend in the medical centre the night they broke in. Was it too late to save him now?

On Chancellor's command, Christian walked into the centre of the room and stood before the audience. His expression was blank and he didn't react at all as Mallory placed a hand on his forehead and lifted his hair away to expose his scalp.

"This subject had a SPIDIR implanted less than forty-eight hours ago," Mallory explained. "The boy is now fluent in six European languages, is expert in applied mathematics and has an unquestioning respect for authority. A new-found desire to exercise will transform his body over the coming weeks." Mallory ran a finger across Christian's forehead. "Notice the lack of cranial scarring due to our patented healing accelerators. The operation takes less than thirty minutes. You can have a skull opened, the SPIDIR implanted, and closed up before anyone knows what happened – especially useful for covert operations."

Someone at the back asked, "Can more information be mapped onto the SPIDIR post-implantation?"

"This is achieved by wireless upgrade – simple," Chancellor said with a snap of her fingers.

As members of the group muttered among themselves, Henry looked away in disgust. So, this was what it came down to – the kids at the Malcorp complex were all part of some experiment to create a generation of emotionless, robotic followers. A technology that Mallory was selling to the highest bidder. And their parents had signed them right up for it – just as long as they kept on getting top grades. Poor Christian.

"You say you have made him into some kind of genius?" a bearded general said sceptically. "He looks like a sleepwalker."

Mallory held up a hand. "He's merely in a fugue mode built into the brain implant. This state can be triggered at will by the subject's operator – usually by a targeted theta wave combined with a command phrase, but for larger scale pacification the trigger could be built into a sound wave broadcast across an entire city. In this state he's highly suggestible, impervious to pain…"

Dr. Chancellor proved this by removing a pin from her coat and pricking Christian on the arm. He didn't flinch.

"…and will remember nothing after the fugue is cancelled. However, he is also fully capable of following orders from an operator. Let me give you an example."

Mallory opened a desk drawer and removed an automatic pistol. Then he took out a sleek silver bullet-shaped object. Pressing a small button on this, he said to Christian, "Initiate."

Christian immediately stiffened to attention at the command word, like some kind of soldier. From his hiding place by the counter, Henry shook his head. It was like looking at a different person – a machine rather than his friend.

Mallory held up his hand so the audience could see the tiny device. "The Initiator is a simple wireless theta-wave command switch used in conjunction with the command word. It also has an emergency kill-switch built in." He pointed to a red button on the other side. "When the Initiator is placed at the base of the subject's skull and the kill-switch depressed, it sends a concentrated electronic burst to the SPIDIR, deactivating it. Only to be used in a last resort, of course."

"Why?" the bearded general asked.

"Because the deactivation is permanent. And it would most likely lead to some brain damage for the subject."

"Most likely?"

"Well, we haven't ever had cause to try it out. Our SPIDIRs are one hundred per cent safe, after all."

"Then why have the kill switch?"

Mallory grinned at him. "I'm overly cautious. Now, back to the demonstration." He handed the gun to Christian. "Field-strip this, Christian. With your eyes closed, please."

Henry eyed the Initiator in Mallory's hand. *If I could just get my hands on one of those,* he thought. It could be used to control the adjusted kids and shut down their SPIDIR implants. Mallory's words echoed in his head: *some brain damage...* But what was the alternative? Remaining one of Mallory's slaves for the rest of your life? He knew that if he had a SPIDIR in his head, he'd be prepared to take the risk.

Across the room, Christian took the gun, moved to the nearest workbench and started taking the weapon apart. Henry noticed the way he laid out the component parts of the pistol in a neat line, as if it was an operation he'd done many times before. Christian had his eyes clamped shut as he did this.

"Military training that would take years has been implanted in seconds," Mallory said as Christian reassembled the gun, slotted the clip into the handle and opened his eyes. He held out the weapon for Mallory's inspection. "Very good, Christian," he said, before turning back to the audience. "But what good is training without the will to use it?"

Mallory took a step back and looked around the room, his eyes falling upon a swivel chair in the corner. "Shoot the chair, Christian."

Without a second's hesitation, Christian raised the gun and put a round through the back of the chair. Everyone in the room jumped as the noise echoed around the room. Mallory grinned at the stir he'd created.

"Quite a shot for a fourteen year old, don't you think?" he said. "Now, Christian. *Shoot me.*"

Christian raised the gun and aimed it at Mallory's head. The weapon trembled in his hand and his face screwed up in concentration, as if he was desperately trying to pull the trigger, but just couldn't do it.

"Shoot me, Christian. *Do as you are ordered.*"

Christian gave a whine of agony as he continued to fight against himself.

"Okay! Stop!"

Christian breathed a sigh of relief and lowered the gun. Mallory looked at the stunned audience.

"Like I said, certain fail-safes are built into every SPIDIR," he explained. "Subjects who have undergone adjustment will do as they're told, but not to the point they can be used against you. The idea of doing anything to harm myself or any other Malcorp employee is so deeply ingrained in Christian's new brain that he couldn't have pulled that trigger, even if he thought I would have caused him terrible harm. *Complete obedience*, that's what we offer, ladies and gentlemen. Imagine taking the most troublesome people in your countries and having them *adjusted*. No more protests... No more annoying Facebook pages and Twitter feeds putting down your governments... Just happy citizens. *Productive citizens.*"

Henry looked in disgust at the approving nods from the group.

Only the bearded general looked unimpressed. "Will he follow *my* commands?"

"If I order him to."

"Good. I want my own demonstration."

Mallory studied the man carefully before saying, "Of course." He looked at Christian. "This is General Aziz,

Christian. You're to follow his instructions as if they were from me. Do you understand?"

"Yes." Christian's voice sounded different. It was flat and dead. It could have been anyone's.

General Aziz stepped forward with his hand outstretched. "Give me the gun."

Christian handed it across. Aziz ejected the clip and inspected it, as if checking to see that the bullets were real. Satisfied, he reloaded the gun and pointed it at Christian's head. Henry stifled a cry... But Christian didn't even flinch.

"Good," General Aziz said with a little laugh. "He'd just stand there and let me shoot him?"

"Absolutely," Mallory said. "If you asked him to, he'd even help you line up the shot." If he was nervous, he was doing a good job of not showing it.

"That's very good." General Aziz handed the gun back to Christian...but the demonstration wasn't over. "Shoot yourself," the man commanded.

"Now hold on..." Mallory said as Christian placed the gun under his own chin.

"I don't need citizens who will stand still for a bullet," Aziz snapped, without taking his eyes from the kid. "I need citizens who will put a bullet in their own heads if I command. Do it, boy! Shoot yourself."

Christian's eyes flicked towards Mallory, who sighed and shook his head. "This is going to take some explaining to his parents," he said. "Go on, Christian, do as the man says..."

Christian straightened a little, finger tightening around the trigger...

"No!" Henry yelled, leaping from behind the counter. "Christian, stop!"

Every head in the room turned towards him. For a moment no one moved – even Christian seemed momentarily confused, although he showed no sign of recognizing his friend. Then Dr. Chancellor grabbed a communicator from her coat and barked into it, "Security breach in demonstration lab!"

A siren sounded in the corridor. General Aziz threw out his arm, finger pointing towards Henry like an arrow.

"Shoot him!"

Christian brought the gun from under his chin and fired twice across the lab. Henry threw himself back behind the counter as bullets whizzed by, impacting the wall. More rounds ripped into the counter as Christian began unquestioningly to empty the clip at his former friend.

"Henry!" Gabrielle screamed from the vent opening. He threw himself towards her, squeezing into the shaft as she crawled back.

"Move!" he said, half expecting to hear the sound of Christian following them. Instead he heard Mallory yelling from the lab...

"Stop! Stop shooting, you idiot! I want him alive!"

25

Security lights flickered on around the medical centre as distant alarms sounded in the background. In contrast to the first time Henry had escaped from the building, this time it seemed they would stop at nothing to catch him.

As they crawled through the vents, the sound of running guards seemed to come from all around. Yet somehow they made it to an exterior vent grille. Henry grabbed Gabrielle's hand and pulled her from the shaft. They'd come out at ground level and, as yet, the guards didn't seem to be searching nearby. Henry ran towards the gate and the cover of the trees, dragging Gabrielle with him. Halfway there, a buggy driven by a single guard whizzed out from the side of the building. Henry saw he had two choices; he could run, or…

Letting go of Gabrielle, he sprinted towards the approaching buggy. The guard's eyes widened, wondering why his quarry wasn't running in the other direction. Henry leaped seconds before the buggy mowed into him… Landing on the front of the vehicle with his right foot, he struck out with his left, hitting the guard in the shoulder and pushing him over the side. As the guard hit the gravel with a cry of pain, Henry half-fell into the vacated driver's seat, wrenched the wheel round and skidded to a halt in front of Gabrielle.

"Get in," he said.

She jumped into the passenger seat and Henry sent the buggy speeding down the drive as more guards broke from the centre. The small vehicle was fast enough to outrun a man and Henry put the accelerator to the floor. The chain-link security gate was closing as they sped down the drive... The buggy whizzed through at the last second, knocking another guard aside as he tried to make a grab for Henry. Then they were clear of the perimeter and racing down the drive into the complex.

"Where are we going?" Gabrielle asked as they drove across the grass behind a set of lodges, headed for the school.

"We need to get to Newton," Henry said. "Find Fox and get out of town. I've got the evidence of what Mallory's been up to on my phone. We can use it to get the FBI in here and shut Mallory down."

"They'll have shut down the main gates," Gabrielle said, as guards with torches appeared ahead of them. "We'll never get past."

"I've got an idea about that," Henry said, steering the buggy towards a line of bushes on the edge of the school grounds. Driving the vehicle into the foliage so it was half hidden, he leaped out and beckoned for Gabrielle to follow him. Hand in hand, they ran the length of the school towards the swimming pool. There was only one person left in the Malcorp complex Henry thought he could trust…

Coach Tyler.

As they reached the side door to the sports complex, Henry looked back over the grounds. Torchlights shone in the night and the sound of men's voices was getting closer. It wouldn't be long before the guards caught up with them.

"Coach!" Henry yelled as he and Gabrielle slipped into the building and ran down a corridor to the main pool. The water flickered, sending blue ripples of light across the glass ceiling. The place looked deserted. Henry just hoped the coach was having one of his late nights. "Coach!"

"Henry?" The stocky man appeared in the door to his office.

They ran over and pushed past him into the tiny office space.

"Henry, what's going on?" the coach asked, following them in and hastily grabbing a bottle of Scotch from the cluttered desk. He dumped it in a filing cabinet at the back and studied them carefully. "Are you in some kind of trouble?"

Taking a deep breath to regain his composure, Henry said, "I know this looks bad, but we need your help. Remember all those things we were saying were weird about Malcorp…"

"Uh-huh…"

"Well, it's a lot weirder than that." Henry looked round as a door slammed somewhere in the building. "I just don't have time to explain everything right now."

Footsteps sounded from the pool area.

"You can't let them catch us."

The coach looked from him to Gabrielle, no doubt wondering where she'd appeared from.

"Please," she said appealingly. "They want to hurt us."

The footsteps got closer…

"Under the desk!" the coach said urgently. Henry and Gabrielle moved fast, but the space was a tight squeeze. Coach Tyler flopped back into his chair and put his feet up. Seconds later, a security guard appeared in the doorway.

"You seen two kids in here?" the guard demanded.

"Uh, no," Coach replied, trying to sound casual about it. Under the desk, Henry and Gabrielle held their breath.

"A security door at the back of this building was left open. You sure nobody came in here?"

Coach laughed, moving to the filing cabinet. "Kids are always going out that way and leaving it unlocked. No matter how many times I tell them not to." He removed the bottle of Scotch and held it up. "I was about to have a nightcap. Do you fancy—"

"No thanks," the guard interrupted, backing away from the door. "If you see anyone…"

"You'll be the first to know," Coach said, pushing his sagging leather chair back and sticking his legs under the desk so they almost kicked Henry in the head. "If you change your mind about that drink, just let me know."

The guard gave no reply. As his footsteps echoed away around the poolside, nobody in the office moved. It was only as a door banged in the distance that Henry and

Gabrielle breathed a sigh of relief and climbed out from their hiding place. Coach Tyler poured himself a drink for real and knocked it back in one.

"I am not cut out for lying," he said.

"You did great, coach," Henry said. "Thank you."

Coach Tyler looked at him. "I could get sacked for what I just did. This had better be worth it."

"It's worth it," Henry replied. "You wouldn't believe what Malcorp is up to."

The coach cocked his head. "Try me."

Henry looked at Gabrielle, who shrugged. If they were going to ask the man for help getting them out of the complex, he at least deserved an explanation. Henry gave him a potted version of events that evening, describing Mallory's plot to implant strange devices into the brains of students in the Malcorp complex, while Gabrielle backed him up.

The coach took a while to register everything Henry had told him, then he poured himself a third drink. "So what do you want from me?" he asked.

Henry reached out and took the glass from his hands. "First, stay sober because you're going to drive us out of the complex. Gabrielle and I will be in the back of your car and you're going to drop us off at the coffee shop in Newton."

Coach raised an eyebrow. "That's it?"

Henry shrugged. "We might need a lift to the city as well. We have to contact the police, but Malcorp controls all communication in and out of this place…"

The coach stood up and began to pace around the office, which wasn't easy considering its size and the amount of junk that lined the walls. "Man, this is crazy," he said. "No one out there is going to believe you…"

Henry and Gabrielle exchanged a look. Although the coach had listened to their story without question, he was obviously nervous about getting involved.

"Come on, coach," Henry pleaded with him. "You said yourself something stunk here. What does your gut tell you?"

"It's turning over!" he replied. "But I thought Mallory was feedin' these kids steroids or something. Not…this brain stuff!"

Gabrielle stepped forward and placed a hand on his arm. "We need your help. If we don't get out of the complex they're going to do bad things to us."

Her tone seemed to calm the coach, because he stopped pacing.

"Please," she continued. "If you don't want to help us after that, you don't have to. Right, Henry?"

"Right," he agreed.

Coach Tyler sighed, then grabbed a set of keys from his desk drawer.

Ten minutes later the coach's ancient Chevy drove across the complex from the pool in the direction of the main gate. In the back, Henry and Gabrielle lay squeezed into the seat well, covered with a rather smelly blanket that had previously been lining the trunk. The Chevy's suspension was practically shot, so they felt every little bump in the road.

"Sorry," Henry whispered as a turn pressed him closer to Gabrielle in the confined space.

"It's okay," she whispered back. "How much further?"

"I think we're almost at the gate." Henry sincerely hoped Hank was on duty tonight and not some other guy who would want to check the interior. If they were lucky, the guards would still be confining their search to the buildings within the complex.

"They did it to me, didn't they?" Gabrielle asked as the car continued on.

Henry looked at her, able to make out only her eyes staring back in the darkness under the blanket. "Did what?"

"Put one of those SPIDIRs in my brain. And now they can make me do whatever they want, whenever they want…"

"We don't know that."

"I do," she said. "I don't feel right… Mallory told me it's taken longer than they expected to get my 'treatment' working. I think the only reason I'm not like Christian and all the others is they haven't finished programming me yet…"

Henry reached out and squeezed her hand. "It's going to be okay, you know. You're still *you*, whatever they've done."

Her eyes bored into his. "Am I? I'm not so sure."

He changed tack. "There has to be a way to shut those implants down. If we could just get hold of one of those Initiators Mallory has…"

Henry thought it over. There had to be more than one of the command switches around somewhere in the complex – either in the medical centre or Mallory's house… John Mallory was a cautious guy, he'd said so himself. He must have an Initiator on hand at all times, just in case his experiment went wrong.

Gabrielle asked again, "Henry, what are we going to do?"

Before he could answer, the car pulled to a halt. They'd reached the main gate. Up front, Coach Tyler wound down the window and Hank's familiar voice asked him if he'd seen anything unusual. The coach did a good job of sounding annoyed at being stopped, saying that he'd already been questioned back at the pool and no, he hadn't seen anything unusual.

To Henry's massive relief, it worked and Hank let them carry on through without even asking to look in the trunk. A few hundred metres up the road the coach gave a little whoop of triumph.

"Yeah! We're out!"

Henry pulled the stinking blanket down from his and Gabrielle's faces and they both breathed a little easier.

"You two had better stay down," the coach said, keeping his eyes on the road. "There might be more patrols up ahead."

"Good thinking," Henry said.

"Thank you, coach," Gabrielle added.

The man gave another whoop. "I feel like I'm in a goddamned James Bond movie!"

Gabrielle smiled, looking a lot happier than she had a few moments ago.

"Thank you, Henry," she said, leaning in and planting a kiss on his cheek. "I'm glad you didn't give up on me."

Henry hoped she couldn't see him blushing in the darkness. "That's okay."

The car screeched to a halt without warning. The coach cursed loudly and then said, "Get out of the road, you idiot!"

Henry closed his eyes as he heard footsteps approach the vehicle. Then he recognized the sound of Steve's voice. Without being invited, Steve jumped into the passenger seat and slammed the door shut.

"What the hell do you think you're doing?" Coach Tyler demanded. "I almost ran you over!"

"Sorry, coach," Steve said. "I was just looking for a lift into Newton. You don't mind, do you?"

Grumbling, Coach Tyler started the car going again. Gabrielle squeezed Henry's hand tighter as Steve began to talk in a monotone about the swim team and sports day in a never-ending stream. The coach gave non-committal replies to his questions, just concentrating on getting them to Newton as fast as possible.

"So, have you heard about the break-in at the medical centre?" Steve asked out of the blue.

"What, another?" Coach replied.

"Yeah. Turns out that girl Gabrielle Henson was involved. The one Henry Ward was asking about last week."

"I thought you said you didn't know her."

Steve laughed. "Turns out I did. And it turns out she's in the back of this car right now."

"What are you talking about?" the coach said, his voice wavering.

Steve looked over the seat, holding up something in his hand…an Initiator! He pressed the green button and said, "*Initiate.*"

Henry felt Gabrielle tense beside him and was caught by surprise as she slipped her hand from his, took hold of the blanket and ripped it away from their bodies.

"No!" he hissed as she rose to a sitting position in the back…

Then he saw her expression…*blank*…just like Christian's had been in the lab…

He tried to get up, but her feet had his legs pinned to the floor with surprising force. Steve looked over the back of the passenger seat and took in the scene calmly.

"Take him out," he ordered.

Gabrielle closed her hand into a fist, drew it back and smashed it into Henry's face. Stars exploded across the bridge of his nose and his vision went blank. Then she hit him again and there was nothing more…

26

"**W**ard!" Fox's voice floated across to him through layers of blackness. "Ward, wake the hell up!"

With a groan he opened his eyes and tried to raise his hands to his nose, which was hurting and felt twice its normal size. His hands were bound behind the wooden chair upon which he was sitting. His ankles were bound to the legs.

"I think my nose is broken," he mumbled, looking blearily around the room, which he recognized as the lounge above the coffee shop. "People keep making me unconscious."

"Stop being a baby," Fox said. "It is not broken. Maybe."

He focused on her voice and saw that she was sitting opposite him on another kitchen chair. Like him, her arms and legs were bound with heavy-duty packing tape. There was a cut on her right cheek and a bruise was appearing; it looked like someone had hit her.

"Are you okay?" he asked.

"Yeah, I'm just great. Tied to a chair in my apartment. Having fun."

Henry sniffed and looked around the lounge, trying to clear his head. The sounds of a struggle came from behind the door to Fox's mom's room.

"They're tying her up," Fox said, seeing where Henry was looking. "Steve and Gabrielle. We have to do something…" Her voice cracked.

"It's okay," he said, looking back at her. "What happened? Where's the coach?"

Fox frowned at him. "What coach? Gabrielle turned up with you five minutes ago, saying you'd got injured escaping the complex. When I opened the door, Steve jumped me. He had a gun!"

"Malcorp has altered their brains," Henry said, quickly explaining about the SPIDIR implants. If Steve was armed, he'd be prepared to kill. "Mallory's turned Christian into some kind of soldier he can control at will. You should have seen it, Fox. It was…" His voice trailed away as he pictured his friend under Mallory's control. *It's not over yet,* he told himself. *Mallory's going to pay for what he's done.*

Fox looked at the door to her mom's room. "We have to get out of here."

Henry strained against the tape around his wrist and felt it give a little. With enough time he could probably pull free…

The bedroom door opened and Steve and Gabrielle appeared. As they closed it behind them, Henry caught a glimpse of Mary Layton with her wrists taped to the bedpost.

"Get the petrol can from the coach's car," Gabrielle said

to Steve, her voice an emotionless monotone now. "You can fill it across the street at the gas station."

Without a word, Steve exited the lounge, leaving them alone with Gabrielle. She walked to the kitchen, extracted a large carving knife from a block on the counter and returned to them. For a moment she merely stood, as if processing something internally. She looked like a different person, Henry thought. Her face was like a mask – expressionless, unmoving.

He said, "Gabrielle, don't do this. Mallory is using you."

She snapped out of her trance, moving swiftly towards him and placing the knife against his cheek. "Who else knows what you have learned?"

"No one…"

She pressed the blade into his cheek so hard he could feel the steel almost breaking his skin. "Who have you told?"

"Leave him alone!" Fox cried, rocking her chair from side to side. "He hasn't told anyone!"

Gabrielle removed the knife from his face and crossed to Fox. Grabbing her hair roughly, she twisted her head back and pointed the tip of the knife at her throat.

"Don't do this!" Fox said, breathing quickly but keeping herself under control. "We're friends, Gabrielle! You have to remember!"

Gabrielle released her hair and lowered the knife. Fox gave a relieved breath and met Henry's eyes. He nodded at her encouragingly. There had to be something left of the original Gabrielle in there beyond Mallory's programming.

"Don't you remember me?" Fox said. "We've been friends since kindergarten. On the first day of school you were crying so I let you have my doll to play with…"

Gabrielle took a step back, rubbing her forehead with her hand. The hand holding the knife fell to her side.

"Remember? And how we used to have sleepovers right here in this house? You always used to love my mom's cookies and you never wanted to go home at the end…"

Gabrielle let out a scream of frustration. "Shut up!" She moved behind Henry, placing the knife against his neck and looking at Fox with wide eyes. "I remember you!"

Fox nodded. "Yes…"

"You were always jealous of me… Always wanted what I had…"

"That's not true," Fox said, shaking her head. "We were friends…"

Gabrielle placed the knife closer against Henry's neck. He leaned back in the chair as far as he could go to avoid it. "You were jealous of my boyfriends. My looks. You wanted to be me, but you never could, could you?"

"Please, Gabrielle, you're not thinking straight…"

"Say it!"

Fox looked at her. "Okay, okay. You're right. You've always been better than me."

Gabrielle lowered the knife from Henry's throat. "You've always been jealous."

"I've always been jealous."

"Now, tell me everything you know about Malcorp and everyone you've told or I'll slit his throat in front of you."

Fox looked at Henry, who could do nothing other than stare at her desperately. She shook her head slowly. "Gabrielle...I'm really sorry."

There was a *clunk*.

Gabrielle toppled forward suddenly. As she hit the floor, the knife fell from her hand and embedded itself in the floorboards near Henry's feet. He looked round and saw Mary Layton standing unsteadily behind him with a baseball bat in her hands. She staggered forward and half fell over him, using the bat to keep herself upright.

"Way to go, mom!" Fox cried out.

"Guess they didn't think the *cripple lady* needed tying up properly," she said as she sat on the floor and grabbed the knife. She slid round to slice through the tape holding Henry in place. In a few seconds he was free and out of the chair. Taking the knife, he crossed to Fox and cut through her bonds as well.

"Steve will be back any minute," Fox said as she massaged circulation back into her wrists. "And he's armed, remember."

"Like I could forget," said Henry, looking around the lounge and taking stock of the situation. They had to move fast. He went to where Gabrielle was lying on the floor, grabbed her arms and started dragging her to the bedroom. Fox got the door and they hauled the unconscious girl onto the bed. Using the bat to walk, Mary appeared in the bedroom doorway. Fox helped her back into her wheelchair.

"Tie Gabrielle up," Henry said, taking the roll of packing tape from the bedside table and tossing it to Mary. The sound of the front door opening and closing came from downstairs. Henry snatched up the baseball bat and moved back to the lounge, followed by Fox.

"What do we do?" she whispered.

"Sit down in the chair like you're still bound," Henry said, closing the bedroom door. "It won't fool Steve for more than a second, but it should give me enough time to get in a decent swing." He took position to the left of the stairs door, both hands clutching the bat. Fox sat back on the kitchen chair and put her hands behind her back, as if they were still secured...

The stairs creaked...

The door swung open to reveal Steve standing with an automatic pistol in one hand and a can of gas in the other...

"Where is Henry?" he asked without stepping into the room. Beside the door, Henry stood poised with the bat, ready to swing – but Steve had to be inside the lounge.

Fox said, "Gabrielle untied him...uh...he needed the toilet..."

Steve frowned. "She should not have done that." He stepped into the lounge...

Henry swung the bat across Steve's back and he staggered into the room, landing on his hands and knees. The automatic flew from his hand and tumbled across the floor, while the gas can clunked heavily on the carpet. Not wasting a second, Fox grabbed the chair and raised it high, ready to bring down on Steve's head. The tall kid was too fast, however, dodging to one side as she brought the chair down. He swung his left hand at her, which was still holding the gas can, and knocked her backwards. Henry cracked the baseball bat across Steve's skull…

The blow would have been enough to put anyone out cold. But Steve merely turned his head towards Henry and looked at him with a quizzical expression.

"Why don't you just give up?" he said.

Henry swung the bat again, but this time Steve caught it by the shaft and wrenched it from his hands. Steve grabbed him by the throat and threw him into the kitchen with a strength that was beyond even a jock like him. Henry landed on the worktop and then fell forward onto the tiles, stunned. He looked up to see Fox throw herself on Steve's back. He picked her off like she weighed nothing and threw her across the room to land beside Henry.

"Jesus," Fox moaned, rolling over into a crouch. "How strong is he?"

"He's superhuman," Henry replied.

Steve picked up the automatic from the floor and tucked it in the back of his trousers. Then he unscrewed the cap on the gas can and began to shake the contents over the sofas and floor of the lounge.

Henry looked around the kitchen for a weapon. They couldn't fight Steve physically. He was too powerful for that. Whatever Mallory had programmed into his brain, it had enhanced his physical ability beyond measure. "What are you doing, Steve?" Henry asked him, trying to buy time.

"Preparing for a fire," Steve replied emotionlessly.

"You'll never get away with it," Fox said, nudging Henry. He looked where she was looking and saw the carving knife Gabrielle had dropped, lying on the carpet less than a metre away from them. He nodded and began to edge towards it.

Steve gave a humourless laugh. "Mr. Mallory can get away with whatever he wants. This has proved the perfect opportunity to catch all you troublemakers together. Such a shame you didn't know that Gabrielle would turn on you with a single command."

"There'll be an investigation," Fox continued. "Everyone will know it was arson."

"People will believe whatever Mr. Mallory tells them."

Fox fell silent and looked at Henry, who shrugged. He hated to admit it, but Steve was right. In Newton, Malcorp was the law.

"Mallory doesn't want me dead," Henry said, clutching at anything that would buy them some time. "He wants me adjusted."

"He *wanted* you adjusted," Steve corrected. "But his last order to me was that if we can't stop you from causing trouble, you're to be killed. Are you ever going to stop causing trouble, Henry? I mean, really? It's just much easier this way – for everybody."

"What about the coach, huh?" Henry asked. "What have you done with him?"

"Coach is out cold in his Chevy," Steve said. "He's going to have a car accident right after I'm finished here. Driving under the influence of alcohol. Guess I won't be the star of the swim team any more. Not his one, anyway."

"Sounds like you've got it all figured out," Henry said, laying his hand on the knife and pulling it behind his back. He didn't know if he could use a knife against another human being, but if it came down to him and his friends' survival, he was going to give it a damn good try. And he didn't really know if Steve could be classed as a human any more…

"Mr. Mallory asked me to take care of you personally," Steve said, with a hint of pride in his voice. "He made me a soldier and tonight I'm going to show him how loyal I can be…."

With a cry, Henry flew from the floor at Steve, bringing the knife round as he did so. Once again, Steve was just too fast, however. He caught Henry by the wrist and twisted. Henry dropped his weapon with a cry of pain.

"He told me it would be better if you were found without bullets in you," Steve said. "But I guess a few won't hurt."

He threw Henry across the lounge, where he collided with a standard lamp and fell to the ground. Steve withdrew the automatic from his jeans…

"Leave him alone!" Fox yelled, bringing a kitchen drawer filled with cutlery down on Steve's skull. He didn't even flinch, turning round and aiming the gun directly at her head…

"Goodbye," he said.

In desperation, Henry grabbed the nearest weapon

available: the standard lamp. He swung it round, hefting it like a spear, the shade falling off as he jabbed it towards the back of Steve's neck…

The exposed light bulb shattered against Steve's bare skin… There was a crackle of electricity… And for a moment all the lights in the building dimmed…

Steve crashed to the floor, making no effort to break his fall. There was a horrible crunch as he landed. He twitched a little, face down.

"Get the tape!" Henry said, leaping on him and snatching the automatic from his grasp. Then he remembered the Initiator Steve had used to control Gabrielle – if Henry could find it, he could use it to shut their implants down. He started to search Steve's pockets…and cursed as he pulled out a broken mechanism. It had shattered into pieces when Steve fell.

Fox ran through to the bedroom and appeared a second later with the roll of packing tape. While Fox wound the tape about Steve's ankles and wrists, Henry held the gun on him, fearing he would come round. Once he was taped up like a parcel, Fox tore off a smaller strip and was about to place it over his mouth when Steve's eyes flickered open.

"Hey!" he said, sounding completely different from before. There was fear in his voice for the first time. "Don't!"

Henry held a hand out to Fox. She looked at him questioningly.

"I think the electric shock fried the SPIDIR implant in

his brain," he explained. "That's why he went down so easy."

On the floor, Steve looked around wildly. "Where the hell am I? Who are you?"

"He's acting," Fox said coldly. "I don't trust him."

"Please!" Steve said, craning his head to look at her. "I know you! You're that weird kid from school..."

Henry slapped a hand across Steve's face to get his attention. "What's the last thing you remember?"

"Huh?"

"Before this. What's the last thing you remember?"

Steve frowned in concentration. "I was...in hospital..." His eyes widened in shock and he began screaming in absolute panic. "Jesus Christ! They're gonna cut open my skull! HELP! HELP!"

Fox jammed the tape over his mouth to stop him from alerting the entire town.

"What does it mean?" she asked, looking up at Henry.

"It means we can short-circuit the SPIDIRs," he replied. "Shut down the implants Mallory's using to control these kids."

"With an electric shock? What are we gonna do? Hit everyone in town with lamps?"

Henry held up the shattered components of the Initiator. "Mallory had one of these and so did Steve. They can be used to control the implants and shut them down. There have to be more around in the Malcorp complex. If I can get my hands on one, we could use it to free Gabrielle and Christian and the rest."

Fox shook her head. "Not much chance of getting back in the complex without being captured. We need a game plan."

Henry considered for a second, before remembering something. *Game plan.* "Coach!" he exclaimed.

Henry found the man in the trunk of the Chevy, which was parked in the deserted street round the back of the coffee shop. His arms and legs had been bound and his face was a bloody mess, as if he'd been beaten with something hard.

"Take it easy, coach," Henry said as the man struggled into a sitting position in the open trunk. Using the carving knife, Henry cut through the tape.

"That kid Steve went psycho!" he exclaimed. "He pistol-whipped me! Where the hell did he get a gun?"

"From Mallory, I think."

"Jesus."

Henry took Coach Tyler's arm and he cried out in pain. "I think it's broken," he said, almost apologetically.

"Can you make it inside the building?"

The coach nodded and, leaning on Henry for support, allowed himself to be led up a fire escape at the back of the building.

Back inside the apartment, Henry sat him in one of the armchairs and went through to check the bedroom. Mary was watching Gabrielle and Steve, who were now lying side by side on the bed. She had the gun in her hand. Steve was thrashing wildly against his bonds, but no one was in a mood to trust him, even if his SPIDIR really had been shut down. Fox took one look at the coach and went through to the bathroom to fetch her first-aid kit. She set to work patching up his face.

Henry leaned in the doorway to the bedroom, feeling suddenly exhausted. His nose was still throbbing and after their battle with Steve he felt as if he'd just run a marathon. And he guessed the night was far from over. Mallory had set Steve on them with express instructions to catch them or kill them; he was sure to be waiting for his soldier to return to confirm he'd done the deed. Which meant they didn't have long...

"We have to get out of here," Fox said as she finished with the coach. "All of us."

Henry nodded his agreement, stepping back into the lounge. He checked his cell phone – zero reception. All they had to do was get far enough outside Newton to be able to contact the authorities... His eyes fell on the telephone on the kitchen counter. He ran over and snatched it up, wondering if he'd get through to somewhere outside Newton if he dialled 911...

"*Hello?*" a woman's voice said on the other end of the line.

Taken aback, Henry replied, "Hello? Who is this?"

For a moment there was silence. "*This is the operator. Who would you like to call?*"

"Uh..." Henry looked at Fox and placed his hand over the receiver. "Some woman says she's the operator."

Fox rolled her eyes at him. "Hang up. It's them."

"Emergency services are on the way to your location," the woman on the phone said. *"Please stay where you are—"*

Henry tossed the phone back on the counter. "I guess they know Steve and Gabrielle weren't successful."

Mary Layton wheeled herself to the bedroom door. "You two have to get out of here now. They'll be coming any minute."

Fox shook her head. "We're all going together…"

Mary pushed her chair forward and took her daughter's hand. "There's no time for that. And someone has to stay here and watch those two." She nodded in the direction of the bedroom. "I'd just slow you down. Get the hell out of Newton and tell everyone what's going on here. And when you come back, be sure to tell me what the hell is going on here too, okay?"

Fox laughed, although there were tears forming in her eyes. "I don't want to leave you."

Her mom reached up and stroked her face. "I'm sorry, hon. We should have got out of this town a long time ago. I guess after your dad walked out I was just scared of losing what we had left…"

A car passed in the street outside, screeching to a halt abruptly.

Henry took Fox's arm. "We need to move now."

"Look after my girl," Mary said as he pulled Fox towards the fire escape.

Henry nodded and looked at Coach Tyler. "Come on."

"I'm in no condition, kid," he replied woozily. "Think

I'll sit this one out. I'm betting the keys are still in the Chevy…"

His voice faded as the glass shattered in the cafe below. Henry pulled Fox through the window out onto the fire escape and they flew down the steps as quickly and as silently as possible. Reaching the bottom, Fox looked back at the apartment above.

"We'll come back for them," Henry whispered, looking round at the Chevy, which was parked a few metres away.

"I'll drive," Fox said, regaining her composure. She ran round the front and jumped into the driver's seat. Henry barely had time to get in the passenger's side before the engine started and the Chevy pulled away along the street.

"How long have you been driving?" Henry asked, steadying himself against the dash.

"Ever since mom has been in the chair," she replied. "Special dispensation."

"Well, you might want to take it a little slower."

"Too late for that!" Fox replied as the Chevy hit the end of the alley and roared onto Main Street, heading south out of town. She looked pretty comfortable behind the wheel and was getting some speed out of the ancient vehicle. As they flew past the last of the shops and by the houses on the outskirts of town, Henry looked out through the back window.

"I think we got away clean," he said. Hopefully whoever had broken into the cafe had been too preoccupied to hear them leaving.

Then lights appeared in the darkness behind them: the red and white flashing lights of a police cruiser.

Trooper Dan was in pursuit.

27

"**W**hat do we do?" Fox asked, a note of panic rising in her voice. She was keeping the Chevy on a tight line as the road wound through the forest surrounding Newton, but the lights of the cop car were getting closer in the rear-view mirror. The ancient car was never going to outrun a tuned-up patrol vehicle.

"We can't stop," Henry said, hanging on for dear life as the Chevy took a sharp turn. It felt as if the wheels on his side of the car were lifting off the ground. He pulled on his safety belt and reached across to do the same for Fox.

"I don't think he wants us to stop!" she exclaimed as the engine of the cruiser roared behind them, like a huge beast bearing down on them. A second later there was a jarring impact as the cruiser slammed into the back of the Chevy. Fox let out a cry, but held the wheel firm, managing to keep the car on the road.

"He's trying to kill us," Henry said.

"No! You think?"

There was a roar as the cruiser accelerated again. Henry looked back in time to see the high-beam headlights approach, blinding in the rear window. "Look for some way to get off this road."

"I'm looking!"

The cruiser engine roared again as it picked up speed to pull alongside. Henry looked across at the interior of the cruiser as it drew level. In the driver's seat he saw the silhouette of Trooper Dan, brimmed hat on his head, one hand on the wheel and one reaching for...

A gun.

"Fox!" Henry cried out too late...

A bullet exploded through the side window and carried right on through the windshield. Henry felt it pass his face by centimetres. Then the interior of the Chevy was filled with flying shards of glass. Fox screamed at a second muzzle flash from the direction of the cruiser and a deafening gunshot. Henry looked round, fearing she was hit...

The Chevy slammed into the crash barrier and carried on through. There was a moment like being in an elevator rising very fast as the car sailed off the road and became airborne. Then it started to come down, but the descent was curtailed when the front end slammed into a tree. Henry clung on to the safety belt around his torso as the world turned sideways, tossing the contents of the Chevy interior like they'd been placed in a tumble dryer. Broken glass, candy wrappers and empty soda cans spun around Henry's head. There was another jarring impact as the vehicle hit the ground side-on and finally came to rest on its roof.

For a moment Henry hung upside down in his seat, held in place by the belt, hardly believing he was alive. He looked left and saw that Fox had slipped out of hers and landed on the roof, which was now the floor. From the rear of the vehicle the smell of leaking gasoline filled the air. Up front, the engine was sputtering away, refusing to die.

"Hey," Henry said, reaching out and shaking his companion.

Fox stirred and looked round at him. He could see she was in pain.

"Are you shot?" he asked.

"I don't know," she said with a groan. "I feel like I've been hit in the back with a sledgehammer."

Henry checked her over and was relieved to see there was no blood. No evidence of a gunshot wound. "We have to get out of here," Henry said. Trooper Dan could only be moments away, but it was the gasoline that worried him the most. At any second, the Chevy could explode. "Can you move?"

To show she could, Fox slid towards the crumpled driver's side door and started squeezing herself through the shattered window. Henry reached for the release catch on the safety belt and found it locked out. Pulling the belt as far as it would go, he slipped from underneath and landed on the roof amid the shattered glass that had collected there. He made to follow Fox, but then had a thought. He reached up and opened the glove compartment; the contents spilled out around him.

"Hurry up, Ward!" Fox hissed through the window. "I can hear someone coming!"

"A second!"

Henry felt through the junk that had come from the glove compartment and found two items that would come in useful: a Zippo lighter and an electric torch. *Nice one, coach!* Clutching them in his hand, he manoeuvred himself back through the window and out into the darkness of the forest. Fox moved to his side.

"He's over there," she whispered, meaning the other side of the crashed Chevy. They began to back away from the wreck, towards the cover of the trees. Henry made out the shape of Trooper Dan moving through the forest towards the car, his silhouette somehow blacker than the night around him. In his hand he held a gun. As they came to the cover of a tree, Henry stopped and waited. Fox tugged on his arm urgently.

"What are you waiting for, Ward? We have to get out of here!"

"Hold on."

The crashed car was now a good ten metres away and in the flickering light thrown out by its headlamps he saw Trooper Dan approach cautiously, bending down to see inside the overturned vehicle.

"Ward!"

"Get ready to run," he whispered back, turning the Zippo over in his right hand and flipping the lid. "Now!"

Henry struck the flint and the lighter flame sparked into life. He threw it at the rear of the car...

There was a *whumpf* as the gasoline leaking from the Chevy's ruptured fuel tank ignited. Henry staggered back. The entire car went up in an orange fireball that momentarily lit up the night. He held up his arm against the heat, trying to make out if their attacker had been caught in the explosion before Fox grabbed his shoulder and pulled him away. They fled through the trees, their way illuminated by the growing fire behind them.

After several minutes, they collapsed against a tree and looked back. In the distance the flames were still visible through the forest.

"Is he following?" Fox asked breathlessly.

"I don't think so," Henry replied.

"Is he dead?"

"I don't know."

"Do you know which direction we're going?"

He shook his head. Fox had a good point – in the confusion of the crash, they'd completely lost their bearings. For all they knew, they could be heading back to Newton. "We need to keep moving." Henry looked at Fox and saw from the dark look on her face that she was as worried as he was: worried about their friends and family…worried that they'd never get out of Newton County alive…

"We're going to be okay," he reassured her. "We're going to find someone who'll believe us."

Fox nodded, and they ran into the night once more.

28

For the best part of an hour they stumbled through the undergrowth of the forest with only Coach's tiny emergency torch to guide them. It was a moonlit night, but under the tall fir trees it was always dark as pitch. They'd considered doubling back to the road, but decided that it was too risky. If Trooper Dan hadn't been killed in the explosion, he'd be expecting them to do that and might be lying in wait. More of Mallory's men might have been watching the roads as well. The safest option, they decided, was to keep on walking. Deeper into the forest.

Fox folded her arms across her chest and shivered visibly.

"Are you okay?" Henry asked.

She nodded. "Yeah…I just started to feel really cold." Her teeth were chattering as she spoke.

Henry removed his jacket and made to put it round her.

"I'm not a damsel in distress, Ward," she said, pulling away.

"You're experiencing shock. We've been through a traumatic event and you need to keep warm. Perhaps we should stop for a moment."

She shook her head. "We need to keep moving."

"Then take the jacket."

"Okay, okay," she said, allowing him to drape it over her shoulders. "But don't start looking at me like I'm helpless or something."

He grinned and said, "You just drove us out of town with a psycho cop on our trail. I think you're allowed to be a little shook up."

"Well, you seem to be holding up pretty well."

"Trust me, inside I'm a mess. Besides, I had time to freak out earlier when they were going to cut out my brain."

"Really?"

"Oh, yeah. I did the whole screaming, crying thing."

"I wish I could have been there to see that."

They walked on. In the moonlight, the stillness of the forest was peaceful. *You could almost forget a psycho cop is on your tail*, Henry thought.

"Can I ask you a question?" he said finally.

"Go on."

"About your nickname. Fox. What's with that?"

For a moment she said nothing, to the point when he thought she wasn't going to reply. Then she said, "You don't tell this to anyone. And you don't laugh. Okay?"

"Okay."

"It's my real name," she said. "Fox. My mom and dad were obviously on some kind of back to nature trip around the time I was born. It's a lame hippy name, so I tell everyone it's my online nickname and pretend my real name's Michelle. Wait a minute... Are you laughing?"

"No!"

"Your shoulders are shaking!"

"I am not laughing!"

"I knew I shouldn't have told you!"

"Well, I think it's a good name."

"*Right*."

"I do!"

"Ward, you are so full of it…"

Her voice trailed away as a noise split the silence of the forest. A low droning sound that got louder as it got closer. Then the sound changed, the unmistakable *thwok thwok thwok* of helicopter blades.

"Over here!" Henry said urgently, pulling Fox towards a fallen tree trunk lying in the undergrowth. He killed the torch as they squeezed into the hollowed middle. Seconds later the chopper passed overhead.

"Do you think it's Malcorp?" Fox whispered as it went.

Henry nodded. "It didn't see us. The trees are good cover, but they won't hide us for ever. For all we know they've got thermal imaging equipment on that chopper."

Fox raised an eyebrow at him.

"What? Haven't you played Modern Warfare?"

"Strangely, no," Fox replied, pointing off to the left. "I think I see something through the trees over there."

She led the way. Henry couldn't see anything among the trees at first. It was as they ran over an incline that he made it out against the dark night sky: a three-storey wooden house standing amid a clearing in the heart of the forest. A couple of rusting pickup trucks stood off to one side and the garden, such as it was, was overgrown with long grass and brambles. The side of the house nearest to them was weather-beaten and the paint was peeling, as if no one had cared for it for a long time.

"It looks deserted," Henry said as they stopped at the edge of clearing and checked the way ahead. They would have to cross open ground to get to the house and the sound of the chopper was getting louder, making another sweep of the area.

Fox looked at him. "But it's our best chance. Right?"

Henry nodded and they ran from cover. The ground was uneven and halfway to the building Fox tripped. Henry caught her arm and pulled her on with him. They reached the house and looked back in the direction they'd come.

"That helicopter's coming back!" Fox exclaimed.

Henry didn't waste time responding. Instead, he moved along the wall to where a low covered porch led to the front door. He pressed the doorbell. In the depths of the house, a buzzer sounded, its tone off-key. There was no response, so he pressed it again.

"Come on, Ward!" Fox said urgently. "We need to get in there!"

Henry nodded. He tried the handle and, finding it locked, started looking around for something to break a window. A heavy-looking frog ornament was sitting on the floor by the welcome mat. He picked it up, ready to throw it at the window by the door...

"Wait!"

Henry stayed his hand as Fox bent down by the mat and flipped up the edge to reveal a key. She grinned at him, picked it up, and fitted it into the Yale lock. It turned. They hurried through the door into the hall and slammed it shut behind them…

29

They stood in the silent entrance hall. Henry strained to see through the window beside the door. Outside in the moonlight it was possible to make out the overgrown grass being flattened as the chopper hovered overhead. For a moment the machine hung there, but then it began to fly north, back in the direction of Malcorp.

"They're leaving!" Fox whispered, though there was little need. The stillness of the house encouraged quietness somehow, like a library or a crypt.

"Yeah," Henry said with a frown. The fact the chopper had paused over the building suggested the men inside knew they were sheltering there, so why hadn't they landed and come in after them?

"Look at this place," Fox said, turning her attention to the interior of the building.

Henry flashed the torch around the hallway. There was a dusty smell in the air, as if the house hadn't been cleaned properly in a long time. Somewhere in the building a clock ticked loudly, like a metronome counting down the seconds to something.

"Looks pretty deserted," Henry said, wondering if it

had been abandoned when Malcorp came to town. Perhaps the occupants had left Newton rather than work for the big corporation. Perhaps it had been bought up, like everything else in the area, and left standing like a mausoleum. An artefact of a previous existence.

Henry shivered. There was something about the place he really didn't like. He resisted the urge to flick the nearest light switch. The torches would be less visible from outside.

"We need to find a phone that works, right?" Fox said. Henry could tell from her tone of voice that she was feeling pretty much the same as he was.

"Right," he said.

"Well, let's do it then."

Fox walked across the hall to the lounge, closely followed by Henry. This room was even darker than the hall and just as dusty. On a small table by an old-fashioned-looking sofa stood a phone – the type with a coiled cord linking the receiver to the dial pad. Fox picked up the receiver, and put it to her ear. She looked at Henry and shook her head.

"It's dead."

Henry reached past her and held up the cable dangling from the back. It had been cut a few centimetres from the phone. "No wonder," he said.

Fox put the receiver down and shook her head. "That doesn't mean the main line has been cut, right? There could be a working phone in the kitchen…"

"Or bedroom."

"Right."

"I'll check upstairs," Henry said, handing her the torch and already moving for the hall, using the moonlight streaming through the windows to see. "You go…"

"For the kitchen, I get it," Fox said as he headed out of the room and up the stairs. "You know, when you're in a spooky old house it's usually a really bad idea to split up!"

If Henry heard her, he didn't respond. Waving the torch around the deserted lounge, she saw a door leading through to what appeared to be a kitchen and pulled it open.

The kitchen looked like something from the 1950s. There was faded linoleum on the floor, yellow-painted doors on the cabinets and plastic chairs around a table with spindly metal legs. Although the worktops were clean and there were no dirty dishes in the sink, there was a slightly bad smell in the air, as if something had been left to go off in the fridge or one of the drawers. Fox decided not to look too hard for that.

She walked to the counter and peered through the window onto a backyard that was just as overgrown as the front. She ran her hand over the counter and was surprised to find that it was dust free – as if it had been cleaned not long before. Which must mean someone still lived there…

"Focus," Fox said to herself, looking around the kitchen. "You've got a job to do."

There was no telephone. There wasn't even a telephone point that she could see. But that didn't mean there was nothing of use there. She thought of the ancient pickup trucks out the front. There had to be keys for them somewhere – and her mom had always kept the car keys in the kitchen, back when she could drive. There was no set of key hooks on the wall, like they had in their apartment, so she began opening drawers. One was filled with cutlery. Another with napkins and dishcloths. Another with yellowed coupons for the Newton supermarket. And one with two sets of car keys.

Fox picked up the keys, weighing them in her palm. They had to be worth a try – they were going to get a whole lot further even in the most decrepit vehicle than on foot. She was about to risk a walk out front to check if any of the keys actually fitted the pickups, when she spotted something else, wedged at the back of the drawer behind a box of bullets.

A wallet.

Fox reached for it and flipped it open. The money flap was empty, but a number of credit and store cards were nestled in various pouches. She chose one and removed it. The name on the card made her frown.

Stuart Richardson.

The journalist she had contacted! The one who'd disappeared. It couldn't be a coincidence, could it? The next card she removed confirmed that it wasn't – a laminated ID for the paper where he worked. *He'd been here, in this house.* So where was he? And why did he leave his wallet?

Fox looked round the kitchen again, feeling a sudden chill, as if she were being observed. For the first time she noticed a door standing ajar on the far side. It was dark beyond, but possible to make out steps leading down into a basement.

And on the floor by the door there were multiple scratch marks in the linoleum, as if something...or someone...had been dragged towards those steps...

On the second floor, Henry moved between the bedrooms as quickly as possible, checking for telephones or anything else of use and then moving on. The moonlit decor here was just as old-fashioned as on the floor below: fading, striped wallpaper, beds covered with frilly-edged quilts and thick, dusty carpet on the floor.

Having checked all of the bedrooms on that floor, he came back to the landing and looked at the narrower flight of steps heading up to the third floor. He could hear Fox moving around in the kitchen below and considered going down to join her... But what if there was a phone on the floor above? Not likely, he realized, but he had to check.

Henry headed up the uncarpeted flight of steps; they creaked loudly as he put his foot on them. At the top he pushed open a door covered with peeling, green paint.

It was an attic space that had been converted into a room. The sloped sides of the roof formed the walls, with a circular window at the far end, overlooking the front garden. The floorboards were bare and dusty. The place was cluttered with packing crates and boxes. Henry sniffed – not much chance of finding a telephone up here. But then something caught his eye...

Near the circular window was a metal-framed bed. The sheets were rumpled, as if someone had slept there recently. Henry started towards it, making out framed pictures standing on a bedside table. He picked one of them up and squinted at it, interested to see who actually lived there.

The picture in his hand was old, perhaps taken twenty years before, judging by the clothes the people were wearing and the washed-out colours. He could just make out a couple in their fifties, grey-haired and standing on either side of a much taller, good-looking man, who Henry guessed was their son. He realized that the picture had been taken on the porch of the house, at a time when the place was well-painted and there were hanging baskets brimming over with flowers. He turned his attention to the younger man in the middle and realized with a shock that he recognized him...

Although he was wearing a T-shirt and jeans rather than a cop's uniform, it was unmistakably Trooper Dan.

Henry's mouth fell open. He hadn't noticed who it was at first because the trooper's expression in the photo was friendly and open. He was grinning broadly at whoever was taking the photo. Henry turned his attention to the other pictures on the table. He narrowed his eyes to pick out the details in the gloom. There were more of the older couple. A graduation photograph from a police academy.

Dropping the photo on the bed, Henry was certain of one thing: *they were standing in Trooper Dan's house.*

And they had to get the hell out. Fast.

Headlights and the sound of a vehicle moving outside made him cross to the window and look out.

The familiar police cruiser had pulled up out front, sending a cloud of dust into the air. The car door swung open and Trooper Dan stepped out. He reached back into the vehicle, produced a pump-action shotgun, and then walked towards the porch.

30

enry felt his way across the attic room as swiftly as he could without making a racket on the floorboards. As he reached the top of the narrow stairs he heard the front door bang open. Trooper Dan's boots clumped into the hallway, making no effort to disguise his presence. Henry listened for a moment. He couldn't see, but he sensed the cop standing in the hall, listening to the silence of the darkened building. Clearly, the men in the helicopter had seen them run into his house and alerted the trooper. And now here he was.

There was a loud, metallic rasp – the sound of a round being jacked into the chamber of the pump-action shotgun; Henry recognized it from a million cop shows.

"Yoo-hoo!" Trooper Dan yelled into the house. "I just came to let you kids know, y'all picked a real bad place to hide."

Henry closed his eyes as he heard the man begin to walk across the hall, no doubt towards the lounge and then the kitchen… Where Fox would be hiding…

Before he really knew what he was doing, he brought his foot down heavily on the nearest stair. A loud creak echoed through the house. Below, the sound of the cop moving stopped.

"I can hear you, you dumb little punks!" Trooper Dan called up. "Don't make me come up there. Or it'll be worse for you!"

Henry stood still for a moment, waiting for the cop's next move. When he was greeted only with silence from below, he realized that the trooper was waiting for him to act. He licked his lips, which were incredibly dry. Suddenly, he remembered something he'd seen in one of the bedrooms on the second floor – an open fireplace...and beside it a metal poker. His best chance of a weapon against the man. And at least it would give Fox the opportunity to make a break for it...

"Come and get me!" Henry yelled, bolting down the stairs to the second floor. Even as he reached the landing the sound of Trooper Dan thundering up the main staircase made the walls shake. Henry didn't look round. He hit the half-closed door of the nearest bedroom and ran towards the fireplace, snatching up the poker and throwing himself down beside the bed...

Trooper Dan jumped into the doorway and froze there, the shotgun trained on the room. There was no emotion in his eyes, but he was breathing heavily, excited.

"I know you're in here," he hissed.

Hidden by the bed, Henry held his breath and gripped the poker tightly in his hands. He knew he would get just one chance against his enemy. He had to wait for the man to step into the room.

"You should have given up when you had the chance," Trooper Dan said, walking into the room. "Now it's gonna have to hurt…"

Henry expected the cop to check the bed first, but was surprised when he headed for the other side of the room. He looked around and, seeing a cupboard standing ajar, realized the trooper thought that was where he was hiding. He'd been given a chance. All he had to do was wait…

Trooper Dan passed the bed, shotgun aimed at the cupboard as he approached.

"I'm gonna count to five," he said. "One…two…"

Henry tensed, ready to spring as the cop took another step past him.

"Three…"

He gripped the poker as tight as he could and focused on the back of Trooper Dan's neck.

"Four…"

Henry leaped from his hiding place, raising his weapon above his head as he flew at the cop…

Who spun round lightning fast, bringing the muzzle of the shotgun up. Henry skidded to a halt on the carpet, the poker going limp in his hands.

"Five!" Trooper Dan said with a grin. "You think I'm stupid, son?"

Henry allowed the poker to drop from his fingers. It landed heavily on the carpet and he started to back away towards the bedroom door. Trooper Dan followed him, keeping the shotgun aimed at his head.

"Please," Henry said, hoping desperately that Fox had

used her chance to get away, "I haven't done anything wrong."

"*Haven't done anything wrong?*" Trooper Dan said. "You've broken into my house, boy. I've got every right to shoot you."

Henry backed through the door and out onto the landing.

"I didn't know…"

"*I didn't know*," the man mimicked. "Well, I'll tell you what *I* know. You've got about ten seconds to live. Say your prayers. If you do pray, that is, city boy."

Henry's back touched the bannister. There was nowhere else to go.

"I knew you were trouble from the first moment I laid eyes on you," Trooper Dan said as his finger tightened around the trigger.

Henry grabbed the bannister and pitched himself backwards. He fell a short distance…then hit the stairs on his side. The thick carpet cushioned his fall, but the pain was intense along his arm. With a cry, Henry began to tumble uncontrollably, coming to a rest on the floor of the entrance hall. He struggled to get up, but his leg buckled underneath him – he'd twisted it in the fall.

Thud!

Trooper Dan leaped over the bannister and landed perfectly on the stairs before him. Henry rolled over onto his back and began to push himself away in desperation.

"Hoo-eee, boy!" Trooper Dan said with a whistle. "That was some acrobatic move! I didn't think you had it in you!"

Henry managed to get to his feet and started staggering back towards the front door, which was standing open, shafts of moonlight brightening the porch.

"Come on, son," Trooper Dan said, making his voice sound reasonable, friendly almost. "You didn't think I was really gonna shoot now, did you?" He laid the shotgun down on the hall table as if to prove his point. "I ain't gonna do that. It wouldn't be fair. But I am gonna beat you to death…"

He moved forward and aimed a kick at Henry's stomach that connected with the force of a locomotive. Henry flew backwards, through the open door, across the porch and onto the dusty ground at the front of the house. He clutched at his gut and gasped, trying to suck air into his lungs as pain exploded through his diaphragm.

Taking his time, Trooper Dan strolled across the porch, pulling on his leather gloves a little tighter and flexing his fingers. As the cop got close, Henry grabbed a handful of dirt and threw it at his face.

"That ain't nice," Trooper Dan said, dodging to one side and then reaching down to take Henry by the shirt front with his left hand. He hauled him to his feet and drew back his right fist.

"No!"

Trooper Dan's fist stopped in mid-flight as Fox's voice rang out from the porch.

"Let him go right now or I'll put a bullet in your head!"

With a surprised look, Trooper Dan released his grip on

Henry's shirt, allowing him to fall back to the ground. They both turned to where Fox was standing… On the edge of the porch… The shotgun in her hands…

"Hey!" the cop said. "That's my gun!"

"Back off!" Fox ordered, taking a step towards him across the porch.

"You're gonna put a bullet in my head?" Trooper Dan said. He tapped a gloved finger on the centre of his forehead. "Right here?"

"Yes!" Fox said, clearly struggling to stop the shotgun from trembling in her grasp. "Put your hands up and stay back!"

Trooper Dan slowly raised his arms. "It's okay, missy. I ain't gonna do nothin' stupid."

"Take out your gun and toss it over here," Fox ordered.

Trooper Dan began to reach towards the revolver sitting on his hip.

"Slowly!"

"Take it easy," Trooper Dan said as he picked the Magnum from his belt with his thumb and forefinger.

"Toss it over here."

The cop threw the weapon so it landed on the porch steps between them. "There you go," he said. "I ain't armed no more. Now what?"

Fox licked her lips and shifted the gun in her grasp. "Henry, are you okay?"

Henry moved to the side and caught Fox's eye. He could see she was terrified. "Just run," he said.

Trooper Dan grinned and started moving forward again.

"Are you gonna run, girl? Ever fired a weapon before? You know you've got to squeeze the trigger, right? Squeeze it real slow…"

"I know how to fire a gun!" Fox said, her voice high and strained. Beads of sweat stood out on her forehead. "Stop moving!"

Trooper Dan sniggered. "Just give that shotgun here and we'll forget all about it, what do you say?" He lowered his left hand and reached out for the weapon.

"No deal," Fox said with determination. She waved the end of the shotgun at him.

The cop stopped moving and lowered his hands slowly. His voice hardened. "Now, let's not do anything stupid."

"Fox, get the hell out of here!" Henry said, struggling into a crouch. He could barely stand on his left leg.

"Shut your mouth, boy!" Trooper Dan snapped, not taking his eyes from the shotgun barrel. "Nobody's goin' nowhere until I get my gun back. Now, you hand it over and there's no hard feelings…" His right hand began to creep round towards the back of his belt… "I'll just take you both back to Newton and we can have a good talk about everything that's happened…"

The shotgun wavered in Fox's hands, as if the effort of holding it up had become almost too much to bear.

The trooper reached out towards Fox with his left hand. Henry looked to the cop's back and saw the fingers of his right hand closing around the handle of a knife concealed in his belt…

"Fox, watch out!" he yelled.

Trooper Dan whipped the knife round in a smooth, well-practised motion. Fox squeezed the trigger…

The sound of the shotgun was deafening.

Trooper Dan's left hand exploded as the shell ripped through his open palm.

The recoil from the blast threw Fox back against the side of the house as if she was the one who had been hit.

Henry staggered back in shock as a fine red liquid like the lightest of rain fell through the air across his face. Before him, Trooper Dan sank to his knees, clutching his left wrist with his right hand. A terrible, siren-like howl broke the silence of the night air. It took Henry a second to realize that it was the sound of the cop screaming in agony. He looked to where the man stood, holding his left arm. Nothing remained of the fingers of his left hand. Only the lower part of his palm and the thumb remained. Still stunned, Henry looked around on the blood-splattered dirt, expecting to see the cop's severed digits lying around, but they were nowhere to be seen. Perhaps they'd been completely destroyed by the force of the shotgun shell.

"*Oh, Jesus,*" Trooper Dan whispered. His hat had fallen off his head and was lying to one side in the dirt. Henry noticed that the pupils of his eyes were huge and black and locked on his damaged hand. "*Sweet, holy Jesus.*"

31

Henry stumbled to the porch, giving the kneeling cop a wide berth and noticing that the knife had embedded itself in one of the wooden posts circling the house. Fox was sitting on the floor with her back against the wall, staring at Trooper Dan with a shocked expression. The shotgun lay to one side.

"Are you okay?" Henry asked, crouching down beside her.

Fox gave no response. She was either too shocked or stunned to respond.

"Hey!" Henry said, shaking her shoulder roughly.

She snapped out of it, looking round at him. Reaching into her pocket, she produced two sets of car keys. "I found these."

"Great," Henry said, looping his arm under hers and lifting her up. "We're getting out of here."

"Did I get him?"

"Yeah. You got him."

He began to manoeuvre her across the porch, stopping to pick up the shotgun awkwardly with his free hand. Tucking it under his arm, he stooped to get the Magnum as well. He didn't intend to leave either of them lying around for Trooper Dan. The cop had stopped staring at his hand now and was gazing at them both with a completely blank expression.

"Stay the hell down!" Henry snapped, waving the second gun at the cop as he moved to get up. "You know we'll use this now!"

Trooper Dan stayed on his knees, but his eyes followed Henry as he passed. The cop's skin had gone deathly pale, making the splatters of blood on his face stand out in high contrast, almost black in the moonlight. He grinned, exposing two rows of perfectly white teeth. "You're dead," he hissed. "I'm gonna kill you."

"Yeah? Well you'll have to catch us first."

Henry carried on past the cop, half carrying Fox, who was too shaken up to put one foot in front of the other unaided. Up ahead the ancient pickup trucks stood waiting and Henry made a beeline for the slightly less wrecked of the two. It was a monster of a vehicle with rusting green paint and cobwebs in the windows, but the tyres appeared intact. As they reached the door he looked back at the house and was shocked to see that Trooper Dan had got to his feet and was staggering in the direction of a barn over to the side.

"You have to help me out here," Henry told Fox urgently. "That cop isn't finished."

His words seemed to bring Fox to her senses a little, because she unhooked her arm from his and stood up straighter. She caught sight of the guns he was carrying and her face went pale once more. "I don't want those anywhere near me."

"It's okay," Henry said. "I'm getting rid of them."

With a cry, Henry heaved the shotgun through the air. It disappeared far into the undergrowth at the edge of the property. He did the same with the Magnum and then pulled on the pickup door handle. It opened with a screech of rusted metal. Henry pushed Fox into the passenger seat and then limped round to get behind the wheel.

The first set of keys fitted in the ignition and when Henry turned them the engine gave a protesting howl. The entire frame of the vehicle shuddered as if it were about to fall apart.

"Try again," Fox encouraged as she reached over to wipe away the grime from inside the windshield with a rag she'd found on the floor. Already she was beginning to sound more like herself again, much to Henry's relief. Nothing kept her down for long.

Henry turned the key again, but shook his head when the engine failed to spark a second time.

"Maybe we should just make a run for it," Fox said.

"We need a vehicle," Henry insisted, remembering the helicopter. They weren't going to make it very far on foot. As Fox wiped another section of the windshield they saw Trooper Dan emerge from the barn through the smeared glass. He was headed directly for them, left hand now wrapped in a bandage and covered in a thick, black substance that looked like tar – as if he'd smothered it to stop the bleeding. In his right hand he held an axe.

"Oh no," Fox said, reaching over to lock her door.

Suddenly Henry regretted getting rid of the guns and almost considered making a run to get them, but Trooper Dan was already too close. For a man who had just lost most of his left hand, he showed little sign of pain now. In fact his face, with those black, inhuman eyes, had a look of insane determination that gave him the aspect of an unstoppable machine.

"Come on!" Henry said, almost pleading as he turned the key and hit the gas again. The truck began a rhythmic juddering, as if it were on the verge of ticking over…

Outside, Trooper Dan came within a metre of the vehicle and raised the axe high with a cry. He brought the shining, highly sharpened head toward the windshield.

The engine of the pickup roared into life. Henry threw it into reverse and it sped backwards as the axe came down, scraping across the already dented surface of the hood. He spun the wheel and the pickup skidded 180 degrees, so it was facing the driveway out of the property. The truck handled like a beast, but instincts honed by years of playing racing games kicked in… Henry threw the stick into drive like he'd been behind the wheel for years…

"Floor it!" Fox yelled.

In the side mirror Henry saw Trooper Dan running at them, axe swinging in his hand. He hit the gas hard as the blade of the axe ripped through the flimsy metal of the passenger door, centimetres from Fox's leg. Then the pickup shot forward, down the gravel drive that wound through the trees, and out onto the main road.

"I hope this leads somewhere!" Henry yelled as they took a sharp turn. If anything, the drive seemed to be getting narrower...before it suddenly opened out onto a main road. Henry struggled to keep control, gripping the wheel hard, but it was more luck than anything that got the truck on the road and headed in the right direction. The tyres squealed as they burned rubber along the tarmac.

Then they were heading away from Trooper Dan's house as fast as the truck could carry them, which was about 40kph. Henry leaned his head back and took a deep breath. The head of the axe was still sticking through the door – it had been wrenched from the cop's hand as they sped away. He looked round at Fox, who was focused on the road ahead with great intensity, knuckles white on the dashboard.

"Are you okay?" he said.

Fox nodded. "I'm okay. I just..." Her voice trailed away, as if she'd just thought of something terrible. Her eyes darted to the rear-view mirror. "He's in the back!"

Henry jerked round in his seat, looking through the back window into the empty back of the truck...

There was nothing there. He took a deep breath. "He's not there."

Fox laughed, a little manically. "Sorry. Getting paranoid."

They took another corner fast. Henry was riding the gas hard, trying to put as much space between them and the cop as possible. He wondered just how much Trooper Dan had in him. The wound to his hand had been serious, but he'd shown little sign of pain. Had he been *adjusted* as well? The cop's resilience reminded him of their fight with Steve. An implanted SPIDIR would have allowed him to shut off the pain, but how long would it be before the blood loss caused him simply to collapse? Henry took another glance through the back window, half expecting to see the police cruiser in pursuit, but the road was empty. He looked up. No sign of the helicopter in the sky either. Perhaps they'd got lucky.

"Henry!" Fox exclaimed.

He looked round in time to see the headlights of a cop car speeding towards them. For a second he thought it was the trooper, but then realized there was no way Dan could have come from that direction. Also this vehicle was white with blue markings, more like the patrol cars he was used to seeing in the city. He watched the tail lights recede into the distance in the side mirror. But then the car stopped and began to pull round. Red and blue flashes lit up the dark sky.

"It's following us!" Fox said. "Why is it following us?"

The randomized *whup-whup-woo* of the siren grew closer as it sped back up the road after them.

"Well, let me see," Henry said. "They just passed two kids driving a forty-year-old pickup with an axe sticking out of the passenger door. I think they might have noticed."

Fox shot him a glance. "Do you think they're with Malcorp?"

Henry considered as he watched the cop car grow huge

in the mirror. "No. Those are city cops. I can tell by the colours on the car."

"What does that mean? They could be working with Mallory too."

"Maybe," Henry said. "Or maybe they're just passing. They'll have a radio. We can call for help."

Fox nodded, but didn't look convinced.

"PULL OVER TO THE SIDE OF THE ROAD NOW," a cop's voice blared from a speaker set into the front of the pursuit vehicle.

"We can't outrun that car," Henry said.

"I hope you're right about them," Fox replied as he eased off the gas and brought the truck to a halt by the side of the road. Behind them, the patrol car stopped a good ten metres away.

"Just stay there," Henry said to Fox before opening his door and stepping out with his hands raised…

"FREEZE!" a lean, thin-faced cop screamed from the other car. He was halfway out of the passenger door and already had his automatic in his hands. "Police officer! Hold it right there or I will shoot!"

32

"**P**lease!" Henry called back to the cop. "We need help! We're being chased!"

The driver's door of the patrol car opened and another officer, much stockier than the first, emerged. He had a shotgun in his hands and crouched down, using the door as a shield.

Henry went on, "There's this crazy—"

"STOP TALKING AND LISTEN CAREFULLY!" the thin cop bellowed in a voice that made Henry shut up immediately. "Get on your knees and place your hands on your head. Do it now!"

Henry did as he was told. As he kneeled down, he glanced at Fox through the open door. Although she looked as terrified as he felt, she still managed to roll her eyes at him as if to say *told you so*.

"Who else is in your vehicle?" the cop yelled, keeping his gun trained on Henry, even though he was kneeling as instructed.

"My friend," Henry said.

"Tell her to put her hands on the dash and keep still," the cop ordered.

"Keep still," Henry said to Fox.

"Yeah, I heard," she replied, placing her hands where the cop could see them.

Satisfied that they were complying, the thin cop said something to his partner and then started walking towards the pickup, all the while keeping his gun trained on Henry. As he approached, Henry saw that he was indeed a city cop – dressed in a different uniform to the brown Newton County trousers and shirt that Trooper Dan wore. A gold name tag on his chest read *Myers*. He gave the pickup a wide berth as he approached, looking into the front at Fox before turning his attention to Henry.

"Do you know you've got an axe sticking out of your vehicle?" he asked.

"Uh, yes sir," Henry replied. "I do."

"How old are you two?"

"Fourteen."

"Little young to be driving, don't you think?" Rather than waiting for a response, the cop asked, "What's that on your shirt?"

Henry looked down at the front of his T-shirt and saw the flecks of blood all over it from Trooper Dan's hand, drying to a dark red now. He winced as he said, "It's blood."

"Your blood?"

"No, sir."

"Her blood?" Officer Myers asked, nodding at Fox.

"No, sir," Henry replied. "It was this cop..."

"*A cop?*"

Henry shot a desperate glance at Fox, who shook her head slightly.

"He's crazy," Henry went on. "His name's Trooper Dan, but he's insane. We were in his house…"

"You were in the cop's house?"

"Yeah…"

"Breaking and entering?"

"No…we…"

"How'd you get his blood on you?"

"He…" Henry swallowed heavily. "He got shot. But it isn't what you're thinking…"

Officer Myers moved fast, grabbing a pair of handcuffs from his belt and moving behind Henry. "Don't you move a muscle," he ordered Fox as he snapped the cuffs over Henry's left wrist, pulled his arm down his back and then cuffed his right wrist to it.

"You've got this all wrong!" Henry protested. "We're in danger!"

Myers grabbed his arm and hauled him to his feet. "In danger? Well, don't worry, kid. We're gonna lock you up in the back of our patrol car where you'll be real safe. Your girlfriend too." He turned to Fox. "Get out of the truck nice and slow. Then start walking towards my partner with your hands high as you can. Got it?"

Fox nodded. She opened her door and began walking as she'd been instructed. Myers started leading Henry in the same direction, keeping a few paces behind Fox.

"What's your name, kid?" asked Myers, who seemed a whole lot more relaxed now his prisoner had the cuffs on.

Henry told him his name. "Well, you've got some explaining to do, Henry."

"I'm trying to explain!" he protested. This wasn't going at all as he'd hoped. It looked like the cops were going to put them in the car and drive them right back to Newton and into the waiting arms of John Mallory. And who would they listen to then? The kid with blood all over his T-shirt or the billionaire businessman? He could almost imagine Mallory's words...

They're runaways, officer... Problems with drugs... Delusional... Yes, we'll take very good care of them from now on...

"Please, you at least have to make a call on your radio," said Henry, knowing he was running out of chances to convince them.

"You'll get to make your call at the station," Myers said. Fox was now standing with her hands on the hood of the patrol car. Henry met her eyes and gave an exasperated look.

"Great," she said. "Take us to the city..."

"We're taking you to the nearest sheriff's office," Myers said. "Which I'm thinking would be the Newton County department."

"No!" Henry said. "Not Newton! Trooper Dan's in charge there!"

"Who's Trooper Dan?" the other cop asked, speaking for the first time.

"The insane cop!" Fox persisted. "You have to listen to what we're..."

Her voice trailed away at the sound of another vehicle. They all looked round and saw the blinding headlights of a sandy-coloured police cruiser appear a few hundred metres down the road. It stopped, as if the driver was deciding whether to approach or not.

"That's him!" Henry said. "That's Trooper Dan!"

Myers opened the back door and bundled Henry inside. "Sit in there and stay quiet if you know what's good for you."

Henry twisted round to protest – it was difficult trying to sit down with his hands cuffed behind his back – but Myers simply slammed the door in his face. On the other side of the car the second cop opened the back door and, taking Fox's arm, pushed her inside.

"I ain't gonna cuff you," he said more softly. His name badge said *Clifton*. "But if you cause any trouble, I will. Just sit tight and it'll all be okay."

Fox began, "But…"

"Leave this to the professionals, huh?" He slammed the door.

Fox turned to Henry. "We have to get out of here!"

"I know," Henry said, looking around the inside of the car. There was no handle on his door – it could only be opened from the outside. And with the cuffs on, he wouldn't be getting very far anyway. He looked through the back window. Trooper Dan's cruiser had started moving again. It rolled to a halt ten metres down the road. The driver's door swung open and the huge cop unfolded himself from inside. Although it was the middle of the night, he was wearing his mirror shades to hide his crazy eyes and had a jacket zipped over his bloodstained shirt.

"Oh, my god," Fox whispered as they watched the trooper greet Myers with a smile and a wave of his good hand. He approached the patrol car and as he came closer, they saw that his left hand was now covered in a fresh, white bandage. The driver's door of the patrol car was open beside the cop called Clifton, so they could hear the exchange between the trooper and Myers.

"Howdy," Trooper Dan said. "You boys are kinda outside your jurisdiction, ain't ya?" His voice was suddenly like a country hick – not too smart, but very friendly.

"You can say that again," Myers said with a laugh. "Our sergeant sent us up here on a wild goose chase. Some reporter went missing. Guy called Stuart Richardson. Ever heard of him?"

"Can't say I have," Trooper Dan said coolly.

"Turns out he's the mayor's nephew, so the whole world has to stop. Sent us over here in the middle of the night to check out the GPS on his iPhone. Dumb idiot probably got lost in the woods up here."

Through the window, Henry watched Trooper Dan grin and shake his head like he felt Officer Myers's pain. It was a great act. And, as before, if his damaged hand was giving him any pain now, he was expert at hiding it.

"We tried calling the Newton sheriff's office, in fact," Myers went on. "There was no answer."

Trooper Dan shrugged. "I'm pretty busy."

"We've been trying to call for two days," Myers said.

Suddenly there was an edge to his voice.

"Hmmm," Trooper Dan said. "I'm sorry, I didn't get you boys' names."

Myers introduced himself and Clifton and rattled off the name of their precinct in the city. But Trooper Dan wasn't really listening. Instead he started looking directly at the back of the patrol car, checking out Henry and Fox in the back. When Myers finished, rather than offering his own details, Trooper Dan just stared at his prey.

"Have you hurt yourself?" Myers asked.

"Huh?" the trooper said, as if he'd been disturbed from a trance.

"Your hand. That looks nasty."

Trooper Dan held up his bandage as if he'd forgotten it was there. "This? It's nothing."

"What happened?"

"Looks like I owe you city boys a drink," Trooper Dan said, ignoring the question. "You've picked up a couple of runaways I've been huntin' all over these woods."

Myers glanced back at the patrol car. "Runaways? You know one of them is covered in blood?"

Trooper Dan looked at him. "Blood?" He shook his head. "God knows what kids get up to these days..."

As the trooper continued to spin the standard yarn about runaway kids and drugs, Fox let out a little gasp, as if remembering something.

"What is it?" Henry asked.

"I found this in the house!" she said, pulling Richardson's wallet from her jeans. "It belonged to that reporter!"

She leaned over the passenger seat and waved it to get Clifton's attention.

"I thought I told you to…" Officer Clifton's voice trailed away as he took the wallet from her and opened it. Stuart Richardson's ID cards were plain to see. "Where'd you find this?" he asked.

"In that cop's house," Fox said.

"Hey, Sam!" Officer Myers called out to Clifton. "Looks like those two belong to the trooper here. Want to get them out and put them in the back of his cruiser?"

Clifton was silent for a moment. Henry and Fox looked back again to where Trooper Dan was standing, still glaring at them from behind his mirror shades.

"Perhaps we should call this one in first," Officer Clifton said, tossing the wallet on the dash of the patrol car and shifting the shotgun in his hand.

"You sure?" Myers asked, and once again Henry sensed a silent understanding passing between the two cops.

"Yeah…I'm sure," Clifton replied. He climbed back behind the wheel and snatched up the radio mic from the dash. "This is patrol fifty-one calling mobile dispatch, come in…" All that came back was static.

"Please, you have to un-cuff me," Henry said, leaning forward. "You don't know what Trooper Dan's capable of..."

"Just sit tight," Clifton said. "We'll deal with this." He spoke into the mic again and got nothing back.

Outside the car, Trooper Dan was getting impatient. "What you got to call this in for? Those kids are my problem, not yours."

Myers looked at him apologetically. "Procedure. My partner's a real stickler for procedure. You know, sometimes I think he wouldn't take a leak without filling in a form."

"I know the type," Trooper Dan said with a sympathetic shake of the head. "Let me tell you what I think of procedure…"

He pulled a gun and calmly shot Officer Myers in the head.

In the back of the patrol car, Henry and Fox recoiled in shock as the sound of the gunshot reverberated across the road. Officer Myers seemed to fall in slow motion, pitching to one side, his skull practically obliterated by the force of the bullet at close range. Trooper Dan's spare gun was an automatic that was much smaller than the Magnum but no less lethal. As Myers hit the ground, Trooper Dan turned towards the patrol car and fired.

The back window exploded. Henry and Fox ducked down as Officer Clifton, breathing fast and with beads of sweat pricking his forehead, leaned in to the front seat. A second bullet ripped through the vehicle, punching a hole in the windshield.

"Get us out of here!" Henry yelled. But instead of driving the car, Clifton leaped out with a shotgun in his arms. He fired twice in quick succession, but his hand was shaking and the bullets flew way off target. He kept on moving to the cover of a ditch on the other side of the road. Trooper Dan fired after him.

In the back, Henry and Fox exchanged panicked glances.

"What do we do?" Fox asked above the noise of another round of gunfire.

Between the front seats Henry could see the key chain dangling in the ignition. Attached to it were a couple of smaller keys – undoubtedly for the cuffs.

"Get those keys," Henry said. "At least I can slip these off my wrists."

Keeping as low as possible, Fox reached through to the front and grabbed the keys from the ignition. As she got them, Henry stole a look through the back. Trooper Dan had retreated to the cover of his cruiser and was slotting a fresh clip into the automatic. Meanwhile, Officer Clifton fired his shotgun more steadily now, hitting the front of the cruiser, but missing his target.

"Here," Fox said, fitting the small keys into the cuffs. Henry almost laughed with relief as they sprang open. He turned round and grabbed the keys from her.

"Let's get out of here," he said, squeezing through the gap between the front seats. He fitted the keys into the ignition and put his foot on the gas. The engine turned over easily, not like the truck. Through the open driver's door he saw Officer Clifton crouched in the ditch across the road.

"Get over here!" Henry called out to the cop.

"Stay where you are!" Clifton called back. "Do not move!"

Henry shook his head. "He's going to kill you!"

Clifton rose from the ditch and fired the shotgun at the cruiser once more. "I said—"

A bullet from Trooper Dan's gun hit Clifton in the throat

and he staggered back into the ditch, out of sight.

"Just go!" Fox cried from the back.

Henry floored the gas and the patrol car roared away so fast the driver's door slammed shut. Easing himself into the seat behind the wheel, Henry struggled to keep control as Trooper Dan fired after them down the road. At least one bullet hit, shattering a side window.

"Are you okay?" he asked Fox as they sped out of range of the gun. "Are you hit?"

"I'm fine," Fox said, crawling over the passenger seat into the front. "Can you drive?"

"Just about," Henry replied. "Is he following us?"

Fox looked through the open back window. "Not yet… No, wait… Here he comes!"

Henry checked out the passenger mirror. Sure enough, Trooper Dan's cruiser was approaching at high speed.

"Try to outrun him!" Fox exclaimed. "Put your foot down!"

Henry gritted his teeth as they flew around a corner, almost going off the road and into the trees in the process. "I'm going as fast as I can without killing us!"

Henry could hear the roar of the pursuing car and didn't need to check the mirror to know it was right behind them. He suspected that Trooper Dan's vehicle had a few speed modifications that weren't strictly by the book. A second later the cruiser impacted the back of the patrol car. Henry just managed to hold it on the road.

"See if you can get anyone on that," he said to Fox, indicating the police radio.

She picked up the handset and started speaking into it, asking for any response. Henry checked his mirror, seeing the trooper coming again. This time he swerved to the side, avoiding most of the impact. One thing he didn't want was for Trooper Dan to pull alongside them where he could fire off a clear shot.

"I can't get anything on this!" Fox said. "Malcorp must be blocking the signal for miles!"

"Keep trying!"

Ahead, the road straightened out somewhat. On the left, the moonlight illuminated what appeared to be a quarry between the trees – a giant wound in the earth, evidence of the industry that had been in the area before Malcorp arrived...

Bullets ripped through the hood of the patrol car, almost causing Henry to brake in shock. For a second he thought it had been Trooper Dan, but then he realized that it couldn't have been. They'd been hit from the air. The helicopter! In his effort to concentrate on the road and their pursuer, Henry hadn't heard the whir of the blades. He looked up as the chopper passed overhead, coming round for another pass. One of the Malcorp security guards was hanging out of the back with the machine gun in his arms.

"Dammit!" Fox said. "This isn't fair!"

"I know," Henry said, coming to a sudden realization. They'd never escape both the trooper and the helicopter. It was time for drastic action...

He threw the wheel to the left, sending the patrol car down a wide dirt road that ended after a few metres with a large gate. He didn't slow for a second, smashing through the gate and carrying on in the direction of the quarry.

"What are you doing?" Fox demanded as they sped down the road, passing giant mounds of rock and sand that stood amid decaying buildings. The place was deserted. "This is a dead end!"

"I know," Henry replied, sending the car round one of the mounds and then weaving behind another. For a moment he lost sight of Trooper Dan in the mirror. The helicopter was still back over the road, no doubt waiting to see if they tried to double back. He looked at Fox.

"You need to jump out when I say," he said. "I'll try to slow as much as possible. Then you need to stay out of sight and get away."

Fox shook her head vehemently. "There is no way…"

"Listen!" Henry said. "They're going to catch us! This way one of us can get the story out there. Understand?"

Fox's face fell, but she nodded. "Henry…"

"No time!" he said, as he drove the patrol car behind another mound of sand. Trooper Dan had collided with a different mound and lost ground. He hit the brakes. "Jump out. Now!"

Fox didn't need telling twice. She pushed the door open and leaped out, hitting the ground moving and bending her knees so she rolled into a crouch. In his mirror, Henry watched her run for cover and find it as Trooper Dan's cruiser heaved into view.

"Okay," Henry said to himself. "Let's see how fast you can really go."

He put his foot to the floor. The engine of the patrol car screamed and it jumped forward at a startling pace. Passing out of the little mountain range of sand piles, Henry hit a relatively straight dirt track that took him between two of the larger buildings on the site. Beyond them he could see the edge of the quarry – a two-hundred-metre wide indentation in the ground.

Suddenly, Trooper Dan's cruiser smashed into the back of Henry's car. Henry was thrown against the wheel. Ahead, the edge of the quarry loomed closer. He tried to turn, but the steering had locked out. He hit the brake… But the cruiser slammed him again and stayed there, pushing him down the track…

The patrol car flew through a warning barrier and the road ran out a second later. Trooper Dan's vehicle came to a halt with a squeal of brakes. The patrol car carried on, unstoppable…

Over the edge and into space…

Half a kilometre back down the track, Fox staggered from the hiding place she'd found behind one of the sand mounds. From her elevated position she'd seen everything: the pursuit, the patrol car pushing the cruiser, and finally Henry's car sailing off into the quarry. An explosion lit up the night sky as the car hit the bottom, a hundred metres down. By the quarry, she saw Trooper Dan get out of his cruiser and walk to the edge to admire his handiwork.

"No," she cried. "Henry!"

She stood for a moment, lost. Henry was dead. Trooper Dan had killed him. Her first instinct was to run down the hill screaming…to attack the man who had murdered Henry…

But she had to escape. To tell the world. Save her mom and Henry's mom and the coach – if they were all still alive.

Somehow, she managed to get her legs working and started running between the hills of sand and rock, back in the direction they'd come. If Trooper Dan thought she'd died in the patrol car as well, then he'd call off the search.

She had a chance…

A howling wind rose, sending rock dust and sand flying. Fox shielded her face with her hand and tried to struggle forward, but the wind became a gale, forcing her back.

The helicopter rose over one of the mounds and began to descend before her. With the shock of seeing Henry slide into the quarry, she'd completely forgotten about it. Fox considered trying to run back in the other direction – but Trooper Dan was there. And the security guard leaning out at the back had his machine gun trained on her as the chopper landed. Defeated, she raised her hands in the air.

A slim-looking guy in a white lab coat emerged from the helicopter and ran over to her, grabbing her arm just as Trooper Dan's cruiser roared up and came to a stop before them. The giant cop emerged. Fox saw that his bandage, formerly white, was now soaked red with blood.

"Where d'you think you're taking her?" Trooper Dan

demanded, shouting above the noise of the helicopter blades. "She's mine! She owes me!" He held up his injured hand to prove his point.

The white-coat didn't let go of Fox's arm, but he did tense a little. "The boy's been neutralized. We're taking this one back for adjustment. We need to find out who else she talked to."

"What about me?" Trooper Dan yelled. "Take a look at my goddamned hand!"

"We'll fix you up. But first you need to clean up that mess you left back on the road. No more mistakes." The white-coat reached into his pocket and produced a bottle of pills that he tossed to the trooper. "These will keep you going until you can get back to Malcorp for treatment."

With that, the man started pulling Fox towards the chopper.

"Hey!" Trooper Dan called after them. "You boys can grow me another hand, can't you? Right?"

The white-coat merely pushed Fox into the back of the helicopter and climbed in after her. The machine rose swiftly into the air.

Fox pressed her head against the window in the back. She had a bird's-eye view of the burning wreck of the patrol car at the bottom of the quarry as they headed north, back to Newton... Back to Malcorp...

They'd failed... Henry's sacrifice had been for nothing.

33

For a moment when Fox awoke, she thought she was back in her attic bedroom above the coffee shop. Maybe it was the firmly pressed sheets of the bed she was lying in. Or the brightness of the room, which reminded her of the early morning sun that used to stream through the skylight.

It only took a second for the illusion to be shattered. She saw the bare white walls, steel door in the corner and observation window in one wall and realized that she was somewhere in Malcorp. The room smelled like a hospital but looked like a prison cell.

She rose to a sitting position and tried to swing her legs out of bed, but found they weren't obeying her commands. Leaning back against the pillow, her head spun.

The door clanged open and Fox tensed, although she knew she was in no position to do anything. Malcorp had her.

"Hello, my dear," John Mallory said with a smile as he appeared in the doorway. "So nice to finally meet you."

Fox watched without saying a word as he entered the room and sat on the end of the bed. Despite all her protests against Malcorp and research on the man, this was the first time they'd met in the flesh. He was taller and better built than she'd expected. And despite everything she knew about him, there was something strangely personable about his manner. The play-act of a ruthless man, she reminded herself.

Finally she said, "What have you done to me? I can't move my legs."

"Oh don't worry about that," Mallory said dismissively. "Just a temporary side effect of some pre-operation drugs we gave you."

A chill went through her at the word *pre-operation*.

"Okay then, what are you *going* to do to me?" she said, trying to keep her voice strong when she felt anything but.

Mallory smiled at her. "We're going to make everything better, Fox. And not just for you. For your mom as well."

"My mom's here?"

Mallory nodded. "Yes, and don't worry, we've been taking very good care of her."

"I want to see her."

He held up a hand. "All in good time. You know, she and I have been having some very interesting chats while you've been running around the countryside causing problems. She told me all about her condition. Multiple sclerosis is a terrible—"

"Don't you talk about her!" Fox cried. If she could, she would have leaped from the bed and pummelled Mallory's smug, grinning face with her fists.

"Calm down," he said. "I was merely going to say that

after the adjustment process, she's not going to have to worry about that any more."

Fox blinked twice at him. "What?"

"I'm sure you know that MS is caused by demyelination of the axons of the brain, affecting its ability to communicate with the spinal cord. Your mother's adjusted brain won't have that problem." He spread his hands like a magician performing a trick. "No more MS! Ever. She's going to be able to walk again, Fox. Now, isn't that good news?"

Fox had no answer. Tears welled in her eyes and she wiped them away.

"Don't you see?" Mallory said, leaning forward a little, eyes sparkling with passion. "We're trying to help here. Eradicating brain diseases, mental problems. Making the brain a more efficient application. All you're fighting is progress!"

"You really believe that, don't you?" Fox said.

Mallory nodded.

"But what about my mom *after* you give her a new brain?" Fox asked. "Who will she be?"

"Why, she'll be all better!"

"No, she won't. I don't think she'll be my mom at all."

Mallory snorted. "Nonsense! She'll be perfect in every way—"

"A perfect copy that you control," Fox snapped. "And what about Henry? Can you bring him back?"

Mallory looked down at the bed sheet. "I would have preferred it if he hadn't been killed, but he forced my hand. After he escaped Steve – my best soldier – I had no choice but to resort to Trooper Dan." He looked at Fox almost apologetically. "Dan was one of our first adjustments, you know. When we arrived in Newton, he had a somewhat different attitude to our plans. He was quite a vocal opponent of our operation here. He had a habit of sneaking around our facilities, looking for clues, just like you and your friends."

"So you *adjusted* him," Fox spat. "And now he's insane."

Mallory shrugged. "We've found that adjusting an adult brain leads to certain…instabilities. We think it's something to do with the maturity of the system. Our adolescent adjustments have been by far the most effective." He patted her on the knee through the covers. "But don't worry, we've come a long way since Dan. Your mom is going to turn out just fine, I'm sure."

He rose and walked back to the door.

"Please," Fox said, disgusted by the pleading tone in her voice. "Don't do this. We don't want this!"

Mallory looked back at her one last time. "People never want things that are good for them, do they?"

He closed the door.

The old man was dozing in his seat by the gas station window when the sound of the truck horn blared through the night. He woke with a start, eyes falling instinctively on the clock on the wall opposite. Almost 5 a.m. *Who was making such a commotion outside at such an hour?* He rose irritably from his chair, thinking that he might just refuse to serve them for disturbing his sleep…

The truck engine howled as its driver floored the gas.

The old man pressed his face to the glass just in time to see the vehicle, a twenty-tonne quarry truck, speeding down the road towards the pumps. At the very last second, the brakes squealed and the vehicle swerved, but not before it completely demolished the big board showing the gas prices out front.

"Goddammit!" the old man cursed, reaching for his shotgun from under the counter. Nobody smashed up his forecourt and got away with it…

The truck gears crunched and the engine whined as the vehicle went into reverse, backing round fast towards the shop. With a cry, the old man threw himself back. Somehow the driver managed to stop the truck before it flattened the building. Still, the back smashed into the window, shattering it. On the floor, the old man screamed as he scrabbled around for his fallen shotgun.

"YOU. INSIDE THE SHOP." A male voice from the cab blasted from a loudhailer set onto the side of the truck. The volume was turned up so loud, it sounded like the voice of god.

The old man got slowly to his feet, hands in the air. He didn't reach for the shotgun.

"CAN YOU HEAR ME?"

"Yes, I can hear you, dammit!" the old man yelled back. "I ain't deaf!"

"I NEED YOU TO DO SOMETHING FOR ME."

The old man stuck his chin out indignantly and yelled back, "You almost ran me over!"

The driver gunned the gas to show he still could if he wanted to.

"Okay, okay!" the old man yelled, waving his arms. "What do you want?"

"CALL THE FBI. TELL THEM TO GET TO THE MALCORP COMPLEX NEAR NEWTON. THERE'S A SITUATION."

"What kind of situation?"

There was a pause as the driver thought it over. "TELL THEM A TERRORIST SITUATION."

The old man snapped his fingers. He knew it! "Terrorist situation? Sounds like you need Homeland Security more than the FBI."

"JUST CALL THE FBI."

"Or the CIA—"

"JUST CALL THE FBI."

"What number?"

There was another pause. "DO YOU HAVE THE INTERNET? GOOGLE THEIR CONTACT NUMBER."

"The what...and do what?"

A sigh echoed through the loudhailer. "JUST CALL THE OPERATOR AND SAY YOU HAVE A TERRORIST SITUATION ON YOUR HANDS."

"Who are they?" the old man asked. "I saw some guys with beards pass through here just a couple of days ago..."

"JUST DO IT."

The engine roared and the truck pulled away from the

gas station, headed in the direction of Newton. Still stunned, the old man snatched up his shotgun and ran to the telephone behind the counter. With a trembling hand, he picked up the receiver and dialled the operator.

"Alright, alright," he said as a woman answered. "Shut up and listen. I've got a goddamned terrorist situation on my hands here…"

Time passed in the windowless room. Whether it was minutes or hours, Fox found it impossible to say. Her head was still fuzzy and for a while she fell into a kind of doze, all the while willing herself to get out of bed, to try for some kind of escape plan… But she was just too exhausted.

Finally, the door opened again and a male nurse entered with a wheelchair. He threw back the sheets, lifted Fox out of the bed and placed her in the chair. She tried to struggle, but the nurse was too strong. He informed her coldly that if she caused any trouble he'd give her another injection of sedative. She played it cool after that – the last thing she wanted was to be knocked out again.

The nurse wheeled her down long corridors that gave the impression they were in some kind of underground facility. Finally they came to a door marked *Pre-Op Lounge*.

"Mom!" Fox exclaimed as the nurse pushed her through.

Her mother was sitting half asleep in a similar wheelchair on the other side of the waiting room, which was empty except for a couple of sofas and a television in the corner. As the nurse closed and locked the door behind her, Fox struggled from her chair and walked across the room, feeling shaky on her legs.

"Thank god you're alive!" Mary Layton said as she threw her arms around her daughter.

"I'm sorry, Mom," Fox whispered. "We couldn't get away."

"It's okay. We'll find a way out of this. And don't think for a second I'm going along with anything that crackpot Mallory told me. I've just been playing for time."

Fox smiled with relief at her mom's words, though she found it hard to share her confidence. She turned her attention to the other side of the room, where the coach was lying on a sofa in a semi-doze. His broken arm was in a sling. Beside him sat a younger, smart-looking woman. Fox could tell instantly from her face that she was Henry's mother.

"My name's Fox," she said. "I'm a friend of Henry's..." The name caught in her throat, but she forced herself to go on. Henry might be dead, but he'd want her to make sure his mom was okay. And to get them all out of Malcorp if she could. "Are you alright? How did you end up in here?"

"I'm fine." Jennifer Ward frowned. "I was supposed to stay a few days in the city. Mallory said it was an emergency, but when I got to the Chicago lab there didn't seem to be a problem... That seemed a bit odd and I was worried about leaving Henry alone after everything that had happened anyway, so I rented a car and drove back here." Henry's mom went silent for a moment, rubbing her tired eyes.

"And when you got back...?" Fox prompted.

"I was stopped by security guards. I couldn't believe it – they pulled out some kind of stun gun and...shot me!" She looked around agitatedly. "John Mallory is behind this! Henry tried to warn me and I didn't listen."

Fox placed a hand on her arm. "Take it easy."

"Where is Henry?" Jennifer asked, sitting forward slightly.

Fox struggled to find words. Finally, she just shook her head. "He died saving me," she said. "He was a hero."

The woman looked at her blankly. "Henry's not dead."

Fox looked down. "I'm sorry but I saw…"

"It's okay," Jennifer Ward said. "I know he's not dead. I can feel it."

Fox looked at her mom, who gave the barest shake of her head. Jennifer was clearly in shock.

"We have to get out of here somehow," Fox said. "Mallory is crazy."

Her mom nodded and looked across to the other woman. "Are you okay?"

Jennifer Ward's eyes snapped into focus at the sound of her voice. She'd been lost in her thoughts. "Huh?"

"Jennifer, we need to get out of here. Can you help us?"

For a moment Fox thought Henry's mom was merely going to look away again, but then the same kind of resolve came over her that Fox had seen in Henry's face before. "Yes. We're going to get out of here and find Henry. And then Mallory is going to pay."

Fox met her eyes and nodded. She began hesitantly to walk back across the room, trying to get her focus and strength back. Jennifer Ward joined her, looking equally unsteady on her feet, as they began looking for a way out.

34

Hank the security guard checked his watch and yawned. It was almost 5.30 a.m. and just getting light outside. No one had passed through the main gates of the Malcorp complex in hours and a memo had been circulated that Henry Ward, who had previously been flagged as a security risk, had been *neutralized*. Whatever that meant. He flipped the lid on the Dunkin' Donuts box that sat on the bench in his cubicle and sighed. He'd finished the last of them earlier that afternoon and now his stomach was rumbling. There was still a good two-and-a-half hours until the end of his shift and the cooked chicken that was waiting for him in the fridge of his lodge. There was only one thing for it.

He reached into the desk drawer, pulled out his iPod and thumbed on down to the hypnosis album he'd downloaded the week before – the one that was supposed to take his mind off food and make him feel good about taking positive action in his life. Taking a quick look around to make sure that no one was watching, he flicked off the camera from the manual control on the wall outside. Sure enough, less than ten seconds later, he got a call on the desk phone from central security.

"We've lost the feed from the gate camera," said Higgins, his shift commander.

"Uh, yeah," Hank replied, sounding surprised. "The light's off on the side. Must be on the fritz again."

"Dammit," Higgins said.

Smiling, but not sounding like he was, Hank said, "You gonna send someone down to check it out?"

"No. It will have to wait until the repair crew comes on duty in the morning. Can you manage?"

"Hey, I'm a professional."

"*Can you manage?*"

"Yes, sir."

The line clicked dead. With a satisfied chuckle, Hank put his feet up on the desk and his headphones in his ears. He pressed play and the soothing voice of hypnotherapist Benjamin P. Bonetti warned him not to drive or operate heavy machinery while he was listening. *No intention whatsoever*, Hank thought, closing his eyes. Except there was an annoying buzzing sound in the background. He opened one eye in time to see the cab of a truck the size of a small house flying towards the cubicle…

With a cry, Hank threw himself through the door, moving faster than he had in years. As he hit the grass, the truck ploughed through the cubicle and smashed into the security wall, shattering its windows. The reinforced wall hardly registered the impact, but the front of the vehicle crumpled like paper. For a moment the engine whined and the wheels spun on the grass, churning the dirt into the air. Then the driver cut the engine and the door of the cab swung open.

On the ground, Hank fumbled at his belt for the taser that was clipped there. One of the headphones was still in his ear and the hypnotist was still speaking...*you might find yourself feeling very relaxed while you're listening to my words...*

Now the driver jumped down from the cab and landed deftly on the grass amid the shattered remains of the cubicle. He had a shovel in his hands.

...it's like dreaming, but you'll remain fully aware...

Hank gave a little cry as the taser refused to come free from his belt.

...and not lose consciousness...

"Hiya, Hank," a voice said, as the head of the shovel swung towards his skull. There was a *clunk*. Then nothing...

"Wake up!" A hand slapped Hank hard across the face. He groaned and reached for his alarm clock on the bedside table.

"I'm awake, I'm awake!" Hank protested as he fumbled for the snooze button. For some reason his hand found only grass...

Then he remembered.

Eyes snapping open, he sat up abruptly and immediately regretted it as pain shot through his skull from where the shovel had hit him. He looked up at the hulking wreck of the truck, making out the lettering on the side for the first time: *Henderson Quarry*.

"Take it easy, Hank," a male voice said. "You were hit over the head."

"Yeah," Hank muttered, reaching for his belt, "by you! You son of a..." He stopped talking as his fingers brushed the empty holster where the taser was supposed to be.

"Looking for this?"

His attacker held up the squat, plastic weapon so he could see it. Hank focused his vision and recognized the kid: Henry Ward.

"Henry!" he said, getting up as quickly as possible. "But...I thought you were supposed to be dead or something."

Henry pointed the taser at him so that the little red laser target flicked over his face. Hank shielded his eyes and almost fell on his ass again.

"Easy, man!" he protested. "You can blind someone doing that!"

"Make any sudden moves and I'll tase you in the face," said Henry, his voice hard and full of business.

"Why'd you want to do that, man?" asked Hank, aggrieved. He'd always been nice to the kid – and his good-looking mom. "You can kill someone like that!"

"Because you work for some bad people, Hank," Henry replied, keeping the taser aimed at his forehead. "And they've done some bad things."

"Hey! That's not me! I'm just an employee!"

Henry gave him a disappointed look. "I don't think that defence is going to hold up in court, do you?"

Hank shook his head slowly.

"But it might look better if you could say you helped out one of the good guys."

Hank frowned, thinking this over. "What do you want?"

Henry nodded at the gates to the Malcorp complex. "Help me get inside."

"Uh…Mr. Mallory gave very specific orders that no unauthorized persons—"

Henry jerked the taser at Hank's face to shut him up. "Screw Mallory! Now get the gate open!"

Hank shook his head as he reached for the remote on his belt. "You're making a tactical error, dude. They've got cameras watching this entrance."

Henry actually laughed. "Looks like those cameras are turned off, Hank. Who do you think did that?"

The security guard's shoulders slumped a little as he pressed the button on the remote. The gate slid open and Henry poked him in the back to get him moving. "You're coming with me."

Hank did as he was told, closing the gate behind them. "If anyone comes by here," he said, "don't you think they're gonna notice the big truck halfway through the security fence? You'll have every guard in the complex down on you in five minutes."

"Then we'd better be fast," Henry said, pushing Hank towards the wall to the east.

Hank glanced over his shoulder at him. "Where are we going?"

"The nearest security substation," Henry replied.

"How d'you know about them?"

Henry poked him with the taser. "Just keep moving, big man."

Trooper Dan sat in the leather chair with his eyes closed, listening to the soft strains of "The Star-Spangled Banner" as it echoed around the chamber.

"You're feeling no pain," the voice of one of the doctors floated across to him through speakers concealed in the curved walls of the adjustment chamber. "No pain at all. In fact, you're feeling strong. Stronger than you ever have."

Trooper Dan shifted in the seat and opened his eyes. He looked at the subtly changing tones of the colours on the walls. In some areas they were projecting images of trees and fields, no doubt intended to make him feel more relaxed, not that it had much effect. He was feeling tense and frustrated, although the pain from his damaged left hand had subsided to a dull ache under the suggestive words of the doctors (and the drugs they'd pumped into him).

He looked down the length of his left arm. All that remained of his hand was the thumb and lower part of the palm – the rest had been obliterated with the blast from the shotgun. The doctors at the medical centre had been to work, cleaning the wound and stitching it up properly. Then they'd attached a temporary prosthesis – a set of metallic digits that looked like the talons of some kind of bird of prey. Dr. Chancellor had promised the trooper they would be able to link the motor controls in the metal hand to his brain, so he would have control while they grew him a new hand from stem cells (which could take up to a month, they told him). Until then, the claw was just a lump of dead metal clamped to his wounded hand. He turned it over thoughtfully, looking at his reflection in its shiny surface. Even though he couldn't move the digits yet, he sort of liked it.

"Your body will heal at an enhanced rate," the voice ordered through the speakers. "Your mind will divert all its energy towards healing your damaged hand and accepting the neural implants for your new prosthesis."

Trooper Dan closed his eyes and tried to empty his mind, just like the doc had asked – it made the process easier for them, apparently. But there was something bothering him… Something about seeing that kid sailing over the edge of the quarry in the stolen police car. The memory should give him pleasure, he realized, but for some reason it didn't. Something was wrong…

Was the kid definitely in the car when it went over?

He'd seen the vehicle explode at the bottom of the pit, but could he have jumped free at the last minute? Clung on to the side of the quarry, out of sight? In all the panic of cleaning the dead cops off the road and the increasing pain from his hand, he hadn't taken the time to go back and check the wreckage. A bad feeling started in Trooper Dan's gut – the same bad feeling he always had when he'd done something wrong, like when he was a kid and his pa used to lock him in the basement for getting into trouble.

He was suddenly certain of it: that Henry Ward kid wasn't dead. And if the kid wasn't dead, then he'd be coming back to rescue his friend.

The girl.

The girl who had shot him.

Eyes snapping open, Trooper Dan leaped from the chair and strode across the chamber to the part of the wall where he knew there was a concealed door. Before he even had to bang his good fist on the wall to be let out, the door opened and one of Dr. Chancellor's lackeys stuck his head inside the chamber.

"You're not supposed to be out of your seat, officer," said the white-coated man, his voice several octaves too high. It seemed that everyone in the medical centre was terrified of him. "Dr. Chancellor says you have another fifteen minutes of brain readjustment therapy…"

"Get out of my way," Trooper Dan snarled, pushing past him into the corridor. He glanced left and right – everywhere in the underground facility looked the same to him. "Where are you holding her?"

"Holding who?" the lackey replied.

"The girl who shot me."

"Dr. Chancellor says—"

Trooper Dan grabbed the lackey by the shoulder with his good hand and brought the claw up to his face.

"Sub level two!" the lackey gasped, wide eyes locked on the claw. "Take a left then the emergency stairwell up two levels."

"Thanks."

Grinning to himself, Trooper Dan released the lackey and strode off down the corridor. Using his claw to push open the double doors at the end, he thought about the girl who had shot him.

He just couldn't wait for her to see his new hand.

35

Hank placed his hand on the scanner outside the entrance to substation nine – a discreet box located amid a little grove of trees. As it scanned his fingerprints, the security guard glanced round at Henry, who was standing just a metre away with the taser trained on his back. He wondered if he just threw himself at the kid…

"Don't even think about being a hero, Hank," Henry said, raising the taser so it was pointed at his head again.

"Uh-huh," Hank said, as the magnetic locks clicked and the door swung open, revealing a flight of descending concrete steps. He started down, and Henry followed closely behind. After about twenty steps, they reached another door, which opened into a small room with a console and a bank of monitors. There were two leather chairs, but the place was empty.

"Take a seat," Henry said and the guard did as he was told.

"They've probably found that truck by now," Hank said as Henry found the *on* button for the console. The monitors sprang into life, showing a computer desktop on one and multiple views of the security cameras on the others.

"Doesn't look like it," Henry said, indicating the camera views. The complex was as quiet as the grave. "What exactly is the point of this place? The substation, I mean."

"It's a fail-safe in case the complex is ever attacked," Hank said, trying to remember the induction talk they'd given him when he'd landed the job six months before. "If the main command and control is knocked out, security operatives can access some systems from the substations."

Henry sat on the edge of the console and gave Hank a hard stare. "Who were they expecting to attack the complex?"

Hank struggled to remember. "Uh…they said something about the FBI. Hmmm. Does sound kinda suspicious, now I come to think of it."

Henry actually laughed. "How did you get this job, Hank?"

The security guard reddened. "My uncle works in personnel."

Pushing himself off the console, Henry turned his attention to the monitors, grabbing the mouse and scrolling through programs on the desktop. He quickly found access to a second screen of security cameras, which seemed to be located within the medical centre, and stifled a gasp of relief. One of the screens showed a view of a room in which Fox and his mom were standing. He also made out the coach and Mary Layton. They were alive! And judging by the way Fox was searching around the room, they had yet to be adjusted.

"Hey!" Hank said, pointing to another view. "It's that terminator guy!"

Henry switched to the other screen. Trooper Dan was striding along a corridor, an insane look of determination on his face – as if he were about to kill someone. He also appeared to have some kind of a metal claw for a hand.

Hank shook his head. "I practically pee myself every time he comes through the front gate. He is one scary son of a bitch."

"We need to access the broadcast system," Henry interrupted. The fact that Trooper Dan was loose in the same building as his mom and Fox meant there was no time to waste. He had to do something drastic.

Hank shook his head and folded his arms. "You do what you like, kid, but it's more than my job is worth…"

Henry grabbed the arms of his chair and pushed it back against the wall so hard Hank almost pitched out the side. "Listen to me, you idiot!" Henry said, waving the taser in his face again. "You work for the bad guys! You're just too stupid to have figured it out! But when the FBI gets here—"

"The FBI is coming?"

"*Yes they are*, and when they get here they're gonna want to *shoot* the bad guys. And that's *you*, Hank."

"But I'm not a bad guy!"

"You could have fooled me."

Hank sat in silence for a moment, glaring at Henry. Then he sat forward abruptly and took the mouse, scrolling to an application called *Emergency Broadcast Portal*. As he logged in, Henry lowered the taser and patted him on the shoulder.

"You're doing a good thing, Hank."

"Just tell that to the FBI when they get here," the guard said. "What now?"

Henry leaned in and looked at the options on the screen and pointed to one labelled *Star-Spangled Banner*. "Bring that up."

"Not many Americans appreciate a good smoke these days," General Aziz said, leaning back on the sofa in Mallory's residence and taking a slow puff on his cigar. The glass coffee table Henry had destroyed had been replaced with an identical model. Aziz now had one of his highly polished black shoes resting on the glass, much to John Mallory's displeasure. Mallory had been up all night dealing with the situation created by Henry and Fox and, of all his "guests", Aziz had proven impossible to get rid of. The general seemed quite content to hang around in the midst of the crisis. In fact, he seemed to be enjoying it.

Rather than revealing his annoyance at being unable to shake the man, Mallory reached over to tap the end of his cigar into the ashtray resting in the middle of the table. "Well, I'm not your average American."

"And I am not your average customer," Aziz said, looking around the interior of the house. The lights were dimmed and soft music played in the background, piped in through hidden speakers. "That's a nice piece of music. What is it?"

"Bach."

"And infused with a hypnotic suggestion designed to make me more agreeable to purchasing your product, no doubt," Aziz said, giving him a wide smile. "I'm trained to be above such crude methods. I'm not one of your teenagers, Mr. Mallory."

The head of Malcorp nodded and looked towards the kitchen, where Blake and Gabrielle were standing stiffly to attention, at the ready in case they were called upon. The girl was showing no signs of resistance to the adjustment now, but Mallory wanted to keep an eye on her all the same. There had been enough mistakes in the last twenty-four hours. "Cut the music, Blake," he ordered and his grandson disappeared into the kitchen area. A second later, the music stopped.

"I shouldn't have underestimated you, General," Mallory said.

"I thought you might have worked that out when I didn't run away like your other prospective buyers following the incident in the lab and the trouble overnight…"

Mallory held up a hand. "That was a mere glitch, which is now fully under control. It was good of you to stay through all that…commotion."

"Please, Mr. Mallory. There's no need to thank me. I know that every organization has its enemies – terrorist insurgents seeking to destabilize progress. Look at my own country. My uncle's government is hanging on by a thread! A democratically elected leader!"

Mallory smiled thinly. "Your uncle got ninety-eight per cent of the vote in the last election, didn't he?"

Aziz threw up his hands. "It was a landslide! But still they're not happy. That's why we need your technology." He clenched his fist and slammed it into the palm of his other hand. "Stability is the key."

Mallory nodded. "That I can give you, General."

Aziz looked round at the kitchen. Blake had now joined Gabrielle and both were staring blankly ahead. "Very impressive indeed. Tell me. Do they really do everything you order, Mr. Mallory? Or rather, *anything* you order?"

The head of Malcorp sat forward on the other side of the table and said, "I think you'll find there's very little..."

The sound of music from outside the building stopped him short. The familiar, distorted strains of "The Star-Spangled Banner" began drifting across the complex from the emergency speaker system. There was a crackle as the volume on the complex-wide speaker system was cranked up to the loudest possible level.

"What the hell?" Mallory said, standing up and looking at the window, which showed only the century pool. Beyond, the complex was cloaked in early-morning mist. "They're playing that way too loud!"

General Aziz chuckled and leaned back on his sofa. "Another demonstration, Mr. Mallory?"

"Uh, yeah. I think..."

The speakers crackled again and a voice began to speak over the slowed-down anthem. *"This is Henry Ward,"* the voice said, *"and this is a message for kids of Malcorp High.*

You have been lied to. Your parents have been manipulated by John Mallory and Malcorp. They are trying to control you, but I'm here to tell you that you can take back the freedom that has been stolen from you…"

"He's messing with the theta wave," Mallory said to himself. He snatched the communicator from his jacket, looking round at Gabrielle and Blake as he did so. They had not moved. If they were hearing Ward's orders, they didn't show it.

"Alpha team to my house now!" Mallory snapped into the communicator. "Lock down the complex!"

Aziz sat up, interested now as Henry continued to speak.

"Malcorp is not your friend," he said. *"You owe it no loyalty. The Malcorp complex needs to be destroyed. Destroy all Malcorp property. Tear it down. If Malcorp security forces try to stop you…you have the training to fight back and defeat them. I also say to any Malcorp employees, do not attempt to stop me or any other free citizens from doing what we want within this complex or Newton. If you are holding members of our families, set them free immediately and you will not be hurt. The FBI has been notified and agents are en route to this location. The best thing you can do now is to give yourselves up. That is all."*

Just as the message came to an end, the anthem began all over again. Henry's words were on a loop, repeating every few minutes, to make sure no one could escape them. Blake raised a hand to his forehead and closed his eyes.

"Malcorp," he whispered.

Mallory grabbed an Initiator from his jacket and held it at the ready.

"What is going on here, Mr. Mallory?" Aziz asked, rising to his feet. "The FBI?"

"A bluff!" Mallory exclaimed, taking a tentative step towards the kitchen, where Blake and Gabrielle were standing.

"Are they going to attack us?" the general asked, moving to Mallory's side.

The head of Malcorp snapped his fingers at Blake. "Who do you serve?"

"I am loyal to Malcorp and yourself, sir," he replied snappily.

Mallory laughed and shook his head. "Crazy kid thought he could subvert months of programming with one message." But the message was still repeating all over the complex. He looked round at Aziz as the security detail he had ordered buzzed the front door. "Take a seat, General. I have a troublesome young man to deal with."

"What about these two?" the general said, eyeing Blake and Gabrielle a little nervously. "I need protection."

Mallory sighed and tossed him the Initiator. "Take my spare if it will make you feel better."

Aziz nodded and weighed the switch in his hand. "It does," he said, walking back towards the sofa. "Now go and deal with your problem quickly, so we can get on with our business."

With a final glance at the two teenagers, Mallory hurried down through the house to the main entrance and the waiting guards.

Rather than sitting down, Aziz walked over to where

Blake and Gabrielle stood. With a quick check to see that Mallory had gone, he turned his attention to Blake.

"Put out your hand," he ordered.

Blake raised his right hand, palm up. Aziz took a final puff on his cigar, before dropping it, lighted end first, into the boy's palm. Blake didn't even blink.

"Get rid of that for me, huh? And fix coffee while you're at it."

As Blake turned and walked through to the kitchen, General Aziz moved so he was standing directly in front of Gabrielle. He reached up and stroked a finger through her hair.

"You know, I'm a very important person to Mr. Mallory," he said quietly. "You could say that I'm part of the whole Malcorp family. So you can take orders from me, just like you would from him."

Gabrielle's fixed expression shifted, coming to focus on the general. "You are part of Malcorp."

"That's right," Aziz said with a smile.

"Just like Mr. Mallory."

Aziz nodded. "Just like Mr. Mallory. You should be nice to me."

Gabrielle reached up and closed her hand around General Aziz's. There was a sickening crunch as she jerked her arm back, breaking every finger on the man's hand just above the knuckle. Aziz let out a howl of agony and sunk to his knees before her, looking in disbelief at his mangled digits. The Initiator dropped from his other hand and skidded across the floor. Gabrielle seemed to look right through him.

"Malcorp is the enemy," she said, turning to Blake, who was watching her from the kitchen without expression. "It must be destroyed."

A momentary look of confusion passed across the boy's face, but as Henry's message echoed through the house, he nodded and reached for one of the kitchen drawers.

"Please," General Aziz spluttered, gripping his right wrist tightly in his left hand. He started shuffling across the floor towards the fallen Initiator. "D-don't."

Gabrielle didn't move, but there was a clatter from the kitchen. General Aziz watched, wide-eyed, as Blake reappeared with a mallet-like meat tenderizer in his hand.

"No!" Aziz exclaimed as the boy approached. "You can't do this!"

Hesitating, Blake looked at Gabrielle with a question in his eyes.

She said one word. "Malcorp."

General Aziz let out a final cry as Blake stepped forward with the meat tenderizer raised…

36

Fox and Jennifer Ward had just about given up trying to find a way out of the holding room, when they heard the sound of running footsteps from the corridor outside.

"Someone's coming," said Fox.

"Get behind the door." Jennifer pushed Fox towards the corner of the room. "When the door opens, you slip out while I keep him talking."

Fox nodded and pressed herself to the wall. They could hear fingers punching in a key code, followed by locks clicking. The door swung inward and a harassed-looking guy in a white coat stepped into the room.

"We have to get you out of here right now," he said urgently.

"What about my son?" Jennifer demanded, trying to keep the man's attention from the corner where Fox was hiding. "I want to know what happened to him."

The white-coat stepped forward to grab her arm. Henry's message hadn't penetrated the basement of the medical centre, but word had travelled fast across the complex, sending the staff into a blind panic. "No time! The FBI is coming and I need you to tell them I'm not one of—"

Wham.

The white-coat pitched forward and hit the ground as Fox brought a plant-pot down on his head. The remains of a rubber plant scattered the carpet around his now-unconscious body.

Jennifer looked at Fox and smiled. "That worked."

"What was he saying about the FBI?"

"Don't know, don't care," Jennifer said, kneeling beside him and snatching the key card from his belt as Mary and Coach Tyler came to their side. She stripped the coat off the unconscious guy and slipped it on. "We're all getting out of here, okay?"

An alarm began to sound in the corridor outside. "Is that for us?" Mary asked.

"I don't think so," Fox said. "Something must be happening." She looked at Jennifer Ward, who nodded at her.

"Henry," they both said together. Suddenly Fox shared the woman's certainty – Ward wasn't dead. He had come back for them – wishful thinking maybe, but it made her smile.

Fox helped her mom into the wheelchair and pushed her across the room. "Are you okay to walk?" Jennifer asked the coach as he shuffled to the door.

"Just watch me," he said, cradling his broken arm. "What's the plan?"

Jennifer looked around. "We get to ground level, find a car and smash the hell out of this complex. If anyone stops us, I'll say I'm a doctor transporting you out."

"What about Henry?" Fox asked.

"He's here somewhere," Jennifer said. "I'm going to get your mom and the coach to safety and then go looking for him."

"I'll be coming with you."

Jennifer Ward opened her mouth to argue, but saw the determination in the girl's eyes. "Okay. Let's get moving."

She moved to the door, stuck her head out and, after a quick check, beckoned for the others to follow. They slipped out as a group, Jennifer marching at the front with the confident air of a doctor who had every right to be walking around inside the medical centre. They reached the end of one corridor and passed through a set of doors into another, with turnings branching off to left and right.

"Do you know where you're going?" Fox asked as Jennifer led the way forward without breaking her stride.

"There's got to be a lift here somewhere," she replied as another set of doors to the left flew open and a female nurse came running towards them. For a second they all tensed, but the nurse went running on by.

"What's going on?" Jennifer called after her.

"Whole place has gone nuts!" the nurse yelled over her shoulder. "Forget the patients! Save yourself!"

With that, she was gone. Jennifer looked at her companions. "Whatever's happening, it's going to give us the cover we need to get out of here."

The doors flew open again as someone else pushed through…

Trooper Dan.

"Run!" Fox exclaimed, pushing her mom's chair towards the opposite end of the corridor.

Trooper Dan quickened his pace on seeing them. As they reached more doors and went through into another, almost identical corridor, he was hot on their tail.

"Keep runnin', girl!" he yelled after Fox. "I can keep this up all day!"

Fox met Jennifer's eyes as they raced down the corridor to the next set of double doors and realized they were thinking the same thing: for all they knew they could have been running ever deeper into the facility. As they made the next set of doors, Jennifer grabbed hold of Mary's wheelchair while Fox held back, allowing the others to go through. Rather than following, she pulled the doors shut and slid the emergency lock into place. Jennifer and the coach appeared at the window on the other side.

"Keep going!" she called through to them. "Get my mom out of here!"

Ignoring their protests, she turned round...and faced Trooper Dan, who had stopped halfway up the corridor.

"It's me you want," she said, meeting his insane eyes. "Not them."

Trooper Dan cocked his head on one side and studied her. "Well, you are just about as brave as a young girl can get, ain't you?" He raised his left arm, showing off the hard metal of his new hand. "I'm gonna kill you slow."

Fox broke from her position, throwing herself at the nearest door as Trooper Dan ran at her. The door flew open and she staggered into the darkness of one of the labs...

37

The Malcorp complex was already in chaos as Henry emerged from the substation. Several of the lodges were on fire, casting flames high into the night. A buggy screeched past with one of the security guards trying to hold the wheel as two kids Henry recognized from his French class clung onto the front. The buggy veered off the road and all three ended up sprawled on the grass. The security guard got to his feet first and started running along the road as the kids began to tear the upturned buggy apart with superhuman strength.

"Oh, my god," Hank mumbled, appearing at Henry's side. Somewhere in the complex there was a muffled explosion. "What are they doing?"

"What they've been ordered," Henry replied. "They're smashing up Malcorp."

"When are they gonna stop?"

Henry gave him a look. "When there's nothing left. Hey, Hank, maybe you should just get out of here. And lose all of those Malcorp badges, huh?"

Hank stared down at the logos on his jacket and hurriedly removed it. "What are you going to do?"

Henry looked towards Mallory's house, which was all lit up in the distance. "I'm going to finish this," he said, and started running.

"Hey!" Hank called after him. "Do you think I'm gonna get in trouble when the FBI get here?"

But Henry didn't look round, running between the trees and past a group of lodges that had been set on fire. Men and women stood on the grass, gazing in shock as their children charged around the buildings with flaming torches in their hands. As Henry passed, someone grabbed his arm.

"You!" said the man who had grabbed him. "You did this!"

Henry yanked free and rounded on his assailant. It was Christian's dad. He was standing in his dressing gown and his eyes were wide, terrified. Somewhere in the distance of the complex there came the sound of a vehicle crashing, followed by an explosion.

"No," Henry said. "*You* did this." In the background, his message was still repeating, muffled now by the chaos it had caused.

"Like hell I did!" Christian's dad yelled back. "This is just the kind of thing we've been worried about. Juvenile delinquency…looting… This is what we came here to escape! And you brought it with you from the city. If Christian wasn't so goddamned weak…"

"Weak?" Henry said with a shake of his head. "He's one of the only people round here who was ready to stand up to Mallory."

"Mallory... We just wanted what was best..."

"Adjusting your own children's brains?" Henry snapped. "Mallory's been putting implants inside their heads! Did you know that?"

The man's face fell, as if he was only just realizing the insanity of the situation himself. "Th-that can't be right," he stammered. "Mallory said it was just...a new educational process...minor hypnotic suggestion..."

"And you believed that?" Henry said with a shake of his head.

The man looked at him helplessly. Henry waved a hand around the complex. "Take a look around!" he said. "You think this is normal? Mallory's turned your children into machines waiting to go crazy at the first wrong command."

Christian's dad looked at the chaos going on all around and then down at his feet.

Seeing there was nothing left to say, Henry turned to run, but the man grabbed at him again. "Please! Mallory's got my son..." His voice broke. "We just wanted to do good!" He looked around the chaos of the complex. "Not this."

Henry looked at the man and it was impossible not to feel sorry for him. "I'll find Christian," he said, looking around the other adults. They looked shell-shocked, like the survivors of a war. He guessed seeing everything that Malcorp represented being destroyed was pretty traumatic for them. "Get these people to Newton. It's not safe in the complex any more."

Christian's dad nodded frantically, as if grateful that someone had given him an order. "Okay," he said. Then he said again, in a pathetic tone, "We just wanted the best for our kids. You understand that, don't you?"

Henry didn't answer. He ran on, past more destruction. In the distance he could see the sprawling school complex on fire. In the light it was possible to make out the shapes of students running away from the conflagration. *No more French lessons,* Henry thought with no little satisfaction.

He kept on running.

"What the hell is going on here?" Mallory demanded as he walked into the foyer of the medical centre, accompanied by echoes of the destruction across the complex. "Somebody shut that goddamn broadcast off." He was flanked by four armed security guards – his most loyal men. As a technician rushed off to follow Mallory's order, doctors led by Chancellor were piling computer hard drives, boxes of files and medical records in the middle of the floor.

"We are destroying the evidence," Chancellor said breathlessly as she started throwing gasoline from a can over the pile of documents and computer equipment. "This operation is compromised."

Mallory shook his head. "One little problem, and you start to panic."

Chancellor threw the can down on the ground and advanced on him. "A little problem! Those kids have gone nuts. The FBI is coming!"

Mallory looked round as the door leading to the elevators opened and Jennifer Ward appeared. She quickly tried to back away, but froze as one of the guards levelled a gun at her. Raising her hands, she stepped into the foyer, pulling the door shut, Mary and Coach Tyler hidden behind it.

"Well, well, well," Mallory said. "Here we all are."

"It's over, Mallory," Jennifer Ward insisted. "Give up before this goes too far."

"Goes too far? I've barely even started."

Mallory nodded to one of his men, who ran over and grabbed Jennifer by the arm roughly, making sure she couldn't run.

"This is insane," Chancellor said. "They will put us on trial! We have to get rid of this evidence!"

Mallory gave her a sad look. "But you don't understand. You and your doctors *are* the evidence." He looked at his guards. "Take them to the transport truck."

Dr. Chancellor and the others protested as the guards shoved them towards the exit. One doctor who put up too much of a fight was silenced with the butt of a rifle in his face. The man went down on his knees, blood pouring from his nose and mouth, and was dragged along by his colleagues before he was hit again.

"You're insane," Jennifer Ward said in disgust as Mallory walked towards her. "You treat people like cattle."

"Not at all," he countered. "I actually like cattle."

Mallory pulled a gun from his coat and grabbed her arm. "And none of this would have been necessary if your son hadn't kept poking his nose into my business." As he manhandled the struggling woman towards the main door, he passed the head guard. "Clean out the rest of the medical centre. We have the head doctors – the rest are expendable. Burn the place to the ground with them in it. Just make sure none of them get out. I'm offering a million dollar bonus for every man in your team."

"Yessir!" the guard said with a salute, before signalling his men to move into the medical centre.

"Where are you taking me?" Jennifer demanded as Mallory pulled her outside.

"I'm getting a helicopter, my dear," he replied, jamming the gun into her back. "And you're insurance to make sure your son doesn't cause any more problems."

Henry ran around the side of Mallory's house towards the patio and swimming pool at the back. Here one of the windows had been shattered, as if something had been thrown through it. That something turned out to be General Aziz, who was crawling on his hands and knees through the broken glass. His face was bruised and bloody and his suit was torn. Upon seeing Henry, he cowered in fear.

"Don't hurt me!" he said.

"I'm not going to hurt you," Henry said, kneeling down beside him. He tried to summon up some sympathy for Aziz, but it didn't come. This was, after all, the man who had ordered Christian to kill himself just the day before. "Who did this to you?"

"Those kids," Aziz said, spluttering blood. "They're maniacs."

Henry gave him a hard look. "That's what you wanted, isn't it? Trained killers?"

Aziz reached out and grabbed his arm. "I think my leg is broken. A million dollars if you carry me out of here."

Henry pulled away from him in disgust.

"Two million dollars!"

Henry stood up slowly and looked down at the general. "The main gate is that way," he said, pointing. "I suggest you crawl."

With that, he walked through the broken glass into the house, ignoring the curses General Aziz was throwing at his back. The interior of Mallory's house had been ripped apart. Books had been pulled from the shelves and strewn about. Paintings torn from their hangings. Ornaments dashed against the wooden floor.

Henry went straight for the office area. Mallory's desk was relatively untouched. He searched through papers and books, looking for a single object: Mallory would have one of the SPIDIR Initiators in his house. He was sure of it. Casting stuff aside on the desk, he found nothing and tried the drawers…locked. Then he saw it: an Initiator. It was lying right on the floor – Mallory must have dropped it. He snatched it up and cast his gaze around the interior of the building, noticing for the first time the smell of burning coming from the kitchen. He followed the smell and saw devastation: pots and pans thrown all around…knives jammed into the wooden work surfaces…

And in the middle of all the chaos sat a single figure.

Gabrielle.

She was cross-legged on the floor with a pair of kitchen scissors in her hand, all her attention focused on cutting what remained of a Picasso painting into tiny pieces that she had arranged on the floor in front of her. Henry approached cautiously, but she showed no sign of knowing he was there.

"Gabrielle?" he said, kneeling before her. "It's me. Henry."

She didn't look up from her work. "Henry? Aren't you supposed to be dead?" Her voice had a distant, lifeless quality to it.

Henry placed a hand on her shoulder…

Lightning fast, she lashed out with the scissors, almost slashing his throat. Henry caught her wrist and held her firm. The girl's eyes blazed with an insane fury.

"Destroy!" she spat. "Malcorp!"

"No!" Henry said, holding her arm tight. "It's over! Do you hear me? Malcorp is finished. It's over!"

He held the Initiator to the base of her skull. *I hope this works*, he thought. *If it doesn't, forgive me.* He pressed the red button…

For a few seconds Gabrielle continued to stare into his eyes, but then something seemed to crumple within her and her whole body went limp. The scissors dropped from her fingers and her head fell forward. She let out a sob.

"Henry," she said, leaning towards him. He put his arms around her, praying he'd done the right thing – that shutting down her SPIDIR implant hadn't caused brain damage.

"Gabrielle?" he asked softly. "Are you okay?"

For a while she was silent…motionless… But finally she spoke. "I couldn't stop myself… I hurt you…"

"It's okay," Henry said, almost laughing with relief. She could talk normally, which surely meant she wasn't permanently damaged. "You're going to be okay."

He looked around at a sound from the direction of the kitchen. There was someone else in the building.

"We have to get out of here," he said, rising to his feet and pulling her up. "We need to find Fox and the others."

Gabrielle looked at him through tear-filled eyes and said, "Blake."

Before Henry could react, the kid ran from the kitchen, hitting him full force. They flew across the room towards one of the intact windows and smashed through, landing in a sea of glass. The Initiator flew from Henry's grasp and landed on the other side of the patio. Groaning with pain, he rolled onto his back, but Blake was already rising into a crouch.

"Hello, Henry," he said with a smile as he raised a fist. But then a look of confusion crossed his face.

"It's over, Blake," Henry said, jumping to his feet and holding up his hands. "Malcorp isn't in control of you any more. You don't have to do this."

Blake shook his head violently, as if trying to clear it. "My grandfather…" Blake's voice trailed away. His expression was full of pain, as if he were having to fight the ingrained programming harder than the other adjusted kids. Henry guessed that was the result of being Mallory's grandson... an extra layer of brainwashing because of the family ties. Poor kid.

"Your grandfather was using you!" Henry said. "Just like he used all the other kids at Malcorp High. He turned all them into robots...test subjects..."

Blake's face contorted, his mental struggle clear. "And now you're the one giving us the orders. Is that right?"

Henry shook his head. "No. I'm setting you free..."

He stopped talking as Blake reached behind his back and produced a twenty-centimetre-long kitchen knife. He looked at the blade in his hand and then at Henry.

"I'm sick of having all of you in my head."

From the house, Gabrielle gave a cry. "Blake! No!"

Blake's expression flickered and he looked at her with recognition in his eyes. "I'm sorry," he said softly. "But this has to end."

With a cry, he flew at Henry, slashing the blade in front of him. Henry ducked to one side as the knife swiped in front of his face. His back was to the edge of the pool and there was nowhere to go as Blake came at him again, bringing the knife low to catch him in the stomach. Instead of trying to dodge – Henry knew from their previous encounter that Blake was faster and stronger than him – he threw himself at his attacker. They collided and Blake staggered back, completely off-balance. Henry used his weight to twist them over into the pool.

They hit the water and sank to the bottom, still holding

on to one another. As they touched the bottom of the pool, Blake's mouth opened, expelling a stream of air bubbles. He struggled to slash at his opponent with the knife, but Henry held his arm firm. He released just a little air from the corner of his mouth and tried to stay calm...

Blake thrashed his legs in an effort to kick towards the surface, but Henry wouldn't let him go. Outside the pool, the big kid had the upper hand, but he was in Henry's world now. *You might have super strength*, Henry thought grimly as he held on for dear life, *but I'm a swimmer.*

And I bet I can hold my breath twice as long as you.

Sure enough, as the seconds ticked away, Blake's efforts to free himself became more desperate. He had expelled all of the air from his lungs, but Henry still wasn't letting him go. Blake's mouth opened reflexively and he choked... The knife slipped from his fingers and was lost at the bottom of the pool... His movements were weaker now... His eyes rolled into his skull...

Henry allowed a little more air out from his mouth as Blake's body began to go limp. Just a little longer... He couldn't risk giving his attacker a second chance...

Blake's body gave a spasm as he gulped water into his lungs, beginning to asphyxiate...

Henry kicked towards the surface of the pool, dragging Blake with him. Unconscious, the other kid had become a dead weight that threatened to slip through his fingers, but Henry gave it everything he had. If he didn't get Blake out of the water, the kid was dead. Breaking the surface, he gasped air into his lungs and tried to heave his attacker out.

His muscles screamed with the effort… Blake began to slip down to the bottom of the pool…

Gabrielle reached down and grabbed Blake by the back of his shirt, heaving him up with a cry of effort. With the last of his strength, Henry pushed too. Between them they hauled Blake onto the patio, where he lay motionless.

"He isn't breathing!" Gabrielle said.

"Get him on his back," Henry said, pulling himself out of the pool. As Gabrielle pushed Blake over, Henry kneeled by his side. He laced his fingers together and placed his hands on Blake's sternum, trying to remember what he'd learned in life-saving class. He pushed down hard, forcing the lungs to expel the water they'd taken in. Blake's body shook. Henry pushed again…and again…

Blake choked, coughing up water. His breathing came in ragged gasps, but he was alive. Whatever fight had been in Blake was gone now.

"You did it!" Gabrielle said, cradling Blake's head in her lap as he gasped for breath.

Henry didn't waste a second, moving for the fallen Initiator. He retrieved it from the other side of the patio and repeated the process he had used to shut down Gabrielle's SPIDIR. Then he looked at the kid who had been intent on killing him just a few minutes before. Blake stared back at him blearily.

"Henry?" he croaked. Then his gaze fell upon Gabrielle and it was as if he was seeing her for the first time in a very long time. He reached out and took her hand and smiled at her. Finally he said, "What happened?"

"You didn't make the swim team," Henry replied, placing the Initiator in his pocket. "Where's Mallory?"

"He went to the medical centre," Gabrielle answered.

Henry nodded and started towards the house.

"Be careful!" Gabrielle called after him. "He's seriously mad."

Henry looked over his shoulder at her. "So am I."

Crossing through the wrecked house, Henry ran down the stairs leading into the garage. He looked over the vehicles, his eyes falling to rest on the largest: a Hummer with a sparkling black paint job. Practically a tank.

Perfect.

The keys were behind the ignition. He grinned. *Guess Mallory never thought he'd have a car stolen from his own garage.* Turning the key, the giant engine roared into life. Directly ahead the automatic garage door was closed. Henry looked around. No sign of a door control.

No problem.

A second later the Hummer smashed clean through the garage door, sped up the ramp onto ground level and screamed across the complex in the direction of the medical centre...

38

"**C**ome out, come out…wherever you are!"

Trooper Dan stood in the doorway of the lab. Globes in the ceiling illuminated rows of medical equipment and gurneys covered with sheets. The cop closed the door behind him and locked it with the key, which he placed in his pocket.

"No way out," he called into the room, scratching his cheek with the metal claw on his left hand. "You may as well give yourself up."

He took a few paces towards one of the gurneys – the space below it was hidden by a sheet.

"Come on, girl," he said, voice reasonable. "I ain't gonna hurt you… I'm just gonna rip your head off…"

He grabbed the gurney and slashed his claw through the sheet. There was nothing underneath. With a cry of rage, he picked up the trolley and threw it against the wall.

"Get out here now!" he screamed, veins bulging in his neck. "Don't make me search for you!"

At the far end of the room, Fox crouched behind a vat of what appeared to be human brains, trying to still her beating heart. *Have to stay calm*, she told herself. *Have to think.*

There was only one way out of the lab – through the locked door. And the key was in Trooper Dan's pocket. Fox looked around for any other exit from the room. There was nothing…no doors…no accessible ventilation shafts…

Which, she realized, meant one thing…

If she was going to get out, she had to fight the cop.

There was a crash as he attacked another gurney, slashing at the sheet and then kicking the trolley against the wall in frustration when he found she wasn't hiding beneath it. He continued forward. It would only be a matter of time before he found her…

She looked around for something to use against him. She was no match for his physical strength, of course. Even the damage to his hand didn't seem to be affecting him – if anything it had made him meaner. And goodness knows what they'd pumped into him to take away the pain.

Another crash and a table went over.

"I think I'm getting warmer!" Trooper Dan said. He grabbed a rack of surgical equipment and pulled it over with a mighty clatter.

Fox looked around. Near her were several pieces of electrical equipment: what looked like an ultrasound device, some type of centrifuge and somethi͟ recognized from hospital dramas on the TV. /
– one of those machines they used as a last
a patient's heart pumping again. It basically

electric shock. The machine sat on a trolley, its two paddles resting in cradles on the front.

Checking round the edge of her hiding place, Fox saw that the cop was still ten metres away. Although he appeared to be out of control, he was taking his time over his search – systematically working his way from one end of the lab to the other. *He's enjoying this*, she realized.

"You know," Trooper Dan said, his voice almost conversational once more as he threw over another trolley, "when I'm finished with you, I'm gonna go find your cripple momma and put her out of her misery. Would you like that?"

Ignoring his words, Fox crept across to the defibrillator and reached up to a *power on* button on the side. Flipping it, she winced as the machine emitted a high-pitched whine. A light on the side indicated that it was powering up. A sign read *Do not use until fully charged*.

Fox took a glance round. Suddenly she couldn't hear Trooper Dan's movements any more. She looked back at the machine, which was still charging. *Come on!*

There was a footstep to her right. Trooper Dan leaped out from behind the vat of brains.

"Gotcha!"

Fox staggered back as he approached, slashing the claw at her. She backed up against the wall. There was nowhere left to go. Desperately, she reached round for something to use as a weapon… Her hand brushed a shelf of jars and she picked one up blindly, throwing it at the cop as he ran her…

Trooper Dan screamed as the jar smashed, clear liquid splashing the right side of his face and instantly starting to burn through his skin. Shocked, Fox looked up at the shelf – the jars were labelled *hydrochloric acid*. The cop went down on one knee, pawing at his face with his good hand. He screamed.

Not wasting her chance, Fox ran for the defibrillator. He reached out and grabbed her leg as she passed. Fox went down hard on the floor and then Trooper Dan was on top of her. The side of his face where the acid had hit was red raw and giving off a chemical smoke as the liquid ate through his skin. He took Fox by the shoulders and slammed her against the tiled floor. She gasped as the blow knocked the air from her lungs, and pain exploded up her spine. Then the cop lifted her like she weighed nothing and threw her down on the top of a gurney near the brains' vat.

"Don't you move," Trooper Dan spat. His voice was slurred now, as if some of the acid had eaten into his mouth and tongue. Fox lay helpless on the gurney, too stunned at that moment to do anything. She looked round at her attacker and recoiled in shock and disgust – it was like the right side of his face was made of wax that had been melted with a blowtorch.

"Please," she said. "You need a doctor."

Trooper Dan actually smiled, revealing his molars through a hole in his cheek. "Yuh thunk am gunna need sum plustic surgry, huh?" He looked around, eyes falling upon a tray of surgical equipment. He grabbed it and threw it down on the trolley beside Fox. She tried to sit up, but he forced her down with his claw hand, the metal talons digging into her flesh so that she cried out.

"Stuy stull," he ordered, running his good hand over the scalpels in the tray. "Thus ain't gunna hurt a bit..."

"Don't do this," Fox begged, trying to squirm away. "We know what Mallory did to you. He adjusted you like all the others. Made you crazy..."

Trooper Dan smiled as he picked up a cranial saw from the tray. "Crazy," he repeated as he flicked the button on the side. The metal blade began to spin. He moved it towards her skull...

"No!" Fox cried, grabbing his wrist and pushing him back with all her might.

"Iz okay," Trooper Dan said, pressing down. "Juz wunna see whut yuh brain luks like..."

Fox tried to push him away, but he was just too strong. The spinning blade came closer and closer to her skull...

Desperately, she reached down with her free hand and found the metal claw they'd placed on his wounded arm. She closed her fingers around the metal and wrenched it free with all her might. Trooper Dan howled as the prosthesis was ripped away from his hand. He staggered back. The cranial saw dropped, still spinning, from his fingers and started grinding against the tiles. As he reached for her again, Fox slashed at him with the metal claw. It made contact with his neck, and stuck there. The cop fell back, clutching at his throat.

Rolling off the trolley, Fox staggered towards the

defibrillator, aware that the big man was rising behind her. Nothing kept him down for long. Snatching up a paddle in each hand, she spun round in time to see him flying at her...arms flailing...the claw still sticking out from his bloody neck...

Fox threw out her hands instinctively. As Trooper Dan's chest connected with the paddles she pressed the trigger on each. There was a whine as the electricity was released...

The cop flew back as if he'd been hit with a wrecking ball... He hit the floor of the lab and lay there on his back... gave a final violent twitch.... And then lay still.

For a second Fox stood motionless as the defibrillator recharge hummed. She dropped the paddles and fell to her knees, every part of her body shaking. She gazed in horror and relief at Trooper Dan's body, and noticed that smoke was rising from it.

With great effort, she moved to stand in front of the fallen cop. Somehow, lying out on the floor, he looked even bigger than when he was standing up. His previously blue eyes were wide open, but they'd been fried white by the electricity that had coursed through his brain and blasted his implant.

There was a strangely peaceful look on his face.

She reached down and retrieved the lab keys from his pocket, then headed out to find the others.

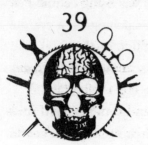

39

Henry drove the Hummer up the medical centre driveway at full speed, not stopping for a buggy that had jackknifed in the entrance. He simply ran over it, obliterating it completely.

The last of the doctors were making a run for it. Henry ignored them as he brought the beast of a vehicle to a screeching halt on the gravel and jumped from the cab – they'd be rounded up eventually, he hoped. He was only interested in his friends and his mom. Having seen most of them on the monitor in the substation, he guessed they were probably still inside. Christian was surely being held in the complex somewhere too, most likely well away from the effects of Henry's message, adjusted and completely at Malcorp's mercy. Henry had to shut down his SPIDIR, just like he had with Gabrielle and Blake.

"Henry!" a familiar voice called from the side of the building.

He looked round to see Coach Tyler and Mary Layton hiding in the shadows. He ran over to join them.

"The whole place has gone nuts!" the coach said. "Mallory's got a bunch of killers dressed as security guards taking out all the doctors. We decided to hide it out."

"Where's my mom?" Henry asked.

"Mallory took her hostage," Mary answered. "And my daughter is still in the building. That cop is after her."

Henry weighed up his options and came to a difficult decision. "Get her to the Hummer," he ordered the coach, who looked like he was barely able to walk himself. "I'm going after Fox."

"Be careful, kid," the coach said as he started manoeuvring the wheelchair to the vehicle.

Henry ran to the main doors and into the familiar foyer...except now the place was filled with the stench of burning. And the floor was littered with the dead bodies of doctors. He took in the shocking scene and ran for the security door. As he got there it opened and he tensed, ready to face one of Mallory's killers...

It was Fox. She looked as if she could barely stand, staggering towards him... Henry caught her in his arms.

"It's okay," he said as she clung to him, a sob racking her body. "I've got you."

She mumbled, "Trooper Dan..."

Henry looked past her towards the security door. "Is he...?"

"I think I've killed him," she said flatly, pulling away and looking him in the eyes.

Henry placed his hands on her shoulders. She was clearly in shock. "You did what you had to do," he said. "Now we have to get out of here. Okay?"

Fox looked at him blankly for a second, but then her eyes focused. "My mom…"

"Is waiting for us," Henry said, taking her hand and leading her across the foyer.

They hurried out of the building and Henry put Fox in the passenger side of the Hummer, before running round to take the driver's seat. "I'll come back for Christian once I'm certain you're all safe. And what about my mom – where did Mallory take her?" Henry asked as he fired up the engine.

"We overheard his men saying something about a helicopter," Mary said from the back.

"There's a helipad on the east side of the complex." The coach pointed to the left through the window. "That way."

"Strap yourselves in," Henry said as he put the car in drive. "This could get bumpy."

The Hummer tore away with a screech of gravel, just as a guard with a machine gun exploded from the foyer of the medical centre.

"Everyone down!" Henry cried as bullets strafed the windshield. Rather than trying to avoid their attacker, he swerved the Hummer towards the man, clipping him with the boxy front of the vehicle. The guard flew back and smashed against the wall of the centre. Henry drove on.

It seemed every building in the Malcorp complex was on fire. Henry had ordered the adjusted kids to destroy everything. And they had certainly done that. Now the kids and their families were standing around in the open spaces between the buildings, looking dazed or huddling together for protection. They were like refugees from some war. *So much for Mallory's vision,* Henry thought grimly as he steered the Hummer around them, the heel of his palm on the horn.

"Over there," the coach said, pointing towards a raised area set away from the buildings up ahead. The early-morning mist had cleared now, and the helicopter sat on the helipad for all to see, its rotor blades turning slowly as if gearing up for flight. Henry put his foot on the gas, heading straight for it. He wondered what would happen if he drove the Hummer right into the tail of the machine...

"Take it easy, kid," the coach warned. "Mallory's got your mom, remember."

Henry eased off as they came close, hitting the brake to bring the giant vehicle to a skidding halt at the edge of the helipad.

"I don't see any guards," Henry said, peering through the windshield, hoping to glimpse his mom.

"It's Christian!" Fox exclaimed, pointing to the front of the chopper. Sure enough, Henry saw his friend sitting in the cockpit, one hand on the joystick, staring ahead blankly. Fox reached for the door handle, but Henry stopped her.

"It looks like he's still under Mallory's control," he said. Two figures appeared round the back of the helicopter: Mallory and Jennifer Ward. The man turned and Henry saw the gun he had pressed into his mom's back. Mallory made a beckoning gesture with his free hand.

"What's he want?" Fox asked.

Henry took a deep breath, trying to stay calm. "He wants me to go out there."

Fox shook her head. "Don't be crazy. He'll kill you!"

"Maybe," Henry said, half opening his door. "But this has to end somehow."

As he started to get out, Fox reached over and grabbed his arm. "Be careful, Ward!"

He gave her what he hoped looked like a confident grin. "Get behind the wheel. If he starts shooting, get out of here."

Fox nodded and slid into the driver's seat as Henry stepped out of the Hummer.

It was a cold, still morning now. The part of the compound in which the helipad was situated was quiet apart from the thrum of the chopper blades speeding up. On leaden legs, Henry walked towards the helicopter. As he approached, Mallory grabbed Jennifer and moved from under the blades.

"I could have left five minutes ago," Mallory shouted above the noise. Jennifer struggled against him, but he jabbed her in the side with the automatic.

"Why didn't you?" Henry asked, knowing this was what Mallory wanted. He met his mom's eyes for a moment, and she managed a twitch of a smile to show she was okay.

"I wanted to see you one more time, Henry," Mallory said, "to have words with the kid who wouldn't play ball."

"It's over, Mr. Mallory," he said. "The complex is destroyed. The authorities are on their way. Everyone's going to know what you've been doing here."

378

Mallory let out a roaring laugh. "You think this is the end? You haven't destroyed anything, just put me back a little. In a month I'll have a new face and a new set-up twice as good as this place! There are plenty of countries begging me to give them my technology."

"Plenty of dictatorships, you mean," Jennifer said, trying to pull away from him.

Mallory shook his head and held her tighter. "Don't be so naïve. There isn't a country in the western world that wouldn't kill for the control I can offer. Adjustment is going to work and it's going to make the world a much happier, simpler place."

"Just as long as you're one of the people pulling the strings," Henry said.

Mallory sneered at him. "There are two types of people in this world, kid: the controllers and the controlled. Look at you. You've caused all this destruction and what have you really achieved? But me? I've got your mom. With a little adjustment, I think she's going to be very happy as the new Mrs. Mallory…"

Jennifer jerked her head round at him. "In your dreams."

Mallory laughed. "Oh, you will learn to love me." He looked back at Henry. "And I've got my new son, Christian. A son who'll never let me down. Not like the others."

Henry slowly began to move towards Mallory, hoping he was too caught up in his monologue to notice. *If he could just get the gun…*

Mallory continued, "We're going to be one big happy family, Henry. But I'm afraid there's no place for you at the table. You just don't fit in…" He whipped the gun round so it was pointing at Henry's head. "That's close enough!"

Henry froze and raised his hands to chest height.

"You can't beat me, son," Mallory said viciously.

"I can see that," Henry said, choosing his words carefully. "What about Christian? Why hasn't he been affected by the theta signal?"

Mallory glanced quickly back at the helicopter and Christian. "We had him tucked away in the medical centre for more upgrades. So luckily he didn't get to hear your set of instructions…" His voice trailed away and a look of understanding passed over his face. "Very clever. Trying to keep me talking? Hoping the FBI is going to come running in to save the day?" He shook his head with mock sadness. "It doesn't work like that. This is the bit where I take everything you care about and carry on business as usual. And you get to be a hero." He sighted down the gun at Henry's head. "Just like your dad."

Henry tensed, waiting for Mallory to pull the trigger…

"Stop!" Jennifer Ward's voice rang out above the helicopter roar.

Mallory shifted his grip on the gun. "What? You want some last words with your son?"

Jennifer kept her eyes on Henry. "I'm sorry I didn't believe you."

"It's okay, Mom," Henry said, his voice thick as he saw the tears in her eyes.

"And I'm sorry for giving you such a hard time these last months…" Her voice broke.

"It's okay," Henry said, holding her gaze. "Sometimes you have to put your foot down. Know what I mean?" He flicked his eyes down to her feet and then up again. An understanding passed between them.

"Yeah," she said.

Mallory held up the gun again. "Very touching. Now let's get this done..."

Jennifer Ward raised her leg and rammed the heel of her shoe hard onto Mallory's foot with a crunch. He howled in pain. There was a roar as the gun discharged in his hand

A bullet flew past Henry's head...

...but he was already running at Mallory. He hit the man, driving him down onto the tarmac of the helipad. The gun flew from his grasp as they landed in a heap with Henry on top.

"Run, Mom!" Henry yelled, trying to disentangle himself. Jennifer started for the Hummer and soon Henry was on his feet too, about to follow...

Mallory grabbed at his leg. "I'm gonna kill you! You little son of a bitch!"

Henry spun round and kicked out at Mallory, catching him in the face and driving him back down. Then he turned and ran, aware of Mallory scrambling for the fallen gun as he fled. The Hummer roared into life and drove onto the tarmac, screeching round to form a protective barrier as Jennifer passed.

"Henry, watch out!" Fox yelled through the open passenger window.

He ran full pelt for the vehicle. A gunshot rang out.

Henry jumped at the front of the Hummer, flying across the hood and landing on the other side next to his mom as bullets slammed into the side of the vehicle. Everyone inside ducked for cover as Mallory emptied the automatic at them.

As the shooting stopped, Henry looked round the front of the vehicle in time to see Mallory toss the empty gun and run as fast as he could for the chopper, blood streaming from his nose where Henry's foot had connected.

Henry didn't hesitate for a second: running out from the shelter of the Hummer and across the helipad as the chopper started rising into the air. He was vaguely aware of the voices of his mom and Fox calling after him as he ran, but he was focused on one thing…

Saving Christian.

Through the side windows of the chopper he could see Mallory in the back, hunched on the seat, cupping his broken nose in his hands. In the front, Christian was expertly piloting the vehicle – another of his new skills. As Henry approached, the helicopter was almost two metres into the air…

Henry put on a spurt of speed…

Leaped…

And grabbed onto the landing strut with both hands.

The chopper continued its inexorable rise, carrying Henry with it high into the night air.

40

Great plan, Henry thought as he clung onto the helicopter landing strut for dear life. *Really great.*

With every ounce of strength in his body, he managed to swing his legs up so they caught the strut. From there he was able to pull himself round so he was lying on it. Looking down for the first time, he saw that they had passed the compound and were now flying towards the endless treetops of Newton County. At least a hundred metres below, he made out the southern road winding through the forest.

A wave of vertigo passed over him and it was tempting simply to cling on for dear life, but he knew that he had to get off the strut somehow. Who knew where Mallory was going or how far? Henry was already shivering with the cold of the higher altitude and he knew it would only be a matter of time before his muscles weakened and he fell off the side. He looked up at the doors to the front and back compartments of the chopper. At the moment, Christian and Mallory seemed unaware that he was on the side, which meant he had the advantage of surprise.

With great effort, Henry pulled himself up so he was

crouching on the strut. Then the chopper made an unexpected course adjustment and he had to grab the handle of the cockpit door to avoid being thrown off. He took a breath. *Now or never.*

He flung open the door and pulled himself into the seat next to Christian. The other boy didn't even look round, so intent was he on piloting the chopper. Mallory, in the back, was a different story, however.

"Christian!" he screamed, still clutching his nose. "Kill him!"

The other kid immediately sprang into action. Releasing his grip on the joystick, Christian turned in his seat and locked his hands around Henry's throat, slamming him first against the front window and then against the side door…

…which flew open. Henry grabbed the side of the chopper to stop himself falling out as he felt the wind on his back. Christian's leg brushed the joystick and the chopper went into a slow dive, although the pilot showed no sign of noticing. He was completely focused on his latest command.

"Christian!" Henry managed to cry as his friend's fingers tightened around his throat. "It's me!"

Christian looked at him blankly, no recognition in his face. In desperation, Henry braced himself against the door frame and kicked out with his left foot, driving his attacker back across the cockpit. As Christian flew back, he hit the joystick again, sending the chopper rolling in the opposite direction. Through the front window the trees below spun dizzyingly.

"Take the controls!" Mallory cried from behind.

Christian turned his attention back to the stick, pulling the chopper out of its dive. Henry realized that, in the chaos of the cockpit, using the Initiator that was stashed in his pocket wasn't an option. He could only take one shot at frying Christian's SPIDIR properly if he didn't want to mess up his friend's head for good, and he couldn't risk it in a spinning helicopter. Instead he looked around for something to use as a weapon. If he couldn't take out Christian's SPIDIR, then he'd take him out of the equation by cruder means. It would mean getting the chopper down by himself – but what choice did he have? A fire extinguisher hung behind the pilot's seat. Henry snatched it up and raised it high...

"Sorry, Christian," he said as he moved to bring the cylinder down on his head...

But Mallory reached through from the back and caught Henry's arm, holding him firm. Henry looked round to see the man staring at him with an insane hatred in his eyes.

"I should have killed you when I had the chance!" he hissed.

Henry reached for the top of the extinguisher with his free hand as they struggled. "Too bad you were so busy talking. Like always." He pulled the firing pin free and depressed the trigger. White carbon dioxide gas flooded from the extinguisher nozzle, blasting Mallory back. Seeing his master attacked, Christian let go of the joystick and launched himself at Henry once more...

But this time Henry was ready, bringing the cylinder round. It connected with the side of Christian's head with a *clunk*. The kid spun and slumped unconscious against the helicopter controls, sending the vehicle into a steep dive.

Henry moved fast, grabbing Christian and hauling him out of his seat. Choking against the CO_2 that was flooding the cockpit, he pulled back on the joystick, levelling the chopper just before it ploughed into the forest. The tops of the tallest firs slammed against the landing struts, rocking the interior.

"Henry, take the controls, boy!" Mallory screeched, trapped in the back. "Fly the chopper!"

Henry linked his arm through the unconscious Christian's and pulled him towards the still-open side door. As the helicopter began to lose altitude again, the front brushing the treetops, he took a final look back at Mallory. The head of Malcorp was gripping the back seat, his face terrified.

"You're the genius," Henry said to him. "You fly it."

He paused on the edge for just a second. Directly below was the canopy of trees. Taking a breath, Henry jumped from the helicopter, taking Christian with him...

Free fall lasted for a split second, then they hit the top of a fir tree. Needles and branches ripped into them, but Henry kept his grip on Christian's arm...he couldn't let go...the boy was helpless without him.

They hit branch after branch, ripping them away from the trunk as they fell from one to the next. Henry cried out in pain as his leg caught against a thicker limb, spinning both him and Christian round 180 degrees. They continued to fall, the ground visible now and rushing up with nothing to stop the impact…

With a crunch, Henry landed on a branch five metres above the ground. It didn't break. He hung there, trying to ignore the pain that racked his body. A great weight was pulling his arm almost out of its socket: Christian was dangling below, held only by Henry's grip. A grip that was quickly slipping. With a cry of effort he hung on for just a second more, but it was no use. Christian fell silently, hitting the ground with a soft thud.

Henry grabbed the branch he was lying on and with some difficulty pulled himself into a sitting position. Although his body was covered in minor cuts from the tree branches, and his clothes were shredded, no bones seemed to be broken. A glance up the length of the trunk showed how far they'd fallen – at least fifty metres. Each branch had slowed their fall just a little.

In the distance, the sound of an explosion made Henry look round. Somewhere in the forest the light of a fire grew between the trees. *The helicopter.* It was time to move.

Edging along the branch, he reached the trunk and lowered himself down a series of smaller branches until he could jump the remaining two metres to the soft floor of the forest. Christian was lying face down in a crumpled heap amid the fallen leaves and bracken. He ran over as fast as his battered legs would carry him.

"Christian!" Henry said, kneeling down and gently turning him over.

The other kid groaned and opened his eyes slowly. Henry removed the Initiator from his pocket, held it to the back of his head and pressed the red button... Christian's body twitched, but when his eyes opened, there was recognition there.

"Henry?" Christian said. "Where am I?"

"It's a long story," Henry replied, breathing a sigh of relief. "We have to get out of here. Can you stand?"

Christian nodded and pushed himself into a sitting position. "I feel like I've been pulled through a hedge backwards," he said, rubbing the scratches along his arms.

Henry glanced up at the tree and grinned. "Something like that. You don't remember anything?"

"Uh-uh."

"That's probably just as well. I'll tell you all about it when we get out of here." He stood up and offered support as Christian tried to do the same.

"I think my leg is sprained," Christian said with a wince. Henry put an arm round his shoulder.

"Which way do we go?" Christian asked.

Looking through the trees, Henry could see the fire from the crashed chopper was clearly spreading. "As far away from that as possible," he answered.

They walked into the forest, supporting one another as they went.

"I think I'm getting some flashbacks of the last couple of days," Christian said after some time. Their progress was painfully slow due to his twisted ankle and the uneven ground.

Henry looked at him. "Yeah?"

"Yeah. I kinda remember firing a gun at you."

Henry nodded. "Yeah. You did that."

Christian thought it over for a moment. "And I kinda remember kicking your ass a bit. I felt like a jock."

Henry laughed. "Oh yeah. You should join the football team."

"And I think I can fly a helicopter. And speak Arabic. And Mandarin. I hate to say this, but it's pretty cool. My dad's going to go nuts. Finally I can do something better than my brother."

Henry gave him a look. If his SPIDIR was shut down, shouldn't he have lost all of the knowledge implanted by Mallory's doctors? Or could it still be active in some way? Made dormant by the Initiator, but ready to be reactivated… That wasn't a nice thought.

"What's wrong?" Christian said. "You're looking at me weird."

"Nothing," Henry said quickly. "I was just thinking about the last time I saw your dad. You know what? I think he's just going to be glad to see you again."

The trees opened up at that point, onto a cleared area with a building and up ahead a road. A neon sign hung over a set of tired-looking pumps. Behind the crumbling building was a corrugated iron outhouse. The words RESTROOM stood out in white paint on the side.

"I don't believe it," Henry said, shaking his head.

"What?" Christian asked.

"This is where it all began," he replied, looking round the dirt yard of the gas station where he'd first met Gabrielle Henson. Holding Christian up, he started across the yard towards the main building with renewed energy, thinking about finding a phone and getting in touch with what was happening at the Malcorp complex. The day was really getting hot now. How long had they been wandering the forest? An hour...two?

"FREEZE!"

Henry and Christian stopped dead as a figure stepped from the shadows at the side of the building, the unmistakable shape of a double-barrelled shotgun aimed directly at them.

"One wrong move and I'll plug you!"

"Easy!" Henry said, putting up his free hand. "We just want to use your phone!"

The figure stepped forward, straining to see better, but not lowering the gun. It was the old man from the gas station. "It's you," he said, peering at Henry. "The kid with the girl. And *you* were the one with the truck who smashed up my forecourt. Tell me I'm wrong! I recognize your voice!"

Henry swallowed heavily. "Uh, yeah. Sorry about that…"

The old man lowered the gun and stepped forward, clapping a bony hand down on Henry's shoulder.

"Sorry?" he exclaimed. "What the hell are you sorry for, boy? I've had 'em all here this evenin'. FBI. CIA. SWAT.

WSIL news. They're kickin' up one hell of a stink at Newton. And they are all buyin' gas!"

Henry and Christian looked at one another and then at the gun in the old man's hand.

"Pardon me," he said, leaning the shotgun against the side of the building. "Can't be too careful here. Gotta watch out for them fortune hunters tryin' to get a souvenir of the place where the story of the century began."

Henry frowned at the man as he began to lead them towards the front of the gas station. "Story of the century?"

"Hell, yes!" he replied excitedly. "There's got to be a film deal in all this. TV mini-series at the very least. I figure we go fifty-fifty on any contract, seein' as I was your sidekick and all…"

As they stepped onto the forecourt, Henry saw that the FBI had set up a roadblock restricting vehicle access to the road leading to Newton. News vans were piled up around the gas station and there were several ambulances and police cars...and a black Hummer sparkled in the brilliance of the sun. Amid the emergency vehicles was a tent where refugees from Newton were being treated.

Fox was sitting on a gurney by one of the ambulances. Her face lit up as she met his eyes and she waved to him excitedly.

"Come on," Henry said, pulling Christian across the forecourt towards their waiting family and friends.

"Okay, sixty-forty split!" the old man yelled after them as they went. "But I get to say who plays me in the film!"

Against the protests of a doctor who was bandaging a cut on her arm, Fox ran over to meet them as they reached the road.

"You're alive!" she cried. "You're both alive!"

"Just about," Henry said, wincing as she gave him a hug. "Easy. I just fell down the side of a tree."

And then Henry's mom and Coach Tyler appeared with Mary as well. For a moment they stood, hugging one another and laughing with relief.

"What happened?" Henry asked, nodding at the FBI roadblock.

"They came in just a few minutes after you left," the coach explained. His broken arm was finally bandaged. "They rounded up the last of Mallory's special security team. Sounds like they had some help from an insider."

Henry smiled. Hank had finally done something right. "What about Mallory?" he asked. "He went down in the helicopter. Have they found the crash site?"

Fox grabbed the arm of a passing FBI agent and demanded news of the helicopter crash. The agent, a tall guy in a perfectly pressed grey suit, looked at them with an expressionless face, weighing up what he should tell them.

"We're the ones who called you guys," Fox said. "Come on!"

"We reached the chopper crash site ten minutes ago," he said, as if reluctant to give out any info at all. "Whole thing was burned up."

"And Mallory?" Henry asked.

The agent looked at him. "They didn't find a body, but trust me, nothing got out of that explosion. Most likely he was vaporized in the extreme heat."

Henry and Fox looked at one another. "*Vaporized?*" they said in unison.

"Yeah," the FBI agent replied, as if they were being slow. "Happens more often than you'd think. Believe me."

With that he walked away. Fox shook her head slowly. "I don't buy that."

"I don't buy that at all," Henry said, starting to walk after the agent…

Jennifer Ward placed a hand on his shoulder. "And where do you think you're going?"

Henry looked at her with exasperation. "But, Mom! The creepy FBI agent…the vaporization…"

Jennifer gave him one of her immovable expressions. "Firstly you are going to get some medical attention. Then you are going to get a good meal." She looked at Fox and Christian. "None of you look as if you've eaten in days. And then…" She placed her hands on Henry's shoulders. "We are going to get our butts back to the city where we belong. How does that sound?"

Henry grinned at her. "Great. I've had enough of the countryside to last me a lifetime." He looked around his friends. "It's really dangerous out here."

EPILOGUE

Henry Ward stood in the middle of the corridor and closed his eyes for a moment…

The sounds of kids laughing and shouting all around… Locker doors being slammed noisily… Running feet screeching on the polished floor…

He smiled to himself… It was good to be back in a real school. This was so unlike the silence of Malcorp High. Four months had passed since the events at Newton and he was back in the city, attending a school of over a thousand, shouting, screaming, arguing kids. And he loved it.

"Hey!" a girl yelled, bumping into his arm and carrying on past. "The corridor ain't for standing, idiot!"

"Sorry!" Henry said, opening his eyes and raising his hand. The girl gave him a dismissive wave and he walked to the row of lockers over to his left. As he flicked the combination wheel on his padlock, he saw the note sticking from the edge of the door. Depositing his bag inside, he opened the note.

Have a story you need to look at – Fox.

With a grin, he crumpled the note and headed across the school to the janitor's closet that had been converted into the office of the school newspaper.

When Henry and his mom had moved back to the city, Fox and Mary had followed soon after. In the aftermath of the Malcorp incident a special fund had been set up by the company's new owner to help the victims of Mallory's experiments – and the fund had bought Full of Beans for a very generous figure. Generous enough for Mary Layton to set up a new cafe in one of the trendiest neighbourhoods in the city. And for a high-school dropout, Fox turned out to be some kind of genius – placed in every gifted and talented programme going. The art teacher kept raving about how she was the most gifted painter she'd taught in twenty years, although Fox's main interest was the school newspaper.

Up on the second floor Henry stopped at a door with a handwritten note Blu-tacked on the front: *Newspaper Office – Private*. He tried the handle and found it locked. With a sigh, he knocked three times and waited.

The door opened a crack and the round, bespectacled face of Roland, Fox's assistant editor, peered through suspiciously.

"Yes?"

"I'm here to see Fox," Henry said, trying to keep the impatience from his voice.

"Do you have an appointment?"

Henry pushed the door open and stepped in past Roland, who gave him a murderous look and then sat back at his desk in the corner. The newspaper office was windowless and about three metres square, but in that space they'd managed to cram two desks, a filing cabinet and a stack of aging computer equipment collected from around the school. On the far wall a pinboard was filled with newspaper clippings and web printouts of stories associated with the Malcorp affair. Fox looked up from her monitor as Henry approached and cast his eyes over the story wall.

"Quite a collection," he said, noticing a story he hadn't seen before. There was a photograph of Blake under the headline *Teen Malcorp Heir Vows to Dismantle Company*. In the image he was smiling and relaxed, with Gabrielle at his side. Next to it was a postcard from Christian – *Greetings from Quantico*. It seemed the FBI were making use of his new skills and, by the sound of it, he was having the time of his life as the youngest and most rebellious candidate on their *special entry* programme.

"It gets bigger every day," Fox said, handing him a printout of a blog entry. The title was *John Mallory Lives*. A quick scan of the text was enough to tell him everything: the usual conspiracy theory about how Mallory's body was never found in the chopper crash…that he had fled to a South American country, where he had set up a new clinic… experimenting on native tribes…

"Maybe it's time to stop collecting," Henry said, handing it back to her. "Malcorp is over. We have a new life now." He waved a hand over the clippings. "Dwelling on everything isn't…healthy."

Fox was about to respond when her laptop emitted a beep. She leaped back to the screen, her expression excited.

"What is it?" Henry asked, moving round so he could see.

"I've got a news monitoring service installed," Fox said as a new window opened. "It trawls the web for keywords. You know… Malcorp…Adjustment…Mallory…"

"Right."

"And look what it just threw up," Fox said, scanning the story that had opened on her screen. Henry leaned in a little closer so he could see better.

It was a story on the website of a local newspaper from some nowhere town in Ohio. A student had been arrested on the campus of the high school when a semi-automatic weapon and what appeared to be an improvised explosive device were found in his locker. Local police thought he was planning some kind of attack on the school. The student's name was Stephen Lehane.

Henry shrugged. "So?"

Fox gave him a look that said he was being slow. "I fed the names of all of the Malcorp High students into the tracker. They've been scattered all over the country. Some of them have even been given new names. But a few are starting to show up. This Stephen Lehane is…"

She scrolled down to a picture at the bottom of the story. It was a blurry shot of a cop shoving a handcuffed kid into a cruiser. Henry recognized him immediately.

"It's Steve," he said.

Fox nodded. "Once a soldier, always a soldier."

"But his SPIDIR was fried by the electric shock from the lamp," Henry said. "Wasn't it?"

"Maybe," Fox said. "Maybe not. Remember, the deactivated SPIDIRs were left in the brains of Mallory's adjusted kids, right?"

Henry nodded. "Because it was too dangerous to try removing them."

"So what if Mallory's Initiator didn't deactivate them fully. Maybe they're still following orders."

Henry looked at her. "What do you mean?"

"Perhaps Mallory embedded some deeper programming in the adjustment process. Who knows what he was planning to do with his little army of robots? But now he's not there to control them, perhaps that programming is going a little haywire. Hence our friend Steve here – planning to kill his classmates and teachers."

"They could be a bunch of time bombs waiting to go off," Henry said quietly.

"And nobody knows when or where."

They sat in silence, staring at the screen for a moment. Finally, Henry said, "Show me what else you've found."

About the Author

ANDREW TAYLOR was born in New Zealand and grew up in East Anglia. He studied English Literature at Sheffield University and teaching at Cambridge. For the last ten years he has worked as a teacher in England, South Korea, Poland and Australia. He currently lives in Melbourne with his partner, her whippet, his Italian greyhound and numerous computer games consoles. He has not been adjusted (yet).